AFTERIMAGE

J. Kowallis

Cover design by Hayden Halvorsen.
The text for this book is set in Palatino Linotype.

Title ID: 5420916
ISBN-13: 978-1511626514
ISBN-10: 1511626518

Library of Congress Control Number: 2015906602
CreateSpace Independent Publishing Platform, North Charleston, SC

Love you, Grandpa.

AFTERIMAGE

"The replication of theistic architecture through science and the advancement of human capabilities, is the greatest offering we, as mankind, have to make for the world."
–Dr. Martin G. Lobb, *Modern Mankind*

—REGGIE—

The clashing images subside. Vibrant reds and deafening shouts drift off into the haze of morning shadows. I lay still on my side, not allowing myself to move because I know when my eyes flutter open I'll be wrenched off my body-oil-stained mattress and taken to Dr. Dryer. I'm not ready. I can't do it today.

The truth is I'm never ready. I haven't built up a tolerance to the drugs or the pain. After all this time, I can't. I don't think anyone could.

I've thought about attempting to alter the images to throw them off. Even if I could, if I somehow could figure it out, they'd know and he'd be furious. Dryer would dig into me, torture me for it, but not killed. No, they can't destroy their precious device; their prize pet. They would never risk it. The pain is always *enough*. Enough to make my brain feel like it's been sliced through while never actually causing any damage. This way I'm supposed to know who's in control.

I keep waiting for the right time. I don't know when it will be, but I know it will come. The day I leave. The day this all ends. Even if I have to make it happen myself.

I control the air in my lungs very carefully, slowly releasing it before I take another slow shallow breath, trying to mimic the REM sleep I've just left behind. The doors to my cell whisper open, and my heart plummets to my stomach. My face jostles around the fabric and familiar smell emanating from my mattress, and my head is pulled back before they wrench my arms behind my body. Men grumble and bark at me.

"Get your ass up."

"Come on!"

"I know," I say firmly while I'm dragged along. My rough bare feet scratch along the brilliant white floor beneath me. I stumble between the two men, striking my toe into the slick marble. Of course, this just makes me trip again. One of them, the guard on my right, swears at me again.

Rotten peppers radiate from the man to my left with every breath he exhales. The smell is something I'm forced to inhale every morning. Spicy and putrid. The perfume of cigarettes and musty saliva linger like a bad aftertaste. My tongue curls in the back of my throat. I never forget him. Not just because of the rancid zing fermenting in his stomach, but his hands always wander where they shouldn't.

The contrast between my dark gray linen clothing and my surroundings leaves me feeling like a crusty smear on shimmering crystal. The hallway is sickly illuminated by fluorescent lights; draining and cold. No warmth to them. No sunlight. Just manufactured and fake. The combination of the light, the tile floors, and the bright white walls nearly blind me. Cold aluminum chairs sit outside each cell door we pass. Sharp and bare.

Like every other morning, Pepper-Man leans forward to the ocular scanner. It beeps three times and the door unlocks. The doors slide apart and I'm led into Dryer's control cell. The walls are made of solid Duralen metal, and straight rows of recessed lighting shed a glow on the room from above.

I spend less time here than in my own cell, but I know every corner of it. A body-length medical chair on an elevated stand is in the center of the room with a tray of instruments next to it. Standing to the right of the chair is a machine housing four cylinders full blue, yellow, and clear liquids. The cylinders are attached to long thin tubes with hair-thin needles on the end.

They twist my arm to force me into the seat. The force of their hands give me skin burns. Without reaching over to nurse my throbbing arm, I rest my head back against the vinyl headrest of the chair and stare into the bright overhead lights that watch me with unblinking eyes. The pain's not that uncommon.

I wait until I hear the door open once more. The sound of footsteps tap across the floor. My gaze drops from the light to stare into the face of another man. Blurry white fireworks, the residual burnish of the overhead lights explode in my eyes, yet I can still make out the dark brown eyes that approach me. Set along his ear is a small round device.

"Good morning, Reggie. I trust you slept well."

I sigh wearily and close my eyes. "Can we just get started?"

"Are you ready?" he asks me. At the moment I open my eyes, I see him smiling at me. The wrinkles around his mouth scrunch together as if his skin isn't even attached to the muscles beneath; it's loose, almost liquid.

"Of course not."

His smile weakens and he strokes my mousy brown hair with his hand. The touch turns my stomach. It's too soft. I jerk my head away.

"Don't touch me."

Dryer chuckles deep. He reaches across me and grabs the first thin needle. A few taps to the inside of my elbow, and he gently drives the needle into the light-green vein snaking under the surface. He repeats the same with the second needle, shoving it into my right arm where repeated uses of the needles have left dark scars.

My nose crinkles at the smell of Dryer's weighty musk cologne while he grabs two anodes and places them on my temples. The cold slimy stick of each anode clings to my skin and causes small goose bumps. Two more go behind each ear, and the last two are set on my forehead.

"All right, Reggie, I want you to relax," he says, standing by my side. "I'll go into . . ."

"I know," I cut him off. "We do this every morning. You don't need to remind me."

He smiles again, and continues his sentence. ". . . the next room and you'll take us through your dreams. Just visualize what you've seen. Follow them in detail when they come back to you. Let the antimorphaline guide your visions and we won't have to worry." He pauses.

"Will we?"

His finger traces alongside my jaw and my teeth grind. Seemingly satisfied, he walks off and I hear him over the intercom. "Reggie, close your eyes and count back from five."

I can see him in the room above, behind the wide panel of glass. My mind begins to slip away. My body starts to tingle with antimorphaline. My eyeballs loll lifelessly to the right while the drug turns my waking mind into a blurred echo of the present. The room and everything around me interfere with the visions I'm re-experiencing. For a brief moment I see pictures projected like a hologram directly in front of Dr. Dryer and he starts to direct the images around the projected screen behind the glass, much like a symphony conductor.

My eyes close slowly, weighed down by the drug. My mind focuses on my dreams. Everything is still in pieces. Not . . . all. No. All there, but . . . never . . . whole. Never in a timeline. Like . . . like watching half of . . . third act . . . play. Then jump. Jump back to . . . beginning. Barely know . . . the story line.

Three people walk down a dirt road. No, one man. Dr. Dryer in a well-decorated office on a phone with a man he calls "Comrade." A gun drops. Clang, clang, it hits a white tile floor. Numbers on various objects – signs or maybe vehicles. Their licensing. Two, two, nine. Eighteen, eight, five, and twenty-seven. It's raining . . . no, it's not rain. Then it stops. The feeling of cold clear water trickling down someone's face. My face? Not mine. A man's. I can still feel it. A vehicle carries people through a forest area. A yell. An engine revs and drops off, echoing. Dryer flicks a cigar. Someone whispers, "Do you think—" and the voice trails off.

For a brief moment my thoughts run away with me in tow, and the dream images slip away. Under their influence I begin to think semi-straight once more. I'm not spinning out of control anymore. I don't feel normal; only "normal" to the way the drugs affect me. They do that.

"Do you think you'll be all right here?" a woman's voice asks me.

I think back to the day I was brought inside The Public. I remember the surgery. They never told me why. A nurse seemed, at the time, to be very kind to me.

"Just wait right here." She left me. I never saw her again. She placed a drink pouch in my hand. It tasted like fake grapes. I remember my head hurting so much.

Sometime later I realized a chip had been placed along a small area at the back of my brain, under my skin, threading through my skull. It malfunctioned repeatedly, giving me migraines and seizures. They had to take me into surgery again.

The chip is how Dryer taps into the images. They can't be played for him on the large screen during what Dryer refers to as the "Initial Stage" when I'm dreaming. He's tried that before. The dreams overpowered the equipment and it froze. No one could explain it then. When I recall the images as a memory, they're weaker, but the collecting still works.

A deep and blinding shock of pain travels through me, forcing me back to the images. It's a reminder from Dryer. My mind shouldn't wander.

A man smiles. The image jumps. It's fuzzy and disconnected. The smile appears again. It's carefree. He's of medium build, black hair, Asian descent, and there's a tattoo across the back of his neck that says something in Korean. I understand it: Loyal. The second is younger, maybe sixteen. Very skinny; blonde hair and a large birthmark on his temple. He is filling a duffle bag with bloody meat. There is a third.

He's back again.

He's the tallest. I've seen him before. I don't know why. Dark brown hair, almost black. He's tired. Worn, with stark blue eyes. I never forget them. A phone rings in the distance. Laughter. The image of the Asian man returns. He lingers longer than before. He wears an old United States military jacket and he's talking with a woman.

Another image begins to creep up behind my eyes. The antimorphaline starts to wear off too, and I can control my thoughts. I hold the image back and everything goes black. I open my eyes and stare up. They drown in the bright heavy lights.

"That's it?" Dryer asks over the intercom. I can just see his hands still moving images and files around the large projected display with each word he says.

"That's . . . it," I whisper.

He frowns and he looks at me as though he almost feels sorry for me. I know better.

A shock of pain goes through the chip in my body. My teeth slam together and I feel a very fine fragment break off. "Reggie, you know that's not true."

Another wave of sharp stings ripples through my arms and legs, bouncing around in my skull. The metallic taste of iron glides down the back of my tongue and I realize I've bitten into my cheek. I breathe out hard, gasping for air.

"There was," I groan and lick the inside of my mouth, trying to gain focus, "a name on the . . . jacket. Irie. I. R. I. E. That's it . . . I, I promise."

Without acknowledging me, he turns his back and the images on the large screen vanish. I can't see, but he speaks to another man who's in the room with him. My vision is slightly blurred, and my hearing isn't clear. There's a conversation between them. I want to hear. I can only make out insignificant words like "no" and "common." He turns around again, looks at me with his repulsive smile. A deep bleary version of his voice hits my ears, "Good job. Thank you, Reggie. Take her back to her room."

The two men remove the electrodes and pull me off the chair. Although the antimorphaline is beginning to wear off, the room still spins. Each time I attempt to step, the floor slides to the left. The guards jerk my arms up and drag me to my "room." If you can call it that.

They push me inside and the door whispers closed. My feet can barely feel the floor and I crumple to the ground without strength in my legs. The walls still spin around me, making my eyes beg for steadiness. I rub my hands up and down my arms, trying to warm myself up. Although I've never really been warm, between the temperature of the room and the drugs, which slow down my circulation to barely above minimum, the warmest I ever get is at night when I do whatever physical exercise I can.

Fifteen years of this, and it still doesn't feel real. This can't be my life. Still, it is. Day after day I go to bed, wake up, and have images ripped from my mind. What's worse, I only remember the past fifteen years. In my entire life—all I can recall—has happened here. This room, the chair. I don't even know how old I am. I think maybe twenty-four, but how can I be sure?

My long hair falls out from behind my ear and I tuck it back. My stomach whines at me, reminding me that I haven't eaten yet. I move over to my white mattress. The coils poke and jab at me. I have to shift to one side to avoid the worst one. If I lay on it, the coil snaps through the fabric with a sharp barb.

Pushing aside my early memories, I think about the men I saw in my dream last night. They all had smiles on their faces at one point. All except for him. For weeks I've seen his face. I've memorized the lines in his forehead, the color of the waves in his hair. His eyes. Always just a glimpse. I can't get them out of my head. Never, in all my visions have I seen him smile. There are never any laugh lines on his face. Plenty of tiring wrinkles and shadows—though he seems too young to have them. He's always tired and his shoulders hang, making him look like he's in his early forties, much older than he probably is. I understand how that feels.

My hand slips into a slit in the mattress that I made and pull out a spoon I'd managed to save from my dinner plate years ago. I look at myself in its blurry surface. Wrinkles are lightly prominent at the corners of my grey eyes and light purple circles swaddle them. I should look younger too. By my estimates I'm at least under thirty. I feel like I look so much older, though. With my gaunt face, pale silver blue eyes, and bland brown hair color, I look less than plain.

The hatch in the wall to my left slides open and a shiny silver tray glides out for me. On it is a bowl with a large ladle-full of the lukewarm brown liquid they give me every meal with small chunks of potato. I shove the spoon into the mattress and walk over to take the bowl.

The soup-like liquid is tasteless. I drink it slow and try to savor the potatoes. I suck on them until all the juice is siphoned out. Then I slowly chew on each bit of potato until it dissolves down my throat. One more spoonful. I have to remind myself not to eat too fast. If I do, my stomach won't be able to handle it. I've learned that the hard way.

I set the bowl back on the silver platform and it slides back into the hatch from where it came.

With fourteen more hours in the day, I sit down to do what I normally do: practice keeping The Public out of my mind. If they have the ability to record my dreams at night through the chip in my brain, who's to say they can't watch my thoughts by day? I sit on the bed, cross my legs and lean back against the wall. For two hours every day, I focus. Focus on finding a way to shut off my mind and block it all out.

—NATE—

Twigs and rocks poked at Nate's stomach and stabbed his chest after he lowered himself to the ground. He hugged the rifle tight into his shoulder and focused on the moose through the crosshairs of his scope. The animal was probably twelve to thirteen hundred yards in the distance. An easy shot if he'd had his military-issue rifle, but this might as well be a plastic child's gun at this range. Nate's finger curled tenderly around the trigger. Soft, like touching a woman's cheek. He couldn't afford to miss this shot. Nobody had had meat in months—just canned artichokes and white rice. Since the war, animals were scarce. Most had died off like everything else.

The gun kicked back into his body after the shot fired and he kept his eye on the animal. The bullet spliced right between the moose's eyes. The animal shook its head wildly and bolted to the left, running east from the hunter.

"Damn."

"It still amazes me," Liam said from behind. "We could have gotten closer you know. Thousand yards off and you still hit it with that POS."

"Twelve hundred," Nate corrected. He didn't say it to be cocky. It was the truth. "I know we could have gotten closer, but I didn't want to risk losing him. We're already too far away from the community, and we still have to track him down."

"Gunshot to the head. How far could he have gone? Fifty feet?"

"I've seen 'em make it a mile."

"Yeah, with a shot to the lungs, maybe. An artery. That was a kill shot. Plus, how in the hell do we get it back to the group?"

Nate peered through the scope and stood up, brushing himself off. The dirt and pine needles clung to his jacket and thick olive green pants. "Waddya know?" he mumbled. "We got lucky. It's not far. Take a look."

He took the scope off his rifle and handed it to Liam. "It collapsed two hundred feet from where I shot it. As far as *how* we get it back . . . that's why I brought you along. You're the brains. You tell *me* what will work since we're twenty miles from everyone."

"Brains? I thought you brought me along for eye candy." Liam handed him the scope.

Nate lifted his eyebrow at Liam and rested the rifle strap over his shoulder.

"Did Nathan Naylor just cock his eyebrow at me? Shit, from you, I'll take that as a smile. I may just have to journal this holy event." Liam straightened his face and looked down across the hillside in front of them.

After glancing back to where they'd come from Nate grunted. "You wanna clean it there? That should take off some of the distance we'll need to carry it. One of us will just have to walk back to get the ATV." He pulled the twelve-inch combat knife out of the holster at this belt and hiked toward the dead moose.

Liam picked up both of their packs and followed. "You know, it wouldn't hurt you to crack a real smile. We finally have decent protein and fat to put some warmth on our asses! Don't you think that's something worth pissin' in a real toilet for?"

Nate shook his head and pulled the corners of his lips down in thought. "Not really."

"Not really? If you think about it, that dead animal is the happiest thing to happen to us in weeks. Of course, *he's* not really that happy because he's dead." Liam smiled at his friend and lightly punched him in the shoulder. He waited for Nate's response. For nearly four hundred feet, Nate said nothing.

Liam cleared his throat. "Okay, I'll give you that one. That joke was stupid. I can do better."

"L.O.L." Nate's voice was low and dry.

"What's that mean?"

"Nothing," Nate responded and continued hiking.

Liam brought the first pack around and pulled out a length of rope, handing it to Nate. "Should I know what it means?"

"No. Just something my mom used to say to me." When they reached the Moose, he hunkered down next to the moose and held out his hand for the rope. Nate tied the moose's hind legs and kept his eyes off of Liam. "\Why don't you go get the four-wheeler and bring it around. After I get finished bleeding this I'm gonna need the ax."

Nate's obvious dodge of their conversation was meant to signal to Liam that the topic was finished. It actually managed to work, and Liam nodded. "Sure. Give me about an hour. It's a ways back there." He set the packs down next to Nate and jogged through the forest toward where they'd left the ATV.

When Nate finished getting the animal on a slope, he tied the animal's legs open and tossed the rest of the coiled rope to the side. Grasped tight in his hand, Nate drove the knife into the shallow cavity at the base of the throat and sliced across the main blood vessels with a wide deep cut. The blood flowed away from him and the animal, creating a small black stream.

He didn't mean to be such a beast. It was just the simple fact that he still remembered what it was like before. Perhaps that was the reason he couldn't accept what his life had become. These days there wasn't anything worth, as Liam so beautifully stated, pissing in a real toilet for.

A crack in the woods sent him into alert and he reached for the gun in his back pocket. A basic nine millimeter. Aiming it into the tree line around him, he listened closely. There was nothing. No more sounds. Hell, it could have been a squirrel and he'd still jump. It never stopped. Never went away.

Nate cleared his throat and put the gun back in its place. He then finished cutting through the skin and muscles of the animal, and was ready to eviscerate it. Blood splattered across his pants and shoes, staining the mud underneath his fingernails.

An hour later, Liam showed up with the ATV. Its engine revved and growled with each bump over the dirt and fallen logs. "Oh good, you're just as broody as when I left you. I'd hate to have missed anything," Liam said, turning off the engine.

"I'm not brooding." Nate pulled the knife back and wiped the dripping red blood off on his pants. "Just painfully aware. Hand me that ax, will you?"

"Got it. Here you go."

Nate lifted the ax in the air, swung down, and broke through the breastbone. Blood spattered his face and sprayed drops of blood onto his shirt. "When we get this cleaned we need hang it up so it can cool before we head out."

The two men finished the work and used the four-wheeler to pull the carcass up into the air with the rope and a tree limb up above. With the moose hanging securely, Nate reached up for the fur, made a few cuts, and started peeling it back.

"What?" he asked, noticing the verbal constipated look on Liam's face.

"Nothing."

"You're standing there looking like you ate shit. You want to say something. So, say it or stop making me look at you."

Liam sighed and leaned up against the tree, folding his arms. "I'm worried about you, Spud. You know that."

"Yes, I do. You tell me on an almost *daily* basis. Then I always tell you that everything is fine, which it is. And I wish to hell, each time, that you'd stop being a woman and bothering me about it. Then shortly after you say the same thing all over again. So believe me," Nate grunted, putting his full body weight into pulling the hide off, "I'm fine." He sliced through the tissue where it was tougher. "Life's not like it used to be, and I accept that. You deal with it in your way which works great for you. I deal with it in mine. Now let's just drop it." Nate looked over at Liam and kicked the hide over to a fallen tree.

Liam raised a hand in defense. "All right, Giggles. Fine, I get it. While you're doing your job I'll go ahead and start dinner."

Nate ignored him and finished with the animal before pulling out a large jug of clean water. He rinsed his hands off and wiped them off on his shirt. He hated it when Liam tried to get him to talk, or even smile. Of course, as much as he tried to keep Liam off the subject of his depression, he knew the constant jokes helped to keep his mind off everything that haunted him. That, and the kid, London.

"Nate, did we pack matches?"

"There were only a few boxes left back with the community, so I took a flint stone instead. Front pocket of my pack."

Liam grabbed the pack and pulled the stone out to start the fire. With a dinner of soup cooking in their cans, and the stars starting to poke through the hovering debris of smoke and pollution in the sky, Nate finally sat down and pulled his boots off. They were completely worn, but they were the only pair he had. He stuck his finger into his soup and when he gauged that it was hot enough, he picked it up with a cloth and started eating.

"So what did London say when you told him to stay behind with Ben and the girls?" Liam squatted down next to the fire.

"You know London. He told me I was being too protective and that I wasn't his dad and all that crap."

"He's got a point you know."

Nate looked up from his soup and raised his eyebrow. "I'm not his dad? You're right, I'm not. His eyebrows are way too thick."

Liam smiled. "You just made a joke."

"Don't get used to it." Nate cleared his throat and dug around in his soup can.

"Well, what I meant is, I think you might be too protective. Spud Junior's fifteen now, Nate. I started hunting with my dad when I was seven. It may have been technically illegal at the time, but he took me anyway. I think you need to give him a chance."

Nate took another spoonful of his soup.

At Nate's silence, Liam shifted. "You know what? Even if you were going to respond I already know what you're going to tell me and let's just say I'm all bummed out for the night." Liam was quiet for a moment before he blurted out, "You know what I miss?"

Liam talked more than any woman Nate'd ever known.

"Hmm," Nate answered with a grunt.

"Girls. Don't get me wrong, it's not like Olivia and Sophia aren't cute, but I miss Santa Monica Pier. The bikinis, the fake blondes, the short shorts. Oh, man. The sundresses. It may be sunk two miles under the ocean now for all I know, but I hope the mamas are still there. You ever think about that?"

Nate swallowed and nodded his head slightly. "Sure, I guess."

"You guess? You're a thirty-three-year-old man, Nate. Don't tell me your libido's sunk too."

"I guess I'm more concerned with staying alive."

Liam ignored him and continued. "Olivia'd be a real looker if she'd stop wearing her dad's old clothes. A little shape on her would—"

"They're all she's got," Nate grunted before taking another spoonful.

"Now Sophia. There's a reason she's engaged to Greyson. She knows how to work the pout. You ever noticed that?"

"A chemical explosive went off ten feet from her when she was young. Scar tissue built up in her lips and right cheek when she healed. There's a reason she pouts. She can't help it." He slurped back the rest of his can.

Liam set his spoon in his can and stared at Nate with a less-than-surprised smile. "Can't you just once have a normal conversation? I used to talk this way with Dan and Shawn all the time. We're not dead yet!"

"What, like they are?"

The moment he'd said it he knew he'd gone too far, and the shock on Liam's face was proof. Never in all the years he'd known Liam had he thrown something like that that in his best friend's face. Liam's brothers weren't the only ones gone. He couldn't believe what he'd just done. Nate shook his head and set his can on the ground. "I'm sorry, I . . . I don't know where that came from. I didn't mean it like that."

Liam nodded and quietly took another spoonful of soup, barely slurping it. "It's okay, man. I know you don't mean it. We've all got our demons."

Silence spread between them. Nate pulled his sleeping bag close and got inside. "I have to go to sleep." He closed his eyes, but underneath he was wide-awake. He felt like a complete jackass. He just wanted to forget everything.

Not that that would be easy.

It was harder for him to fall asleep these days. His mind constantly listened for planes or sirens, even though there hadn't been any attacks for almost seven years. Even when he did get to sleep, all he ever dreamed of was gun fire and war. The screams of men echoed in the night. Power shot pelting through their bodies; their flesh boiling from chemical raids. The fighting was over, but it didn't feel like it. He felt trapped, no matter what he did or where he went.

There were two choices: stay with the community, fighting each day to live, or allow himself to be caught by The Public. Fighting for life was better than dying in a cage.

"Nate."

He kept his eyes closed and grunted in response.

"I'll walk back tomorrow. You can drive the kill back."

Nate's eyes opened slightly. The glow of the dying fire burned in his sight. "It's all right. I brought my good boots. You drive back and I'll be four hours behind you."

"Your *good* boots? You only *have* one pair of boots, Spud." Liam's voice sounded exhausted.

"Don't worry about it, Liam. You just get the meat back to them. I'll be fine."

"You sure?"

"Yes," Nate grumbled and then rolled onto his other side. Liam said something else to him about the trip back. He chose not to respond. He was tired. He had a ten hour walk ahead of him with all the equipment. His eyes closed from the weight hanging over his body and he slipped into darkness.

—REGGIE—

Watch to your . . ." the voice cuts out. A truck. Wind
blowing through my hair. A scream comes from
somewhere close. Laughter. The numbers two, two, nine,
eighteen, eight, five, and twenty-seven. Again, I see them. One's a
road sign. Pine trees and the dark sky. A blurred image of a door
lock with a key pad. A man tumbles on the floor, his eyes dead, still
looking at me. It's a guard. I'm running down the bright white
hallway. It's the same one I've taken every morning. Then, his face.
The man who doesn't smile. "Nate!" a voice calls. The image slows
down. He cringes at me. His eyes are darkened with hate and
bitterness. There's death inside.

"Reggie," his voice trails off.

My eyes burst open. My chest pounds and sweat drips off
of my face and rolls down my chest. Liquid soaks my shirt,
making my clothes stick to the already stained mattress.

He said my name. My name. How? I don't understand. It
doesn't make sense. Why does he know me?

Always, without fail, my mind puts me in the place of
someone else. This is different. It was me. *I* was running. *I* was
looking at him. He called *my* name. There's no way I can let

Dryer know. I wonder if they've been waiting for something like this. Have they been expecting it? How could they?

Without hesitating, I sit up and look at the two men ready to take me in for my report. "I'm coming," I whisper.

"Stop moving so slow." The man curses behind my back. The butts of their weapons prod me down the hallway. "She's shaking."

The other chuckles. "Don't worry. Dryer will take care of it."

My feet pad along the cold hallway while I try to figure out how to hide the fact that I was in my own vision. All the practicing I've been doing hasn't helped. To keep my visions blank is near impossible. Dryer can't find out. Again, I'm led to the room with the chair. Dryer comes in with one other man. He has a smile on his face that reminds me of a clown doll I saw once. A little boy had it. The smile's wide, painted, false.

Dryer affixes a needle to a syringe. "Morning, Reggie. I see that last night must have been difficult for you."

"Yeah."

"Injection?"

I hesitate to say anything. I can't show him that I'm nervous. He'll know. Sometimes when I get the injection I can't control where my mind takes me. I forget what I show him. I'd like to forget this one before he hacks into me. "I don't want it. It makes me feel sick."

"Every day, Reggie?" Dryer reaches across me and inserts each needle and then places the small bud electrodes in their places. He smiles at me while repeating the same words he has every morning for the past fifteen years. "Relax." "Visualize."

As if I could possibly forget.

I set my head back and try hard to focus. The drugs keep my control slippery and out of reach. All the years of practicing to keep The Public out of my mind seems like stupidity. A picture begins to appear and I quickly push it aside. My view spins around to a different scene.

Laughter. The numbers again. The keypad. The trees and the wind. The man.

Everything but me. I think I'm sweating—straining to hold the image of myself back; to hold back the man from saying my name.

The images become choppier and unexplainable while I work to see nothing. Black. Darkness. Focus on nothing. Empty. It has to work. I have to block it. I know they mean something. Someone is going to get me out of here and I have to protect that. It's mine. He can't have it.

Words trail off, cut mid-sentence. Images are shown in black and white instead of full color. Lastly, the third man, the one with blue eyes, is the last thing I see before I push that image aside too. "Nate!" the name reverbs back and forth in my mind. He opens his mouth to say my name.

Then it goes black. There's nothing. I'm finally holding everything at bay. It feel like nothing I can explain. Pushing, resisting. Almost like a door is trying to open in my mind, but I'm barely able to keep it closed. It's so hard.

"Reggie?" Dryer's voice resounds deep, slow, and unclear. "Is that all?"

I try to open my eyes. The drugs still weigh heavily in mind. I nod. At least I think I do. Focus. Focus is all I can do to hide my future from him. I don't know what it means or if it's even a good future. My visions could be trying to tell me I'll die. They're talking to me.

I lay there in the chair, propped back, and everything is silent. My pulse rate is slow and my fingers feel ice cold.

A blinding jolt of pain travels from my head to my toes and every muscle, vein, and tendon in my body seems to curl, pierced by a vine of thorns, squeezing.

"Reggie, Reggie, Reggie. *Sweetie*. We know you're trying to keep us out. So why don't we try this again?" Dryer looks down at me from the window above. Tears involuntarily drizzle from the corners of my eyes. I nod and close them.

I feel my bare feet running down the bright hallway. The scratch of my dry skin can even be heard. The wind in my hair. Nate, he looks at me with . . . not pain . . . distrust, and disgust. Death. Hate. The guard falls to the floor with his lifeless eyes looking straight into mine.

Scuffles and hurried words fill my ears. I can't tell if these sounds are part of my vision or happening in the waking world. The door opens and closes various times. Tears continue to fall from my eyes and I think I've finished. I don't want to open them. I don't want to come back to reality. Even though I'm trying to shut out what's around me, the hands still grab my arms. The needles get yanked from my veins too quickly and warm trickles of blood travel down my forearms.

The guards pull harder than usual, and lead me back to my cell. Everything is blurry and I keep tripping over my own feet. My muscles still spasm from the shock, and shudder at the thought that I couldn't do it. Years of practice to keep them out of my head and I couldn't do it.

When my body hits the cool floor of my cell, I curl into a ball, my mind continually replaying the look on Nate's face. I could feel his emotion. The look on his face said it all, and it scares me. He's going to take me away from here, but he won't be doing it to help me. He won't trust me. For the first time in the weeks I've been seeing him I'm afraid. It was my first vision of myself—something I want to protect, something

I've wanted, something that I thought would change my life and make everything all right.

But . . .

This dream, this vision isn't the same as the others with Nate. Even if I do get out of here I don't know what will happen to me. What if I don't want that future? What if it gets worse than this? Much worse.

Maybe I'll never know. Now that Public One knows what I've seen, they'll do anything to keep it from happening.

—NATE—

Nate finally arrived at what used to be the city limits of Hudson, Wyoming, the old Sinclair station sitting there, empty and lifeless like the rest of the town. You could scarcely see the painted dinosaur on the side of it anymore, and the only words that were still legible were the last letters in "Pennsylvania," ANIA, and MOTOR.

His foot caught the edge of a small hole in the ground and the packs on his shoulders slid to one side. He was only feet from the edge of the community and soon he'd be able to rest. Liam must have arrived hours ago with the meat. People would have divided it up and already taken home their shares.

He saw a woman running down the street to meet him. Long dark ebony hair swished back and forth in the ponytail at the back of her head. Her large baggy jeans held up by a fraying fabric belt, stained tank top, and unbuttoned flannel shirt gave her away. Although Sophia and Olivia looked similar, Olivia was taller, and her father's pants could barely stay around her small waist. Her ponytail made her ears look like they stuck out even more.

"Nate! Ya made it back," she said in her very light southern drawl. Olivia stopped in front of him, holding out her hands for some of the things on his back. "We were beginnin' to worry. Liam said 'at chu both left ten hours ago."

"We did." Nate grunted under the weight of the pack and sleeping bag he handed her. With the rifle, a pack, a sleeping bag, and the rope still on his back, they started walking. "But I found a stream just two miles out. I stopped to test the water and see if it was clean to use."

"And?" She scrunched her turned-up button nose.

"It's good. I'm gonna tell your dad so that a few of us can go out there."

Olivia smirked. "Good. We're really low. 'Specially since the new guy, Isaac, decided tuh take a small bath a day ago."

Nate's mouth dropped slightly and he shook his head. "What? Who's Isaac? Didn't Ben tell him it wouldn't be possible?"

"Oh yeah, you weren't here. You and Liam left just three hours 'fore he got here. He's new and don't know the rules." Olivia hoisted the pack higher on her shoulder and smirked. "You know Dad. He'll say no at first. Then they get that look in their eyes . . . an' he caves like a mud slide."

It was true. Ben Woodstock, the man who could be known as the "ringleader" of the community, was a child of the old days. Born in the early nineties, he had a continual positive outlook on life. He'd seen the growth in technology, a time of world peace—however briefly in the late nineties—and even experienced times when what used to be the United States was a grand country. Now, sixty-three years old, he didn't know how to tell people "no" to things that used to be essentials and were more like luxuries.

Nate looked over at Olivia as she walked beside him. At her core, she was her father's daughter, but she behaved nothing like him. She was stubborn, hard-willed, and had a right hook that could rival Nate's. For a moment, he remembered what Liam had said to him the night before. She was attractive in her own way. Sweet looking. A lot like his own sister had been.

"Of course," Nate nodded. They walked until they arrived at the abandoned house that Nate and London were living in and had called "home" for the past six months. Had it already been six months? It would only be a matter of weeks, maybe days, before the community packed up and left again. It was dangerous to stay in one place for too long. The Public had a way of knowing where Nomads were.

Nate dropped his load on the old couch in the front room and walked into the kitchen where the large cooler was. "Want one of the last two bottles of water?" he asked.

"Nah," Olivia set the other things neatly on the floor. "Save it fer London. He'll be happy fer it. He's been going crazy the last couple days without ya'll here. I think he should go with next time."

Nate took a swig of lukewarm water. "Hmm."

He swallowed half, spit, and put the cap back on the bottle. "Liam talk to you about that?"

"Nah," she frowned, "It's just hard to see him cooped up here. He's a teenager now, you know. You're gonna have to get used to the idea that he's not a kid anymore. 'Specially not now."

"What do you mean, 'especially'?"

"Nate, yer the one going on and on about how horrible life is."

"Yes," he nodded, "all the more reason to give London a semi-normal life."

"A normal life includes huntin' before the age of fifteen!" Olivia sounded exasperated, but she tried to keep her voice light.

Nate's jaw shuffled around and he stared at the floor. "You weren't there, Liv."

"Whaddya mean I weren't there? I saw the look on his face when you two took off and left 'im."

"No," he growled. "When we found him. When I opened that pantry door and saw him on the floor pointing that gun at me."

London was fifteen now, but back then, he'd just been eleven, clutching tight to an old pistol. He'd hidden in an abandoned home's pantry. The area was hit with missiles three years before. It was only when Nate stumbled through the small Arizona city—he couldn't remember which one now—that he opened up the pantry of a random home looking for canned foods, that he even knew the boy was there.

Olivia sighed and picked at the threads on the corner of her shirt. "The gun was empty, you know that."

"It's not that." He massaged his neck, thinking back to the day. "He was so . . . afraid. No child should ever experience that. I promised myself I'd never let him go through that again, no matter what it took. So you can judge me for being 'overprotective' or a horrible guardian, but it's my *job*."

Just then, the door swung open and a lanky teenager came through the door holding a plastic bag of what looked like moose meat. London's jeans didn't fit him either. Thirty-four inch waist on a boy with a twenty-six. Even though his red Chicago Bulls t-shirt had a tear in the seam, he grinned when he saw Nate and made his way over. London's light blonde hair was ruffled and darkened slightly by the tinge of dirt swirled up by the Wyoming wind. "Nate, man. You made it back! You know, I could have helped carry all that stuff back from the kill sight," he said with a slight squeak in the middle.

Olivia raised her eyebrows and folded her arms.

"Yes, but your voice would have cracked like that and scared off the animal before we got to it," Nate pointed out, ignoring the look in her eyes.

London smiled with embarrassment and shook his head. With sarcasm, he said, "Thanks."

"No problem, kid. You got our share?"

"Yeah, and Mr. Woodstock's having a meeting down at his place. He didn't tell me what it was about. He wanted me to bring you back if you were home." London placed the bag in the cooler—not that the cooler would keep the meat good for long. Fresh meat would keep for a day, enough for one meal. After that, they'd have to dry and cure it.

"Okay. You stay here with Liv, and I'll be back when it's over."

"I'm goin' too, you know," Olivia said as she opened the front door.

Nate nodded. "Fine. London, stay here then and . . ."

"Mr. Woodstock told me to come back."

"Is Ben your guardian?" Nate started to follow Olivia out the door.

London's face fell and he took a few steps. "I'm not a kid, Nate!" His freckles seemed to get darker from the rush of blood that came to his smaller face.

"Stay here. I'll be back."

Nate shut the door behind him and joined Olivia out on the road.

"That's what I'm talking about, Nate."

"What?" He stuck his hands in his pockets.

"London. If Dad feels he's adult enough to be at this meetin', then maybe he should be."

Nate dug his heels into the ground even harder with each step. Olivia and Liam weren't even close to being parents. Not that he was either, but they didn't understand. Everyone was quick to judge when they didn't have to deal with the consequences.

The two of them made it to the house just a block away and walked through the front door. Sitting on a couch by himself was a stranger, someone Nate had never seen before. His clothes were dirty, but they were of excellent quality. Fabric like that didn't exist outside of The Public. The man was in every aspect of the word: perfect. He seemed to be in peak physical shape, kind of a pretty-boy with a strong straight nose and square jaw, clean-shaven, quiet, and had had a recent haircut. Not like the choppy haircuts Sophia gave. This was professional. Immediately, Nate knew what the meeting was about.

"Glad you made it back, Spud. Deuce take longer than normal?" Liam walked through the archway to the right. He'd just been in the dining room talking with two other men.

"Found a clean stream," Nate responded, ignoring Liam's following burst of laughter which he attempted to cover. "What's going on?"

"Not quite sure, myself. If I were a bettin' man, and," Liam raised his eyebrows, "let's face it, I am, I'm guessing it has something to do with the clone over there."

"Nate!" An excited voice called from behind. Ben's drawling voice wasn't booming. On the contrary, was quite light and breathy for such a large man. "You made it."

"Yeah, I did. I was just explaining to Liam that I took a detour and found a clean stream just two miles outside city limits. We'll need to take some men out there."

Ben took a deep breath and sighed. His bushy strawberry blonde eyebrows had turned almost white over the last three years, and his hair was thinning. Ben was tall, even more so than Nate. With the lack of consistent food, he was much thinner than he should have been. "Good. Ya'll have no idea how good that news is."

"Ben, what's going on?" Nate whispered.

Ben took a sidelong glance at the man on the couch and motioned for Nate and Liam to follow. "Nate, Liam. This is Isaac Quigg. Isaac managed to find us just after ya'll left to go huntin'. He's got an interestin' history, and even more interestin' information. I wanted to wait 'til you two got back 'fore we did anythin'. I think ya'll need to listen to him." The man stared and passed a glance between him and Liam. "Go ahead, Isaac."

The man shifted in his seat and nervously looked at each face in the room. "As Ben has said, my name is Isaac. First," he spoke hesitantly, "I know you don't trust me. I can tell."

"You think?" Liam said sarcastically. "You're a Public manufactured clone. PMC, made right in the heart of the Public."

"I'm *not* a clone," his voice was hard, though Nate could sense that Isaac was trying to stay calm, "and I'd prefer if you listened without talking." The man waited to see if someone else would talk before he continued. "Yes, I am from Public One."

An immediate burst of excited whispers erupted in the room from the other ten adults that were there. Ben waved them down and then urged Isaac to continue.

"I'm not your enemy. I escaped from Public One two weeks ago. I needed to find someone that would help me, and I thought that if I could get outside of the limits of the government, I'd be able to find Nomads. I'm glad I did. You see, there's a reason why The Public is able to find others like you so quickly. When was the last time you had a run-in with them?"

Ben folded his arms and leaned back slightly. "It's been a little over three years. We don't give 'em much chance to find us because we keep movin'."

"It doesn't matter," Isaac said, shaking his head. "It doesn't matter if you move or not. It doesn't matter if you hide, or even if you dig into the earth and live like moles. You people think that if you stay in run-down areas, or the colder climates that they won't find you. That's naïve bull. That may have worked fourteen years ago, but not anymore. The city government is rumored to be in possession of something that makes them almost invincible. They can protect themselves, round up Nomads, and prevent any attack on their society. They have a Precognitive."

"What the crap is a Precognitive?" Liam asked, shaking his head.

"A weapon. More importantly, it's the only one known to be in existence. Rumor has it that fifteen years ago, a precog showed up at the gates of Public One. This precog foresees the future. The immediate future. This precog shows them like dreams would be to us. Only in this instance, they aren't dreams. They're reality. What we need to do . . . is steal the Precognitive. Then," he shook his head, "the public can be stopped."

"Wait a minute," Nate spoke up. His eyes had narrowed more and more while the man talked. "You want us to break into Public One, go into, what I'm sure is an impossibly secure area, and steal something that we're not even sure exists? You said yourself it's a rumor, so why should we risk ourselves and our families to help you?"

Isaac looked at Nate with stoic eyes. "Because I need to save my family too."

"You've got a family? Where are they?" Nate folded his arms.

Isaac looked at the ground. That wasn't a good sign. "They're still there."

"Hold up, hold up, hold up," Liam interrupted. "You . . . *left* your family behind? I guess a better question would be: you *have* a family? Wait, wait . . . *better question* . . . a woman voluntarily let you into her bed?"

"What do you think I am?" Isaac asked.

"I've heard about the nutso stuff going on in there. You're not real. Not like . . ."

"You? How are we different?"

Ben held up a hand as Liam was about to retort, and pulled up a chair next to Isaac. Nate was becoming increasingly wary, but watching Ben handle the situation made him realize why Ben was the one in charge. "Isaac, you say ya aren't different, but we *have* heard stories and we need the truth."

Isaac took a deep breath and spoke straight to Ben. "I'm *normal*. I promise. From the inside of my guts to the hair on my head. My dad was in marketing; my mom was a pre-school teacher. My children—"

"Who you left behind," Liam interrupted again. This time it was Nate who gave him a look to keep him quiet.

"—my boys," he repeated and paused, "are a different story. I love them. I love them as if they were my own."

"They aren't?" Nate asked.

"Ah," Liam grinned, "it all makes sense."

"Shut up, Liam," Nate turned on him, sick of the incessant buzzing and prodding. He just wanted to be able to think.

Isaac's eyes swiveled onto Nate. "Thank you."

"It wasn't for your sake. Keep going."

Isaac nodded with a sigh. "Any child living within The Public is below the age of ten. None of the others are living."

"What do you mean?" Ben asked.

"Three years previous to the oldest Public child, the precog showed up at the gate. The Precognitive is genetically modified. Tweaked and engineered. It was apparently a U.S. project. The Public tested it, learned from it and within three years were creating their own versions. My two kids are a product of The Public's experiments. They . . ." Isaac licked his supple lips, "are made of my genetic DNA, but they don't belong to my companion and me. They belong to The Public, or at least, they'll return to being the property of the public when they reach the age of four where they're housed for two years. Training, classes, whatever they do. They're creating the perfect society. That's their goal. That's what they do."

"How do ya mean?" Ben asked, folding his arms.

Isaac looked down at the floor and clasped his hands, folding his fingers. He looked frustrated, very antsy. "I was seventeen when my mom and I were found outside of what used to be Atlanta. I almost thought," Isaac shook his head, "I almost thought that it was good that they found me. They fed us, bathed us, gave us beds to sleep in, a vaccine. It was like a dream. I never saw my mom again, though. The second day they took samples from me." He went quiet again, staring at his hands. Something made Nate feel like Isaac was holding something back, but he let him continue.

"What kind of samples?" Nate shrugged his shoulders.

Isaac looked directly up at him and then back down at the floor. "Body fluids. Blood, urine, semen."

He said it so quietly, Nate wasn't sure he heard him correctly.

"Look, I'm not perfect, but I watch my kids and I can't," he shook his head, "I can't give them back. I thought I could, but I can't."

Nate cleared his throat. He didn't want to believe any of this. It was too farfetched. Even so, he looked back at the whimpering man. "What does The Public do with the children when they turn four?"

"The children go to the Ponanki Building, or the training center, Public building, whatever you want to call it. We don't know what happens there."

"What's so wrong with your kids being perfect?" Liam baited him.

"How would you like it if your son and daughter had part of you, part of your companion, plus fifty parts of fifty other people, then twisted into something else? They're pieced together with selective DNA, with strings of mutations added."

"Mutations? Are ya saying these kids are like comic book characters? X-Men?" Ben asked.

"What's a comic book?" Liam asked. No one except for Ben registered any type of shock. They were all wondering the same thing Liam was.

"Look, I don't know what these *Ex-men* are, but what The Public is doing, it's not perfection." Isaac licked his lips. "It's disgusting. It's one man's idea of perfect. Please, you have to help me. We have to take the Precognitive and get it away from The Public. Once we do that, they won't be able to see. It'll be like blinding them. It's the only way to weaken them."

"But we're prime targets on the way in, right?" Liam spat.

Nate shook his head and hissed in disbelief. He'd had enough of listening to this story and just needed to get out. Liam's shoulder jerked back when Nate shoved him to the side. The pounding of his boots echoed even on the dirty floor of the home. The second screen door squeaked on its hinges and slammed closed behind him.

In his haste to leave he heard Ben say to Liam, "Watch him." Ben followed Nate out of the house and called for him to stop. Nate stopped at the edge of the sidewalk and then turned around to face Ben.

"What are ya thinkin', Nate?"

"He's lying."

"How do you know? Just 'cause it's odd don't mean it ain't true. You told me yerself that while you was in the military you'd heard rumors of the government doin' experiments exactly like this. Don't this confirm that rumor? I mean, I'm not sayin' I'm completely on board with everythin' Isaac says, but how is this false and the other true?"

Nate shook his head and quietly looked back at the house. "Something's not right. I'm telling you I've got a feeling in my gut. This guy is hiding something."

"Is that jest an excuse for not wantin' to trust a soul anymore?" Ben replied.

Nate stood there, his chest rising up and down. He ran his hands through his dark hair.

"We need to talk about this as a community and I need you in there more 'an anyone else."

"You think that anyone is gonna want to act on this?"

Ben shook his head and looked back at the house. "I have a feelin' they might."

Nate bit down on his lips and blew out a breath. Before he knew what he was doing, he nodded. Though, quite against his instincts.

He followed Ben back into the house. Questions were still being fired at Isaac from others in the room, and he was having a difficult time with it. Isaac's face was now scarlet red, though he attempted to keep his composure. His fingers kept knotting together while he leaned forward and then back. Over and over.

"All right, that's enough," Ben said, the others parting enough to let him through. "I need everyone in the back room so we can talk. Let's see . . . Liam, keep watching Isaac. London, Liv, the rest of you, follow me."

Nate heard London's name and his head snapped around. He saw the tall body and the back of the boy's head bobbing behind Ben down the hall. Nate cursed under his breath and pushed through the others to grab a hold of London's shirt collar. A slight gagging noise crackled from London's throat before he turned around.

"What are you doing here, London? I told you to stay home."

"And Ben told me to be here. I have every right."

Nate took a deep breath and exhaled. He pulled London's shirt collar just a little tighter and London came closer. "You have to *earn* the right. And you don't do that by pulling stunts like this."

"You're right, because you won't even give me the opportunity!" London harshly whispered back.

The rest of the adults had filed into the back room. He knew London was right. He knew everyone was right. He just couldn't risk getting London involved. This kid was all he had in the way of family. It had always been his goal to do anything and everything to keep London safe, and perhaps blissfully unaware of how horrible the world was. Despite that, he knew he wouldn't be able to protect him forever. Nate let go of the shirt and London rolled his shoulder back. "Fine, but you'll stand next to me and keep your mouth shut." Nate opened the door and led the boy inside. When the door shut, voices exploded.

REGGIE

I hear the sliding door to my cell whisper open as I finish my fiftieth sit up. My eyes open wide. My thoughts go blank. For only a moment.

The guards never come to get me during this time of the day. What's going on? It doesn't make sense. My anxiety rockets. Coursing waves of blood thump through my chest. This isn't right.

"What are you doing?" I ask, my voice frantic. I slap away one of the guards' hands. He lashes out again for my arm and grips it tight behind me. "Wait! Why are you taking me?" The two men seize my wrists and arms, yanking me to my feet; the force of which snaps my head back from my shoulders. Sharp stings speed up and down my neck. The whiplash triggers the chip in my head and my whole body seizes. My teeth crack together and my brain throbs. Limply I hang from their arms like a rag. The shock tires my muscles, but I feebly continue to pull my arms away.

"Where am I going?" I say breathlessly when my jaw starts to loosen. "Leave me alone!" My voice gains power.

"Don't . . . *touch* me!" I try pulling my arms out of their grasp. The pull of their grips are tight enough to leave red skin-to-skin rashes on my arm. The natural oils and salt on their hands makes contact with the raw skin. Twisting my arm rubs the oil in even more. The sting of it lingers the longer they hold me down.

The man with over-ripe pepper breath threatens me and calls to his partner to calm me down. The other pins my left arm further behind my back and I feel the bone in my socket grinding against my shoulder blade. It's close to popping out.

I scream out and pull to the right. At that moment, a blunt object cracks against the back of my head and a burst of white explodes in my eyes before it goes dark.

As if my heart has climbed its way into my brain, a repetitive thump, thump, thump beats against the inside of my skull.

"Get her ou . . ." a voice orders. My head swings around and I'm looking into almond-shaped eyes.

"Reggie." The voice sounds like a whisper drifting from the bottom of a pit. My head beats again, and again. Muted echoes Dopplerize and rebound against my eardrums. Now, there's significant pain. Everything is dark. I try to open my eyes, but the blinding light above burns through my retinas.

"Reggie, you can open your eyes," the voice coaxes. It's too cavernous to know who it is. I try to open my eyes again while my head pounds more and more. I can feel a large bump on the back of my head as it rolls to the side to avoid the light.

"Open your eyes, Reggie."

Once more, I peer through the cracks of my eyelids and a blurred form is in front of me. Like a shadow in the air.

"We need to talk about what's happening, Reggie."

It's Dryer. His voice is warped, but I recognize it. My head pounds again. The throb moves through my entire body, ending in a tingle at the end of my toes.

"You weren't very cooperative," Dryer smoothes back my hair, "when the guards tried to bring you in. Why were you acting that way? Hmm? You know that wasn't a smart thing to do. I hope you realize that now, because this process is going to run much smoother if you simply answer my questions, all right?"

My head rolls to the side again in pain. Dr. Dryer takes this as if I'm saying no. "Ah, Reggie. Reggie, my girl. I know you don't want to, but you've seen something that has . . . concerned me. I think you know what I'm talking about." With each word he says my head throbs more. I can barely hear him over the pain.

He sighs, and it sounds like waves crashing on rocks. He motions to someone else. "Inject her with selabraxatine."

Another form appears at my side and cold metal presses into the side of my neck. A hiss of air, a slight pinch, and immediately the fog in my head lifts. The pain disappears, and the tears dripping down the side of my face cease and begin to dry up. The drug leaves behind a taste of smoke in my mouth, and the sudden urge to vomit. However, I don't.

"Now that you're no longer in pain, this might actually work. Reggie, this . . . is going to be more complicated than usual. Last night, you had a vision of yourself. You dreamed of yourself. Do you understand that?"

I don't move. Even if I wanted to, I'm strapped. It's more than that, though. A mixture of rage, fear, and obstinacy holds me back. Now I know why they've brought me in. They think I can answer questions and fill in holes that my visions left out. Never mind that I've not seen a single one of those faces in my waking life. Ever.

I tried to keep them from seeing Nate say my name and now they think I know more.

"Reggie, drugs are the last thing I want to use because you won't be able to give me clear answers, but I will if I have to. Now, are you willing to answer my questions?"

I continue to stare up at the ceiling and my throat starts to close off. The odd gagging reflex just before acidic vomit arrives. I swallow it down.

"Are you going to answer?" The words come out of his mouth with so much force, yet his voice is smooth and sweet as honey. His face is cold and expressionless. My eyes graze over to look at him.

"What if I don't? Dryer, are you gonna hit me?" I close my eyes to focus on my rolling stomach. "See," I wince, "I know you, too. You want to beat me. But you won't."

His breathing is calm. "No. You're right. Reggie, you've always been stronger and smarter than these others have expected. That's why I love you like my own. You realize this is your home, don't you? You may see other possibilities, but this one . . ." he leans forward and I can smell the fusty trace of canned fish on his breath. He gently runs his repulsively soft hand over my hair. "This one won't come true. Do you know why?"

I continue to stare at him.

"Because it's not possible. No one knows about you. No one cares about you. No one but me. This is your life and there is none different. We've taken care of you for years, and we always will. The life you see is impossible to live. It's not safe like it is here. Understand that? Now, why don't you stop being stubborn and answer some questions, all right?" He turns to grab an instrument next to me.

"Everything I see comes true. And you know it."

The raise of Dryer's eyebrow accompanies a look I've never seen before. "Do they? Do they come true? Reggie?"

Dryer walks around the head of the slab they have me resting on and trickles his finger over my collar bone. "What if I was to tell you that every vision you've had we've not only been able to corroborate, but impede and even change?"

"Impede?"

"Of course, Reggie. All those people we've taken care of. They've been brought safely inside the city. Just like you."

"Just like me? You . . . you use me to capture people?" A million memories flash through my mind. The people I'd seen before, the events. "The man last week. The one I saw. You said he was a traitor." I furrow my eyebrows. "I remember the look on his face."

"We don't capture them. We rescue. And we find and stop criminals."

"Criminals who escape? Ones like that man?"

Dryer folds his arms. "He escaped, did he?"

"Why are you asking me? You already know the answer."

"How do you know he did?"

"You know better than anyone that I have eyes. Not just the ones in my sleep that you take upon yourself to pilfer and tamper with. You, and everyone else I've seen. You've been different. You've been worried since he left. I can see it. You never got him, and he could be anywhere, talking to anyone."

The doctor lifted his chin while still looking down on me. "Reggie, why did you try to keep your vision from me this morning?"

I start to answer him, but the room slowly pulls back, stretched from end to end like stretched elastic. My eyes go cloudier and my vision tunnels deep.

I can't see the interrogation room anymore. I'm not on the chair anymore. I'm sitting on wood steps. I can feel the prickles of bare wood beneath my feet, and a hole under my big toe. When I bend down to feel it, I hear a creek behind me.

It's dark, and the moon is shining brightly in the sky. It's impossible. I was just in the compound of Public One.

The creek groans behind me again and I jerk to look in its direction. It's him. One of the men from my dream is walking up to me from behind. Nate was his name. Can he see me? He won't look at me. I hesitate to say something to him, but I can't help but want him to sit next to me. I clear my throat and he looks over at me for a moment before looking ahead again. The look he gives me. Stormy. But there was something else there too. Whatever presence I carry brings him a sliver of trust. I can see it. The night is quiet. Still. The air is so tense, so thick, I almost can't breathe.

Dryer's voice echoes throughout the night. "Reggie," it says, demanding.

The world disappears around me and my head throws back in agony. The chip signals my pain center and pulls me back.

The interrogation room forms around me again and I'm back. I'm trying to control my breathing. I don't know what just happened. This has never happened before and if Dryer saw . . . .

My thought trails off. I don't say anything. Dryer is glaring down at me, a small twitch in his right eyebrow is the only flicker of movement I can see before he says, "Is something the matter, Reggie?"

"Of course not," I say, my voice shaking lightly from the shock.

He looks at me curiously, not saying a word. He picks up the needles and begins to insert them into my veins—my wrists strapped down to the chair.

"I really didn't want to do this, Reggie. But you're being stubborn. And I need to know everything."

In a matter of moments, my mind becomes cloudy. There is so much spinning and I can't stop it. I close my eyes. Everything continues to spin behind my eyelids.

"Reggie, can you hear me?" His question is trailed by the shock of my chip. My toes stiffen and jut in different directions. My heart races.

"Yes," I whisper with a slur. I don't know why I'm talking. I don't want to.

"Why did you hold your vision in reserve this morning?"

The vision? Which vision? I feel my lips almost wanting to mouth it. "Because . . . it . . ." I breathe a few times while my brain swims freely around behind my eyes. Another jolt blasts through my limbs from the chip in my brain. My fingers clench and dig into the center of my palms. "It was mine!"

"Do you know the men in your vision?"

My eyes roll to the left and I feel my mouth begin to open, but I hold my words back.

"I'm warning you, Reggie. I'll push the button again. Do you know them?"

"The men? The men. I . . . I don't."

Electrical pulses seize my abs and I feel the contents of my stomach rocket up through my esophagus once more.

"Do you know them?!" he yells.

Tears slide down my cheeks, mixing with the vomit drooling down the side of my face. "No," my voice shakes.

"You saw a keypad in your dreams. Can you tell me if there was a code?"

"No."

A jolt of pain sears through my body again, rendering me paralyzed in agony. More tears flood down the trails on my face.

"Was there a code, Reggie?"

"No," I sob very lightly and my head joggles back and forth as much as it can. There was no code. Random numbers, yes. But, he wasn't asking for numbers.

"Good. Lastly, do you really believe we'd let someone take you?"

My head rolls again and I try to make my groggy eyes look in his direction, even though I can't see him. "No."

—NATE—

People talked over each other, disregarding what others said, only wanting to hear their voice above the sea of clamor. Nate stood silently near Ben, looking between the faces of each adult in the community. No one agreed on what to do with Isaac's information. Everyone had their own opinion, and frustration creased in Ben's face. Every once in a while, Nate looked over to his ward, still wishing the kid was back at the house. He just wanted London safe. Why couldn't he just stay away?

There were so many thoughts bombarding Nate that he could barely sort them out. London. Isaac. He hated the guy. Something didn't sit right. Did he distrust him because the man was from The Public, or was there a valid reason? He usually felt he could trust his gut, but this . . . he just didn't know. Ben's comment about Nate not trusting a single soul had resonated to his core. Was it true? Did he simply not trust anyone anymore?

The one thing that held him back from making a snap judgment was something else. He'd seen something.

Something in Isaac's face was familiar; something Nate understood. When Isaac said he wanted to protect his children, he'd meant it. There was no denying it. Who was Nate to decide who died and who got to live out their life— captured or not? Whose job was it? It definitely hadn't been God. God had abandoned them years ago. No God he wanted to know would allow human beings to wipe each other off the face of the planet, separating children from parents.

"This man is from *Public One!*" one man called out. "Does that mean nothing to the rest of you? We've spent the last twelve years running from them, and the previous ten just trying not to get killed by other bullshit bombs!"

"But what if we could stop 'em? Or at least weaken 'em? Wouldn't it be worth it?" Sophia's lilting voice spoke up. Sophia was Ben's youngest. She was petite long black hair that cascaded down her back in a braid. There was so much more of Ben in her than in Olivia. Ben's wife had been killed years before, and Nate had never met her, so it was hard to say if she had any characteristics of her mother. Sophia was trusting, warm, sympathetic. Exactly like Ben.

"Are you stupid? Worth it? Worth risking our lives over? Our families' lives? I'm sure you'd have us try to take down the other four Publics while we're at it. Because that's about as sane!"

"He's trying to lure us inside. I'm telling you, The Public is just using this as a ruse to get us."

"I agree."

"That's the most ridiculous thing I've ever heard. If they wanted us, and he was really in communication with them, they'd sweep in and already have us. I think what he's proposing is a good idea. He seems to be telling the truth, believe me! I studied body language extensively at Harvard, and I know what I'm talking about."

"Oh, shut up, Hugh!"

"Hold on a minute!" Olivia called out, and everyone went quiet. "We're gettin' nowhere and all this fightin' ain't helpin' the situation. We need to make a decision based on the facts. So, can we just sort those out first?"

"Yeah, the facts are that what he's asking us to do is physically impossible!"

"Are they?"

The others continued to bellow and talk before Ben put his hand in the air, silently asking them to stop. "Nate?" Ben looked over at him, his eyes squinted in thought. He kept two fingers over his mouth as he spoke. "What ya think?"

Nate shook his head, closed his eyes, and then looked back up at the group. "I've been standing here trying to come up with every conceivable reason why going into that compound is the worst idea in the world. Let me say, there are *thousands*."

"Yes," a man murmured.

"Nothing that man says makes sense. What he's gone through, what they're doing, the weapon. It sounds like aliens and space shit to me. There's no way in this world, or the next, that I will ever believe it."

"Yes!" A murmuring moved through the group.

"*But* there's one thing he's not lying about. He wants to protect his family. I trust that in him, and that alone. I don't trust him." Nate rested his hands on his waist. "I can't believe I'm gonna say this, but, I think rescuing his family might be or *should* be something we need to act on."

Ben nodded and exhaled loudly, covering his mouth with his hand. Many in the room began to demand that no one go, others sighed in disappointment. Some were already throwing out suggestions that Nate lead the team. Ben just stood, looking at Nate; shock and worry etched around his eyes.

"I'll do it, Ben. If you think that's best. I'll support whatever decision you make."

Ben looked back at Nate and then nodded. A heavy sigh, weighed with the worries of an entire community. He looked like he wanted to hold his words back. "Then I've made up my mind. We're goin' to help him."

"I'm going with Nate." A short muscular man raised his hand. Greyson Peters had his arm around Sophia's waist, but for the first time during the meeting he'd said something. Greyson's curly blonde hair was pulled back into a ponytail and a tendril hung to the side of his face. "If Nate thinks this is a good idea, then I'm going with."

"I didn't say it was a good idea."

"You said we should act on it. So I'm acting."

"Me too," another stepped forward. It was the same who'd studied at Harvard. He was newer in the community, but had already came in tow with an annoying aura that followed him. A little self-important—holier-than-thou. Nate thought his name was Hugh. He was older—perhaps forty-five, and more book-smart than survival savvy. Nate eyed him with apprehension, but nodded.

"I'm goin', as well." Olivia folded her arms.

Of course she'd want to. That wasn't a surprise. Hearing her volunteer still made Nate's gut squirm, though. He cared about her. She was like family to him.

"I'm goin', Pa."

"No, Liv," Ben started.

"Me too," Sophia spoke up.

"NO!" both Greyson and Ben shouted simultaneously. Greyson glared protectively at Sophia and kissed her forehead.

"Dad," Olivia spoke again. "Keep Soph here. I'm goin'. I might be able to do things as a woman that the men can't. I can survive just as good as Greyson, and I can hold my own. I'm not goin' to argue 'bout this, I'm goin'." She'd dug her heels in. Nate knew that even if Ben said no again, Liv would find some way to get onto a truck.

"Just as *well*," Hugh whispered out loud.

"Me too," London said.

"No, you're not," Nate stated. "Not even close."

"Ben, I volunteer," London said again. "I can do it."

Ben looked from London to Nate. "I wish I could say yes fer your desire's sake. But I can't. I don't want to, son. That's fer Nate to decide."

Nate looked over at London, the latter did not return the gaze but stood straight, his chest rising and falling faster and deeper. "Then that settles it," Nate said. "Me, and four others. I'm sure Liam will come too. When I explain it to him. It's best we keep the party small."

London's shoulders sank, and his jaw jutted forward in frustration. Nate ignored it. The kid could throw a tantrum for all he cared. He wouldn't be going.

Even though the community didn't fully agree with what had happened, they walked back out together. Many faces were blank. Emotions ran high and anxiety clouded the air. When Nate stepped out into the front living room again, and saw Liam sitting across from Isaac, neither man looking at each other, he knew that they'd spent the entire half-hour in silence. Liam was picking at the skin and dirt on his finger tips, and Isaac stared at the ground, his clean hands lightly clasped in front of him.

Nate tried to prepare himself for the reaction Liam would have when he learned they'd be going into the city. How could you come up with the right words to say, "We might die this week?" Even during the war, it'd never come out right. That was one blow you couldn't cushion.

"Liam." His voice was low. "We're going." That was it. He turned on his heel and quietly left the house.

"What?" he heard called out behind him. Liam jumped up from the chair and the sound of his heavy boots could be heard clomping over the hardwood floor behind Nate before they both burst out of the house.

"What do you mean we're going?! I thought you didn't *trust* him. This is stupid, Nate! What happened in there? Don't tell me you're doing this to save London from some hard shit or something like that because we both know that you can protect him without doing this. Hey! Turn around and say something, man!"

Nate stopped walking down the sidewalk, took a breath, and then looked back at his friend. "I may not trust him, but this isn't about that. I'm not some passive-aggressive supreme being, and I don't get to pick and choose who I help. Come on, Liam. Don't make me beg."

Liam huffed and placed his hands on his hips. Shaking his head, he looked down.

"Liam."

His friend paused, silent. When he spoke, there was a noticeable lilt to his tone. "If you want me to do this with you, I'm gonna make you. I wanna see you beg."

"Don't mess with me."

"No." Liam looked him straight in the eye. "I wanna see you beg. Beg like a little bitch. Get on all fours, and beg." He gave Nate that look. The one reserved for the rarest of occasions when he was not actually kidding.

"Do you *want* a broken arm?"

"Hey, if I'm going to risk my life for a damn clone, I want to make sure it's worth it."

"And seeing me beg would make it worth it?"

Liam's eyes widened. "Do you not know me?"

He was going to kill Liam for this. Inside, his heart pounded with irritation and just a touch of blazing fury. Each bend of his two knees jostled. When he reached the ground, he looked up at Liam whose face was filled with joy. His eyes danced like a six-year-olds at a carnival.

"Liam," he growled quietly, "please, come with us."

His best friend bent at the waist slightly and put a cupped hand to his ear. "Come with you where?"

"To the Emerald City, jackass."

"Do you really think I'm gonna say yes to a man who insults me?"

"Screw you," Nate rumbled, standing to his feet.

Liam reached out to grab Nate's shoulder. "Wait! Okay," he sighed. "I'll come. You got me."

"Good. We leave in a half hour." Nate turned.

"You sure about this?" Liam's tone dropped again.

Nate kept walking. "I don't know."

He continued to walk back to his house. If they were going to leave, the sooner the better. The old station still had about a hundred gallons of gas left in the underground tanks and it'd be enough to get them back and forth from Public One's outer walls. He went over everything in his mind on what they'd need, where they'd get it, and how impossible this was going to be.

"Nate! Hold up!" London yelled from behind. Nate had nothing to say to the kid. He'd be staying here.

"Nate! I want to go," London said again when he caught up. "I *am* going to go. You can't leave me behind this time."

"Watch me." Nate opened the door to his house and immediately picked up the pack and items that had just been dropped on the floor from hunting. "You broke the rules, London." Nate threw a thick jacket into his pack.

"*That's* why you won't let me come with you guys? Come on, that's bull, and you know it. I'm old enough to do this." London picked up the rifle sitting next to Nate's knee and held it up with Liam's bag.

"What, are you nuts?" Nate whipped the gun out of London's hand and set it next to his own. He reached over and grabbed the bag that London was trying to pack and tossed it across the room. "I'm doing this for *you*. Some of us may not come back. I don't think you understand how dangerous this is."

"I don't *understand*? Seriously, Nate? You have the nerve to tell me I don't understand? I spent three years trying to provide for myself after my family was killed. My own mom died in front of me. Her face went purple as she suffocated. I watched every person I knew, and every person I didn't know, either be dragged to The Public, suffocate, rot, or die before I got to them. I had to try and rely on a broken pistol to keep me safe from looters. Don't tell me I don't understand!" Spit flew from his mouth, and when London finished, his face was scarlet.

Nate took a deep breath and hung his head. There was rarely a time that London talked about his life before. Somehow Nate had figured that London's brain would have tried to close off those memories. Obviously the teen had been holding onto them for years.

"I know. I didn't mean that. But I can't have you risk your life when yours is the one I'm trying to protect. I'm sorry, London. The answer is 'no.'"

"Bullshit," London responded adamantly.

The bag of first aid equipment Nate was about to stuff in fell to the floor. "I'm sorry, what did you say? You've got some balls speaking to me like that."

"I learn from the best." London narrowed his eyes. "Look, you told me I couldn't go to the meeting, and I still went. What's to keep me here after you leave? We have extra ATVs. I'll just get on one and catch up after you're too far away to bring me back."

Nate folded his arms and took a step forward.

"Now, I can either come with you guys who are prepared, or I can come by myself with no protection. It's up to you."

"Fine." Nate leaned over and grabbed a pair of handcuffs attached to his pack. He stood up quickly and gripped London's wrist dragging him backward. The kid swore and cursed the whole way to the banister while Nate locked him up.

London kicked at the solid mahogany wood and swore again.

"Ben'll be your guardian 'til we get back. Believe me, kid, I'm doing this for you."

"Like hell you are!"

A knock came at the door and Olivia let herself inside. With one look to London cuffed to the banister and Nate standing with his hands on his hips, she rolled her eyes.

"Seriously?"

"As long as it keeps him here." Nate walked back to the bag he'd left on the ground. "Listen, we're leaving in half an hour, so you better get ready if you're still going." Nate turned around to pick up the rest of his gear before he saw Olivia's reaction.

"Excuse me? Yer just gonna leave him here like that?" She seemed to be waiting for a response, but he raised his eyebrows and dared her to challenge him.

"Yer an idiot. And why the hell are we leavin' so soon?"

Nate gave her a look, a silent gesture to tell her he didn't want to discuss London. "The sooner we get our butts on the road, the better the advantage we have. We're already screwed as it is if The Public knows we're coming. Science fiction bullshit." The last part was mostly muttered to himself. He nodded to the kid, who tried to kick at him when he walked by, and left the house with Olivia trailing behind.

He wouldn't leave London there. The moment before they left, he'd give the cuff key to Ben and tell him to keep the kid from the ATVs. That would give them enough time to get far enough to discourage London from coming after them.

They walked down the street to the three community trucks parked just outside the old clinic. Hopefully they were all repaired now, ready to drive longer than ten minutes. They would be taking the last of the supplies inside, and using the last hundred gallons of fuel from the underground tanks at the gas station that were still available.

Nate threw his things into the back of the pickup and then turned to Olivia, placing the key in her hand.

"Here, take this to your dad. Tell him about London, but tell him to leave him there for a good twenty minutes after we leave. Make sure he keeps the other ATV keys locked up. Or else London will come after us. Get your other things together too. Meet back here in fifteen." Olivia shook her head and jogged up the street, her flannel shirt flying behind her.

"And make sure you grab Isaac on the way back!" he added on.

He went into the clinic to find as many spare supplies as he could get his hands on. Even with what they had, it was still not enough. It'd take a miracle to make this entire thing work. Every time he started to imagine how this would all pan out, he got a sinking feeling in his stomach. So he started pushing it out of his mind.

Minutes later, Liam strode down the sidewalk toward them, a few of his things slung over his shoulder. The hole-ridden, tatty, button-up shirt he'd been wearing was tied around his waist and he simply wore his jeans and wife-beater. The Korean tattoo he got when he was younger was visible at the base of his neck. "Did you bring my other bag?" his voice was dry.

"I've got it tied down in here." Nate jumped into the back of the truck and hefted up the rest of Liam's things.

"I heard some strange noises coming from your house when I walked by, Spud." Liam cocked his eyebrow.

"Oh yeah?"

"Mostly a lot of cursing and squealing grunts. What'd you do to the kid? Hog tie him?"

"He may as well 'ave," Olivia said, reappearing with a bag slung over her shoulder. She handed it to Nate and he glared at her. "The psychopath cuffed London to the banister."

A whistle rang from Liam's lips. "Nate finally cracked, huh?"

"Shut up, and help us put everything in the truck, Liam." Nate placed another plastic tote of ammo and communications that he'd set on the gate of the truck bed.

Liam saluted. "Wow, ya twist his arm and he gets incredibly pissy," he whispered to Olivia.

"You talk to your dad, Liv?"

"Yes, *Ma*," she folded her arms. "Don't worry. Dad's got it all settled. By the way, he thinks yer a psycho too. Oh, hey. What's that?" Olivia said as Liam walked by. "Since when did you get a tattoo?"

"Ah, hell, girl," Liam smiled, "I've had this since my time in Germany."

"What's it mean?"

"Semper Fi in Korean. Language of my father, symbol of my bruthaz. 'Always Loyal.' I guess that's why I'm taking this death trap with Nate." He smiled overly sweetly at Nate and continued to explain to Olivia about his time across seas and the pair of German twins he'd been with that night.

At that, Nate jumped off the bed of the truck and walked into the clinic. When he heard a faint, "You're disgusting," comment from Olivia, he knew exactly what part of the story Liam had just rehearsed.

He gathered the last two flashlights and batteries and went back out just when Hugh and Greyson arrived with Isaac. Isaac carried no supplies, and he sauntered with his arms crossed while Greyson and Hugh carried the bulk of their provisions. Nate immediately knew this plan would include Isaac sitting on the sidelines while the group did all the work. He eyed the man out of the corner of his gaze. Isaac simply stood there, clasping his hands together. No incentive to help, no offers. He seemed to be at a loss for what to do, although not concerned about it.

"Hey," Nate called to him. "Toss those last two things of gas up to me." He climbed up into the truck bed and waited for Isaac to realize he was the one being spoken to.

"Oh, yes, sorry."

Nate rolled his eyes before the first five-gallon gas container was handed to him.

"I can't tell you how grateful I am for what you're doing for me. I know you're risking a lot."

"Do you?" Olivia asked as she stepped up to the truck. "Because it seems like ya aren't worried at all."

"Believe me," he said. "I'm terrified."

REGGIE

The guards throw me back into my cell and the door slides closed. My eyes can barely focus enough to find my bed. Every time I move I feel like I'm falling backwards. I reach out and pull myself onto the mattress, slowly lying down. My eyeballs feel sluggish and lazy, moving on their own accord around in my sockets. I press my fingers to my closed eyelids to stop the movement. Whatever's happened, whatever I've seen, it's scared Dryer. I could tell by the look on his face; by the tone of his voice. There was more intensity and anxiety than has ever been there before.

What's happening to me? I think to myself.

My brain starts to swim again. My own words aren't quite clear to me. Even inside my own head.

I don't know—

You know you're not leaving now.

But I've seen what's supposed to happen, I reply to myself. *What could happen. What if Dryer is wrong?*

They can stop it. They can stop you from ever leaving. They can stop the whole thing from happening, despite what you've seen.

They'll continue to gather information from your visions and they'll be prepared. Just like they always are. You know how they work.

Then I'll stop sleeping. They can't know what will happen if I don't sleep.

"You think you can . . . stop? Day after day after day?" my speech slurs, my breath rattles, and I close my mouth again. *Never mind the fact that you just had a vision without sleeping. What now? What if it comes again?*

I shake my head sluggishly back and forth on the mattress. *It's never happened before. We don't know if it will ever happen again. It's a fluke.*

But I want it to happen again!

The feelings I had, the vibrancy, the calmness I'd felt. That vision was not like any other I'd had. It was different. It was so real. For a moment, I felt like I was somewhere else. Somewhere away from Public One. The man who'd hated me in other visions, hadn't looked at me with hate or distrust. Even *he* had changed. He looked at me with trust, almost a . . . friendship. In that vision, it was all different.

They don't know I'm seeing events while—it is almost too tiring to think to myself—*I'm awake. They don't have to know.*

They'll find out. Dryer already suspects that something happened. He may be waiting and watching for you to do it again. They'll hook you up to those chemicals indefinitely. They'll never be able to predict your visions during the day, afraid of missing them, they'll inject you all day, all night . . .

". . . for the rest of your life." The last part hissed out of my throat, separate from my inner dialogue as if some other being had said it. I open my eyes long enough to see the room spinning above me.

They can't do that. They've tried it before.

You don't think they'll try it again? This time they won't be gentle with you. They don't care. Not now. If they ever did.

I can't help crying and a few tears slither over my temples into my hairline and ears.

Do you think what we've seen is impossible?

Do you?

No. But everything you say . . . it's true.

I don't want it to be. We merely have to face the truth. Dryer will find us out. They don't trust us. Do you think that they ever have?

No. It'll never be the same again. They won't believe it. I wouldn't.

I open my eyes again. My head feels heavy. Like it will fall to the floor. "How did it happen? How did it happen?" I repeat again, out loud to the world.

It was the hit. The guard's blow to your head did something. That has to be it.

I think you're right.

But how is it possible?

I slowly reach up with my arm and roll to my side in order to feel the back of my head. The selabraxatine I'd been given to mask the hit cleared up my pain, but the inflammation is still very much there. It's just below the base of my skull and I wonder how the drive of the hit didn't break my neck. All I know is that I'm still alive.

It's so big. Apparently it was hard enough to shake my mind loose, just not enough to damage me.

They would have preferred that, I think.

I know.

I stay on my side and pull my legs up to my chest. The exhaustion from the day is too much and before I know it, I feel myself wanting to sleep.

The remains of a dying fire smoked up through the trees while the group stood watching the two men yell at each other.

The mix of fresher air and pine along with burning embers filled the area. Since leaving the community, very little had been said until the fire.

Nate had driven one of the two trucks all day with Greyson in the cab with him. Liam drove the second truck where both Isaac and Olivia sat with him, and Hugh had ridden in the back. Back at the community, there had been some discussion as to who would ride with Isaac to keep him guarded. Olivia had won, explaining that Hugh wouldn't know what to do if there were problems. "What are you going to do? Analyze him to death?" she'd asked. "Get in the other truck."

It had taken a two-day drive to get within twenty miles of the compound's limits. They were still close enough, and with the rising sun rays bouncing off the smoke patterns, now it was even more obvious.

"What were you thinking?" Nate shouted. "Piece of shit Harvard graduate?! We're just miles away from the Public and you go and build a fire?"

"Nate, it's nineteen degrees outside. Nineteen! It's so cold I can feel my own veins freezing inside me. Besides, no one can see it from here!" Hugh yelled back.

"Do you honestly think within that deeply educated mind of yours that the compound is dumb enough to *not* patrol around the limits of the city? Do you have any clue how dangerous it is that we're *this* close?"

"It's just a fire!"

"It's smoking!" Nate turned around and kicked more dirt onto the fire. "Why do you think I said 'no' when we got here?" He took a few steps toward him, an inner fire boiling beneath his chest. "Dammit, Hugh!"

"Hey!" Olivia ran in front of him, heaving his shoulders back with the thrust of her hands. "Stop it!" She turned to Hugh. "You should've known better, Hugh. But fer the love of—" Liv's words cut off before she turned her anger back at Nate. "Fightin' isn't gonna get us anywhere. Not now," she said, trying to calm the two of them down. Her eyes were red from being awake for over fifty hours—identical to everyone else's. "We're not goin' to work well as a team if we're fightin'."

"Liv, you know how dangerous this is!" Nate pointed to the fire.

"Yes, I do! It was a stupid choice but it's happened and now it's *over*," her voice was hard, and then she looked back at Hugh. "I don't care how uncomfortable we are, how frigid it is, or how the sweat pours down yer man parts, but don't you *ever* do somethin' like that again. Un'erstand? Now, we're only twenty miles out. We need to focus on what's gonna happen tonight when we get there. All right?"

Nate's chest rose and fell. Fury bubbled deep within him the longer he stared at Hugh. "Fine. Just make sure he doesn't do this again." He twisted around and headed for the truck.

"I'm an adult, Nate! I think I deserve to be treated like one," Hugh called after him.

"Then start acting like it, dick!" Nate called over his shoulder. Hugh replied with a less than appropriate name before Nate reached the truck. He pulled the door open and unlocked the glove compartment, swearing to himself in whispers. In one move, Hugh could have destroyed the entire mission.

Nate shuffled through the papers and finally pulled out a large sheet of paper, the last he had left, and brought it out with a pencil. "Go get Isaac," he told Liam when he turned back around.

"Aye, aye. Hey, Clone. Get over here." He immediately called out to Isaac who was sitting on the bed of the truck, sipping a cold cup of instant coffee.

Nate went to the hood of the truck, placing the paper down and looked over to Isaac when he strode up. "We need to have a plan. None of us know what the city looks like or how it's laid out."

"Okay."

"We'll need to plan for three groups. Obviously we're going to stand out like bunions around everyone else, so we'll need to go at night. One of us can go with you to your home and get your family. One group will need to break into whatever building is holding this *precog* and the other will need to be ready to pull us out, monitoring whatever we can."

"Three seems like a lot of groups. Why not two, and we can monitor each other?" Isaac asked.

Nate took a deep breath, attempting to control the curt answer he wanted to use. "Because that leaves room for error that we don't have time for. I'm not risking more lives than we need to. Now, draw me a map of the city. We need to know what we're up against here. Include any security you know of and any possible security that you *don't* know of." He slid the paper across the metal hood toward Isaac. The man pulled the paper to himself and with the pencil began drawing up a very crude map.

"Now, the way that I got out is going to have heavy security at this point, unfortunately. And, it used to be the least monitored route."

"Why's that?" Liam asked, putting his hands on his hips.

"It's the waste dump." Isaac continued drawing. "Now, our best chance would probably be to enter where they wouldn't expect it. Which is also the most obvious."

Liam folded his arms and leaned forward to look into Isaac's face. "What? You want us to knock on the front door, get them to open it up, and then gust 'em?"

Nate's eyes narrowed.

"Essentially . . . yes," Isaac answered.

Liam laughed. "This man is nuts."

Nate pulled the paper closer to himself, causing Isaac to drag the pencil across the paper. "You're kidding, right?" Nate could feel his anxiety rising. They'd traveled all the way out here, wasting whatever gas they had left just to learn that entrance to the city would be impossible.

"Once you're through, the sensors on the gate are down for about five minutes. If we can get through during that time, then we'll just need to tap into the security system. I saw the equipment that you have, and I . . ."

Nate held up his hand, cutting Isaac off. The sound was faint, but he heard it. Rumbling. An engine; the rumble of it bouncing off trees and humming in his eardrum. He looked up and tried to gauge where it was coming from. Southwest. It was coming in from behind them.

"What is it?" Olivia asked.

"Sonofa . . ." he muttered and swung on Hugh before looking back to Olivia. "Someone's coming. It could be other Nomads, or it could just be Public guards. Arm yourselves. If you don't know how to use a gun, hide in the cabs." He said the last part looking right into Isaac's face.

Each of them grabbed at the nearest weapon and took cover behind the trucks, the trees, anything that would block them. Nate crouched with a rifle in his hands behind the hood of the truck. He peered through the scope, waiting for the vehicle to come into view. If he could maybe pick them off before they were in range of the camp, they might have a shot.

The sound was getting closer. His heart thudded in his throat, but his hands were still. In the scope, he finally saw it come into view. He narrowed his eyes and placed his finger on the trigger, tucking the butt into his shoulder. When the vehicle became clearer, an ATV, he felt his stomach boil. He recognized the driver. Aiming the rifle at the ATV's headlights, he shot once and then twice. Both lights immediately went out and he could hear the rider's voice yell out.

"Dammit." Nate moved around the truck and Olivia tried to grab at his ankle to keep him back.

"Nate! Where are you goin'?"

"It's London. That skinny piece of crap."

"What?" She and everyone else jumped from their spots while Nate walked toward the approaching ATV, his rifle still raised.

When London was in yelling distance, he stopped the four-wheeler and raised his hands. "It's just me, Nate! You don't have to shoot out my lights!"

"I know." Nate shot the dirt near the ATV, sending up puffs of earth. The force of the dust must have stung the kid because he kept jumping.

"Nate!" he yelled. "Are you nuts!?"

"I should be asking you the same question! What are you doing here, London?"

"Exactly what I told you I'd do!" London stepped off the ATV.

Nate fired the rifle again near London's feet and the kid shot up in the air.

"Dammit, Nate! Stop it!"

"I should just shoot you now, London."

Olivia grabbed at Nate's arm from behind and tugged. "Knock it off, Myron Beddings," she said, referencing the President Dover's 2025 assassination shooter. "Now that London's nearly pissed his pants."

"What do you mean, *nearly?*" London squeaked, looking down at his pants.

"I can't believe you!" Nate barked at him. "I explicitly told you to stay with Ben!"

"Yeah, and I told you I'd come anyway!"

Nate's chest tightened and he handed off the rifle to Liam as he approached. "Kid, I'm gonna kill you."

London stepped forward. "Good. You'd better do it then, because that's the only way I'm leaving."

"He is here already, Nate. We can't just send him back," Liam muttered. "We'll have a better chance of keeping an eye on him if we keep him with us."

Nate glared at Liam.

"Or you can shoot him. Your choice, really."

He shook his head and turned on his heel, heading back to Isaac. "I guess I have no choice." Nate leaned over the hood of the truck again, trying to control his breathing, trying to keep his fist from flying into the nearest face.

"Isaac!" he snarled. "Tell us how we're supposed to get through the gate. We need to know about these damn sensors you told us about."

Isaac took a breath before stepping closer and looked at London who joined them. Nate gripped the paper.

"The gate is an open archway in the walls of the city. Looks as inviting as a country English manor, but the gate is actually a grid of laser beams unseen to the eye. Once you walk through, they are set off and need time to reconnect. Everything is well-oiled and high-tech, but even then . . . there are still glitches."

"And you're telling us you have no clue how to tap into the security? We're supposed to come up with that little detail?" Nate's eyes widened.

"Of course he doesn't," Liam said, holding onto London's elbow like a prison guard.

Nate mumbled a curse and ran his hand through his hair. "Liam, what do you think? Could you figure it out?" He slid the paper they'd left on the truck toward Liam.

Liam shoved the teen to Olivia and glanced over. "Well, this doesn't tell me anything except that Isaac here is out of his mind. I mean, look at this city. I have no idea what the system is like. I don't know what exactly we need and it's not like we can drive right up to the gate. We'll have to leave the trucks at least two miles out to begin with, and carry what we need." He laughed again. "It's just not possible. We might as well go home now."

"NO!" Isaac yelled, slamming his fist into the truck. "We can't go! We *can* get in!"

"Isaac, what about deliveries?" Olivia asked, coming into the conversation. "Does the city produce everythin' for themselves or are there other shipments made to the compound by other means?"

"None. Food is all grown by the city. It's closed off except for . . ." He paused. "Except for water. There's a pipeline that runs from the Rockies down to the city. There's an entrance point about twenty feet outside the city for maintenance. It's not big though. Only large enough for a person who's about ninety pounds." He drew a pipeline heading out of the west side of the city.

Nate looked at Liv.

"Nuh uh. As much as I'd love it to be me, I weigh about ten pounds more," she immediately responded.

"Would she fit?" Nate asked Isaac.

"No. Even at ninety, it'd be extremely tight with female hips."

"I could do it."

Nate closed his eyes and shook his head. The sound of London's voice piping up felt like a gunshot to his chest. He couldn't let him do it. It couldn't and wouldn't be the boy.

"Hell, no."

"I'm the only one that will fit, Nate! I'm just over a hundred and twenty. No one else here weighs less than I do," London said.

Nate shook his head. "Then we'll find another way in."

Isaac nodded. "No, he's right. If London could get in he would be able to get to the security box and break in. Liam, you could walk him through it. At that point . . ."

"Dammit, I said no!" Nate interrupted. "We'll do it another way."

"Nate," Liam started, but Nate cut him off again.

"We'll find another way. Even if I have to actually take Isaac's crap plan and knock on the door to get in, then that's the way we'll do it. So here's what I propose. The city has a precog. Odds are, this thing is going to know we're coming. And The Public will know it if they don't already. We need to come up with five different strategies and then decide on one once we get there. No matter what, communications stay on at *all* times. Do you understand?"

Liam nodded and raised his eyebrows. "Sure."

"This needs to be researched. Not simply a smash and grab job, Nathan." Hugh came up behind.

"We can't research it because our inside man doesn't even know the inside," Nate grumbled.

"Why don't we get some sleep first. Then we can decide on the details," Greyson advised. Nate could tell that he was trying not to step on toes, but he bit back at him anyway.

"You want to sleep? Go ahead. I'm getting these worked out now."

"He's right, Nate. We've all been awake for fifty-one hours. We need to sleep. I'm not going to trust you in zombie-mode to save us if the time comes." Liam's head tilted.

Nate sighed in defeat. "Fine. Everyone go to bed. I'll wake you all up in five hours so we can go over details." He turned back to the crude map, and the others broke away slowly.

"Nate," Liam interjected.

Nate looked squarely at him.

"We'll have Greyson wake us up. He, Isaac, and Hugh already slept about four hours. *You* go to sleep."

"I can't."

"You can. And you're gonna."

"If I go to sleep, you won't."

Liam smirked. "That's just a risk you're gonna have to take."

"No, it's one I'm not going to take. It was my decision to come. I stay awake." He went back to pouring over the map, making notes here and there. Scribbles really. His eyes were too tired to write full words.

"Nate, it may have been your decision to come here, but we all decided to follow. We've all got jobs. We're not going to be able to follow you if you're not functioning."

Nate thudding his palm onto the truck hood. "You didn't choose anything. I made you come."

"First of all," Liam raised his eyebrows, "thank you for implying that I'm your slave . . ."

"That's not what I—"

". . . and second of all, I chose to come. I already said it. Always Loyal. I've held my fingers in your femoral artery as blood was pumping out—I know I promised never to talk about it again but let's face the fact that it was a bonding moment for us—I've given you mouth to mouth, I've even given you the last of the toilet paper when we've run out, Spud. I'll follow you to the edge of Hell if need be."

After taking a deep breath, Nate ran his hands over his face. It wasn't fair. He shouldn't be the one to rest, but he was so damn tired.

"Just to the edge?"

"Well, you know me. I burn like a marshmallow."

He chuckled at that. Sighed. "Fine."

Liam pounded him on the back. "Good."

He walked to the bed of the truck, pulled out a blanket and took it into the cab. He had just enough room to lie on his back with his knees tucked up. It wasn't the most comfortable situation, but he made it work. The sky was gray which provided just enough cover to keep the sun from blinding him. A near-frozen fly kept buzzing around the cab, bouncing off the windows as it flew around in the air, struggling to find a way out.

Nate thought to himself how impossible everything was. He worried that with each choice they made they'd be bouncing into windows, like the fly. No solution, and most likely to die before escaping. What was worse, London was here now. Stupid kid. Out of everyone, he had to make sure London made it out alive, even if no one else did. He hated himself for thinking, and hoping, that it would be Isaac and Hugh who wouldn't make it over anyone else.

Who was he becoming? He'd never wished for the survival of one person over another. Not people on the same side anyway. In Korea, there were nights just like this though. Every evening he would lay down on the hard ground with only a military issue bag. He never slept. Each time a gun would be shot, or a muted CDM bomb would drop, he'd reach for his rifle and pray it hit another North Korean. Not just one, but as many as possible.

But this? This feeling? It wasn't him. He closed his eyes, his thoughts still interweaving. The weight of exhaustion caught up with him faster than he thought.

—ISAAC—

A boot kicked against his foot, shocking him out of the shadows of his dream. He looked around, lost for a moment in the darkness. The pipes above, the hard bed. Where was he?

The rich pungent smell of earth and old gasoline revolved around him. A drip of oil on his forehead made him jerk and he realized he'd been sleeping under a pickup. It all came rushing back to him.

"Wake up, clone. You've slept more than any of us, and we're actually the ones doing the work. Camp's down and we've done everything without you, now let's go," Liam called to him.

Isaac pushed himself up and felt the rocks and hard ground roll under his spine. His clothes smelled like his fetid armpits and he wished more than anything to have a shower, or at the very least, deodorant. Maybe the extended time without a bath and proper food would desensitize his nose.

He knew bathing would be impossible once they were in the city. He felt he was becoming more and more like the Nomads he had convinced to help him. A part of him hated that, but he knew once he removed his family, they'd end up the same way.

He rolled up the thin sleeping bag and put it into the bed of the truck where most of the other gear was already tucked. The others had already packed up the rest of their day camp and the sunset and early stars were barely peeking behind the thick evening clouds to their backs. With night setting in, even in June, the area was uncomfortably cold. Since the war, the floating debris and gases in the atmosphere had messed up the regular weather patterns. Frost in July. A heat wave in December. It was always hard to predict what you'd get from day to day. Isaac rubbed his hands up and down his arms, eager to get inside the truck and turn the heat on.

"All right, everyone! Let's head out!" Nate got into the second truck.

"Clone? You. My truck," Liam added, passing by.

"My name's Isaac. How many times do I have to tell you?"

"Right, you're also 'human.' That doesn't mean you deserve to be treated like one." Liam smiled, although obviously not happy.

Olivia swore at Liam with a frown, but turned to her right. "Get in the truck, Isaac." She held the door open.

Everyone got into their respective vehicles again and the roar of the engine made Isaac's heart leap out of his chest. He hadn't seen his family for months. Sadly, Audra wouldn't even be worried. Every year The Public would require annual immunization injections. Included in the injections was something they weren't told about. An additive. Thiarigyzine was an emotion suppressive. It didn't take everyone's full emotional range away, but lessened it to the point of contentment.

Last August he'd missed his immunization. Because of a mix-up at the hospital his name had already been checked.

Even though he continued to ask for it, they'd sent him home. It took five months for his system to completely clear of any remaining drugs. The feeling was unlike any other; as if a blind fold was removed from his eyes. He started to feel real love for his companion and happiness when his boys growled at him playfully. Audra had looked at them in a way that broke his heart. The boys' natural playful demeanor meant nothing to her.

Since he'd left, Audra wouldn't have even noticed the worry. Maybe confusion. He didn't know how to explain everything to her. Or the boys. They'd never known anything but The Public. He'd be saving them. As long as they got out that was all he cared about.

He glanced over at Liam and then to Olivia. She was the only one who looked back, and gave him a smile. It was so quick, he wasn't even sure she had.

These people wouldn't all make it out alive. Maybe none of them. He knew they wouldn't. They didn't understand how impossible it was. He didn't care, though. It wasn't personal, it was life or death, and he was doing everything he could to ensure life for his family. It's how you played the game.

The twenty-nine mile drive to the city limits seemed even longer than the hundreds of miles that they'd driven to get to the day camp. Perhaps it was his anxiety—which he hadn't felt in a long time—that was adding to the length. Perhaps it was his uncertainty of the plans they'd devised without him. He knew he shouldn't have fallen asleep again. It's just that he wasn't used to sleeping less than eight hours a day, and his body just couldn't keep up with the endless waking hours the Nomads were used to.

Trees passed by the truck and the wheels bumped every once in a while across the damaged highway. The forest ended like a curtain being lifted back from a stage. Liam hit the brakes and pulled into the trees, waiting for the second truck to draw up. Isaac leaned forward to look out the side window while Nate and Liam spoke.

"What do we do now that we lost tree cover? Think it's best to keep going this route?" Liam asked.

"My gosh, it looks like they tore down the trees in order to build the city," Olivia muttered.

"They didn't. This was one of the first war zones. That's why they chose to build the public here. The land was already desolated," Isaac answered her.

"Well," Nate leaned forward. "We're still a few miles out. I can see the city lights from here and if they're monitoring this highway, which I assume they are, we need to get there soon as possible. Isaac?"

Isaac leaned closer. "Yeah?"

"Are there any places closer to the city that we can hide a truck for communication and surveillance?"

He paused, thinking it through. "The old guard station might work. It's a small building about six hundred feet from the front gate. They don't use it anymore because it's too vulnerable."

"Then that's where we'll park the second truck. We'll leave this one here and pile into the back of yours, Liam."

"Saweeet." Liam thumped the steering wheel and lightly revved the engine.

Nate, London, and Hugh left their truck, bringing their gear with, and joined them. Within minutes they were ready to head out.

"Liam," Nate said through the back window, "hit the gas."

Liam smirked and a glint of excitement bounced in his eyes. "No problem."

Isaac could hear Nate call, "Hold on!" to the others in the back. The truck lurched forward and the speed increased dramatically. Each gash in the road caused the truck to leap up into the air. Isaac spun around to make sure the others in the back were still there. Nate had his arm lashed around a rope attached to the truck while his other kept London's head down. He winced with each bump. Greyson and Hugh had also lashed ropes around their arms to the side of the truck and were grasping the bed with both hands.

The city loomed before them. Its extravagant grandeur was exactly the way he'd left it. He could remember what New York City used to look like before the war turned it into an uninhabitable sink hole. This was more complicated. Much more. Traffic systems not only ran along the ground, the main being called The Tunnel, but above, webs of public transportation rails slithered through the air.

"Holy sh—" Liam whispered, his voice getting lost on the wind.

"Yeah," Isaac replied with a nod.

The walls of the city were made of steel and rose three hundred feet in the air. Large skyscrapers and domed buildings loomed over the walls. Lights of blue, white, and faint greens radiated from different windows. Added to the faint sunset glow bouncing off the glass of each building, it painted iridescent shimmers that brandished the darkening sky. Directly in the center of the city was government headquarters—the Ponanki building. Records claimed to be the tallest building remaining in the world. At three thousand feet, it was absolutely majestic amidst The Public city horizon. Shining like a glass javelin against the burning sky. But that's where its glamour ended. Isaac had ideas about what went on in there. And it made him sick.

Minutes later, the truck stopped dead behind the small guard building, about the size of three trailer homes. It was less than a mile from the city, farther than Isaac had estimated, but that had its benefits. It was obviously uninhabited, and fully concealed them and the truck.

Isaac followed Olivia out of the truck while the other men climbed out of the bed.

"Okay, Spuds. What are we doing?" Liam stuck his hands on his hips. "Plan one, two, or three?"

"Obviously, if we all knew what plan we wanted to go with and voted on it, the precog would probably still have the information. So, I have stones."

"Well," Liam snickered, "I always wondered about that."

"Liam, stop being a dick. Put your hand in and pull out a rock." Nate's weight shifted.

Liam jestingly punched Nate's shoulder before shoving his hand in and pulling out a rock. Scratched faintly into the surface was the number three.

"Three it is. You ready, Nate? Olivia?" Liam asked, tossing equipment to them from the truck.

"Yup," Olivia responded digging a small bud into her ear and handed the other to Nate.

"All right. Give 'em hell, you two."

Nate and Olivia walked around to the side of the guard station and Isaac strained to see them jog the shortened mile leading to the front of the gate. The "gate" as it was called, was wide open. It wasn't actually a gate—it was an open archway. Silent and invisible laser signals couldn't be seen, but they were running from one side to the other. The Public did it on purpose. The gate welcomed anyone to wander inside. Once inside, the lasers announced any person's arrival.

Liam kept an eye on the two of them as they moved for the gate. While they waited, Isaac collapsed on the ground and leaned against the station wall. At first he pulled his knees up and rested his forearms on his knees. When the breeze blew his own body odor to his face, he grimaced and lowered his arms.

From where they crouched, Liam was obviously straining to see Nate and Olivia. They were out of everyone's sights now.

"I think they made it," Liam said hesitantly.

A power-gun blast echoed in the air and Isaac jumped to his feet.

Liam swore and held out his hand. "A bud, Hugh, a bud!"

Hugh tossed a small device to Liam and he shoved it in his ear. "M' kay, Greyson, Isaac, you're coming with me." Liam spoke while noises continued to ricochet from the gate. He placed a com bud in his ear. "Hugh, you remember what to do, right?"

Hugh, using a flashlight, pulled out the communication equipment and nodded.

"We don't have much time, let's go!"

Greyson shoved Isaac and he stumbled over his own feet. Getting hold of his balance, he raced after Liam. Olivia and Nate had tripped the lasers thirty seconds before they moved. That meant there was only four and a half minutes time for them to make it through the gate. Four and a half to run nearly a mile. Isaac's legs burned, and Greyson was passing him. The darkness hid them from the view of the guards the closer they got to the gate.

The guards forcibly wrapped large metal cuffs around both Nate and Liv's wrists, and activated the magnet connection in them. Even though they'd planned on this happening, it didn't stop the knots from twisting in his stomach.

"Hurry," Isaac breathed. "The gate's only disabled for a couple more minutes."

"HEY!" A guard shouted from inside the city and Liam skidded to the ground, laying flat on his stomach. Isaac and Greyson quickly ducked into the shadows of a slight mound of dirt—most likely an old ditch that had once been used for farmland. Isaac looked toward the gate to see what the guard had been yelling at. Thankfully, they hadn't been seen. Nate had elbowed one of the guards in the stomach and both he and Olivia were being given injections.

"What did they just give them?" Greyson whispered.

"A relaxant. It'll wear off." Isaac watched the guards leave one man behind to watch the gate until they returned. A soft hum barely tickled the air again, and Isaac cursed. That was it. Over. Just like that, it was over.

Isaac closed his eyes and dropped his forehead to the ground, small rocks grinding into his skull. Dust and clay swirled in his lungs as he breathed in. "The gate's already active again. We'll be noticed when we go through."

When he looked up, Isaac watched Liam throw a fist to the ground and slowly pushed himself up. The other two men followed and quietly jogged back to their position with the others behind the station. With each step, Isaac's feet became heavier.

"What do we do, Liam?" Greyson asked, breathing hard. His hair was falling out of the elastic band it was in and plastered to his face with sweat. "Isaac says the gate's already active."

Liam shook his head, frustration and anger brushed across his face. "I don't know. Let's get back behind the station, though. Hey," he smiled weakly and his voice jiggled as he ran, "that rhymed."

Isaac rolled his eyes at Liam's careless attitude and inanity, anger burning in his chest, and the three men hurried back around the corner of the old station, coming up behind London and Hugh. London was sitting in the cab of the truck with a pair of headphones on his head, listening to Nate and Olivia's earpieces.

"What happened?" Hugh took off his headphones.

"We're *screwed*, that's what happened," Isaac said. "Liam hesitated, we missed our window, and all he cares about is making jokes."

"Hey, clone!" Liam harshly whispered. "We *all* ducked."

"So, what do we do?" Greyson looked at the very small blank TV screens that Liam had brought to view the security feed once they hacked into The Public's access.

"What about me?" London asked, taking off his headphones. "What about Isaac's idea with the water pipe?"

"Nate would gust me, kid," Liam replied with a shake of his head.

"He might be killed anyway, Liam, if we don't do something. He'd never have a chance to murder you if The Public kills him first." London looked resolute. With none of the others against his involvement like Nate, the corners of Liam's mouth pulled down in consideration.

"It's the only other chance we have," Isaac said. "Someone has to get in, and the water line isn't secured."

"Without Nate and Liv, it's the only plan we have. But, it's extremely dangerous. You sure you're up to it, London?" Greyson asked.

"I wouldn't have said anything if I didn't want to do it. Come on, you guys. I'm not stupid. I know how dangerous this is, but it's the only other option we've got," London's voice cracked.

The realization of London's age slammed into Isaac. He was only a teenager. The kid should have stayed home.

"Shit. Nate's going to gust me," Liam mumbled, took a large breath and let it out. "All right, Isaac, show us to that water pipe entrance."

A sense of hope swirling in massive amounts of panic rested on Isaac. He peered around the corner of the guard station. No one remained at the gate. Isaac motioned with his hand to have the others follow him and they all sprinted across the hard barren ground. The water pipe was farther away than the front gate, and it took fifteen minutes of jogging to find what he was looking for. Through the darkness ahead, Isaac could see the large dark circle in the ground. The maintenance hole. All he could do was run. Run and pray that the teenager would be able to fit. Pray that the water wasn't being brought into the city tonight. His legs were burning, his lungs having more and more difficulty. After living in The Public for so many years, he felt guilty about not being able to keep up physically like the others.

As they got closer, the small entrance point appeared to get larger. Barely large enough. "That's it," he whispered.

"Are you yanking me, Clone? London can't fit in that!"

"Yes, I can. I just need to—" London sucked all his air in. He looked like a stripped string bean.

Liam scoffed at the site of London's lean body. He and Greyson leaned down to lift off the cover. Each of them dug their fingertips under the top and they grunted as they pulled it back and slid it across the ground. The large lid landed on the ground, making a hollow thump.

Isaac looked in. "No water. That's good."

"It's more than good. Come on kid, let's see if you fit." Liam stepped away from the hole and London walked over. Only darkness was visible. London set himself in and struggled to get his shoulders through. He twisted his body to the right and dropped one shoulder down first.

"Can you move?" Liam asked.

"I have enough room to crawl on my stomach," he responded. "It kinda pinches my chest, but I can move."

"Here," Liam handed him down a pistol, a head light, and an ear bud. You'll need to take the last guard out, and you'll need to move fast. You got that, Spud?"

He was silent for a while, and Isaac could hear the gun being handled carefully. He could just imagine the thoughts running through a teenager's head at that moment. Being handed a gun with the intent to kill someone. It was overwhelming. A feeling of darkness. London finally replied with a "Yes."

"You know how to use that thing?"

London replied affirmatively. "You only practiced with me every night Nate was gone."

"Just wanted to make sure you hadn't forgotten. Keep talking to us on the piece and we'll get you though, all right?" Liam swallowed hard.

"All right."

"Go, go, go!" Isaac whispered. He watched the teen's feet shimmy out of site.

The men hurried back to the truck. Ten minutes later, Isaac put the com-bud in his ear to speak to London. "You almost to the main pool?"

"Uh," he breathed through the headphones, "I don't think so. The only thing I can see is, well, nothing." The shift of his elbows and stomach on the metal pipes echoed through the earpiece. "Wait, there's an opening ahead."

"That should be the main reserve pool. There's a grate you'll have to open. The pool is only nine feet deep. Once you're in, there's a ladder that leads up to a door."

"K," his voice was breaking up slightly. "How do you know this?"

"I used to work for city water services. Main office, but, we went down to the pool there once to see how things worked."

"Big wig, huh?" London's voice was strained. He was obviously having a difficult time taking deep breaths. "'K, I think I see it. There's only one light on in here."

A loud dragged-out creak came across the headset. London was pulling the grate's rusted hinges down. Then, the sound of a loud splash.

"London?" Isaac called.

"Crap. I dropped the gun."

"In the pool?"

"Yeah. Is that bad?"

Isaac sighed, frustration and anxiety coursing through his body. "It'll still work, but you'll have to swim down to get it. Make sure you take the bud out first. Got that?"

"Yeah," the boy grunted.

A rustling sound came over the ear piece and then there was silence. In the background, Isaac could hear another splash of the water. Then it went silent again. Twice this happened. London kept coming up for air. Isaac felt as if he'd been holding his breath for a half hour before London's voice came back onto the piece. "I got it," he sputtered.

"Good," Isaac sighed. "Do you see the ladder?"

"Yeah, I'm climbing up now." Through the ear bud, the faint brush of movement against iron came through, but mostly it was silent.

"All right, I'm through the door. I'm soaked, though. And I'm dripping everywhere," he whispered. "What if someone sees?"

"It's all right. There's no evening shift and the hallway will dry before morning. There's a second door in front of you that leads right out onto the street."

"What?" Liam asked. "You're sending him right out in the middle of the city?"

"Did you think he was going to leap from building to building? I know how to get him through," Isaac responded.

"You know, that's another thing. Why didn't you take this 'special' route when you escaped?"

Isaac raised his head and glared. "I can't fit."

There was a click of another door and London spoke again. "*Wow*, this place. It's amazing."

"Go to your right, London. Go down that block and then make the first left. The guards stay in that last building. Now, you will need to knock on the door. They keep it locked. As soon as he opens the door—"

"I shoot him," London's voice broke again.

Isaac nodded to himself. "Yeah."

"Have you ever shot anyone, Isaac?"

Isaac looked up at Liam's cold hard face while he answered the kid. "Once. Before I was taken. My mom and I were homeless during the war. I made a lot of choices then that I'm not proud of."

"Me too," London said. "I was alone too. But I never actually had to shoot anyone. I carried an empty gun with me though. It scared off some people."

Isaac nodded. "That's tough, kid."

"Doing all this will make things better, right?"

He paused. The fear in London's voice was apparent, and Isaac didn't have an answer for the boy. He closed his eyes and, he lied. "Of course."

"Where is he?" Liam asked.

Isaac held up his hand to Liam. "Where are you at, London?"

"Walking down Stafford? I think that's what I saw. There's no one on the streets. It's freakin' me out," he whispered.

"He's almost there," Isaac replied to Liam. Then to London he replied, "It's curfew. No one's allowed out after six."

"It's the building on the right?" London's voice came through again.

"Yes."

Isaac's heart pounded like a hammer in his chest. He couldn't remember a time he'd been so nervous. Even watching Nate and Olivia surrender to the guards hadn't felt so severe. London was just a kid.

Isaac listened closely when a faint knock came across the other end of his earpiece.

"Who are you?" the guard asked, his voice stern. "Hey! Come here!" There were sounds of shuffling feet, a grunt and a cry of pain from a younger voice. It had to be London. Isaac heard London's hard breathing through the earpiece and a thud.

Isaac swore under his breath.

"What? What's going on?" Liam's eyes were wide.

Scuffles sounded again through the headset and then there was a groan from the guard. Then, a gunshot, and Isaac stopped breathing.

REGGIE

My arms pump my body up and down off the floor and small beads of sweat roll down my face, splashing in miniature puddles in front of me. My anxiety rises like a heat wave, and I pump my arms harder. Prickles of lactic acid releasing in the back of my arms continue to irritate me. I don't know what's causing it, but I have to shake it. I have to get rid of this crushing agitation.

. . . *two eighty-one, two eighty-two, two eighty-three* . . . I count off inside my head.

There is an odd disturbance to how I feel, though I can't quite explain what it is. I've never felt this before. Not quite like this. A few years ago I had a vision that had shaken me more than usual, but even this feeling is not the same. I continue to count up to four hundred and I let my arms give out underneath me. With each rapid breath exhaling from my lungs, I feel more and more lightheaded. I roll over to my back while sweat soaks through the top of my shirt and sops on the floor. I look up at the bright lights above.

Soon, the normal exercise exhaustion becomes more intense. Visions of zooming starry patterns cloud the room, and the vertigo I feel becomes stronger and stronger. I can't control my eyes from rolling to the back of my head, reaching further and further to hit the back of my skull. I can still see what's in front of me despite my undulating eyeballs. The only difference is that the scene is changing.

I'm no longer standing in my cell, but walking cautiously down the brightly lit hallway of the building I know so well. Something draws my attention to a sealed doorway. It looks similar to mine, except it's not. The numbers are different, and the hallway is slightly unfamiliar. There is a shape to one side. It's square, white, and nearly blends into the wall. I let my fingers lightly brush the flat panel on the wall. Sequential numbers appear on the pad.

I rack my mind to remember the numbers from my previous dreams. Each time my fingers touch a number, the colors of the screen ripple away from my fingertip like a drop on a pool of water. Two, two, nine . . . eight, five. The pad turns a bright green, the numbers vanishing. I step back, my bare feet scratching the floor. The door glides open.

At first glance I see two pairs of legs hanging off the bed near the wall. I get closer to looking around the corner and see that one pair belongs to a woman with dark black hair. Dirt is smudged on her face and her hair is pulled back, glistening from weeks of oil and sweat. She's still one of the most beautiful women I've ever seen. She pulls her head off of the other person's shoulder and looks at me in confusion.

Then I see him. It's the man from my visions. Nate. His left cheek is swollen and red. It's nothing compared to his eye. Dark shades of purple and red colorize the mound of swollen tissue that keeps him from being able to open it.

He moves to guard the woman and I clearly hear him ask me with force, "What do you want with us?" His voice is muted in my ears—almost like a resonance, an echo of the future.

I don't know what to do. Can I communicate in my vision? I stand there in a stupor, but I eventually will my lips to move. "You're Nate. What are you doing here?"

He rushes at me and crushes me up against the wall, his forearm digging into my throat. "What do you mean? You're not a guard, so who are you?"

"I . . ." I claw at his arm. His words are delayed and separate from his moving mouth, and the force of his arm crushes down on me. "I didn't say . . . I was a," I try to swallow, "guard."

"You're lying."

"I'm not . . ."

"Wait," the woman's inflectional voice reverberates through, "what if she's tellin' the truth? Isaac never told us that the precog was a human."

Lying? About what?

"Right, and it just happened to drop in our laps?"

He presses hard into my windpipe and I feel my eyes get blurry, my head lighter. I can barely breathe. Out of the corner of my eye, I see the walls begin to melt.

The scene in front of my eyes changes and I can feel my vision pulling me back to my cell. My exhaustion gone, I thrust myself off of the floor and look wide-eyed at the door to my cell.

I can barely catch my breath. I can still feel the force of his arm pressing into my airway. I reach up to finger my throat. It's sore and pulsing—the blood struggling to swim back to my brain. The warmth of his arm can still be felt on my skin. One thought enters my mind above any others:

They're coming.

If only I knew exactly when they'd be here. I guess it doesn't matter. I just have to find them. Even though he reacted in anger, I sensed more fear and protection behind his attack than hate. I may not be able to trust them, but I'm going to need to.

I've never really thought out how I would escape from here. Imagining it always ended the same way: punishment, torture, maybe death. In my mind, Dryer always finds me, always brings me back. That's why I stopped hoping. It was too miserable, and I couldn't let myself be like that. Knowing the code to their cell is necessary, of course, but it doesn't help if I can't free myself.

The small door that delivers my meals opens and the bowl of liquid and potato chunks slides out toward me. I quickly drink down the soup and return the bowl. It slides back and the small door closes. The lights in my cell immediately disappear and the darkness envelopes me.

I feel around in the air for the edge of my bed and when my shin lightly taps the bed frame, I climb up and lay down. My legs curl up to my chest and I close my eyes.

My breathing is harsh. My heart pounds.

I need help.

"G reat," Nate murmured, blinking back the intensity of the lights above. It wasn't enough that he didn't know where he was, so of course, his head had to be throbbing as well.

He attempted to reach behind his neck to stretch out the soreness in his body, but his arms wouldn't move. He opened his eyes fully and found himself lying on a slanted metal bed. It was bare and cold. Along with the cuffs holding him down. They wouldn't bend. Wouldn't break.

In one cursory glance he noticed he was still wearing his own clothes. A low hum of electricity could be heard and he craned his head around to look up at his wrists. Wrist bars held his arms securely to the bed. With no welcoming food, shower, or clean clothes, he knew his captors were not going to treat him with the same care they treated Isaac with when they first found him.

"I almost thought that it was good that they found me," he'd said to Nate just days ago.

Yeah, right, Nate thought.

He squinted through the room's bright white light. In front of him, the wall opened and one man entered. Nate figured he had to be in his late sixties. The man wore a white lab coat that fit straight down over a white shirt and pants. The darkness of his skin was a stark contrast to the brilliance of his teeth—his face was stone cold. His watery eyes were somewhat yellowed, and crinkled in the corners. "Nathan Lewis Naylor. Age thirty-three. Member of the former United States Marine Corps. Am I right?"

If Nate hadn't been surprised before, it couldn't be hidden anymore. "How do you know who I am?"

"Simple DNA analysis and a comparison to old public records. Surely as a military man you know about the United States government's public database, don't you?"

Nate didn't move. "Who are you?"

The man held his hands behind his back and smiled. A disturbing coolness graced Nate's spine like a dozen spiders. "Dr. Charles Dryer. Two thousand eleven Yale medical school graduate. I spent my own years in the service of the U.S. government in the Central Intelligence Agency, and . . . here I am. So now you know as much about me as I know about you. The only thing is," Dr. Dryer stepped closer, "I need to know more. You've caused a lot of problems for us."

Nate sneered back at him. "What are you talkin' about, doctor? I walked into your city for food and a clean chance of living and you immediately lock me up? You've got a strange definition of 'problems'."

"We're not unintelligent Neanderthals, young man. We've been prepared for you and we know your coming is not for the necessity of food and living conditions. What we don't know is why you're actually here. I'm sure we can ask the young woman who came with you, but she's . . . preoccupied at the moment."

A sinking blow collapsed Nate's chest. "Where is she?"

"You give me what I want, and she won't get hurt." Dryer tilted his head, his hands still clasped behind his back.

"You touch one inch of her—" Nate snarled.

Dryer's hands finally came out from behind. In his palm was a solitary handled object. The only thing Nate could compare it to was one of the old thick knitting needles his mother used to use. In one fluid motion, Dryer lowered it, connecting the tip with the knuckles of Nate's left hand. It felt as if every bone in his hand immediately shattered, sending a shock of pain down his arm and paralyzing his lungs for a split second.

His teeth clenched together and his gasped for a breath, not wanting to move his hand in fear that it might be destroyed.

"Ingenious little rod isn't it? Causes the illusion of breaking bones. Muscles and nerves react as if splintered bone is being thrust through the skin. When I was working for the C.I.A., just before the war, our technical division worked this one out. It's the only one they ever made. It was intended for extreme interrogation, but unfortunately it never had the chance to see the opportunity. Very little force is needed, but it causes intense pain, wouldn't you say?"

Nate panted. "All the technology in the world . . . and all you guys could come up with . . . was a knitting needle?"

Dryer drug the rod across Nate's cheek. Burning, crushing, exploding sensations overwhelmed his nerves. The fire flashed through his face and down his neck toward his heart. Each gentle touch felt like a swift blow with a hammer mixed with thousands of volts of electricity ripping his bones apart.

"Now, Captain Naylor, would you tell me why you came to Public One?"

Nate could barely breathe, and the bursting of shattered bones in his face made it almost impossible to talk. "The . . . great view."

Dryer smiled at Nate. "You're a very strong man. I'm impressed. I'll tell you what, I'll let you sit on this and we'll talk tomorrow. But, just to leave you with a small reminder—"

With that, he aimed the end of the rod directly into the tear duct of Nate's eye, and slid it down into the socket. Nate's eyes immediately shut, closing down over the tool, causing even more pain. The sensation was like the bones in his face were shattering all over again, cracking and shifting to the sides. Pieces felt as if they were digging into his teeth and might fall out back into his throat. For two minutes, the writhing pain of his face collapsing in on itself overwhelmed him.

Screams ripped through his throat. His heart fluttered and he knew it would give out soon. When he felt the rod slide out of his eye socket, he convulsed and rolled to the side and wretched onto the table. With the angle he was laying at, the vomit slid down the metal slab, hitting his shoulder and pooling against him. Then the blackness overtook him, and Dryer disappeared.

"Nate?"

Olivia's voice broke through the cloud of noise and shadow over Nate's head and he managed to open his eyes. The jagged beams of light above him pierced his vision and he clenched his eyes closed again. When he realized it wasn't the light that hurt him, he reached up and touched his eye. The flesh and skin around his eye socket was swollen and felt sickly. When he was finally able to open his left eye, he looked over and saw Olivia sitting next to him on the floor. She looked relatively unharmed. Just a small bruise to her cheek, her hair mussed and oily.

Olivia buried her face against his arm, her words muffled. When she raised her head, he could tell that she was trying to keep herself from crying. "I'm so glad you're all right."

"Yeah." His voice was rough. "You all right?"

"I'm just fine. Don't worry about me. You look like hell."

"What did they do to you?" Nate grimaced, pushing himself up. He flinched again as he pulled his right hand up, and took the pressure off. When he managed to look at his knuckles, they were red and sore, but nothing seemed to be broken.

"Nothin' really. They questioned me. That was it." Her voice quivered. She was lying. "I've been stuck in here fer hours. I had no idea what happened to you. I thought maybe they'd—"

"So they did nothing to you?"

Olivia shook her head, her eyes unmoving. Unlike others who looked away, her lies always maintained eye contact. "No." Even though he knew they'd done something to her, he wouldn't be the one to force her to relive it.

"I just hope the others are all right."

Nate stretched his arms. "Me too. I hope we can still make this work. Hey, Hugh?" He waited for a response from Hugh or London, but nothing. "Hugh?"

"What is it?"

"We must have no signal in here. Either that or that stupid rod fried my earpiece." He hissed through his teeth and rested his head back against the wall for a brief moment. He pulled himself up from the bed and walked over to the door.

"Hey! Is anyone out there?" He pounded on the door with his good fist. "HEY!" Nate kicked at the door, but whatever it was made out of was resilient. He kicked it over and over. He drew his fist back before Olivia's arm wrestled it back.

"Nate! You only have one good hand right now. Why don't you save it?"

Nate shook his head in frustration, even though he knew she was right. He slowly pulled his arm back toward himself.

"I think you need to sit down."

He let himself fall back down onto the hard mattress and rested his head back. He tried to open his right eye again and winced. Olivia sat down next to him.

"Hey." She looked at him.

"Yeah?"

Olivia hesitated and took a breath. "I didn't see Liam make it through. Isaac or Greyson neither. I kept my eyes on the gate 'til I blacked out and by that point, I think the gate reactivated."

Nate shook his head. "No, I'm sure they got through. We just—have to trust that they did." He hissed in pain.

"What?"

Nate grabbed at his face again. "My face is killing me."

"I'm sorry."

"You didn't do it."

Olivia sighed and tried to pull Nate's hand away to get a better look at the injuries. "Well, I know that, stupid. You look horrible."

"Don't spare my feelings."

"I'm just sayin'."

They both leaned against the wall and Olivia set her head on Nate's shoulder. Without explanation to himself, he rested his head on hers and reached out for her hand.

"Nate, do you think this'll work?"

"Of course."

She shook her head lightly. "I worry. Isaac told us about this precognitive thing, and we're s'pposed to think that this city weren't warned by it? By this weapon?"

It was a question that had worn on Nate the whole journey to the compound, which was why they'd planned the way they had. If this weapon was powerful and important to the city like Isaac had told them, obviously their coming would have been known beforehand to some extent. Even the doctor had said so. He told Nate they knew.

What if The Public had moved the weapon? What if, now that they were in the city, they were going to be kept here? Obviously, an invisible escape like Isaac's wouldn't be able to be repeated.

"I'm sure they were. We weren't exactly greeted like guests at the gate, were we?"

"Ya think they were expectin' us?"

"I wouldn't doubt it."

Olivia squeezed his hand. "This ain't gonna be a quick job, will it?"

He shook his head. "I don't know."

They both went quiet again. The cell was deathly silent. There was no noise from outside the door, and no obvious source of a speaker where sound could come through. Nate wondered how it would even be possible to find this rumored Precognitive. Even though he'd felt before how impossible this task was, it seemed even heavier now. If they'd had the chance to spend time in the city, get to know the layout, work within the center, they might be able to work it. But this . . . it seemed impossible.

"What if we don't get out? I know I shouldn't say that," Olivia rushed on, "but what if they leave us here? If yer right and they were expectin' us to try somethin', they ain't gonna to be welcome to lettin' us out anytime soon."

Nate barely nodded. He'd known that too. All they could pray for was, at the very least, that the other group would be able to get away. Maybe he'd get the time in here that he needed in order to learn how it operated. Not that he wanted to.

"Nate, I know this's pro'bly the wrong time to ask this. In fact, it's pro'bly the worst time to ask 'bout it. But seein' as if we ain't goin' nowhere, I might as well."

As she went quiet, Nate lifted his head to look at her. She bit her bottom lip and struggled with her words. "Why . . . why haven't things ever worked between us?"

His head immediately jerked back. Olivia frowned.

"What? Where did that come from?"

"I'm sorry, I know. But if you were in my mind, the connection would make sense. I've jest wanted to say somethin' fer a while. Nathan, we've known each other fer years. You know me, I . . . I *think* you like me. How come Soph and Greyson can make a relationship work and we can't?"

"Where is this coming from, Liv? Is it just because we're here right now?"

"Yes. And no. Actually, I was gonna say somethin' when you got back from huntin' but I chickened out." She took a deep breath and stared at the ground. " I just wanted to say somethin' because *you* never have. Nate, I've had the biggest crush on you since I was nineteen. The day I met you. You was this big, macho, military guy, and I was young, and I just thought you were—" She shrugged, not coming up with a word. "I think I've always cared for you."

"I care for you too, Liv, but I don't think I ever really felt the same way you do."

Olivia nodded with a sheepish smile and let go of his hand. "I understand. I'm like your li'l sis right?"

"Exactly. I care about you so much though. I love you. I love you like I've known you my whole life. You're my sister. My friend. Family."

Olivia swallowed hard. "Yeah, I get it." She knotted up her fingers and then looked back at him. "Are ya waitin' fer somethin'? Fer someone else to come into yer life? Have you giv'n up? Do you even care?" She held up her hands defensively. "I'm not attackin', I'm just askin'."

"Liv, this life isn't entirely conducive to romance. You know that."

"Do I? Greyson don't seem to think so."

"Yeah well, Greyson's . . . a crackpot."

Olivia smiled at him. "Are you telling me that my future brother-in-law is weird?"

The corner of Nate's mouth drew up and he set his head back. "Very."

"Nate?" She was serious again. He knew this wouldn't end until he gave her a real answer. Truth was, he didn't know the answer. Maybe at one point he thought *maybe* he could love her differently, but, all their time spent together had more or less made her his sister. That was it.

"Yeah," he said. Not really a question, but an affirmation that he understood.

"Haven't you never, in the last nine years that you've known me, seen me as someone other than a sister?"

Nate licked his lips thoughtfully. Yes, he'd thought about it before.

"I don't know what to say, Liv. I don't know what you *want* me to say. I feel like no matter what I say, I'm gonna come off looking like a dick."

"Come on, Nate." She reached out and took his hand again. He felt her rough fingers delicately trace the veins in his hand.

He honestly didn't know what to say. First, there was how he actually felt: she was his sister, at least close enough. Second, Liam was right: the hormones weren't completely dead. Plus, if he gave her what she wanted, who's to say he wouldn't come around? His head could catch up with everything else.

"Tell me, Nate. If you were to tell me right now that you've thought 'bout you and me, would you be lyin?"

"No," he whispered. "No. Liv, you're an amazing woman. I'm not blind."

Olivia ducked her head and lightly smiled. "So you think," she whispered.

Of course he could—get his head and feelings to meet. Love could always change. Though he didn't feel it now, at least he'd be with someone who wanted him.

He reached out and pulled her chin up. She had a smudge of dirt smeared across her forehead where she'd constantly been brushing her sweaty hair out of her face. Her lips were chapped, but she kept licking them, adding a glisten to each curve of her mouth and the flecks of skin. He could see flashes of worry and maybe excitement in her brown eyes, even though they were red from the dryness of the air and the lack of sleep. Nate pulled her mouth closer to his and he kissed her softly. She smelled of pine and sweet sap. The nervous beating of his heart was so loud that it could be heard off-beat from hers. When they pulled away, Olivia had a small tear running down her face.

"You must really think we're gonna die, don't you?"

"Do you trust me?" He looked her straight in the eye, trying to hide the guilt that was growing inside. "When that door opens up, you act like the girl I know you are. Huddle in the corner so they think you're not a threat. When those bastards try to take me out, get a hold of their weapons and gust 'em."

Nate shrugged his shoulders, showing confidence, and looked at the wall. "This is going to work."

―ISAAC―

ondon? London, answer me!" Isaac whispered harshly into the microphone. He pulled the com-bud out from his ear and looked at it, hoping there was only a malfunction. But there was nothing. No sounds. Not even the shuffle of feet.

"London?" he asked again after sticking the bud in again.

"What happened?" Liam grabbed Isaac's arm and yanked him out of the truck. The force made Isaac trip over his feet, but the grasp of Isaac's hand kept him from falling.

"What *happened*?" He was nearly yelling now. Isaac's head twisted sharply to the right when Liam's fist connected with his face.

Isaac's body jerked like a rag doll and he fell to the ground. Liam grabbed at his arm again, and a shaking voice pierced Isaac's ear through the opposite end of the ear bud.

"Isaac?" London finally came through.

"Stop! Stop!" Isaac shielded his face. "He's alive!"

Liam's arm froze mid-wind. Deep fear was still frozen on his face.

"He's alive!" Isaac repeated. Liam's eyes widened. He lowered his arm, and Isaac slumped to the dirt.

"London?" Isaac responded, his heart thumping. He wiped at the blood running rapidly down his nose.

"There were two. I didn't . . . didn't think there'd be two. They're dead. W-what do I do now?" his voice cracked.

Isaac hocked and spit a mouthful of blood to the ground. It conglomerated in the dirt creating a thick mud. "You'll need Liam to walk you through it." He ripped the bud out of his ear and reached it up to Liam.

Isaac rolled his eyes as Liam yanked the bud away from him and shoved it into his own ear, asking, "London, you're all right?"

Isaac pushed himself off the ground, blood and dirt still trickling thickly down his lip like syrup, gathering in a pool on his lips. He spit again and stumbled over to the truck. It was difficult to keep the blood from dripping down his clothes and he tried to keep his head tilted back. The blood simply ran down his throat, making him gag.

"Here," Hugh said, tossing him an emergency cold-pack from one of the bags. "That should slow down the flow."

"Thanks," Isaac mumbled, leaning up against the side of the truck. He whispered a curse as he looked at Liam.

"He's not usually that . . . 'friendly.' I think he likes you."

"Obviously." Isaac held the compress to his face and closed his eyes, hoping that the bleeding would soon stop. He reached up and gingerly touched the bridge of his nose. It was definitely tender, and broken. Dammit, he thought, leaning forward to hock and spit again. If only he weren't leaving this glorified Hell-hole with his family the hospital would have him fixed in no time. One shot. A simple shot to his arm. The pain would be gone, and the blood would coagulate. At least he'd miss real medicine. Something he'd never have again living as a Nomad.

He turned his head as Hugh tapped his shoulder. Hugh pointed to Liam guiding London through disabling the front gate and sensors.

"You better get ready to go."

"Here." Greyson pulled off a strip of fabric from the bottom of his shirt, took out his knife and cut off a segment, handing it to Isaac. "Shove it up there. It'll help the blood to clot."

Isaac took the fabric, rolled it and then stuck it up his nose. This forced a little more blood down his throat, and a lot more pain, but at least he would be able to function.

"You got it?" Liam asked London through the piece. "Let us know when we can come through." He motioned to Greyson and Isaac, only taking the time to actually look at Greyson. "Ready? Mm 'kay, London says that the gate's down. Let's go."

Isaac ran close behind Greyson. His jaw bounced while he kept it open to breathe. Entering the gates of the city he'd left just weeks ago was more overwhelming than he thought it would be. He'd see his family soon. All he wanted to do was run until he had his boys in his arms again. And Audra . . . he missed her so much. He couldn't remember a time when he wanted just to smell her again, to tell her that he did, in fact, love her.

He could still remember the day he'd met her. It was like meeting a co-worker on the first day at a new job. She'd been brought into the room, white jumpsuit with a white belt around her hips. At the time, he'd thought nothing of it, but looking back on the experience, she had been beautiful. Her short blonde hair pulled back into a ponytail at the base of her neck, her rare lavender eyes wide and calm at the same time.

Even the slight V in the neckline of her suit accented her sharp collarbone. The feelings toward her had never been more than satisfaction. She was satisfactory to him. His assignment, and he was hers. Less meaningful than an arranged marriage.

When his drugs wore off, when he emotionally woke up, the feelings had grown all on their own beneath the surface. Pushing forward, but stuck behind an unbreakable wall. He knew he loved her. Now he could feel it.

"Where do we go?" Liam asked, breathing hard.

"Follow me." Isaac continued running. He only made one turn to the left before jolting to a stop. The door of the building was slightly ajar and he pushed it open. "London?"

Shuffling came from across the room and Isaac finally saw the boy coming out from behind a darkened doorway. Like a hairline panel of light, the entire center of the room was a massive projected screen with at least a hundred camera angles that were all watching the outer wall. It must have been at least fifteen feet wide and seven feet tall. Not a single camera feed was watching the inside of the city.

"You guys scared me." London walked toward them. "I heard the footsteps and I figured I'd hide, just in case. I mean, I knew it might be you, but I still wasn't sure."

"I know, kid," Liam said before wrapping his arms around him. The boy's thin frame almost disappeared. "You did amazing. I'm gonna open up the gate once more for you to go back to Hugh. By the time you get back there, I'll have him patched into the rest of the security here."

"What?" London frowned.

Ignoring the teen, Liam continued. "Our problem now is that it doesn't look like there are many cameras watching the inner city, which—blows my mind based on the amount of security outside. This brings to question, why? Why no security on the inside?"

"They don't need it," Isaac said, staring up at the screen. "Who needs to guard a population of people whose emotions are regulated? They don't even know what they want."

"Well, if cases like yours keep popping up, that just might change," Liam nodded at him.

"Hey, I don't want to go back!" London shook his head. "I'm already here. Let me help. Hugh can watch surveillance by himself. It's not really a two-man job."

"Actually," Liam leaned over the chair and made a motion at the flat screen, causing fifty files to pop up on the screen, "it's a three-man job. One to watch video, one to monitor audio, and one to coordinate. But all we have is two. London, I need you out there." Liam walked over to the boy and put his hands on his shoulders. "Without you, this whole thing would have failed. You've helped more than anyone else. Right now, I need you back with Hugh."

London shook his head. "No you don't, I can do this. Look what I just did." He pointed to the two guards dead on the floor. It looked like one had hit his head during a fall to the ground and his forehead was cut wide open, and his eyes stared right back at them.

"I see." Liam nodded, feeling sick inside for what the kid had had to do. "You were great. But, I need you for something else."

London licked his lips, and his eyes fell to the floor, defeated. "Fine. I understand."

"Good." Liam turned to the screen again and opened the front gate. "Get moving, Spud."

The boy hesitated at first, but then took off in a sprint, running out of the building. Isaac watched the surveillance videos. London flashed across the screen and through the gate. His hand was raised in a fist, signaling that he was through.

"All right," Liam muttered to himself and moved the files around on the screen. He opened up a box on the screen and a grid appeared in front of him. He traversed it, his fingers moving quickly to uplink through MX to Hugh in the truck. "Hugh, do you hear me?"

Isaac's attention wandered away from Liam's work and he focused on a digital map of the city. He splayed his hand on the map like he was imitating a firework, and the picture narrowed in on a street. A row of homes sitting quietly in the city. The map shots were taken during the day. Each home was identical and geometrically simple. But there was only one that meant anything to him. He could just see Audra now. She'd be warming her hands around a cup of tea. Usually she talked to him about the events of the day: the effectiveness of the traffic, how their sons were reacting to the colors in their rooms, or what she wanted to make for dinner the next day, all the while she'd be staring up into the sky or focused on the dust floating in front of her eyes. At least that's what it had felt like.

He wondered what she'd say with her emotions in full swing. What would she really be like?

"Isaac," Liam called to him.

"Yeah?"

"We need to get going. You'll have to show us to your house."

Isaac nodded. "Hugh's all set? We're in?"

"Done and done."

Isaac nodded once more and then led them out of the building. He knew they would need to be extra careful. It had already taken too long to get into the security and he was surprised that the remaining guards hadn't returned. The chances of seeing security on the streets were extremely high now. "Stay close. We may have problems."

"What do you mean?" Greyson asked.

"The guards should have been back to the building by now, that's what I mean. We'll probably run into them. Plus, we need to take the Tunnel to get to my house."

"The Tunnel?"

Isaac turned down another street, looking from side to side. "The Tunnel. It's kind of like what a city subway used to be like," he whispered even softer. "Have you ever seen an earthworm fly through the air at eighty miles an hour?"

"No."

"You will."

"Wait," Liam whispered from the back, "by using the Tunnel, won't they register us on their security?"

Isaac paused, and then spoke with a clip to his tone. "No. But they'll know we're here when they return to find those guards."

"Yeah, no shit, Sherlock."

Isaac peered around the corner of the next building and then backed up again. A lone guard transport was hovering down the street slowly, headed for the elevated highway.

Not only could Isaac be recognized if they were spotted, but in their hygienic state, even a fool could tell the other men were Nomads. "Get down," he softly said. The men ducked down into the shadows of the building. Isaac watched the transport continue down the road and when he felt they were safe, he stood up and motioned for the others to follow.

"Do you ever get the feeling that this guy's gonna screw us over?" Liam whispered to Greyson behind him. Isaac rolled his eyes.

"Now, Liam," Isaac panted, "What would be the point in that?" He glanced back at Liam before he took off running down the side of the building. "Stay near the walls. We can't risk being seen in the streets." Isaac hurried. They were within a block of the Tunnel entrance. When he saw it coming up, he tucked back against another building and waited for the other two to catch up.

"All right," Isaac breathed. "I'm going to tell you again, we probably don't have much time until we're made. We have, I would guess, about ten minutes total to get to my house, get my family, get back on the Tunnel, and then bolt for the front gate."

"Only ten minutes? What happens if it takes fifteen?" Greyson asked.

"We won't make it," Isaac said flatly.

Liam smiled with unbelief. "Of course."

Isaac looked back at the Tunnel. The next stop was in thirty seconds. "Let's go!" He pulled away from the building and sprinted. The other two were close behind. A lilting mechanical voice welcomed them. "Thank you for selecting Public One's transportation Tunnel. We appreciate your help in keeping our air free of pollutants and welcoming a more perfect tomorrow."

"Are you kidding me?" Liam scoffed and smiled again. "I feel like I'm listening to an old PBS special."

Isaac dropped his head and sat down on one of the clean white seats. He knew they wouldn't all make it. Ten minutes was not only crazy, it was impossible. He hoped that Liam and Greyson would create enough of a distraction that he'd be able to get out of the city with his family. The scuffs of his Public issued shoes created streaks of dirt on the floor of the transporter. Isaac couldn't help but feel a sense of guilt sweep over him. He glanced up at Greyson and Liam and pushed the shame away. He had more to worry about.

Then the transporter stopped.

"We've arrived at section three of Public One. Thank you again for—"

Isaac pulled on Liam's arm and bolted off the Tunnel. "Ten minutes, ten minutes," kept running over and over in his mind. They were only a block away. "Ten minutes."

Isaac rounded the corner to his and Audra's home. One light was on in the living room with almost no movement. The fingerprint lock blinked green, the door whisked open, and he removed his thumb. "Audra? Audra?" he frantically called.

A light clatter of porcelain came from the kitchen and a slight woman with short blonde hair came out to greet him. Audra's face showed nothing but mild confusion. "Isaac? Where have you been?" Her voice was soft and willowy. "Guards have been asking questions, Honey." A large smile parted her lips. "They'll be so relieved to hear you're back. They pressed me so much to know where you were going. I just didn't know—"

Isaac wrapped her up into his arms, stopping her from pushing the pad to her right. "Audra," he stopped and breathed her in. He could feel her muscles stiffen and she was trying to push herself away.

"What's wrong, Isaac?" She reached to touch his broken nose. Isaac brushed her hand away. "Who are these men? They aren't Nomads are they?"

"We have to go, Audra."

"Go where? It's nearly nine. It's almost time for bed. I think you should get some sleep first."

Isaac handed her to Liam. "*Don't* let her call the city. I'm going to grab the boys. Greyson? Little help?" He ran down the hallway of their large simplistic home and up a landing of clear steps. Greyson followed. Tucked away in the corner were two separate bedrooms. The first had a single bed. Splashes of red were everywhere. The bed, the shapes on the walls in intricate planned patterns, and even down to the toys. Red cars, red puzzles and building blocks.

Isaac motioned Greyson to go in and get his other boy out of the green bed room. Isaac hurried into the other, leaned over the bed, and gently stroked his son's blonde hair. The boy shifted, but didn't wake. Isaac lifted him in his arms and met Greyson in the hall. The second child, dressed in green pajamas was barely awake and piggy-riding on Greyson's back.

The men walked back to the living room where Audra was sitting peacefully in a couch with Liam watching over her. "Your wife is weird. She hasn't moved or said a word since you left."

"She wouldn't," Isaac answered. "Come on, Audra. Let's go."

"Where?" she asked.

"You'll have to come to see."

"It doesn't make sense, though." She stood up, curiosity etched into her sharp eyebrows. "Why would we go somewhere at night? It's time to sleep."

"Do you trust me, Audra?"

She stood, her shoulders dropping and she slightly arched back. "Trust?"

"Yes. Do you think I would do something to hurt you or the boys?"

Audra's face became even calmer, if that was even possible. She shook her head so slightly that Isaac almost thought he hadn't seen it. "I just don't understand why we have to leave. We have a good home here. We're safe. Everything we have is taken care of for us. We have no worries, Isaac. Why leave it?"

Isaac stepped closer to his companion, cradling his youngest in his arms. "Audra, do you love me?"

"Love you?" She blinked. The concept was foreign to her now as it had been to himself last year. She slowly looked down at the floor, and then back up at him. "I know you're a good person, you work hard, and you are pleasant to talk to."

"But do you love me?"

He could see her mind working. The concept of love was so unfathomable for her that she couldn't even come up with words to answer. "I don't understand the question. I don't know."

"Isaac, we gotta go, man," Liam stated, looking out the window. "We don't even have enough time to get back to the gate."

"Audra," Isaac's pulse raced. He thought about what might happen if he couldn't get her to leave, "we have to go. You have to come with me."

She barely nodded again. Liam took his cue and pushed the door pad. The door slid smoothly open and he motioned for Isaac and his family to exit the house. Isaac grabbed his companion's hand and pulled her along with him. Greyson followed after with the oldest son, and Liam ran after them.

The air burned Isaac's lungs the faster his legs pumped. Audra seemed to be dragging her feet, not in a hurry to move with him. He pulled on her hand harder, hoping to convey the message of urgency to her. Greyson was pulling ahead of him, and reached the Tunnel before the rest of the group. "Come on, come on," he called, ushering the family and Liam onto the transport.

The familiar haunting mechanical voice greeted them again. "Thank you for selecting Public One's transportation Tunnel. We appreciate—" The voice continued its greeting.

Isaac let go of his wife's hand. She sat down on a seat and caught her breath. He turned to look at Liam who had just removed a gun from the waistband of his jeans. It was an old model. At least thirty years old; didn't even have body heat recognition or instant target capabilities like the ones developed for the war. Isaac had never seen one like it before. Liam clicked the magazine out of place to check it, and then clicked it back in.

"You think we'll have to use it?" Greyson asked, hiking the child further onto his back.

"I know he will," Isaac said, taking a few paces and running his hands down his face. "They'll be waiting for us when we get off of the Tunnel, I'm sure of it," he said quietly to Liam. "I don't know if my family will be safe through the fire."

"We'll get them out," Liam said blankly, folding his arms. "When we get to the right stop, you and Greyson take them to the next car down and exit there. I'll keep them occupied."

"They'll take you down."

"Liam," Greyson started.

"Then as I'm gustin' them, you run for it."

"That's your plan?" Greyson spoke up again.

"You have a better one? You know, I could do cartwheels out of here. Maybe a back-flip, some clogging. I've got a mean Nell Thai dance impression. Might really throw them off." Liam forced a grin and lightly punched Greyson's shoulder. "Spud, we gotta get the family out. Plain and simple. So, you get them to safety no matter what what's happening to me."

The Tunnel began to slow in pace. Isaac grabbed his wife's hand again, holding his son close. Greyson handed three-year-old Peter to Audra and she held him on her hip casually. He braced the child's sleeping head to rest on her shoulder. The men pulled off to the side of the door and left for the next set of doors down when the transporter came to a stop. Liam blocked the door, hand behind his back with the gun. He turned to them and smiled with a raw pleasure. "See ya at the truck."

No, you won't, Isaac thought to himself.

The door slid open and the mechanically smooth voice of the Tunnel could barely be heard over the shouting calls of the guards outside. Liam reached forward, his gun flashed up and he got out ten rounds as he ran out cursing, a grin on his face the whole time. The gun fire from Liam was the only thing that could be heard. In contrast, the return fire of the guards was nearly silent. The noises were getting fainter. Isaac slowly peeked outside the door.

Each of the five guards was hunkered down behind their gun fire shields, facing away from Isaac's gaze. Their guns all locked on Liam. Two guards were already down. Liam must have surprised them before they were able to raise their shields.

"Let's go," he whispered to Greyson. He pulled Audra, running harder than he ever had. The pull of freedom was the only thing keeping him from tripping over his own feet. Audra still held back and he yanked her lightly again. When the gunfire ended, Isaac kept running.

"Liam!" Greyson called.

But Isaac kept running. The beat of his heart pounding in his own head—with no thought to the men behind him.

——LIAM——

H e could feel drone of electricity crackling near his head. The bullets from the guards were just like they were during the war, only upgraded. Each shot hit the barrier behind him, right between his shoulder blades. They detected heat signatures, and the center of his body was a prime target. He twisted his arm back, fired off two more shots, and heard the groan of a man. The pounding of his heart was beating between his ears. This was the closest he'd felt to being at war again, and the tightening in his chest was back. The only difference was he wasn't wearing a gas mask or equipped with everything he needed.

Liam laughed when the gun fire paused. "Aw, man! Don't tell me you give up already!"

"Surrender, Nomad, and you will be treated justly," a voice called back to him.

"Justly? How 'bout you explain what you mean by that."

"Public One criminal policy number two, two, three. All trespassing Nomads with malicious intent are to be retired."

Liam whistled loudly. "Live a life of luxury? It's tempting. But I'm not interested."

"Retirement by death."

He chuckled wryly to himself. Liam swung his arm around the barrier again and fired three times. Each of his bullets would have been deadly to the front guard had they not ricocheted off the shield. He barely noticed the last man he'd hit. It was only a leg wound. And there were three guards left. The dry scratch of sandpaper slid down his throat when he swallowed and checked his magazine. He had four left.

"Surrender, Nomad."

Liam's lips pulled up into a crooked and pained smile. He knew what would happen next. It hit him hard. Even when he was in the Marines, he'd never felt like his time was up. Flashes played behind his eyes—bleeding arteries, boiling flesh, body parts, getting off shots with Nate or someone else next to him—he shook his head to forget them. This was different. No one was backing him up. Not this time.

"Really? I think this is rather fun, don't you?"

Liam took a deep breath, and blew it out slowly. His mind raced, trying to develop something that would work. A strategy. He slipped the magazine out again, double checking. When he clicked it back in, he shoved the gun back down into the waistband of his pants. The odds of this working were almost none. But it was the only thing he could think of. The longer he held them off, the more guards would show up.

It was in that instant he knew there was only one way to do it. He raised his arms. He had only the gun and a few throwing blades on him. Not enough to keep them off forever. "All right, fine," he said with a straight face. He walked around the barrier and prayed that the guards didn't shoot him yet. "You got me."

"Stop where you are."

Liam's feet paused for a brief moment. He took another step again.

"Stop where you are, Nomad and throw your weapon to the side."

"Throw it?" Liam smiled. "You want me to throw it?"

The guards kept their guns on Liam, their bullet shields raised. Two of them fidgeted. Nervous. He liked it when they were nervous.

"All right," he spoke again. "I'll throw it." Liam reached back toward the gun, slid his hands to the side and pulled the three small throwing blades out of his back pocket. Without hesitation, his arm lashed out with the first two knives, each sticking two different guards in their throats. The last guard let off a round of electric shots. The first hit Liam in the center of his chest. The second, traveled through his abdomen, and the third penetrated the right lung. His breathing became difficult. Liam threw the last knife and it sunk deep into the guard's skull. A trickle of blood traveled down the guards face, his eyes frozen open—holding onto the last wisp of life.

Liam lowered himself to the ground, struggling to breathe. He heard Greyson in the distance call out his name. That moron. He knew Greyson would come back. He had told him to keep going. Liam's legs gave out and his body shook in convulsions from the shots. A small electrical burn hole was in the center of his chest. Using his fingers, he could feel the singed edges. He could smell the acrid scent of his own burnt flesh. But there was no feeling. A pinch in his lungs. It was hard to breath, otherwise, he would have felt fine.

The faint sound of running boots on pavement came at him from the distance, but he couldn't control his own movements as the bullet's charge shocked him relentlessly.

"Liam, Liam. Liam, can you hear me?"

Liam shuddered. His body was pulled off the ground and spun around. He looked at the ground as Greyson held him over his shoulder. "Don't worry, you're gonna be all right." Greyson winced under the weight. "I'm gonna get you out of here."

"Isaac," Liam managed to say.

"He took off. I think he's gone already."

A flash of lights alternated down the streets to Liam's right. More guards were on their way. He clamped his eyes shut and his breath became raspier.

"We're almost to the gate," Greyson panted and shifted him on his shoulder again. Liam groaned in agony. "Hold on. Hold on."

"Hugh!" Greyson called into his ear bud. "I don't know how far the guards are behind us, but we need that truck pulled around now." He paused. "No, we aren't with Isaac. Just get it here!"

Liam felt cold. It wasn't the night, because it had been about sixty degrees ten minutes ago with a light warm breeze. The chill was felt first in his fingertips, then his toes and feet. When his chest spread with an uncontrolled icy feel, he closed his eyes against the pain. He shook and convulsed again.

"We're almost there," Greyson choked on his words. "Almost there, Liam. Hold on."

Another spasm spread through his body, and the last image he saw was the guards exiting their vehicles, guns and shields raised.

—REGGIE—

I finger the end of the spoon. It's not sharp enough, but with the right pressure, it'll work. I scarcely slept all night. It's almost time. The guards will come get me for my routine. I close my eyes and lay still on my bed. For the small moment of time that I did sleep, the images that flashed behind my eyes never stopped. My precognition could sense the urgency. Like it took on a personality of its own, forcing as much information into my consciousness as it could.

Each detail, every step from my cell to the gates of the city was laid out in chunks that I've pieced together over the last couple hours. Each one connected to the last. The key pad again, the sharpened spoon, the look of a guard falling down near me, his eyes wide open and dead—an image I've seen numerous times lately. A chair. There was a worn edge on the guard's shoe. He walks on the inside of his feet, wearing the rubber away faster. I saw the cell again. The same one I'd seen last night while awake. The one where Nate and the woman were, or are.

My eyes flash open and I tuck the spoon up my sleeve. Nerves tingle at the surface of my skin. I know I can do this. I've seen it. Knowing that doesn't make it easier.

The door opens in a silent glide and the shuffle of feet follows. Guards take hold of my arms and yank me off the bed. The guard to my right, smelling of molded peppers, holds tighter to my arm than usual. Nothing yet looks familiar yet. Nothing like my vision. I know what's going to happen, I'm just not sure when. I let myself be led down the hall where I'm taken to the room and shoved down into the chair. The sharpened edge of the spoon lightly digs into my skin and I pull it away, sliding it out of my sleeve and tucking it behind my thigh. It's only seconds before Dryer comes through those doors. What will happen when he attempts to lock onto my visions? He'll know what I've seen. It'll never happen.

My heart races with anxiety. I shouldn't move. My mind tells me, *not yet.*

The door opens and Dryer walks in. His eyes are red and there is a definitive sense of exhaustion set in his pupils. He's never looked this way before. Something is worrying him more than ever. It's them. They're here.

He walks up to me and rubs my arm. "Reggie, you had a hard night, I'm sure."

"The drugs you gave me last night kept me awake," my voice shakes and I try to play it off as exhaustion. "You don't look so good yourself."

Dryer's eyebrows drop and he looks deep into my face. "Did you not sleep?"

The words spill out of my mouth. "Not enough."

His chest rises and falls slowly and deeply. Muscles and tendons along his jaw tighten and clench, causing a pit in one side of his face. "This was not what I needed this morning. Go get some sleep Reggie. You're of no use to me if you haven't slept." He snaps his fingers and I hurry to slip the spoon underneath my sleeve again. The guards walk to my side and pull me up. I glance down to my left and notice the guard next to me. His feet slant inwards.

If only they could feel the blood rushing through my veins. If only they knew how scared I am. I can do this. I have to do this.

The hallway is bright and my eyes focus on every detail. Just outside my cell is an aluminum chair. My eyes flash from the chair to the guard. We arrive at the cell door, the guard to my left presses the pad and the door opens.

I won't get another chance at this.

I throw my body weight and the sharp end of the spoon into his ribcage. He's a rock wall, but the sharpened end goes right through. His feet twist underneath him from the worn out bottoms of his shoes. The guard to my right yanks me back, pinching my arms tight behind my back. His grip is too tight. It hurts so much.

Oh, please let me get out of this. I grit my teeth, driving the pain somewhere else.

The guard on the floor stumbles over the aluminum chair, trying to pull himself up and it slides a few feet toward me. I lift my legs, the pain in my shoulders intensify. The chair trips the guard holding me. We both fall over to the ground. His power-gun detaches from its holster and it misfires. It's within my reach.

The images of my precognitive dream replay for me, reminding me what comes next. My hand lashes out and I grab the gun. It's heavy, but I roll over and aim it at the large guard who was holding me. I pull the trigger and the shot slices through his body. Another shot to the guard nursing the spoon in his chest. With one deep breath, he gurgles and wheezes.

It's over. My body shakes. I can't move. I close my eyes to shut out the image of the guards' dead faces, looking right at me. Just like my vision. All over again.

Keeping the gun tight in my hands, I stumble to my feet and run down the hall. The walls around me spin. I've been holding my breath. I'm too shaken. I have to get control of myself. I have to do this. Even if I'm still afraid of what will happen the moment I find Nate and the woman. I take a deep breath and feel a flow of oxygen finally make it to my head. The dizziness dissipates and I run harder. Each cell is numbered. The numbers ascend and I know I'm getting closer.

Twenty-seven.

I come to a halt, sliding on the marble. A burning sensation runs along the skin of my feet, but I ignore it. I take a deep breath and face the keypad. The sound of an alarm fills the hallway. Two, two, nine, eight . . . I press the numbers. My finger hesitates, floating over the five. When it slightly brushes across the number, the pad glows green, the numbers disappear, and the door slides open. Inside, the woman is asleep on Nate's shoulder. The scene is identical to what I witnessed last night. Her face is caked with streaked dry dirt. Her eyes flutter open and she immediately stiffens. Their cell smells of clay and a musty sweat. Odors barely memorable to me.

The alarms in the hallway are blaring in my head. And I look at him. His good eye opens up, and the swollen mound flinches.

"What do you want with us?"

"I'm here to get you. I'm here to help. We don't have any time, we have to move. I'll explain everything later."

He rushes at me. I can feel the pulsing movement of his muscles as he presses me up against the wall, his forearm digging into my throat. "What do you mean? You're not a guard, so who are you?"

Risking it, I drive my fist into his sore eye and he releases me with a stream of curses.

"I'm Precognitive! I saw you coming!" My voice is strained. Coarse. I try to keep my tone calm while a flood of oxygen and runs back into my head and lungs.

A mix of recognition and disbelief expand the woman's pupils. Nate rounds on me, staring at me like insects are pouring out of my eyes. "You're lying. The precog is a weapon. Not a woman."

"Hey," the woman comes closer, "what if she's tellin' the truth. Isaac never told us that the precog was a human."

"Right, and it just happened to drop in our laps?"

He rushes for me again.

"Hey!" She pulls at his arm. "Let her go. She's getting' us out and we're wastin' time!"

He steps back and I breathe deep, stepping towards him with a glare.

"We have to go," I whisper. "Follow me." I dart out of the cell and down the hall.

I rummage around in my mind; through the visions I saw from last night. I look for signs of things that seem familiar. A sudden flash of light catches my eye. It's the glare of the sun through the window. I look down the hall to my right and I know it's the right way. "This way," I say, their feet padding behind me.

"I don't know about this, Liv," Nate's rough voice grunts.

The alarm continues to blare and I can hear the sounds of feet coming down the hall. I reach through my memories again. This time the flash of a picture comes through my mind and I press the pad of the door to my left. It slides open and I run through. Stairs lead down and I begin to follow them.

Blaring red lights revolve on the ceiling above us. I continue to follow the stairs down three levels. I get to the bottom and I feel Nate and the woman hurrying to stay behind me. The last door has a glowing red access pad.

"The doors are now on lock-down. They won't open," I state, shaking my head.

"So we're locked in again? That's great." Nate turns and pulls at Liv's arm. He's taking her back up the stairs.

"Stop!" I yell at him. "We have to wait!"

"Wait?" he asks. "Wait for what? For those guards to come through that door and shoot us down? I'm finding a way out."

"Nate, you have to trust me!"

His eyes flash open, and he looks at me snakes are slithering from my ears. *"How do you know my name?"*

They both stare me down. I look back and forth from one to the other. Olivia's beginning to look calmer, but Nate's face is tight. "I've been watching you for weeks. That's how."

He takes two steps down the stairs and I back away from him. "You've been watching me? What the hell have you seen?"

My shoulders fall. "I don't have time to tell you everything."

A boom from the door above sounds, and our eyes shoot toward the upper staircase. I know that the door hasn't opened yet. I look back at the keypad. It's still red. But it's coming. It's almost time.

"You've been seeing me?"

"In my visions, yes."

"You knew we were comin'?" Liv asks.

"Yes!" I almost yell, now repeating myself for a fourth time. "For a while now."

Another boom. That's two. There's one more. The keypad will unlock.

"What's yer name?" she asks.

"Reggie."

"Reggie . . . what?" she prods, her eyebrows angled down.

"What do you mean?" I ask.

"You don't have a last name?"

A last name?

Boom.

I turn around. The keypad unlocks and I slam my hand against it. The door opens just as I begin to hear multiple sets of feet running down the stairwell. I exit and the other two follow. A single guard rounds the corner. The gun shakes in my hand. I raise it and fire. An electric shot flies by his head and burns into the wall. The guard fires off three rounds, and we all duck. My hands still tremble. I can't do this.

Nate reaches out and yanks the gun from my hands. With one shot, it sears through the guard's chest, leaving a charred hole.

"Liv, go take his gun," Nate says.

She stands and runs for the fallen guard, sliding to the ground and slipping the gun in between her hands. "Liv," I say to her. "In about five seconds, you need to duck!"

"What?"

"DUCK!"

She tucks her head down and firing breaks through the glass windows. Guards across the walkway are raining gunfire on us. Nate and Olivia spin around and rapidly start firing on the guards. Each stumble forward, falling over the hand rails to the final floor below.

Nate's shots are exact. Not a single miss. I study the way his eyes focus, the way his body controls each muscle in his fingers and arms. It's a science.

I start running again. Nate follows after, with Liv taking up the rear. The last door is just ahead. I set my hand on the pad and the door slides open. The blaze of the rising sun, the warmth of its barely peeking rays beat down on me and I want so much to stop. To stop and enjoy the feeling of being out of the building. But I can't. I force myself to keep moving. My feet beat harder against the perfect pavement. I feel tiny rocks lodging between my toes, jabbing the pads of my calloused heels.

"Hugh!" I hear Nate call behind me and I turn to look at him. He's holding tight to Liv's hand and pressing his other finger to his ear. "Hugh! We're leaving the holding cells. Please tell me you're still patched into security!"

I turn back. Apparently they were more prepared than even *I* had known. Most others The Public captured had had hand-held radios. Nothing like this.

"We'll be there soon. I'll let you know when to be there. What? What about Liam?"

I hear Nate go quiet and he curses under his breath. I keep running. I can hear the guard's patrollers on the streets. There are at least six. I know we can't outrun them. A picture from my vision flashes again behind my eyes and I look to the right, waiting for the vehicle to come out of the driveway.

Five . . . four . . . three . . . two . . . one, I think to myself. We pass by. It pulls out onto the street. Its engine will stall. I keep running hard, pushing myself. I have to get out of here. I am never coming back. I look behind once more and the guard's patrollers are caught behind the stalled car.

"We're almost there!" I yell back.

The last time I saw all of this was too many years ago. So much has changed, but the bones of the city are the same. It's grown so much—more expansive, and the grandeur is overwhelming. Ahead of me I can see it. The first thing I ever saw of this nightmare. The gate.

"You'd better be there *now*, Hugh!" Nate calls.

The power grid allows the three of us to bolt through, leaving the city behind. A tarnished beaten-up truck is speeding up to walls waiting. It skids to a stop with dust billowing behind it. I see a man at the driver's seat with a younger boy sitting next to him. In the back of the truck is a brown-skinned man with a lot of security equipment, shutting it all down. Laying on the bed of the truck next to him is one of the other men from my visions. Irie, was his last name. I remember his jacket. The same one he's wearing now. His eyes are closed. His skin, which at one point was slightly darker, has lost its color. He's so pale.

"Liv, get in the front with London!" Nate calls. "You," he glares at me, "in the back."

He grabs my arm and forces me into the back of the truck. Memories of the guards just moments ago spring to my eyes and I shut them out. This is going to be different. It's going to get better.

The engine roars, the gas pushed to its limit. The man with long curly hair turns the wheel with a jerk. I clutch the truck side to keep from falling out. I watch Nate get closer to the man lying down.

"Liam?"

The man doesn't respond.

"What happened, Hugh? Where's Isaac and his family?"

"Liam was shot three times—it's a power-gun wound. The holes have cauterized, but the damage is bad."

Nate pulls down the blanket that's been placed on Liam to keep him warm and fingers the holes in his chest.

"He still has a pulse. But we have to get him to a place with the right equipment. He won't live if we don't. And even then . . ."

"And Isaac?" Nate growls loudly, cutting him off.

"Took off. By this point he probably reached the other truck that we left behind. He used this 'precog plan' to cover him so he could save his own selfish ass. So where is it? The weapon?"

Nate glares up at me. It's the same look I've seen in his eyes before. Hate. And now, it's mixed with the pain of seeing his ally shot. "You're lookin' at her," he calls out over the whipping sounds of the air flowing by the truck.

"Her?" Hugh nods toward me.

"Yep," Nate says sardonically. His blue eyes darken. They are almost colorless. Drowning in fury.

—NATE—

NO!" he pounded his fist down on the hospital bed. "No . . . no, NO!"

Behind him, Olivia inhaled. Tears rolled down her face while the generator whirred loudly in the room. Liam's body, the only injured one in the abandoned hospital, was cold. Nate had felt the weakening beat of his best friend's heart underneath the pad of his own palm.

"No," he groaned again, leaning over the body. "Don't you dare leave us, Liam. Do you hear me? I'll gust you!" he growled.

Since they'd arrived at the abandoned remnants of Pierre, South Dakota, Nate hadn't left Liam's side. Hugh had done all that he could with the limited medical knowledge he had. With the lack of electricity to run the machines, which were most likely broken anyway, the chances of Liam's survival had been slim. The staunch reality of that had not only hit Nate, but was chewing him up and spitting him out. Liam's wounds, though not creating internal bleeding, had damaged his lungs and one of his major arteries. He still hadn't woken up.

Nate could hear Liam's voice taunting him. "Hey man, at least I got to gust a few. What did you do?" He'd say it with a grin. Nate sank lower within himself.

Crackling breaths were still emanating from Liam's mouth. It was more painful to hear the same scraping puffs of air escaping his chest. Olivia continued to monitor the generator that they'd brought along. Its power was decreasing. There was only a short amount of time left before it too wouldn't respond. The power it supplied to the respirator was the only thing keeping Liam with them.

"Nate, he's gonna make it," she attempted to console him, though the expression on her face betrayed another thought.

"Liam," he spoke to the closed eyes again, ignoring her comment, "Liam, remember Santa Monica Pier? You've gotta go back. We'll just stay there. No more moving, no more running. You have to wake up though, or I won't . . ." His gruff voice caught and he dropped his head again to hide the tears threatening to spill out. Nate took a deep breath in and shook his head. "You made it all through the war, and you're gonna let three lousy shots take you out?"

Nate leaned forward to feel the pulse in Liam's neck again. It was fatally slow. His fingers shook, still pressing into the artery. The pulse stopped. There wasn't even a chance to say goodbye. Now he was gone. Nate clasped his hands together, rocking back and forth, his head hung low. The generator was shut off and then he heard Olivia move to his side. He felt her delicate hand over the breadth of his back, pulling him close to her. His body shook—even his organs, his muscles— quavering in fury. The entire thing was his fault. If he hadn't heeded Isaac's pleadings, if he hadn't cared so much about helping that clone, this never would have happened. Liam would still be alive.

It shouldn't have happened.

It couldn't. He'd known Liam for years. He was family to Nate. Not just a friend, but a brother.

Olivia pulled him up to his feet against his will. She laced her arms under his, pulling herself close and weeping. Like a machine he slowly raised his arms around her. Tears ran down her face like a river, drenching his shirt. Nate took a deep breath in, the smell of Olivia's hair filling his lungs. Something in him didn't want to be around her right now. He didn't want to be around anyone right now. All he wanted was to talk to Liam. Quickly, he pushed her away and walked out of the hospital room. Hugh was talking in hushed tones to Greyson and London, explaining what had happened in the hospital room.

When they got there, everything had moved too fast, and too slow all at the same time. Nate had carried Liam's body through the broken down hospital doors and into the nearest room. Hugh had followed close behind, searching for medical tools the moment Liam was rested on the bed. Nate had yelled at him, pushing him to move faster. Hugh struggled to find what he needed in the nearest drawers. Too many things had been looted.

Nate closed his eyes, pushing back the memory of the last half-hour.

The precog sat in a chair by herself, looking out the hospital window blankly. Nate ignored her and spoke directly to the other men. "We need to move on. We can't stay here much longer or they'll find us."

"No they won't, right?" London looked back at the precog. "We have her, they don't. They can't see where we are. Isn't that how it works?" He leaned to peer at the precog.

The girl pulled her gaze away from the window to look at them. Her eyes were devoid of color. Gray, like a thunderstorm, but empty of the life and fury of Mother

Nature. The long, stringy, bland, brown hair that grew from her head fell around her face, casting shadows on the high cheek bones of her face. She wasn't even a real person. There was nothing in her. They'd risked everything, Liam's life, for a science project.

"They'll still find us," Nate continued. "We need to go."

"Nate," Olivia said behind him. "What about Liam?"

"Liam's dead, Liv."

"Yes, but *yer* not. *We're* not. I know you don't want to, but we need to have a," she choked on the word, "funeral fer him. We have the time. He deserves that, an' you know it. How can you jest move on, leavin' him there?"

Nate stared at her. He kept his watch hard and unyielding. "You want to bury him? Burn him? Drop him from a building? Fine!"

Nate turned and walked out the door of the old hospital. He didn't want to do it. Getting rid of Liam's body was permanent. Then he'd really be gone.

Next to the big-city hospital was a worn-out storage shed. Its roof had collapsed, and it looked like the door had been broken down by force. He pulled the large broken door away and looked inside. A rake was missing from its spot, a shovel was still there, some gardening tools were all picked over with a few lying on the ground, a lawn mower with its gas cap missing, and a leaf blower were all there. He pulled the shovel off of its hook on the wall and stepped back outside. Directly in front of the hospital, he started to dig. It was like trying to pick at rock or concrete. Small chunks of dirt flew, not piling up in any one area, but all around him. On the boarder of his vision a set of feet walked out of the hospital toward him. It was Olivia again.

"Nate," she said calmly.

He continued to dig through the small area of dried up grass and dirt. The edge of the shovel ground on the rocks and dry soil that broke apart like chinks in pottery.

"Nate." Her tone intensified slightly. It was full of pain and sorrow. "Nate, I need you to stop an' look at me."

He threw the shovel to the ground. "What?" he yelled at her. "What do you want me to say? I'm sad? I'm pissed off? That this is really hard? I *knew* we shouldn't have come." He drove his finger at her, directly to her face. "Liam knew it too, but he did it anyway. He did it because I asked him to. Dammit, the man made me get on my knees and beg him! I should be the one who's dead. I made us come, not him."

Olivia's eyes filled with tears again. She quickly put her hands on her hips and looked out toward the hillside. She blinked a couple times, keeping her tears back. "This ain't your fault you know."

"Yeah, it's that anus, Isaac. If it weren't for him . . ."

"His family wouldn't be safe," Olivia said harshly. "This is nobody's fault, Nate. Nobody but The Public. You need to know that." She walked up to him, looking him in the face. "You did the *right* thing. Liam did the right thing. Greyson told me what he did to save that family. I," she shook her head, "honestly don't blame Isaac for running off. He's a coward, but he took care of his family the only way he knew how. Liam risked his life for two innocent children. He wanted to, he chose to." He turned his head away and Olivia grabbed his jaw, pulling his focus back.

"How can you say that? Leading other people into a city to be decoys in order to create a way to escape is not . . ."

He didn't even have a word for it. Nate knocked her hand away, but he continued to look into her face. Never before had he seen her so understanding and caring. If anything, he thought that she'd be on his side, furious at Isaac, and furious at everything. He dropped his head shaking it.

"You saved that girl in there, Nate."

Nate scoffed, rolling his eyes. "Girl? Please. She's not even a real person."

"How can you say that?"

"Just because she walks like us, and talks like us, doesn't mean she *is* one of us. You saw what happened when she got us out. She knew exactly when to move, exactly what was going to happen. She knew my name before anyone told her! *That's* not human." He pointed to the hospital.

Olivia looked back at him as if she didn't know him. Confusion and sadness melted into her eyes. She'd never looked at him like that. It seemed as if, ever since he'd known Olivia, she'd always looked up to him, trusted him, even worshiped him in a revered way. Now, none of those were shining through her face. Only disappointment.

"Nathan, I know yer hurtin'. Guess what? We all are. But, how dare you say that?"

"It's true. That thing is no more human than a computer. You can program it with whatever you want, but in the end, it's just a computer. We risked lives, Liam's life, to collect *that thing.*" He said the last two words with so much hate it tasted like poison rolling off his tongue.

Olivia's hand shot up in a flash, branding his stubbled face with a hot red imprint of her hand. He felt the burn begin to blend and spread into the pain of his injured eye. Her dark brown eyes flashed with shades of deep red and amber. "I can't look at you right now. I have *never* been so disappointed . . . so disgusted with you in my life," she said, a well of water building up at the bottom of her eyes. She stormed back into the hospital.

A solitary pair of eyes looked back at him through the window. The gray depths of them could swallow him. His stomach turned.

The smell of death—motor oil, broken sewage lines, chemical leftovers—all filled his mind and he turned away to look out at the city that reeked of destruction.

Hugh and Greyson carried the body to the roof and burned it while London, in his light tenor voice, offered a choppy version of *Be Still My Soul*. The moment he'd said, "the Lord is on thy side," Nate's eyes overflowed with tears, spilling down with heavy weight. What Lord, he'd thought, what Lord is on our side?

Then Hugh called for everyone come together as they pulled away from the burning smell of Liam's flesh. "Liam soared in life. Let's continue with that legacy," he'd whispered.

He couldn't do it. Out of the corner of his eye, Nate saw the precog folding her arms, looking blankly at the billowing flames. Blank. No expression.

Nate felt sick to his stomach that she was even there. He couldn't stay. He turned on his heel and left.

—OLIVIA—

Olivia rolled over onto her side. Although her body was screaming for sleep, her eyes wouldn't close. Sleep wasn't just an escape, though. It was something she needed desperately. But with sleep came peace, and she didn't feel it. Peace was far from her mind and her soul. All she wanted to do was sidle up to the curve of Nate's body and have him hold her.

Olivia looked at him sleeping in the chair. His head kept bobbing. She wanted Liam back. She wanted it too much.

She attempted to blink back a group of watery bombs that echoed on the built-in sleeping bag pillow. A movement on the other side of the room made her jolt and she lifted her head up. Sitting back near the large window of the hospital was the precog. The girl seemed perfectly normal to her, aside from the fact that she knew everything before it would happen. Nate's accusation of her "machine" like qualities had hit a nerve with Olivia. Whatever this girl was, she was greater than they could imagine. She just didn't know how.

Olivia pulled her legs up, and then pushed her body out of the bag. In all the hours the precog had been in their possession, Olivia hadn't said a word to the girl. Her tongue felt like it was glued to the roof of her mouth, but she walked over to her.

The precog had such a plain unworldly look to her. Hair with no luster, skin pale as winter snow. When Olivia got closer, the girl looked up at her. Her eyes were so gray. Gray, but filled with fire and life. They weren't dead or inhuman like Nate had said.

"You can't sleep neither?" Olivia said, sitting down across from her. "I'm havin' a hard time myself." She glanced out the window to see what the precog had been looking at. The worn down city had no visual stimulus that was pleasing to look at. Olivia turned to focus on the girl again. "I have to apologize. I haven't even asked yer name."

Reggie nodded without looking over at her. "You did. But that's all right. It's Reggie."

She remembered. In the staircase, the alarms blaring all around them. No wonder she didn't remember. Olivia finally noticed where the girl was gazing and followed it upward. It was the stars.

"I've never seen them before," Reggie whispered.

"Never?"

Reggie shook her head.

"How did you manage to never see stars?"

Reggie pulled her gaze away from the window and tucked her legs up, hugging them. "The stars?" She hummed slightly to herself as if she'd never heard the word before. "I've spent most of my life, most of what I can remember anyway, in my cell. Before I arrived at Public One, I spent two years wandering the land on my own. There was too much debris and residue clouds in the air that the stars never came out."

Olivia looked up at the stars again. "How many years did you live there?"

"Fifteen."

Olivia's eyes slowly moved back. "You say ya don't 'member anythin' before that?"

"Nothing." Reggie shrugged her shoulders.

"Is that weird? Not knowin' about yer past?"

Reggie pursed her lips and made something like a frown. "Yes." She said it with such a lack of emotion, Olivia wondered if she really meant it. Olivia felt so much anxiety in talking to this person. She couldn't comprehend Reggie's situation. No memories of her past. No knowledge of what a real life was like.

"What are you thinking?" Reggie asked.

"What?" Olivia's pulse raced. "Oh, nothin'. I guess I was just imaginin' what'd be like to be without a family or memories."

"Don't," Reggie simply stated. "You don't want to." After a moment, she added, "Tell me about your family."

"Mine?" Olivia fidgeted with the collar of her dirty shirt. Reggie's eyes drilled into her. Not on purpose, but they were so filled with focus and attention that it was unsettling. " I have one sister, Sophia. She's engaged to Greyson, who's asleep over there." She pointed to the dark moss-green bag on the floor and snickered. "I don't know why they call it an engagement. They might as well jest say they're married. They jest keep hopin' we'll run into a minister."

"The one who's snoring?" Reggie asked with no sense of mocking.

Olivia smiled. "Yes. So I guess I could say he's my brother-in-law."

"And Nate? Is he your companion?"

The question knocked Olivia off guard again and she felt color come to her cheeks.

"No, no. Not—" she hesitated and looked at Nate, sleeping in the chair. His head hung low to his chest while his hands rested on the tops of his thighs. "Not really. It's complicated."

"What about a mother or father?"

"My father's name is Ben. He lives with our community. We're goin' back there tomorra', so you'll get to meet 'im. He's a wonderful man. A little soft, but I think that's why everyone trusts 'im. And my mother? My mother passed away fourteen years ago. I was twelve. There was a chemical raid on California where we were livin' and she didn't make it. I mean, I grew up in Alabama, but my father'd been transferred there a year before. We shouldn't 've been there. Soph, my sister, was there when it happened. It, uh . . . it left scars on her in more'n one way."

Reggie smiled as if everything she heard was the most wonderful news. Olivia felt even more uncomfortable.

"I'm so sorry. I shouldn't smile, I know. I'm really sorry about your mother. It must have been awful to lose her. How lucky you are to have your father and sister. I envy you."

Olivia had never thought of her family that way. Of course, she was always grateful they were still with her, but the loss of her mother was, at times, too much to handle. Now, her thoughts traveled back to Liam.

"I'm sorry if talking about death makes you think about Liam," Reggie whispered as if she knew exactly what was going through Olivia's head.

She looked back at Reggie, and frowned. "Can you read minds too?" Olivia asked.

"Oh, no. I've seen enough pain to know. I've felt it before. In my visions. I just saw it on your face. Did you love him?"

"Liam," Olivia whispered back. "He is . . . was . . . like a big brother. You know, the one who always pulls on yer hair," she smiled thinking about him, "and gives ya Wet Willies?"

Reggie replied with a dropping smile. "No, I don't. But that's all right."

"Sorry," Olivia responded.

"No, I like to hear about these things. I never got to experience them. A wet willy." She seemed to think hard on the words, looking confused. "You know, this may sound out of place, but today," Reggie smiled, "was the first time I've felt the sun on my skin for fifteen years. It was so amazing."

When Reggie broke out into a real smile, Olivia looked at her in wonder. The girl's entire face lit up. It was then that there was no possible way to deny that this girl probably felt emotions much deeper than most other people. If *anyone* was human, she was.

"Can I ask you a question?" Reggie spoke again.

Olivia nodded.

"Why did you come?"

"I thought ya saw the future."

"I do. Bits and pieces. I never really understand what's happening. I'm curious because no one has ever come to the city on their own. Everyone on the outside stays away. I know that because—" Her voice trailed off, hesitating to finish.

"Ya helped the Public seek out and find everyone they brought in," Olivia finished for her.

"Yes." Reggie nodded and looked down at the floor. Her face became hidden in shadow, covering up the emotion in her eyes. "So what made you come?"

Olivia startled at the change of topic, but decided to go with it. "The truth? You. You and another man's family. Someone had escaped the city and he came to find us."

"The man with black hair?"

"You know him?"

Reggie smirked, sharing a private joke with herself. Her cheek formed a deep dimple. "No, but I know *of* him. He came to you?"

"He told us he needed help evacuatin' 'is family from the city. He wanted to rescue 'em, and he also told us that The Public had a weapon. Isaac told us about you. Of course, I don't think he really believed you existed. You were jest the bait to get us to go with him. I don't think he even knew you were human." Olivia shook her head in wonder. "And then you jest came to us."

"He hates me." Reggie stated bluntly.

"Isaac?" Olivia shook her head.

The girl looked over and her eyes fell on Nate. "I worried about what would happen if I came with you. I don't want it to be like it was."

"Of course it won't be," Olivia leaned forward, feeling more and more protective of the woman. "I won't let it. And I don't think he hates you. He's jest looking fer someone to blame. He's been wantin' someone to blame fer a long time. Fer some reason, you seem to be the easiest target fer him. He'll get over it."

Reggie nodded and her eyes fell heavily before she quickly opened them again. The same weight of exhaustion was threatening to pull Olivia under too. She could feel the burn behind her own eyes, and her neck felt sore from holding her head up. The odor of fire and smoke, Liam, still clung to her clothes.

"Reggie?"

"Hmm?"

"I want you to know I trust you."

Reggie looked back at her with the wide gray eyes and a calm shock waved across her face. "Thank you." Reggie's mouth opened again, but nothing came out. She hesitated. "You're the first person I've really talked to in fifteen years. I like it."

"Fifteen years? How is that possible?"

Reggie gazed at her with an emotion Olivia couldn't quite explain. Pain? Acceptance? Recollection?

"When no one knows about you, it just is."

—REGGIE—

I know things will change eventually, I think to myself after Olivia goes back to her bed.

It doesn't mean I'm not terrified, though. I still feel that most of them blame me for what happened today. Especially Nate. He's been struggling to sleep. His head keeps moving, and I can see the muscles in his neck tightening to keep it in one place. I think he keeps waking up, but either he doesn't care enough to find a better spot, or he knows I'm awake and simply doesn't want to interact with me.

I push the thought out and look back out the window and up at the stars. My eyes are so heavy and I desperately want to sleep, but I've never seen them. The idea that there's countless objects like them in the universe leaves even my own intellect whirling. It's like nothing I've ever seen or thought about before. Twice, I've seen two streaks of light travel across the sky; comets burning through the atmosphere like stars are actually falling from the heavens. Reflections of the moon bounce off the windows and I can even see the craters and shadowed areas on its surface. Faintly, but they're there.

My eyes begin to drop again. "Reggie, you need to sleep," I whisper to myself. "They'll come back out tomorrow night."

There's a single blanket on the floor that had been tossed to me. I look at it, wanting it so bad. I make myself slink down off of the chair and unfold the blanket, letting it cover my body. I pull it up to my chin and curl up on the floor. It's not comfortable as my old mattress, which I never thought I'd miss, but I'm happier, and that's all I care about.

Feet pound on a dirt road. White boots of Public guards.

Traveling faster. Wind whipping at my hair. Engines growl. The pounding of my heart is louder than the wind blowing by my head.

The scream of a woman. A tear drops down a child's cold cheek.

Olivia runs down a road . . . no, it's not Olivia. She turns with fear on her face. The woman looks so much like her.

Greyson falls to his knees, dust rising in a puff. Doors slam shut and another scream echoes heavily in my ears. The sky is so clear.

A Public Transport lands in the middle of an empty town. There's a home with a blue door. I feel so much fear, so much panic. People slowly peak from behind doors. A blast of power-gun shots echo in my ears—the pictures warp.

My feet slowly walk down an empty road. Rocks jab the pads of my heels. Wind blows the curtains within a broken home window. "Reggie!" a voice screams.

"Reggie!"

I bolt up from the floor. My palms are sweaty and my heart races. A bead of sweat rolls down my forehead and into my eye, burning my sight. I quickly wipe it away with the heel of my hand and look at Olivia crouched down next to me. Her eyes are wide and there's something she's trying to communicate with her eyes—confusion, panic, and horror.

"Reggie. What's the matter?" she whispers. "I've never seen anyone. Never. I mean, was that a . . ." she's finding it impossible to come up with the right words to say.

"What happened?" My voice is harsh like I've been swallowing barbed hooks all night.

"I've never seen anythin' like that. Yer eyes were rolled back into yer head, but you was lyin' still like you were dead. My word, you were sweatin' so much. Did you see something in the future? Is that what that was?"

I wish I knew what to say to her. Something to explain what I'm feeling.

"I," my voice catches and I swallow. "Olivia, I think I saw your sister."

Olivia's mouth slowly parts and I notice a violent movement from Nate out of the corner of my eye—like he wanted to reach out and hit something, but he stopped himself. He's standing directly behind Olivia, and he sinks down into the chair behind her.

"What?" his voice is firm.

Olivia's head tilts and she narrows her eyes on me. Water springs to the corners of her eyes and the corners of her lips drop, her mouth cracking open. "W–what do you mean you saw my sister? What did you see? Are you sure it was her?"

The woman looks so much like her. A dropping tear down a cold child's cheek. Home. Blue door.

"There was a white home. Blue door. The paint was peeling. Does that sound familiar to you at all?"

Olivia's head jerks up and she looks at Nate. "Nate?" her voice cuts.

"Liv, that's where you guys are living." He turns and glares at me. "What did you *see*, Precog?"

A flash of irritation paints Olivia's eyes, but she looks back to me with the same question in her face. The pictures continue to flash in front of my eyes, and I see them over and over. I don't know where to start. "Your families are in danger. It's Public One. They're after me."

"What, what is it, Reggie?" Olivia's gaze freezes on me. The others in the party gather around and I hesitate to talk. If what I've seen is what I think it is, I fear that we may be too late at this point.

"I saw a transport landing in the center of a destroyed town. The home with the blue door. Every single person in the town was being gathered. Many of them were fighting back, but I saw your sister. Her features were so similar to yours, Olivia, that I . . . I almost thought she was you. I'm almost sure it must be your sister. She was running down the street, and I could *feel* how terrified she was. We have to leave." I finally look up. "We have to go. It might be too late already."

"How were they found?" London says quietly from behind Greyson. I'm the only one who hears him.

"No," Nate speaks up. "We won't be too late. You see the future, and this hasn't happened yet. I don't care what we have to leave behind. Everyone needs to be in the truck in two minutes. We're going to stop this from happening." He looks at the group, his eyes barely grazing over me, and then the tendons in his neck tighten.

"NOW!" he yells.

I kick myself off of the floor, others scramble to gather whatever they can into their arms. Their voices are frantic, yelling at each other. Through the mass of noise and movement, I pick up the bag next to me. I don't know who it belongs to, but I run out of the building following Greyson. My linen clothing is too thin to keep my body warm, and the fabric slips over my shoulder slightly, creating new goose bumps on my skin.

When Greyson climbs up into the truck, his longer curly hair falling into his eyes, I call his name and toss the bag up to him. He doesn't turn quite fast enough and the weight of the bag almost knocks him over.

Everything else happens in a blur—the packing, the clamoring into the truck. Then the truck lurches forward.

The wind rushes past my face, drying out my eyes and calling up salty tears to flow back into my hairline. My hair whips around like stinging barbs against my face. I can barely breathe with the force of air driving down into my lungs, so I duck my head, gripping tight to the rope lashed to the truck bed. The speed of the truck causes an invisible weight, constantly pushing on me.

"Olivia!" I shout.

Her arm is lashed to the truck like mine and she looks over at me. Tears fall down her face.

"We can stop it!" I reassure her, not believing my own words. I don't know if she can see it on my face, but she nods once and ducks her head down further.

I close my eyes and flashes of running feet, blasts of power-guns, and the screams of a woman being dragged into the Public Transporter continue to play in my mind. I can't stop my memory from bringing them back.

GREYSON

Greyson held to the image of his fiancée. If they didn't get to her—

No, he couldn't afford to think she'd be gone. She'd be there still. They'd get there on time. They had the precog and she saw the future, not the present. It was to their advantage. All of it.

His heart pounded, pounded, pounded.

After hours of being on the road, his arm was sore from the burns of the rope wrapped around it. His eyes closed again to keep the wind from drying them out.

He could see her. Just as it had been two years ago. Her sleeves were rolled up to her elbows, and dirt caked along her hands from working in the very small garden they'd managed to grow those months. He'd been dehydrated—sick, and struggling to see three feet in front himself. She was the one to bring him water.

The truck bumped and creaked, flying over a boulder jutting out of the ground underneath them. The truck crashed back to the ground. Greyson bit his tongue. He winced and looked up from his crouched position. The plains were so flat.

Why couldn't they see the town yet? Were they still hours away? Five minutes? Being away from Sophia was an eternity. Especially when he knew she could be hurt. Or . . . he didn't want to think about "or."

For so long he'd lived on his own. He had since his father passed away. It was ironic, his father—being a war veteran, outlasting the threat of The Public, and the only thing to catch up with him was the cancer. When Greyson found the community, they'd been living in the northern arm of Idaho. Ben Woodstock had immediately taken the then, twenty-one year-old Greyson under his arm. Sophia . . . that day . . . she'd come out of the back yard and the sun was radiating off of her raven hair. Glimmers of dark copper strands shimmered among the obsidian strands. He knew he'd felt something about her the moment she brushed his fingertips to hand him the water.

Sophia was like no other woman he'd ever met. Her disposition was tender, so caring, that many times he forgot that life sucked. He wanted to spend every moment he could with her. She reminded him of everything good. A reminder of why he wanted to still be alive. He made excuses to help in the Woodstock's home. Even if it was staying behind when the other men went hunting, knowing full well that Sophia could see his ruse because she'd always smile underneath the cover of her hair. After a few weeks, he suggested he move in with them. But Sophia, she wanted to do everything the right way. Engagement and all, with a real minister. Still, almost two years later, they hadn't found a single clergyman.

Greyson ducked his head again. How long was it now? Twenty minutes? Five hours? Should they be there soon? All he needed was to hold her. To tell her that everything was all right.

The truck bounced twice, running over the edges of a ditch and started to slow down. Greyson opened his eyes up and looked around him. The familiar "Welcome to" words on the city sign glinted in the sun. The streets of the town were deadly silent. There was no movement except for the tall grass alongside the road that wafted in the wind. No one walked the streets. Perhaps they were all indoors eating or staying together.

It was only when he noticed the blasted-out windows that he felt a hook lug on his stomach, pinching and twisting toward his spine. The muscles in his arms shook and he couldn't take his eyes away. Doors on homes were splayed wide open, and curtains blew back and forth hauntingly in the windows. The truck's motor purred and it jerked when Nate hit the brakes.

Greyson unlashed his arm in a fury and jumped off the back of the truck. His legs burned while he ran. Sweat trickled into his eyes, rocks grinding under his feet as he tore for the home Sophia shared with Olivia and Ben. The sidewalk in front of the white house was showered with power-gun blast burns. The door swung lightly from a gust of wind pushing it back. The hollow thud of his boots clamoring up the stairs resonated in his ears before he burst into the house.

"Soph? Sophie?!" His own voice sounded empty.

The home was silent. Every item was where it should be. Frantically, he moved into the kitchen where a cooler of meat from Nate's kill was sitting open, and flies and maggots were already at home. The back of Greyson's hand came up to his nose and it crinkled.

"Sophie?!" he called again.

He left the kitchen and moved down the hall and up the stairs to where the bedrooms were. Ben's room was empty, the covers of the wool blankets piled on one side of the bed, unmade. Ben always made his bed and never left anything out of place.

"Sophie! *Sophie!*" Greyson continued to yell through the house. He went from room to room, leaning in each door way. It was getting harder to breathe, but he knew that she had to be here. She still had to be here.

He ran back down the stairs and bolted out the door. "SOPHIE!" he screamed, his voice cutting and choking him.

"They're not here, Greyson." Hugh ran up the street toward him, panting. "No one is. We're too late."

"No, we're not." Greyson growled. "She's here, I know she is. I'm gonna find her!" He bowled into Hugh, but Hugh held him back, trying to get Greyson to look at him.

"No!" Hugh shouted back. "No," his voice dropped back to a whisper, "she's not."

Greyson shoved Hugh away from him and ran to the clinic. If she was injured, that's where she'd be. Ben would be there taking care of her. Or maybe she was taking care of him. Surely Soph would be smart enough to move anyone to a secure place where they couldn't be found. They had to be there. They had to because if they weren't . . . that would mean she was either captured by The Public, back in that city, or dead.

When he opened up the door to the clinic, he ran into Nate who was standing still in the center of the office. Aside from the heavy breathing making his chest expand and contract, he wasn't moving. Nate's fist clung to a handgun. Greyson watched Nate eject the magazine. It was empty. He half-expected Nate to chuck the gun against the wall, but all he did was set the gun back on the counter and turn around.

"They're not here, Greyson. We're too late. We had most of the supplies with us. They just didn't have much."

Greyson couldn't speak. His jaw was so tight, his teeth could break. She was gone. Sophia was gone.

"No," was all he could say in response.

He couldn't take it anymore. In that instant, his arms shot out and grabbed a plastic chair and he shot-put it out the window, the only one not broken in the building. The chair skidded across the sidewalk and into the street. Glass rained down and tinkled on the concrete. Greyson shuddered and he stalked out of the clinic, headed for the truck. It was only then that he noticed two bodies behind a fence. Two children, left behind. The Pennant's kids. London kneeled down next to them and placed two fingers on their necks. He shook his head and glanced up at Greyson. His fingers gently closed the small eyes and stood up.

Behind Greyson, the pounding of Nate's feet followed without a word or comment.

The truck was shut off, but heat still rose from the engine. Standing next to the truck was the precog, her arms wrapped around her body. She had her face angled toward the sky, her eyes closed. Greyson reached into the back of the truck and pulled a long rifle out. He checked for ammunition and when he knew it was loaded he cocked the gun and immediately held it to the girl's chest. The moment the gun cocked, the girl's eyes flared open and she backed up, almost tripping.

"Greyson!? What are you doing?" Liv ran from the doorway of her home, streaks of tears traveling down her cheeks. "Stop it!"

"It's her! It's all her fault. If we hadn't gone to the city and taken her, they *wouldn't have come for them!* They'd still be *here.* We *never* would have left, and Liam would still be alive!" he screamed. "If we get rid of her, then they have no reason to hold them!"

Nate, without moving, spoke up. "Greyson, you kill her and *we* won't have anything to bargain with. You'll destroy any chance you ever had of getting Sophia back."

"*How do I know she's not already dead!?*" Against the throbbing burn of hate filling his body, Greyson finally let a tear fall from his eye.

"Do you want to believe that she is?" Nate asked.

Greyson's jaw continued to clench tight. The muscles in his body shook uncontrollably. He knew he needed to drop the gun, for Sophie, but he couldn't make himself do it. If it wasn't for this monster, nothing would have changed. Her eyes were hollow, Nate was right. There was no feeling, no warmth. If it weren't for her, for Isaac, it would all still be the same, and they'd be safe.

"Greyson." Nate reached out and grabbed the barrel of the rifle.

Greyson jerked it, trying to keep it aimed while Nate kept pulling. He let it fall, and Nate took it from him, set the safety, and tossed it back in the truck. Greyson was frozen to the spot. His feet wouldn't move. The only thing that brought him around was the pull of Olivia's fingers on his arm. He finally looked at her large eyes and his whole soul fall apart. Their arms wrapped around each other, the only two members of their family. They consoled one another in the passing time, and he barely registered the whispering conversations of the others around him. Until he finally heard, "You're going to take me back."

Greyson lifted his head and pulled away from his future sister-in-law. "What?"

"You're going to take me back." It was spoken by the precog. Her tone was resigned, attempting to hide what sounded like terror. Her face dry, but her eyebrows dropped in concern, aching.

"We don't have enough gas to get back," Nate's voice was firm.

"They want me, Nate. They want me back and they knew if they did this, you'd take me back."

"Don't you dare call me by name. You don't even know me."

Olivia's hand dropped from Greyson's arm, and he rounded on Nate. "If you're not going to return her, I will. Even if I have to walk through a power-gun firing range, I'm going back. I'm getting Sophia back. I'm taking *that*," he pointed to the precog, "and trading it back for Soph. I want your help Nate, but if you don't come, I'll go by myself."

Nate shook his head. "They won't let you leave."

"Then I'll *stay there!*" Greyson bellowed. His eyes burned in their sockets. His throat cut with the gust of his scream.

"He knew," the precog spoke. Her eyes were dropped to the ground. "He knew they'd take you back. He was right."

"What are you mumbling about?" Nate's head shook.

"Dryer told you no one would care about you. No one but him. He's trying to pull you back in, like he always has." She turned half-way, her eyes flitting back and forth across the ground. What she said next was barely whispered. "He told you that you only belonged there. You'd never be free—he knew that, and he told you. No one wants you. That's what he said."

Nate cursed, running his hand through his oily hair. "Great, she talks to herself."

"Maybe she's broken," London assumed innocently, quickly turning his head to Olivia. His eyebrow tilted in worry. "Do . . . do we need to push a button?"

Olivia sighed in disgust. Her head shook and she looked at each man. "Are you guys raggin' me? Would you stop referrin' to her as a machine? You've got London believing it now! I'm not gonna put up with this anymore! Dad would be disgusted with you, Nate. *And* Greyson! This is *not* her fault."

"Then why couldn't she tell us further ahead? We could have gotten here sooner!" Greyson shouted.

Olivia's mouth opened and closed. Greyson could tell that the impact of losing her sister and father was just as hard, if not harder, on her than it was for anyone else there. Olivia turned to look at the precog, trying to find an answer to his question. He knew that there was only one. London was right, the girl was broken.

"Reggie?" Olivia's voice quivered, despite her attempts at keeping herself together.

The precog's lips parted and she breathed out slowly before saying, "I can only see future events as present decisions are made."

"What does that mean?" Greyson tilted his head.

"A few days ago, I saw your community. They knew where it was because I showed them. At that time, you must have decided to go to The Public. Weeks before that I saw you coming because Isaac escaped. Each action sets off a round of other actions. I can't see that you're going to kick a rock, until you consciously notice that the rock is there. Just like I didn't see the raid on this community until The Public decided to take action. They *knew* that. They know me, and they knew where you were. They've studied me, my visions, for fifteen years. The moment they knew what they would do, they moved on it. Their transporters move faster and quieter than our truck could make the distance. They beat us here. Only by hours maybe, but they did." Her eyes narrowed on him and she pointed violently at the ground. "I *can't* go back there. I can't! I can't prove him right. I'll tell you what you need to know, but I can't go back to that."

"You won't," Olivia interjected, scowling at Greyson.

He stepped back, his nostrils flaring. His one chance of getting his fiancée back, and Sophia's own sister was guarding this woman with her life. There was an iron-willed sincerity to Olivia's statement and he knew that she would do whatever possible to protect this girl—human or not.

NATE

The tattered gray rag sopped up the grime and dirt on Nate's hands before he dabbed them into the stream again. He and Olivia had left the group behind to hike the few miles up the mountain to the source of fresh water he'd found days ago. With a dozen five-gallon containers filled, they were almost ready to head back. This was the first time in weeks he'd actually washed his hands. It wasn't with soap, but it was better than the back of his pants.

While Olivia was up higher, taking a break for herself, he took out a small cup, dipped it in the stream and poured it over his head. The water trickled in a flat run-off down the back of his head and soaked his shirt. He shook his head and then ran his fingers through his hair, slicking it back with the moisture.

"We're lucky you found this place, Nate," Olivia said when she returned. "With only one container of water left, I was gettin' worried."

"Yep," he grunted and put the tin cup back into his pack. "Hopefully we can make this last longer since we won't have Isaac sucking our reserves in order to bathe."

She looked at him with frustration, her eyelids half-closed. "I still say we're lucky." Nate shifted the last of the containers on the back of the ATV and used some bungee cords to tie them all down.

"Nate? I think we need to talk about what happened back there."

"With Greyson?" he lifted an eyebrow. "He only pulled that gun because he was angry. I don't think we need to worry."

"I'm not talkin' 'bout Greyson. I'm talkin' 'bout us. In the cell back in The Public."

The corners of Nate's lips involuntarily jumped up and then fell back down again. He felt his left eyebrow rise up. He hadn't thought about that since it happened. Honestly, he didn't want to talk about it, either.

"Oh yeah. That."

"What's goin' on? I kinda need to know if that was all jest because of the moment . . . the possibility of . . . you know, the *end*. Or whether you really meant it. 'Cause I need you to know that *I* meant it. I've thought 'bout it fer years. I jest can't ferget about what happened. I don't want to. Because, what you did really means somethin' to me." Olivia was now standing at his side, her hand on her waist.

Nate was pissed at himself. In truth, part of his actions that night were because he really thought they might not have lived, even if he couldn't admit it to her. Losing his best friend, his brother, was hard enough. He didn't want to re-hash this again right now.

Dammit.

"Sure, I meant it," he nodded and then immediately shook his head, "but that doesn't change how stupid I think it was."

"You think that kissin' me that night was stupid? That telling me you cared was stupid?"

"No! Liv, why do you always twist my words around?" His fingers ran through his hair again, and then down across his stubble.

"I'm not twistin' anything. What yer sayin' jest don't make sense."

"I know," he groaned. "It doesn't make sense to me either."

Olivia folded her arms. "Do ya still mean what ya said?"

All he could do was shake his head. Why? He didn't know.

"Nate," Olivia whispered, slipping her arms around his neck. He flinched at her touch. She softly kissed his cheek, traveling her own fingers through the knots in his damp hair. He closed his eyes trying to keep his own feelings in check. He loved her. Maybe not how she wanted, but he did. He loved her spirit, and her determination.

"Nate, please talk to me," she whispered again in his ear. "We can make this work," she pulled back and looked him in the eye. "If this is what you want. I know it's what I want. Nate, yer my best friend and I trust you with my life."

Nate nodded and closed his eyes. "I know."

"I know you love me. Even if you can't say it. Believe me, I'm afraid too. But I'm not goin' to let that get in the way. Please, don't let your fear of whatever it is take over whatever you have left."

Whatever he had left. At times he felt like there was nothing left. Nothing at all. London, who felt so much like his son, was the only thing that had started to close off that hole. With him, Nate was able to control something. With Olivia, he knew he'd have no control. She had her own mind, and the chances of her being taken into The Public again were heightened.

"Yer still fightin' me. I can feel it. Nate, you have to let me in."

"I can't."

"Can't?" Her hands brushed his arms. "Or won't?"

"Maybe both. I don't know."

Olivia's eyes were full of clouds. Even in their dark brown depths, there was so much confusion when she looked at him. He couldn't blame her. Nothing he said or did made much sense anymore. How could she understand?

Without a word she leaned in and pulled Nate close. Just held onto him. It was comforting for him. If things could stay like this, he thought to himself, then he'd never let her go. He took a deep breath and pulled his hands further up her back and cradled her head against his own chest. He felt protective of her, even though she was strong enough on her own.

"You don't have to carry everythin' on your own. You know that, right?"

Shit, he was just tired. Tired of facing this same question over and over. He just hoped she knew what she was getting into. Olivia pulled away, waiting for him to respond. In the silence, the babbling water in the stream sounded more like crashing rapids. He just couldn't come up with a response. Finally, he knew what he need to say, what he'd wanted to say all along. He softly kissed her.

"Are you sure you can put up with me?"

Olivia smiled teasingly. "If I couldn't put up with you, I would of beat the crap out of you by now. Heaven knows everyone else has wanted to."

Nate closed his eyes and let out a deep breath. He pulled her close again and kissed her forehead tenderly. The salty perspiration of her skin lingered on his lips. "I can deal with that." He wondered how much he meant it.

—LONDON—

Breezes continued to run across London's face, wisping his shaggy hair across his eyes. These were the last remnants of his life over the past six months, and here he was, packing them all up again. A collection of face cards, a copy of an old 1999 encyclopedia—F, and even the same shirt he'd been wearing the day Nate found him. It was his life— get settled in one abandoned town only to relocate a few months later.

Even though he was supposed to keep packing their remaining belongings he couldn't help being distracted. The woman they'd brought from The Public, her clear eyes continued to dart from object to object around the old town. It was like she'd never seen much of anything. Nate had told him to stay away from her. Since she was a weapon belonging to The Public, she couldn't be trusted. But London hadn't seen any reason not to trust her. Nate couldn't tell him how to make every decision.

She seemed just as normal or trustworthy as anyone else. Not to mention, she was also the most beautiful woman he'd ever seen before. It wasn't often that he ran into many other girls—whether they were near his age or not. He'd never had the chance to be attracted to a girl, or a woman. Olivia and Sophia were pretty, he guessed. Not necessarily his type. With the sun going down behind the mountains, he loved the way that the sunset bounced off her light brown hair, creating silvery tones that glimmered whenever her head turned. Even though she was obviously much older than he was, what would the harm be in getting to know her?

London set the only other pair of pants he owned into the bag and quickly ran his hands through his hair, slicking it back. When it wouldn't stay, he tried tucking it behind his ears. That would have to work. He glanced into the side view mirror of the truck where she sat and rubbed a smudge of dirt off his cheek.

It was stupid, but London cleared his throat and did his best to pretend he was looking for something in the back of the truck. He shifted his eyes to the right, not wanting her to think he was looking at her. The strain created a sharp ache, and his eyes struggled to focus. She glanced over at London. Nerves burned heat in his cheeks, and London quickly focused back on the bag he was rummaging through.

"You're London, right?"

"Y-yeah," he stammered, shooting to attention. His struggled to get a hold of his anxiety. "Yeah. I'm London."

"I'm Reggie."

London tried to come up with something to say. Even "It's good to meet you" would be a good alternative to absolute silence, but nothing came out. Reggie tilted her head and she smiled weakly at him.

"Of course, you already know that." She took a deep breath. "I know none of you trust me, and I understand that."

"N-no. No. I think they trust you. You look really trustworthy."

Reggie smiled for real this time, and London smiled back even though he really tried not to. "I guess it would be nice to imagine that was true." She looked back up at the sun setting over the mountains and sighed. The colors were almost neon in the sky. Pink, orange, and a deep dark purple.

London ran his hand down the side of the truck and walked closer to her. "Can I sit by you?"

"Please. I just don't remember the last time I saw a sunset like that."

"Oh yeah," London's voice squeaked and he rolled his eyes. His face flushed again and he tried to hide it. "Um, the pollution and chemicals in the air intensify the colors. Ben told me once that sunsets were never that bright before. So I guess you sacrifice air quality for a pretty sky, right?"

"I just hope this isn't the last one I ever see," she whispered.

London gripped the edge of the truck, feeling his knuckles turning white from the tense pressure. "So, what's it really, you know, like?"

"What's what like?" she asked, still looking out at the horizon.

"Seeing. Well, seeing the future?"

Reggie squinted at him when she turned. "It's different than seeing with your eyes. It depends. When I'm asleep at night and I have visions, it feels like I'm dreaming, but I can feel *everything*. The pain, the weather. Everything is chopped and short. Nothing happens in order." She paused and looked down at the ground. "Lately I've had some other types of visions."

"Like what?"

"It's odd. I started having visions while I'm awake. I don't know what triggers them. I think it started when I got hit in the head. Maybe my chip—" her voice trailed off and her hands flew to the back of her neck, feeling the skin. "Oh no, no, no. I have to get it out, I have to get it out!" Her fingers were starting to dig into the skin at the top of her neck.

London jumped off the truck. "What? Get what out? I don't know what you're talking about." He anxiously looked around, trying to find someone to help.

"The chip! I have to get it out. Or they'll find me. They'll find us!"

"What chip?" he was almost yelling back at her.

"London, I need you to go get Hugh. Run!"

His feet hit the ground flying. She had a chip in her? Was Nate right? Was she not a real person? Not that it mattered, but he'd never seen a machine so lifelike. Would Hugh have to cut into her? All the gears showing? His feet skidded on the broken concrete sidewalk in front of Hugh's home and he bolted through the door.

"Hugh!?"

"What?" Hugh's voice panicked in the back room and he came around the corner. "What is it, kid?"

"It's Reggie. The precog." He took a deep gulp of air.

"Is she gone? Is something wrong with her?"

"I don't know! She just said something about a chip and she's clawing at her neck."

A flinch ticked at the corner of Hugh's eye before he grabbed the cigarette lighter on his counter. "Where is she?"

The flame from the lighter ran back and forth across the sharpened pocketknife Hugh held in his hand. A bright orange glow radiated from the Damascus steel and he flicked the lighter off, allowing the knife to cool. "I'm sorry we don't have any pain killers to give you. We're not as equipped as The Public."

"Believe me, I almost prefer it that way," she mumbled.

London frowned at her, not understanding what she meant.

"Tell me again why you have this chip in your skull?" Hugh asked.

London looked over at Reggie. She lifted her long hair up into an old rubber-band and into a tied-up mess on top of her head. Reggie moved to lay face down over the edge of London's mattress. "It was surgically placed in me when I first entered the city. They didn't tell me about it at the time. It's designed," she went quiet, almost as if talking about it hurt worse than the incision that Hugh was now making. She hissed, flinched, and went quiet, her mouth buried in the bed. ". . . designed to trigger the pain center in my mind. If I didn't do what they wanted, they activated it."

London watched a deep red stream of blood run down the base of her neck and he quickly reached forward with the clean cloth Hugh had handed him, soaking up the liquid. The cut was approximately one inch long at the top of her neck. London felt his stomach lurch, but at the same time was relieved to see what he thought was the white base of a normal human skull when Hugh pulled the skin and muscle apart a few centimeters. Well, he thought, it could also be tendons. Either way, it was physical proof that she was just like them.

Sitting like a little parasite, warm in a human home, was a round black chip, smaller than the head of a thumb tack just at the top of her spine. Blood continued to drown it.

Hugh looked at it from all the angles he could, and wiped his forehead with the back of his wrist. "Well, Reggie, we have a problem."

She mumbled into the blanket—more like a moan. It was then that London realized she was biting into the blanket.

"Believe it or not, I've seen this before. We used to use similar models, more primitive than this one, on psychiatric patients. This chip is deeply imbedded in the spinal cord. In fact, it's laced deep enough that if I try to remove it, there's a fifty-fifty chance I could damage your spine. I'm not a medical doctor, and even with the right equipment, I know very little about surgery. I don't trust myself to do that to you."

Reggie's neck flinched and she moaned again. When she spoke, London barely made out what she said.

"If we don't remove it," she quaked, "they'll find us. They'll find us before we even have a chance to get back."

Hugh turned to look at London and pursed his lips. "I doubt that. If it were possible, they'd have come for you, and not the community."

"Unless they don't want her," London added.

"Maybe," she groaned, "Dryer's trying to prove to me what he said. Wanting me to come back by myself. It doesn't matter. They still could find me," she whispered. "I'm just scared."

"Wait." Hugh peered closer at her neck, "What is this?" He leaned forward, shifting his head. It was like he didn't even hear her.

London peered over Reggie, still holding the rag to her neck. "What?" he glanced at Hugh.

"I think I've found the transmitter. It's extremely small, but it's connected to the chip, here." He pointed to what looked like a small black hair extending from the side of the chip and laying flat against something. Bone? It looked just like a tentacle.

"If," Hugh reached over for a pair of tweezers, continuing to hold the skin and muscle tissue back, "I can disconnect the transmitter from the chip, they shouldn't be able to receive or send signals. Which, theoretically means they shouldn't be able to track the chip either."

Hugh poked the tweezers around the transmitter. It moved slightly back and forth each time Hugh bumped it with the sharp tweezers.

Dozens of tear drops fell to the floor, audibly hitting the short dirty carpet below her. Reggie's fingers, wrapped around the edge of the mattress, were white. Hesitantly, London reached out and set his hand over hers. Her hand gripped his even tighter.

"Sorry, Reggie. Is it triggering?" Hugh's eyes briefly darted to her.

"No. Believe me; you'd know if it was triggered." She blew out a shaking breath.

London looked back at what Hugh was doing. The transmitter was now pulled up. Hugh applied slight pressure to the chip, keeping it from shifting out of place. With the tweezers, he grabbed at the transmitter and gently, ever so gently, pulled it up. The hairline antennae slid up, covered in dark red liquid. After two inches it finally came to a stop and wouldn't come out any further. Hugh set the tweezers down and wiped at his forehead again with his wrist. Beaded drops of perspiration were threatening to run into his eyes.

Hugh swore under his breath.

"What?"

"I . . . Reggie, removing this may trigger the chip. What I'm going to have to do is snap it off. If I cut it, it'll still leave the possibility that it would be reached. Snapping it will bring the entire transmitter off, but it may cause a programmed reaction. It may activate the chip."

Reggie's fingertips dug deep into London's hand. A slicing burn spread down his fingers and then stinging followed. Her nails had dug through his skin, and the salty oils of her hands were getting into the cuts. London had to grip his knee, hiding his own discomfort away.

"Go ahead," she whispered.

Hugh picked up the tweezers and grabbed at the base of the transmitting wire. With one swift move, the wire came completely out. London felt her body stiffen. Even the grinding of her teeth could be heard underneath her muffled scream. He'd never seen anyone scream with a locked jaw. It was a sound he never wanted to hear again. Like a tortured dog being smothered.

Reggie's body seized and blood ran profusely out of the wound. Then, just as quick as the reaction had come, it ended. Reggie's grip loosened and fell dead in his hand. She'd passed out.

Hugh took advantage of the opportunity and pulled out medical thread and a needle. The blood was now completely soaking the rag that he held around her neck and London's fingertips. Hugh finished the stitches quickly and then spread a layer of antibiotic over them before he placed a large gauze bandage and taped it down.

"London, run downstairs and fill up a large canteen of water. She's going to need to drink it when she wakes up." Hugh wiped his hands on his pants. Bloody finger streaks like war paint remained.

London carefully placed the bloody rag next to her neck on the bed where it would be able to soak up the trickling blood, and ran down the stairs and into the kitchen. His own canteen was on the counter. It clinked on the edge of the sink when he picked it up. From the large water container on the island, he filled it with the last of their water ration and dashed back up the stairs. Hugh was quietly speaking to Reggie, her eyes still closed. His hand ran over her back, and there was a white bandage taped to where the cut had been.

"Reggie? Reggie, wake up." Hugh turned around when London stepped in and he stood up. "That trigger from the chip must have been too much for her to handle. It may take a while for her to wake up. Keep an eye on her 'til she wakes up. I'm going to run the rest of this back down to the truck. I'm not packed yet, but I have to finish before we take off." He looked back at her limp body. "If she wakes up and there are issues, let me know. I left two Oxycodones there on the nightstand for her. It won't kill the pain, but it will make it tolerable."

"All right." London set the canteen next to the pills. Hugh left the room and London heard the thunder of his feet down the stairs before they went out the door. Then it was silent.

London walked over to Reggie's limp body and tenderly pulled it further back onto the bed. When her head was no longer dangling over the edge, he carefully rolled her over to keep her airway open and her neck from being strained, slipping a pillow under her neck. A small red drip ran down her lip. She must have bit a part of her mouth.

When she looked more comfortable, he sat down on the floor opposite the bed and leaned against the wall. From the sheath on his belt, he pulled the hunting knife he kept. To pass the time, he started picking at the cuticles around his fingernails with the tip of the knife. Flakes of skin drifted to the floor. He looked back up at Reggie. Her chest was still rising and falling. The glow from the lantern next to the bed was now the only light in the house. The sun was gone.

Nate still wasn't back yet. Which, considering the fact that Reggie was there, was probably a good thing.

London couldn't help but notice how much Reggie looked like a fairytale character. At least, like he imagined one would look. He hadn't seen a children's book since he was little. He knew his parents used to read to him, even if he couldn't remember much of his life before they died. He couldn't remember if he had brothers or sisters. Hugh had told him once it was similar to a fugue state. He only remembered the word fugue because it sounded like "puke." London shook his head, trying to clear his mind. He didn't want to think about that. Just look at her. If only he were a little older, if his voice weren't cracking anymore, or better looking like Nate, he might have a shot.

Reggie groaned from the bed and London shot to his feet. He lunged for the canteen and pills, holding them in his hands. Reggie's eyes fluttered open and then shut again. Her hand rose to her neck and she grimaced.

"Here, Reggie. I have some aspirin for you. It's not anything really strong, but I know Ben used to take it a lot for his tooth aches. It'll help with the pain." His hand reached out with the pills and she slowly took them.

"Help me up," she whispered.

London reached forward with his free hand and supported her back. She pressed her way to a sitting position, her back against the wall. He then handed her the canteen. "Drink the full bottle."

"Do I," she scowled again, "chew them?"

"No, swallow them whole with the water."

Reggie took the pills and deeply drank the canteen of water. London pretended not to notice that a few tears fell down her face as she leaned her head back to drink. Though, she didn't really tilt her head back so much as she just tried to tip the water bottle at a higher angle. This caused water to slosh over her lips and down her chin. She coughed and let out a small cry. When Reggie handed the bottle back to London, her hand shook.

"What happened?"

"Do you remember when Hugh told you the chip would activate when he removed that transmit thing? Well, when he did, you seized up really bad and passed out. Scared the shit out of me. I don't think I've ever seen anyone look like that. I guess it would be stupid to ask if it hurt."

Reggie scoffed painfully, and held out her hand for another drink from the canteen. "Yeah. It hurt." She closed her eyes and drank. The canteen kept clattering against her teeth the more she trembled. When she finished, she leaned against the chipped sheet rock wall.

"Thank you," she finally whispered. "I'll have to find Hugh and thank him. I know this wasn't what you wanted to deal with tonight, but I figured we should probably be safe rather than wondering when they'll track me down." She heaved a sigh and opened up her eyes again. "You guys risked a lot for me. For a person you've never met before. I hope you know how appreciative I am."

London felt burning in his cheeks and along his neck. "Well, it was really Nate's decision."

"No, I meant all of you," Reggie corrected. "Not just you, and not just Nate," she spoke the name with a hint of bitterness and winced, reaching up to gently finger the stitches, "but everyone. I'm just grateful."

The banging of the front door downstairs perked both of them up. London held his breath. He tried to brace himself for how Nate would react to having Reggie in the house. With the way Nate had been lately, it wouldn't be surprising to hear him walk in yelling.

London loved Nate. He was the only one who had really cared what happened to London. He was an older brother, a father almost, but with that responsibility came a lot of weight, and London was definitely aware of it. The responsibility of it oftentimes made London feel he was a burden, even though he knew on some level it wasn't true. Nate sometimes just couldn't handle it all. London braced himself.

The footsteps came directly up the hallway, possibly following the faint glow of the lantern. When Nate stepped around the corner and looked in, his face fell from the frown it was already holding. "What's going on? London?"

"We, uh. We had some issues that needed to be handled."

"There's blood on the bed."

London looked to where Reggie had been lying during the surgery and sure enough a large spot of blood had pooled and soaked into the blanket. "Yeah, it's Reggie's. Don't worry, the rest of us are fine."

Nate seemed to be doing all that he could to avoid looking at Reggie. His eyes flickered to her briefly before looking back at London. "What did she do?" It was just like Nate to blame someone else, rather than London. Not that it was anyone's fault. Now he had a target he could pin everything on. Reggie.

"She didn't *do* anything, Nate. Hugh had to remove something from her spine. Something that The Public planted. She's fine."

I don't care about her, London could hear Nate thinking. But what came out was, "Whatever. She has to go back out to the truck. You too. We need to go."

"What? Can't we get some sleep? Reggie's in a lot of pain. We can't just throw her in the truck and take off."

Nate stood in the doorway. There was an absence of facial expression, and he held the doorknob with a flaccid grip. It was an emotion mixed with superiority and exhaustion. "Come on, London." Nate walked back down the stairs and rummaging could be heard in the quiet house before the door opened and shut once more.

"I'm sorry," London started. Reggie immediately cut him off.

"No. He's right. We can't stay in one spot. We need to go." Reggie pushed forward on the mattress and dangled her legs off the side. Her bare feet were black and brown with dirt, and a large cut dipped from the top of her foot down in between her large and second toe.

"You need shoes." London ran down the stairs, ignoring the, "I'm fine," that drifted after him.

The truck was parked just outside and everyone had started putting their things in. Two ATVs were now alongside the truck where equipment had been secured. As he approached, Olivia was leaning into the cab of the truck and he skipped a few steps to get to her.

"Liv," he called.

Olivia straightened and turned around. "Yeah?"

"Do you have a pair of Sophia's shoes?"

Her eyebrows took a dive. "What? Why?"

"Reggie." He shrugged.

A light of realization went on in her eyes and she nodded. "Of course. I think she had a pair of strapped sandals. Let me run back and check. If I find 'em I'll bring 'em in."

"Thanks."

London went back inside and up to Reggie. She was already trying to walk down the stairs. The moment she took the first step, she grabbed for her neck and her ankle slipped from beneath her. In a few bounds, London was at her side. She tried to hold in a scream by clenching her jaw. Just because she wasn't a member of the community, didn't give Nate the right to turn his back on her. London had always dealt with Nate's mood issues because he wasn't hurting anyone except himself, but this was ridiculous.

For the first time in his life, he was disappointed and furious with his guardian. He'd never felt that way before. Nate had always been the one who had the answers, the one who took control. Now he was just the one who slinked away. Liam—London swallowed and frowned at the thought of him—Liam never would have acted like this.

"Thanks, London," Reggie whispered. "I'm fine."

"Keep telling yourself that." He smiled. "Come on, Gimp."

Reggie managed something like a laugh and walked down the stairs with London's skinny arm around her equally skinny waist. He could feel his own bones sliding around on her rib cage. She may have grown up in the city, but she surely hadn't been treated like the others. That alone was proof enough she could be trusted. At least for him.

—REGGIE—

I tuck further beneath the blankets Nate tossed to me before we left. With London and Olivia in the front, and Hugh and Greyson following behind, I'm alone in the back of the pickup. Wind whips at my face. My hair stings my cheek. My eyes are dried out so I close them, leaning my head against a pack near me. The sliding window to the cab opens and I hear London's voice call to me.

"Are you all right?"

I smile. He's so sweet. "I'm fine."

London swears, the words getting caught in the wind. "Nate, her lips are blue." His voice is soft compared to the wind roaring loud around me.

"Tell her to cover up more," is the response.

"Are you raggin' me, Nate?" Olivia's voice chimes in. "Stop the truck."

The wheels start to slow and the wind subsides. Now all that remains is a bitter-still night. Doors open and shut. I see the lights from Greyson and Hugh's four-wheel vehicles stop directly behind and Greyson calls out, "What's going on?"

Nate climbs up into the truck bed and pushes things aside. "The precog is getting cold. Olivia's going to switch with her. We're only an hour away, but whatever." He grumbles. "Come on."

He reaches out to me and I pull the blankets closer to me with one hand while slapping his away. "Don't help me," I whisper. My legs are so weak still from the exhaustion and the cold of the air that I barely keep from losing my balance. Using the edge of the truck, I pull myself up.

"Fine," he whispers and turns to jump out of the bed. London holds a hand out to my waist and I lean into him to get me down to the ground. When I make it into the truck, London pushes me to the center.

"No, I should sit on the end. I don't need to be in the center."

"Your lips and skin are blue." London holds his hand up and gets in. "You're sitting in the middle."

I turn my head around and watch Olivia climb in the back and give me a smile with a confident raised thumb. I think London overestimates Nate's ability to deal with me sitting next to him, but I do so without a word. I'm just grateful to be in the cab. It's already been seven hours since we left, and seven hours in the cold can numb even someone with fat on their body.

The truck starts up again and the wheels spin out. I pull the thick wool blanket closer around me. It smells of gasoline, mud, and grass in here. Mostly of gasoline. The window behind me is still open and I feel a chill slither down the back of my head and my bandaged neck. I must have shivered because London quickly leans behind.

"Sorry, Liv. Gonna close this."

The window closes and out of the corner of my eye I see London's elbow hesitate. He seems to not know whether to take his arm back or put it somewhere else.

London's arm finally makes a decision and he puts it around my shoulders, careful to stay away from the stitches on my neck. I hear Nate make a noise next to me and I can't help but roll my eyes tiredly. Apparently he's noticed London's action and has decided to gently mock him. I think maybe the coldness from Nate may actually overtake the bitterness of the weather.

I close my eyes and try to recall my last vision of him—the kinder eyes, filled with trust and acceptance. I hear Nate chuckle again and the images go away. London doesn't seem to pay attention. They're very different from each other. At least from what I can see. Sometimes I feel like I see too much. I keep forcing myself to remember Nate's face over and over. The way he looked at me in my past vision. How will things change? When will he change?

I feel London's arm tighten around me, and I'm so cold that I allow myself to be pulled in. The bumps and creaking of the truck rock me to sleep and while I fall asleep, my mind races with images.

The truck comes to a stop and my body is pushed forward by the slight jerk of the dying momentum. London shakes my arm and I push myself up from his shoulder.

"Think this place will work, Nate?"

"It'll have to. I can't keep my eyes open anymore and I saw Greyson flagging me down. So, welcome to Scott City, Kansas." Nate gets out. The door creaks and smashes shut.

London leaves the cab without a word and holds the door open for me. I drag my body out and manage to press a smile, my emotions distant. I'm not fully awake yet, but at least I've warmed up. Olivia jumps down out of the back, rubbing her hands together and blowing on them.

"I don't know how you lasted that long back there, Reg. I feel like my fingers are gonna fall off."

"I'm sorry you had to get back there. I really would have been fine," I lie.

"With the color on yer face, you wouldn't have. So," she turns to Hugh and Greyson, "we need to warm up. Let's get inside one of these homes and find a fireplace. That house looks like it's got a woodpile or," she leans forward, "an old shed got knocked over. London? We need kindlin'."

"On it," he calls and dashes off onto the property lines of another house littered with trees and disappears.

"What can I do?" I pull the blanket off my shoulders and toss it into the bed of the truck.

Olivia smiles. "Well, we'll need whatever necessities we can get our hands on. Wanna go into some of these homes and look around?"

"You're letting her go off on her own?" Nate walks around.

"You've seen her before, Nate. She can handle 'erself."

"That's not what I'm worried about." He looks hard at me and leans against the truck.

"Wow. Nate." Olivia shakes her head. "What's she gonna do, huh? Relax, all right?"

I glare back at him, shake my head without speaking and start walking down the nearest street while wearing Olivia's sister's strapped sandals. I've never owned shoes before and my feet feel odd. My toes wiggle around inside them.

The first house I come to has its door already knocked in. Darkness spills from the doorway of the home. Not knowing what I'll find, I carefully walk up the sidewalk and step inside. It's quite an old style home. Nothing I've ever seen in my visions before. Most likely pre-2000. There's a smell of age and dust. I take a deep breath in. Death. The back corner of the home is completely blown open.

I keep away from that area of the house and move into the kitchen. Decorations of birds and what I think are farm animals are everywhere. "I've never seen real chickens before," I whisper to myself. I move to the cabinets and open them up.

"Empty. Of course it is." There's not much here. If there had ever been, it's been looted by now. After making a quick sweep of everything else, I move on.

The next home is much newer. Perhaps even finished just after the war started. It's huge and white. A large extension of the home hovers fifty feet above the ground like a giant plate. The doors have a sliding mechanical design, just like The Public, and seem to still be locked. The extension above me has a glass floor which I can see through. Almost everything seems to be still in place. I feel my heart pound. It reminds me so much of The Public, I almost can't breathe. I go to the door. The key pad is broken, but a window that extends out over the grassy area has been shattered. There's a five inch ledge surrounding the second extension—barely large enough for my feet. My feet slide out of the sandals and I kick them to the side. I grab onto the railway that frames the outside of the house and start to scoot along the ledge.

While my fingers and toes grip the outside of the home, desperately trying to keep myself from falling the thirty or forty feet to the hard ground, I peek in the house. It's dark and almost untouched. Avoiding the edges of the broken glass, I step in and heave the rest of myself through. The bomb which tore off the neighboring home made some slight damage to this one too, but the damage is not accessible from the outside. Still, a large breeze funnels through the house, whistling through crevices.

I wander down a hallway and look into the nearest room. It's a bedroom with a single large bed and an immense closet. The clothes inside are all made for a younger man. I quickly look through them anyway. I pull out a jacket with a name and picture on it. St. Louis Cardinals. It's a too big for me, but it will keep me warm. I also manage to find a pair of pants made of dark blue denim and a couple shirts. My old linen top slides over my head and I toss it to the floor. Cold laces around my skin and I hug my chest.

A reflection catches my eye and I pause. The mirror at the end of the room shows me what I've not seen in my entire life. Me. My ribs and muscles poke out from under my skin. Sinewy and starved at the same time. I slip out of my linen bottoms and stare at myself. I don't really look human. My eyes almost bulge, my legs are too thin.

Wind kisses me with a chill—goosebumps rising all over my body.

I hurry and slip the first shirt over my head. It's a simple black cotton top—of course, it could be blue or brown. I can't quite tell in this lighting.

I put on a button-up shirt with a brown and red pattern. Then, the jacket. I put on the denim pants that are extremely long on me, even with my tall legs. A belt to keep them on my hips is the last bit of clothing before I leave the bedroom.

I try to look through the other rooms hoping that maybe I'll find a pair of women's boots. However, it looks like whoever lived here was alone. On a second landing is the kitchen and I run up. The first cupboard is filled with pots and pans covered in dust. The second cupboard is the first one to give me a jolt in my stomach. There's real food in here. Cans of meat, dehydrated meals, some expired packaged items, but all in all, still edible.

The tap of a rock on the large windows draws my attention away and I walk over to look. Below, Nate is looking up at me.

"Are you following me?" I call down.

"How'd you get in?" He ignores my question.

"The ledge."

"Any other way?"

I shake my head. I don't really want him in here with me too. But if there is a positive side to him showing up, I know I'll need his help to carry things back. I look to the front door. The lock pad is still functioning from the inside with an intermittent flash of blue light.

"Go to the front."

I walk over and press my hand on the pad. It comes to life and I quickly press the screen where the new buttons appear. With one fluid movement the door opens up and Nate is just coming back up into the driveway. Without a nod or notice I turn around and go back to the kitchen.

"Anything in here?" he asks.

I point to the open cupboard in answer to him while I open another. This one has more food rations. Never even had a chance to be used. I start to pull the packages down, and switch my focus back to Nate.

"Why did you follow me?" I ask again.

Nate pulls the packages off of the shelves and puts most of them into a basket he found. "I hardly think it's hidden knowledge that I don't trust you."

"*Hardly*. But, one has to wonder where you think I'd go. On foot."

Nate takes more packages down while I watch him. "How am I supposed to know what you're capable of? For all I know, they gave you wheels."

A sharp pain causes my chest to collapse. Of course he still thinks I'm machine. Even so, to hear it said is cutting. All this time, and I'd been expecting someone else. Is he really this hateful?

"You still think I'm not human?" I ask, gripping the countertop.

"Come on. You've got things planted in you, you can see the future, you're skinnier than a toothpick but you can take out two guards by yourself. Not a lot of that screams 'I'm human.' I've watched you." He glares at me. "From what I've seen, you don't have any emotion, you can't possibly. With abilities like yours . . . it's not normal," he says in a rational tone.

Fury bubbles inside my stomach. All this time I'd been envisioning my escape—leaving The Public and finally being around people who don't see me as a test subject. And yet here I am, a machine, to him. A toy to Dryer. A prisoner to The Public. I feel like Nate has a higher opinion of slime than of me.

It's too much. The more I think about what he said, the more I burn. Without taking a second thought, my hand flashes out and I pull a large knife out of the round container on the counter. Its blade is made from a laser, not like the small knives the others carry around in their pockets.

"Hey!" he yells at me, backing away. "Are you crazy?"

In one movement, I slash the knife down my hand, wincing, and let the blood drip to the floor. "Does a machine do this?" I raise my hand, the splatters hitting the floor like giant rain drops. "Stick your fingers in there. Dig around if you'd like. It's real blood." I flinch from the pain. "Real tissue. Real bone." My hand stings and I make a face. "What? Don't want to? Afraid of feeling the cold surface of metal? Or are you too weak to deal with the sight of human blood? Come on, Nate. Touch it!"

I keep holding the knife in my other hand. When he doesn't say a word—make a move, I throw the knife on the counter. "No? Fine." I reach for a clean cloth and grimace. Throbbing pain matching the beat of my heart thumps in my hand. I swear at him, wrapping the cloth tight. "Don't you *ever* tell me I'm not human. I'm just as real as you. Just as real as Liam, and I could die *just as quick*. I'm not empty, so stop treating me like I am!"

Nate's eyes are wide and penetrating. His chest rises and falls so fast, I think he's more afraid of me using the knife again than anything else. But he's quiet.

I remove the cloth and look at my bloody hand. Cold air runs across the wound, stinging it. Blood rises to the surface again and drips to the floor.

"You know," I continue, not content to finish with him, "you complain a lot for someone who seems to have everything. Friends, London, a girl who obviously loves you. And I just don't get it. It's as if you can't just focus on what you *do* have instead of what you've lost. Yes, I see visions of future actions, but I've *also* been observing you. So do you want to know what I think?" I look around at him again while wrapping my hand once more. "You're *pathetic*. You're terrified. God only knows why these people trust you, because I don't. I'm scared to death that you're the one in charge, because you're definitely not stable enough." I shake my head and look away from the furrowed eyebrows that are now coming together on his face. "You know what? Find your own food."

I reach for the basket and take it with me, pushing past him and walking out of the house. Anger continues to course through me with each step. Using my good hand, I continue to adjust the basket on my hip. It only takes me a few minutes to get back and I quickly drop the basket next to London and Olivia who now have a roaring fire.

"Wow!" Olivia grins. "Are those real war rations? I haven't seen those in years! Where did you find them?"

"A house down the street." I say dryly. "No one had been able to get in. Hopefully there's enough for a while," I try to sound calm, hiding my hand from them.

"Reggie. Your shoes," Olivia frowns at me.

I look down at my feet. I forgot the shoes. I'd left the house so quickly they're still lying on the side of the driveway. I twist the towel tighter around my hand and hold it behind my back. Hugh's footsteps come up from behind me and I close my eyes, knowing that he's just seen my hand.

"Reggie. Your hand!"

I can still feel the blood soaking the towel and I turn around and look at him.

"What happened?" He rushes to the truck and pulls out the same bag he had before when he'd removed the chip.

I feel a little light headed and I lower myself the ground.

"Reggie?" Olivia's mouth drops. "What . . ." her voice dies off.

Hugh unwraps my hand and he gasps when the wound is revealed. I cut myself much deeper than I thought. The tissue and muscle are puckering and the blood is so dark it's almost black in the dark early morning. Each of my fingers are dyed a deep burgundy.

"It's not that big of a deal. It . . ."

". . . was my fault," Nate's voice carries from my right. My shoes are dangling between his fingers. "In order to get into the house, she had to go through a broken window and she sliced it open. I should have been the one to go in first."

"Nate, how could you let 'er do that?" Olivia tilts her head.

"Well," Hugh mumbles, carefully examining the cut, "nothing was completely damaged from what I can see. It's still bad, though. It'll take a lot of stitches and quite some time to heal."

I find myself wishing I'd thought that whole argument through. If we were in The Public right now, the healing injections they have would seal the wound in twenty-four hours. Much more advanced than a lot of stitches.

"Of course, unless we can find more aspirin or painkillers, I'm afraid you may just have to deal with the pain, Reggie."

I nod.

Olivia swears. "All right. London, Greyson, let's go search through some more and see if we can round up some meds." They leave, and it's just me, Hugh—who is now searching through his bag for alcohol, medical stitches, and a needle— and Nate. I sit down on the ground with Hugh beside me. It takes a half-hour for him to sew my hand up.

I bite down on my lower lip for so long, I can taste the blood rising through. Hugh has me hold my arm between my legs to keep it from jerking. Nate hasn't spoken another word.

When Hugh finishes, he pulls out more gauze and wraps my hand well. "Reggie, if you don't stop cutting yourself open, I won't have anything left to bandage you with," he says with a smile.

"I'll try my best," I manage to smile back. The pain is intense. I blow out a sigh to keep from crying.

"All right. I'm going to go help the others. See if we can find some pain killers. It'd be a miracle if we can find injections of mydrazine." Hugh shoves the bag into the truck and jogs down the road in an opposite direction.

I look over at Nate. He kicks at a rock under his foot and leans up against the truck, putting the shoes on the edge of the truck bed. I don't think either of us wants to be the first to speak. I don't blame him. What I did was probably a stronger reaction than he was planning on. It was definitely nothing I'd planned on. Although, at the same time, it serves him right. I hope that all he's feeling is flooding guilt.

Nate keeps nodding his head every once in a while, obviously having a conversation inside his head that he's trying to work out. I'm growing impatient, and my hand is searing with pain.

"I," he finally mutters, and I glance at him. His face spreads with a deep red color. "I had a pretty great childhood. Two brothers, one sister. My dad was a, uh . . . pharmacist and my mom taught second grade. I grew up, went to Mendocino High School, played football." Nate takes a deep breath, but keeps going. "I was fourteen when the U.S. got dragged into the war. When I turned sixteen, I was drafted. Military families had arrangements to live in bunkers across the states, and my family was assigned to Utah. Hill Air Force base." He goes silent. The pause is so long, that I wonder if maybe his story is over. I don't understand why feels I need to know that. The dark brown hair shakes on his head, just slightly. The tension building starts to saturate the air.

With a husky tone, he speaks again. "I was twenty-four. Stationed across the Atlantic when I got the message that my family was killed. I lost them all. Within two years after that, the United States didn't exist anymore. Not as I knew it. The military was almost obliterated. The president was killed— again. We had nothing to fight for anymore, but, I was so angry I couldn't stop. Each enemy I saw, I killed. No hesitation. Even if they were kids."

Nate ducked his head. "The world practically destroyed itself around me. I had to barter for passage back to the county on a filthy pirated cargo with Liam. That was when I finally realized I was alone. I'd lost everything I'd ever had.

No home, no family, none of my friends, no job. I'm—" Nate looks over at me again after a prolonged glare at the sky. "I'm sorry I've treated you like trash. But you need to understand where I've come from."

I nod slowly. The silence builds for so long, I feel it. My mouth drops down in thought. "I understand. I understand why you feel you have nothing. I didn't have a childhood. At least not one I remember. I didn't have a family. I don't remember school, I don't remember any passions I had. My first memory of my life was waking up alone in the middle of nowhere with nobody, and no identity. I had a total two years of freedom, until I found The Public. Two years of being alone. Then, for fifteen years I lived in one room. I had no friends. No talents, no family, no home. My sole purpose in life has been to exist for the use of others." My lips begin to shake, my voice break.

"So don't you *dare* tell me how hard *your* life has been." I can feel a build-up of burning water, welling in my eyes, but I blink it back. "You have memories. You have people who care about you. I never have. You have a new family, new friends, new goals, freedom, and yet none of that is *good enough* for you. I wish I had even a quarter of the life you've had. So I hope you understand where *I've* come from."

Nate's mouth hung open. Each inhaled breath dried his tongue. He swallowed and stared at Reggie. The emptiness he'd seen in her eyes before was now a raging storm. The rising sun's rays came over the flat plains and made her eyes glow like cold silver. Voices came up the road and he turned around, running his hand through his hair. His ears burned, and he couldn't bear to look at her anymore.

London was out in front, running. "Found some!" he yelled. With each step he took, the sound of each word jerked out of his mouth. London reached into the truck, grabbed a canteen and walked to Reggie.

Behind Nate, Reggie sighed after taking a drink with the pills London had found and whispered a thank you.

"We got lucky. One home had 'bout a year's worth of medical supplies stuffed into the floor of a shed, underneath a board," Olivia said with a smile, slipping her arm around Nate's waist. "We probably wouldn't 've found it except London sunk his foot through the board next to it." Olivia forced Nate to turn around and he cleared his throat. London was now putting the bottle of pain pills into the truck and

Reggie was drinking down the rest of the water in the canteen. *Reggie*, it was the first time he'd actually thought of her as a person rather than a thing.

"I didn't sink through the board. It was already broken." London gave them a crooked grin.

"Okay, so you were clumsy." Olivia grinned. "Where's Hugh?" she asked, turning to Nate.

"He, uh, went the other way, looking for supplies. He should be back soon," he clipped.

Olivia looked carefully at him, kissed his cheek and softly whispered, "Is everythin' okay?" before dropping off her tiptoes.

Nate cleared his throat and looked at her. "Yeah. Good."

"All right," her voice said, but there was doubt hiding behind it. "Well, we need to talk 'bout how this is gonna work. Let's get warm, pick out a house where we can all stay and then talk 'bout what we need to do next."

"Great." London smiled and Nate watched him hold his hand out for Reggie's uninjured palm. He could tell that the boy liked her, but before it had made him nervous for completely different reasons. Now he wasn't sure how he felt. The look in her eyes that had flashed the moment she'd started talking was still burned into his mind. He'd never felt emotionally hit with a cross-hook like that. Never before had he felt that his life was better than someone else's, and he hated himself for it.

"Nate," Hugh's voice sounded behind him. Nate turned to see the man walking back, a large white bottle in his hands. "Found some more Oxycodone. Expired, but they'll work better than nothing if we need to." He tossed the bottle and it rattled with hundreds of pills before Nate caught it.

"Thanks." Nate put the bottle in a bag and stuffed it securely away in the truck.

"Nate?"

"Yeah."

"I need to talk to you about something."

There was gravity to Hugh's low tone.

Nate turned. "About what?"

"What really happened in that house?"

"What are you talking about?"

"Reggie's hand. The tissue and skin were slightly cauterized. Glass didn't make that cut. It looked like it'd been a thermal kitchen knife. I've accidently cut myself with those things hundreds of times in the past while cutting bread. So I know what those wounds look like." He licked his thick lips. "With a mental ability like hers, I worry that she might be having visions that cause her to hurt herself. If that's the case, she may begin to be a danger to others."

Nate's jaw shifted and he looked toward the house as the door closed behind London and Reggie. "No," he sighed. "It's nothing like that. I was telling the truth when I said it was my fault."

"What do you mean? You didn't do it, did you?"

Nate took a deep breath and let it out slowly, trying to postpone what he'd say next. "I said some things to her I shouldn't have. I baited her and, so, she pulled out the knife. I didn't exactly try and stop her because . . . I didn't know what would happen. It just happened so fast, I don't think I could have stopped her even if I wanted to." Nate squinted back at Hugh, the rising sun piercing his eyes. "I shouldn't have said what I did."

"What did you say to her that made her so angry?" Hugh's face had fallen further and he folded his arms.

"I told her she didn't feel. She wasn't human."

Hugh's eyes narrowed and he shook his head before glancing at the house everyone had gone into. "I'm liking her

more and more. It's too bad she didn't slice *your* hand open."
Without another word, he left Nate standing at the back of the
truck alone.

<hr />

"The city isn't as monitored as most people think it is,"
Reggie's voice was calm and soft. "Yes, you've been in the
system, I know the gate and the walls, they're all watched. But
the homes, the streets? Not really. What government would
need to monitor cities when the people are complacent and
emotionless?"

"We know all that. But, how do *you* know about the
people?" Hugh's head jerked to her.

"Dryer used to speak about it like it was a good thing. He
told me all about how people were, and how it was the only
way to protect them."

"Dryer is the doctor that used to collect your visions every
morning, right?"

"Yes. With the city laid out the way it is, we should be
able, once we get in, of course, to take up residence in a home
for the time we're in there."

Olivia took her hand off of Nate's and leaned forward.
"How long do you think we'll be there?"

Reggie bit her bottom lip. "You've seen what happens
when things are done quickly. This will need to be done much
slower. It'll take time. Getting to Dryer and this . . . 'Comrade'
that I saw him speaking with before, whoever he is, is going
to be nearly impossible. Not to mention getting your family
members out of their assigned homes and away from their
companions."

"What?" Greyson's head perked up and Nate saw the
registered fear on his face.

A noticeable deep breath filled Reggie's lungs and then
exited. "Yes. She probably has been assigned a companion.

Perhaps even a baby by the time we arrive. If she's anything like Olivia," Reggie looked over at her, "they won't use her for incubation."

"Incubation?" Hugh looked like he'd hit a psychology gold mine. He leaned forward, his legs uncrossed, and he was engrossed.

"Women who don't have desirable DNA become incubators. It's not their DNA, they're just used for their womb. They give birth to the new children in the city."

Nate looked down at Olivia and then over at Greyson. Both had looks of frightened disgust on their faces. But only Greyson looked sick. Either way, Sophia would not be the same person they'd last seen. Even Nate wasn't sure if he'd be able to stomach entering that city again knowing what he had just learned.

"How do you know this?" Nate spoke up. He tried to make his tone calm so Reggie wouldn't think he was being antagonistic. "I just don't understand how you can live fifteen years in one room and know so much about the city outside your walls."

Reggie's eyes slowly swiveled over to him, her chest rising and falling slowly. "Are you asking me how I know about the city like I knew you were coming? Just because I'd never been outside does not mean I didn't *see* it."

Hugh frowned at Nate before turning back to her. "So what do we do?"

"I'm not a strategist, I'm only telling you what I know. If we come up with a plan, I can tell you . . . maybe if it will work. I can't just see what plan we should make. I know it doesn't make sense, but that's the way my ability works."

"No," Hugh shook his head. "It makes perfect sense. You look tired. You need to get some sleep."

"I'll take her," London stood up and took Reggie's arm. "There's a separate bedroom you can have to yourself down the hall."

At first, she declined, but with London's persuasion she stood up and let him take her away. Olivia laced her fingers through Nate's again and leaned on his knee. "So, let's come up with something before she falls asleep. Perhaps then we'll get an answer."

"Yes," Hugh nodded, still looking down the hall after Reggie, "I think we should."

"Down, down, down!" Nate bellowed, hunkering down behind the broken down PL Hummer. The whistle of a chem soared above, dropping on the hollowed out building nearest to them. After the explosion. There was nothing but gas. Acid gas billowed into the air. Out from another building's shadows darted a dark figure.

Nate rounded the corner of the Hummer, his power gun loaded. One, two, three. Perfect shots. The figure fell to the ground. His gas mask secure, he walked up to the figure, his men behind him.

"No."

Liam?

Nate jerked, reaching underneath his pillow and coming to alert. The gun in his hand targeted at the doorway. The cold radiating from the large windows of the house sunk deep into his bones, but there was nothing there.

What the hell?

He looked to the side and his eyes fell on Olivia sleeping on the second mattress next to him. She was curled up in a ball, her lips a slight tint of purple. He folded his blanket back and carefully dropped his legs over the side of the bed, taking a deep breath.

Sleep was apparently not in the cards for him. Not tonight. Not anymore.

He left his gun and dropped his blanket over Olivia's body before leaving the bedroom. A run would hopefully clear his mind and help him to tire out enough to fall to sleep.

The house was deadly silent except for the deep rumbling snore coming from the living room where London slept. Ever since Nate had known him, the boy had been a heavy snorer, and it was probably the only sound that made Nate feel at home. Silently closing the front door behind him, he froze in his tracks when he saw Reggie sitting on the front steps, looking up at the sky.

"You couldn't sleep either." Her voice was soft, but cold.

"No. I didn't mean to bother you, though. I'm just going for a run," he whispered.

"You didn't bother me." She looked over her shoulder at him. The large t-shirt she'd changed into hung off one shoulder and the bones and tight muscle poked through. "I was just thinking."

Nate hesitatingly took a step toward her. "Did, uh . . . did you *see* something? Something to do with how we should move forward?"

Reggie looked away and back up at the sky, something flashing in her eyes, but he couldn't make out what it was. "Yes. You shouldn't send Greyson in first. It should be Hugh."

"Why?" Not that he objected to that. He'd rather Greyson not go in at all.

"Because I said so."

Nate sat down on the step next to her and forced himself to look at her. She was staring intently up at the sky, but her mind was obviously miles away. Whatever she was thinking caused deep lines of hurt and worry to show in her face.

"Tell me about Public One. What was it like?"

Reggie's eyes flickered for a moment, but returned to the sky. She was ignoring him. He couldn't blame her, though. He knew he'd been an ass.

"I was about seven, I think, when I found Public One," she said, breaking the thick chill of the night. "Wow, has it only been that long?" Reggie dropped her head enough to look at the rooftops across the street and picked at the hem of her shirt. "I guess so." She turned to him and offered a half smile before continuing.

"I don't remember anything before that, I'm afraid. I woke up alone at the edge of a road and forest. Hungry, confused, and I didn't understand what was real. The vision I'd just woken up from, or what I was seeing. Almost like waking from a second life. I could only remember bright flashes of silver that moved around and around. Splashing sounds of a river, and I had gotten wet. I'd fallen in. There'd been a tree with two letters carved in its side with a plus sign in-between them." She motioned with her fingers, drawing a plus in the air.

"I wandered around after waking up, with absolutely no memory. Nothing except how to speak, read, walk, mathematics, theology, philosophy. The basics."

Nate almost choked. Mathematics and philosophy? Basics?

"Three hours later I came to the river. The same river from my dream. Inside a small pond off of the river, a flash of silver moved around. I hurried to the side to see what it was. The movement darted around in the water and then stopped. It was a fish. When it saw my quick movements, it rushed out of the cove and into the main river. I was so hungry, and all I could think about was eating it. I didn't even care if it was cooked, I just wanted it. In my haste, I slipped and fell into the water.

"It was at that point that I realized what my dream was. I hurried up the riverside hoping to see the fish again, but it was gone. When I looked off to the side, there was a tree standing right there. Two letters, H and J, and a plus sign were carved into its face."

Reggie tugged at the hem of her shirt more, but her eyes remained rooted to one spot on the horizon. Nate couldn't look away. Listening to her drew him further in. He wasn't even sure she knew he was there anymore.

"I didn't understand what I was. I was just a little girl. I found Public One two years later through one of my dreams. They used the word 'precognitive' a lot. At first I didn't know they were talking about me. I'm still not sure I fully understand what I am. Sometimes I think I get more confused about the capabilities of my mind instead of finding answers. At least I learned more about Public One—though very little. I'm sure you probably know more about them than I do."

She finally looked at him, and he found he'd been staring at her. Nate jerked his gaze away and focused on his bare feet. "The Public government was the world's answer to what the happened after the war. Imperfect people started the war. I guess maybe they thought perfect people wouldn't ever start one. I don't know much more than you do, honestly."

Reggie nodded and he heard her swallow in the quiet night. "Well, knowing how it is now, I imagine it must have been horrifying before. If this is the answer."

Nate shook his head. "We traded one evil for another. Nothing's gotten better."

"It will," she whispered.

Nate flinched. "You can see that?"

Reggie bit down on her lip. "No. But I believe it will. You know, when I was in Public One, to sleep at night, I would say a prayer. Dryer always tells me that God doesn't exist. That

I'm wasting my time. But theology is just as important to human kind's survival as anything else."

Inside, Nate felt like snapping her awake. He was the strongest advocate against The Public, but if there was anything he did agree with—it was that God was a myth.

"What?" she asked.

"What?"

"You just scoffed at me. Why?"

Nate shifted uncomfortably. "I'm sorry. I find it shocking that someone like you can believe that."

"Like me?"

"You know," Nate scratched his beard, "different."

Reggie frowned and turned to face him. "What does that have to do with anything?"

She was definitely confrontational. Instead of shutting down when being questioned, she turned on him.

"Well, for someone who may or may not have been created without the help of a 'God' or whatever you want to believe in, and for someone who has a high intelligence, you sure place a lot of blind faith in something you've never seen."

Reggie watched him closely. He could feel his soul being drilled into with just her gaze. It was unnerving, but somehow moving.

This time, instead of defending herself, she turned around again and looked forward. She didn't say a word to him. Just started to dig her toe in between the wood slats of the porch steps.

"I don't even know if Reggie is my name," she finally said, completely off the subject. "When I woke up, the word 'REGGIE' was engraved into the black metal band around my wrist."

Nate didn't know what to say. His mind went blank and he couldn't respond. How had she jumped to such a different topic?

Then, Reggie started to talk again. Almost too quiet to hear. "I would pray to see just a sliver of my past. A memory, a face, or a smell that would trigger something." She shook her head. "Nothing. But it got me through each night. Every day. You may be right. There may be no one greater than you or me. But that 'blind faith' kept me alive, and if you ask me, you're no different. If you've truly given up, why do you keep trying?"

Nate hung his head and ran his hand over his oily hair. He took a deep breath. Why did he? He'd told himself time and time again that it was all for London. Sometimes even that excuse felt hollow.

He turned to look at her. The quizzical lines near her eyes disappeared and her face went blank. Nothing. Had she forgotten he was there next to her? Or was her mind making her feel different emotions all at once? Her head slowly dropped forward as if she was drowsy, but her eyes were wider than ever.

"Reggie?" Nate paused. He stuck his hands out and grabbed her shoulders. "Reggie, are you all right?"

Her eyes didn't blink, and her body was at the point of being limp. Nate grabbed her face and brought it around. Her skin was soft like satin, and smelled like sanitizer and synthetic drugs. Although her eyes were open and directed at him, they weren't focused.

"Reggie?"

She rapidly blinked and her eyes finally focused on him. "Nate, has Olivia wanted to go in the city?"

"What? What just happened? That wasn't a vision was it? I've seen you *see* things before."

Reggie breathed calmly. "It was. It was a different kind, but that doesn't matter. *Nate,* I saw Olivia go in the city. You said you planned for her to stay out, right?"

"Yeah. She wanted to go with Greyson, but we told her it'd be better if she didn't. Why?"

"Don't let her go in."

"Why?"

"Just *don't.* Okay?"

Nate nodded. "What did you see?"

Reggie's head twisted around to look at the house. "I think Olivia's awake," was all she said in response.

Not a sound was made. There was no way Olivia was awake. Yet, he didn't understand how Reggie would know. Only the future, right? Not the present.

Perhaps it was her way of telling him she wanted to be alone. Though a part of him didn't really want to leave. Sure, he'd wanted a walk, an escape to get away from the crap of the day but he found himself wanting to apologize to her. "I'm sorry, Reggie."

She tucked her chin into her shoulder, frowning, and then glanced up at him. Her mouth opened to say something. She must have thought better on it and turned back to the sky. Nate followed suit and gazed at the stars above.

"'Be the change that you wish to see in the world,'" he whispered. "My mother used to quote it to me. It was said by a man named Gandhi, years ago who was trying to achieve world peace I guess." He let out a mock chuckle. "Wouldn't he be disappointed to see us today."

Reggie continued to stay quiet, her arms wrapped around her body.

"It seems I've forgotten what my own mom used to say. I claim that I want a better life for London. A better place to live, but I don't really change anything about myself—anything positive at least. With all the shit in the world, I know I should view things differently. I don't think I'd ever really thought about that 'til today, though. You were right. I haven't seen anything good in my life before—I didn't want to see it. I was a complete ass."

"Ah. You and I finally agree," she whispered.

Nate raised his eyebrow and glanced at her. She still wasn't looking at him, but a smile played at the corner of her mouth. She was teasing him. A resigned smile spread on his own face.

"Dryer did that to you didn't he?"

"What?" Nat asked.

"Your eye. Your cheek and knuckles. It has his name all over it."

Nate felt his swollen eye again. "Yeah. With a little help from a precognitive weapon."

"Sorry about that. You were trying to suffocate me."

Nate smiled, and his eyebrows rose. "I guess you could say that. He, uh, do the same thing to you?"

"No." Reggie shook her head. "He was much more intrusive." When she didn't say anything else, he knew she didn't want to talk about it any longer. Whatever Dryer had done to her, it was haunting enough that she didn't want to linger on her memories. "They're beautiful aren't they?"

He looked over at her. Her eyes cast reflections of the moon like ripples on a lake; captured by the stars, by the heavens.

"They are."

HUGH

"Congratulations, Dr. Salinger." Dr. Boggs shook Hugh's hand and looked back at him with a smile for the first time in two years.

"I earned a smile? What happened to 'Dr. Freeze?'" Hugh grinned back at him.

"You're my colleague now. Not a doctoral candidate anymore. I'll admit, I've looked forward to this day. Ever since I singled you out in that first class." The crinkled skin around his eyes folded even more as his smile deepened. "Welcome to the world of Psychology. You'll find that it's rewarding at times. I hope you're up to it."

"Of course I am."

Hugh scrubbed at his hands with the rough plastic brush. A small bowl of pink soapy water sat beneath his hands. He thought back on the day he'd graduated, looking forward to a life of prestige, intellect, and wealth. When he was a child, he'd watched his father, a surgeon, work the late hours while trying to support a family of twelve. With the decrease in healthcare costs, medical doctors were barely able to pay off their graduate loans let alone make a living. Hugh swore he'd never have to do the same work as his father. But he looked down at the blood soaking under his fingernails, dripping into the bowl with the soap and water. It was too ironic. Last night he hadn't been able to see in order to wash it all off, so he waited 'til morning.

Here he was, alone, like he'd always wanted.

"Hugh, I know that your job is important to you. But there comes a time where you have to prioritize. I mean, we've been together for six years! Either you want to marry me or you don't!" Shilo's dark blonde hair bounced when she moved. Usually the bounce of her curls played along with her laughter. Not this time, unfortunately.

"I didn't say I never wanted to marry you. I just said, not yet!"

"'Not yet' in Hugh's dictionary of BS, always means never. You said it last month to the plumber! Thank you so much for ranking me and our relationship in the same order of importance as the guest toilet!"

Hugh shook his head and threw his hands in the air. "I can't talk to you when you're like this."

Shilo chuckled, but it was full of fury. "You're ridiculous, you know that? Just go ahead and brush me off when you don't want to talk. It's what you always do." She walked over to the large bay windows and looked out over the ocean. The stillness enveloped him in a chilly embrace. Even the sunshine outside froze once it entered the room. Shilo's breath trembled. He couldn't see her face with his eyes, but he knew her. He could see her hanging bottom lip, the drooping fiery eyes.

"You want to be left alone so bad?" she finally spoke calmly. "Well, you got your wish. I'm finished."

Hugh dried his hands off on his pants and poured the water out on the ground before putting everything away. A call from Greyson within the house let him know that the cans of tuna and one ration meal for each person were open and ready to be eaten for breakfast. His heart pounded in his chest.

He'd be leaving the group the moment he finished—headed off to The Public by himself.

He went into the house to find Reggie sitting at the haphazardly dusted-off kitchen table; the dust just clumsily swished off like a child's finger-painted artwork. London sat next to her playing a card game, flipping each flimsy card over onto the table. Nate and Olivia were opening up the meals while Greyson packed everything up.

"Wait, wait, wait. You said that you only slap the cards when the Jack is on top!" Reggie smiled.

"Yes, but you can also hit it when doubles are down. You know? A five on a five or a nine on a nine—"

"Or a three on a queen?" Reggie smiled at him, mocking. "You know, I think you're just making up rules as you go."

"Sometimes he does," Hugh patted London's shoulders.

"That's *not* true!" London swiveled in his seat, one eyebrow sagging while the other jumped into the air.

"At least not when he's playin' with a pretty woman." Olivia set two meals down for Reggie and London.

Hugh noticed the bright shade of scarlet that flared up in London's face and neck. It was obvious that London had quite the crush on Reggie. Hugh worried about that, despite the teasing. Reggie was at least eight or nine years his senior. But who was he to judge? Things weren't like they used to be, he supposed. Where else would the kid find someone close to his age?

"Here you go, Hugh," Olivia handed him a packaged meal and he started eating it at the center island in the kitchen.

"Ugh, I don't think I'll ever get used to the old war rations."

"Well," Nate sighed, "they weren't made to be gourmet delicacies. Just edible."

"I don't know if I'd call this edible."

"Are you kidding?" Reggie said behind him and he turned around. Her meal was nearly gone and she now had another full mouth of the re-hydrated food. She swallowed. "This is better than anything I've had in my life." The gray depth of her eyes sparkled like silver and she smiled.

She was fascinating to him. From a mental professional standpoint. A young woman raised in, essentially, captivity with no real human connections. Yet she had the intelligence, social skills, and tact of a person with a college education. Still, a simple meal was the highlight of her day. Of course, if anyone had been raised on a thin watered-down potato soup for fifteen years, even a saltine cracker would be appealing.

Never before had he come across a patient or case with a remotely similar background. Sure, he'd studied the effect of brain development on children kept in the parents' and kidnappers' basements and broom cupboards. Each caged like an animal from the time they were born 'til puberty. Those children had zero linguistic ability, were skittish around other people, and stunted in growth. Reggie . . . had somehow taught herself everything. It didn't make sense.

"So, Reggie." Hugh cleared his throat. "Remind me again why it is that I have to be the first one in the city?"

Reggie looked up with a smile still on her face. It softened with her reply, "Hugh, you're the only one who's never been into the city. The one that won't be recognized, and two . . . you have extremely dark skin."

Hugh still wasn't quite used to her candor, yet. He raised an eyebrow. "Because I'm black?"

"Exactly. A variety of genetic material in the Public's population means stronger DNA. They value other ethnic races far more than Caucasian."

Olivia set the garbage from her and Nate's meals in the sink while Hugh nodded. "It *does* make sense. History is wrought with civilizations that were so focused on purity of genetics that eventually the gene pool became too weak with frequent in breeding, which therefore led to the fall of that society. Although there were many that attempted to create that ideal genetic population and failed. Take the Nazis. Strove for blonde hair, blue eyed individuals and all it led to was the Second World War. It's fascinating really."

Nate scoffed. "I don't think 'fascinating' is the word that I would use. Although, we blue-eyed types do appreciate the compliment."

Olivia slapped his shoulder and quickly left the kitchen to finish getting things together. There was a definite glow to Olivia these days. Whatever relationship she'd started with Nate had been the trigger.

Not surprisingly, the same reaction hadn't really happened with Nate—at least not entirely. But, something was different this morning. Nate was easier to be around. And it didn't take a professional to see that.

"You'd better finish that up, Hugh. You've got to head out."

Hugh stabbed at the mush of food again and looked at Nate. "You're not nervous about this?"

"Are you kidding?" Nate's voice dropped. "I'm scared out of my mind."

The truck bumped up and down along the dirt road. What used to be the highway was torn up in many places. Grass was beginning to grow through, pushing the chunks of concrete up, and splitting the thick pavement into sections.

Even with the windows rolled down, the plastering heat of the day caused streams of sweat to trail down his baldhead and roll down into his shirt.

"So what are you doing for Christmas this weekend, Hugh? Visiting family?"

Hugh tilted the wine glass in his hand back and forth. The deep red liquid spun around like a soft cyclone. "No, I won't be. Not this year. My brothers and sister are all choosing to be with their in-laws this year, so I'll be soaking up plenty of Bermuda sun." He grinned through his lie. There was no need to tell his colleague that he'd had a falling out with his siblings since his father had passed away. And there was no need to mention that the reason they weren't talking was because he hadn't attended the funeral. It was well enough anyway. Waking up to the screaming joyful cries of his nieces and nephews over their presents at four in the morning was not his idea of a vacation.

"Well aren't you a lucky S.O.B. Takin' Shilo with you?"

Hugh sipped his wine without looking at him, and then swallowed. "Of course." Another lie. Part of him was still upset over Shilo leaving, but there was a good chunk of his mind that was relieved at the same time.

"Living the life, aren't you?"

"Sure am," Hugh whispered, resting his elbow on the windowsill and squinting at the road ahead. The overwhelming urge to stop for a bathroom break took over his desire to keep going.

He hit the brake and he pulled the truck to a stop. When the engine quit, Hugh got out of the truck while the bittersweet smell of warm gasoline filled the air. It wasn't two seconds into unzipping his jeans that he heard the thump of feet leaving the bed of the truck and hitting the ground.

"Holy sh—" He quickly zipped his pants back up again and spun around. Olivia rested her elbows on the truck bed and smiled at him. "Olivia, you scared me half to death! What are you doing here?"

"Oh, please," she motioned at his pants, "finish."

Hugh sighed. "Answer the question, Olivia."

"Ugh, okay, look. I know Nate wanted me to stay back, but I weren't gonna let ya'll have all the fun. Besides, who's gonna protect yer black butt when ya can't tell a good lie?"

"Who says I can't lie?"

Olivia grinned as she opened the passenger door and jumped in. "No one. But let's face it, Hugh, yer not exactly a cunning persona."

There wasn't enough gas in the tank to take Olivia back, and he knew it. Even if there was, there wasn't a guarantee that the others would still be there. At least this way he'd have some company.

"Fine. Let me . . . walk away a bit, relieve myself, and we'll keep going."

Olivia chuckled. "Relieve yerself? Come on, Hugh. We both know yer takin' a piss, so just say it. Loosen up a bit."

"I'm loose," he jumped in to defend himself until he realized what he'd just said and Olivia burst out laughing. "Ha ha," he mocked, "I think we're a little old for these childish jokes."

"I'm sorry," Olivia called from the truck with a lilt of humor in her voice. "I really am."

Hugh sighed and walked farther from the truck, a good distance away from Olivia's eyes and snide comments. What was the woman thinking? Sneaking off like this was sure to screw things up somehow. Hell, Nate was probably bursting a gasket. Not to mention the fact that Olivia had already been arrested once. They'd know her for sure.

When he finished, Hugh went back to the truck and started the engine. "Look, Olivia," the truck sped up again, bouncing over the gashes in the road, "if you're comin' in with me, they're going to recognize you."

"Already planned ahead. It may not be the greatest plan, but I brought a pair of scissors. Cuttin' my hair is prob'ly the first thin' I need to change." Olivia fingered the long black braid that ended at her waist.

"The first thing? What's the second thing?"

She glanced over at him. The wind from the open window fluttered the wispy hairs around her face. What she was going to say, he could already tell that he didn't want to hear it. "I'll need to look unrecognizable, Hugh."

"And how do you plan on doing that?"

Olivia's voice was harder but quieter than before. "How good can ya throw them fists of yers?"

pull my hair off my neck and put it into one of the elastic bands Olivia gave me. Since I've never had to deal with the weather before, I'm not used to the extreme temperature changes. I can smell the familiar drugged tang of my own sweat mixed with cotton and soap. I grunt while sliding a crate of pilfered items onto the back of one of the ATVs.

"Anyone seen Liv?" Nate calls from the house and his boots thump, thump, thump down the stairs.

The familiar sensations hit me. My throat tightens and my head jerks back slightly as if someone has tugged on my hair.

"Come at me, Hugh. You have to do it," Olivia's voice echoes. *Her face is straight and hard.*

"I can't do it, Olivia. There's got to be something else we can do."

"Hit me, Hugh!" She shoves his shoulders back and his immediate reaction results in a singular punch to her right cheekbone. The chirp of the crickets around them is deafening. She rounds back again to face him. A large red welt has formed on her cheek along with a deep cut.

Olivia hisses in pain. "Good, a few more like that one and they won't be able to recognize me when we enter The Public. Again."

"Reggie!?" London's hands are at my shoulders, shaking me back and forth. "Reggie, talk to me. Are you all right?"

I gasp for air and struggle to regulate my breathing again. No, no, no. Why didn't she listen to me?

I'm able to nod to London, but I have to find Nate.

"Nate," I whisper, trying to catch my breath.

"What is it, Reggie? What did you see?" London's hand nervously shakes while tucking a strand of my hair behind my ear.

"No." I shake my head and pull away to look at Nate rushing down the walkway. His dirty button-up shirt billows behind him, and his boots still aren't tied.

"Nate, I saw Olivia. She's with Hugh."

"What?" He steps forward and nudges London to the side. "What do you mean she's with Hugh?"

"She shouldn't 've gone with him, she shouldn't 've gone with him." I can't help but repeat it over and over. After what I saw last night, I know—I know what will happen. "She must have snuck into the back of his truck when he left. Nate, she was asking Hugh to disfigure her face so she wasn't recognizable."

Nate curses and kicks the ATV's tire. His fingers curl around the handlebar and the veins protrude from his hands and wrists. He swears under his breath. When he stands straight again, he's shaking his head with his jaw jutted forward. "We can't do much now. All we can hope for is that she knows what she's doing. Get on the back, Reggie. Come on, you two. Let's go."

London's hand brushes mine and he walks away, climbing on the back of the first ATV. Greyson gets on with him and the engine revs up. I straddle the second ATV with Nate.

"Is she going to be all right?"

Olivia shouldn't have gone.

"Reg," Nate coaxes my attention again and I pull my gaze away from the dirt on the ground. His teeth are clenched, and I can smell him standing directly to the side of me. A combination of clay, pine, and ripe body odor. "Reggie, will she be okay?"

My head barely shakes. Even I wasn't sure if it moved. I can't stop my visions from happening if people don't listen to me. Olivia, why?

"I don't know."

"If you don't know for sure yet, maybe we don't need to worry. I know Olivia. She'll be smart."

Smart has nothing to do with it, I think to myself.

"Can you scoot back a little further?"

Numbly, I push myself back. Nate's legs straddle the four-wheeler and I nervously wrap my arms around his torso. To hold myself on, I grab onto the fabric of his shirt. The ATV revs and Nate pulls off of the street. Greyson and London follow, leaving Scott City behind. A trickle of sweat slides down my forehead, over my eyebrow, and stings and spreads along my eyelashes. Immediately, I reach up with one hand, wipe its trail off my forehead, and tuck my head into Nate's back.

For hours, Nate and I don't speak through the roar of the wind rushing past my head. I can feel him taking in breaths to say something, but I can't bring myself to ask what he wants. I already know what it is. I'm sure he wants to know why I'm so worried; what's going to happen to her. I can't tell him. I can barely stop it from playing in my mind. I close my eyes and try to block out the images that come flooding back.

So much blood. I feel myself getting sick and cold.

Dryer told me he was able to change what I saw, didn't he? Perhaps there's still a chance we can change the course. Of course there is. If it hasn't happened yet, then there's still a chance. Dryer said so.

I nod my head as if I'm answering a question. I hear Nate clear his throat and I finally bring my head up to look at the side of his face. "She's not going to die, is she?" he asks.

"Not necessarily. We can change it!" my voice drifts on the wind.

He nods.

"Good! I can't lose both of my best friends in a week. It's statistically impossible, right?" For the second time since I've seen him—Nate smiles at his own attempted joke. It's warm, but simultaneously shaky.

"Tell me about Liam," I call into his ear. "I know it's only been a couple days, but no one really talks about him."

Nate makes no movement. I nearly wonder if he hasn't heard me. I'm about to say something else to change the subject when he takes a deep breath. "I met Liam during my deployment in Germany," he takes another breath. "Let's see, that would have been twenty forty-two. We were only there for three months before we were permanently deployed to North Korea." Nate lets out an ironic chuckle before yelling into the wind again. "Liam used to always say that if we were ever captured, he'd just pose as a Korean spy in order to get us out. Only problem was that Liam didn't know a lick of Korean."

Nate's voice stops. I wonder if that's all he's going to say—maybe all he can say. I shouldn't have brought it up.

"One day," he yells back to me again, "a chemical raid was dropped over our area, about fifty miles east of Pyongyang. Liam's suit was torn around his abdomen." His head looks forward again and he pauses. "Since it was exposed, his skin started rotting and decaying." The story ends again. Bumps on the road keep Nate's attention forward instead of yelling into the wind. When he speaks again, his voice is heavy.

"But he kept firing 'til he collapsed. When I realized what was wrong, I put him on my shoulders and ran like hell for the nearest med unit." Nate keeps talking. Even through parts of the story that I'd imagine no one would ever want to relive again. Not that I want him to stop, but in the past five minutes, he's said more words than the previous forty-eight hours.

"I couldn't breathe by the time I got him there. My oxygen supply was low, and I hadn't even noticed," we swerve around a large cratered pothole, "noticed that I'd taken a bullet to my left shoulder. All I cared about was him. To make sure he stayed alive. I'm . . ." he turns his head forward again, losing some of the words on the wind. When he cranes his neck back my direction, I can tell his brows are scrunched together, and his eyes have misted. "I'm not even sure why we were so close. I guess it's just one of those things where you're meant to be friends with someone no matter what. Or maybe it was just the threat of death for each of us, I don't know.

"It was five days before Liam woke up. He always had this," Nate lets go of a handle and motions across his stomach. I feel each movement of his back muscles and ribs and he moves. ". . . red bubbled scar that ran all along his stomach and to the right side of his back. But he made it. He shouldn't have, but he did. I always," Nate smiles again, twisting his head around, and I can't believe how good it looks on him, "I always used to think he was invincible. Maybe he did too. Maybe that's why he saved my life three times after that. I was never able to really pay him back because I couldn't."

Nate goes quiet and brushes his left hand across the beard on his face to swat a bug.

"He sounds like he was an incredible person," I yell at him. "I'm sorry you lost him."

He takes his eyes off the road again and looks back at me. "Maybe he's the lucky one."

"What's that?" Nate leans forward over the handlebars trying to get a better look. Faint motor noises radiate from different points ahead. "Well, well. I don't think we've run into another group of Nomads for about a year. This could be a good thing for us. Either that or we're in a lot of trouble."

Nate raised his arm, moving his hand from side to side, motioning to Greyson and London. I don't understand what the signal means, but they pull up closer and look to the set of homes in front of us. The town is extremely small. In fact, each of the homes isn't even standard. They are large motorized homes on wheels.

"Mobile community. They don't stay anywhere longer than a week," Nate called back to me.

"Why the mobile homes?"

"Less chance of being caught by the Public, they feel. Ben used to live in one years ago until he got sick of the constant change. Reggie, keep behind me."

"Why?"

"I can't see any women ahead." His voice was grave, and I knew not to argue with him.

I can already see the figures of men walking out of their homes, pulling out guns and rifles. Nate and Greyson slow down their ATVs as we approach the edge of the community. The men of the group are all pointing their weapons directly at us.

"Don't shoot," Nate turns off the ATV and keeps his hands on the bars. "We're not here to take anything, just looking for a safe place to stay for a while."

"What's your name, son?" A man with broad shoulders steps forward, a rifle in his hands. His dark beard has overgrown on his face, but sand-colored eyes peer out at us from under his cap.

"Nate Naylor. This is Greyson Peters, and London Goldman." He doesn't say a word about me.

"What about your woman there?"

I feel the muscles under Nate's shirt tighten, but his voice remains calm and steady. "She's my sister. We don't need anything from you, we're just passing by."

"Passing to where?"

"Northern mid-west."

The man's gun cocks and I feel something hard lump in my throat. "No one goes there. No one smart enough, that is. What do you really want?"

"*You . . .*" A faint female voice chirps up from behind the men and walks forward. But she's looking at Greyson. Her gorgeous blonde hair is cut short, but glistening with body oil. I assume it's been only a couple days since her last shower. But it's her clothes that catch my attention. They're from The Public.

Greyson looks over at Nate. "Isaac's here."

"What?" Nate looks back at the woman. She backs up hesitantly. "You're Audra?"

"How do you know her name?" The man steps closer.

"Her sonofabitch husband nearly got us killed."

"Mommy, mommy!" A little boy with light blonde hair pushes his way through the men in front and wraps his arms around Audra's leg. She quickly picks him up and he looks over at us. When his young eyes hit me, his head tilts.

"Mommy, why is that woman glowing like Sammy?" Audra's gaze runs to me and she frowns, her mouth dropping open.

"What's going on, Audra?" a man breaks through the crowd and freezes in his spot the moment he sees Nate. I recognize him. It's the man who escaped from Public One. The one who left them. It's Isaac.

"Nothing," she starts to say, but Nate swings his leg over the ATV. It doesn't take long—just two large steps for Nate to move from me the man he feels is responsible for Liam's death. In one fluid motion, his fist connects with Isaac's face and Isaac falls to the ground. Audra screams and holds her son closer to her, cupping his head to her chest. She's more affected than her son is, and the stress twists her face.

Nate spits. "You left us to die!" An insulting curse flies from his mouth. A dozen guns point right at his chest. Despite the threat, he continues to yell. "Liam's dead! Get that? DEAD!"

Isaac rolls over onto his hands and knees, blood dripping from the inside of his mouth, and down his lip down onto the ground. "It wasn't my fault, Nate!" He curses as he wipes his nose. "Second time this week!"

Nate starts to go for him again, but Greyson leaps off his ATV and grabs at Nate's arms. "Don't tell me you're complaining because of a broken nose, Quigg. I'm gonna beat the shit out of you."

The boy in Audra's arms stays still through her sobs, but surprisingly, the men have all dropped their weapons.

"Not now, Nate. Just leave him. He's not worth it," Greyson growls at him.

Nate relaxes and Greyson finally lets him go.

"Name's Doran McKendrick," the man says to Nate. He shakes his hand and they both watch Isaac and Audra walk back toward one of the mobile homes. Isaac hobbles up the stairs, but Audra takes one last glance at me before she walks in. Something in her face unnerves me, as if she recognizes me somehow.

Audra helps her companion back into the trailer home and the door bangs closed behind them.

"I heard all about you," McKendrick hoists his gun strap over his shoulder, and my focus is pulled back. He shakes his head and motions a thumb back toward Isaac's mobile home. "Cushioned refugee has done nothing but complain about our lack of supplies. Thank goodness it was you that hit him. I've wanted to do that for two days now."

The crackling snap of the fire was the only sound for miles. By using fresh green wood, the smoke of the fire would definitely be visible to The Public seeing as though they were only a few miles away. Since walking up to the gate would create suspicion, he and Olivia kept their distance, allowing for Hugh to be captured. At that point, Olivia would hang back and sneak in behind the guards after they entered the city.

Hugh picked his teeth with a whittled toothpick and tossed it in the fire along with the bones of the rabbit that he and Olivia just finished eating. He had to give her credit for her cooking skills.

"Hugh!"

He turned around to see Olivia walking through the copse of trees and then stopped, beckoning with her hand. Her swollen eyes were wide—as wide as she could get them—and she breathed heavily.

"Ya gotta see this."

"What is it?"

"Jest come with me." Her blackened bruised face, splitting lips, and swollen cheekbone were a horrendous site. He hated what he'd done to her. He followed her through the pines and trees before she rounded the edge of what looked like a giant boulder that was partially stuck in the ground.

"Come on, Liv. What's so important that you couldn't just tell me?"

Olivia narrowed her swollen eyes at him and beckoned her finger at him to come closer. "I was lookin' fer extra dry wood out here when I found this." Her thumb jutted out to the right, pointing to the boulder. Hugh frowned at her and wondered what in the world she was showing him until he walked around to her side. It wasn't a boulder at all. Two heavy-set steel doors were at the side and locked tight. The leaves and needles cracked beneath his feet in the cold morning air. From what he could see, the door had no handles on it. Dirt, faint chips of rust, and dead brittle vines fell to the ground when he ran his hand along the edges, trying to feel for hinges or some way to get in. He tried pushing on them a couple times, but there wasn't even a jiggling sound.

"What is it?" he finally asked.

"I don't know. That's what I was hopin' you could help me figure out."

"Could be anything. I wouldn't know until we got those doors opened. They're completely sealed. It looks like they open from the inside. They could lead to a storage room in there or," he mockingly raised his eyebrows, "I don't know, maybe Hell? If that's the case, I take pity on Satan 'cause this world is a crap hole." He smiled quickly before his eyes shot open like headlights and he whirled around on Olivia. "Well, that explains everything! We're already in Hell! This must be the way out!"

Olivia slapped his arm and attempted a smile. "Jokes aside, what do you think?"

"Well," he chuckled with a sigh. "I'll get back to the truck and see if there's a crowbar of some kind in there. I think you should keep looking for more wood. We need that fire to keep going until they notice and come to get me."

They both left the doors and Hugh crunched back through the woods to the campsite. He came to an immediate stop when he saw two men around the campfire. Their white uniforms made it obvious that their campfire had done its job. Both men slowly turned around and the first smiled at Hugh.

"Quite the meager meal and living situation. Do you have a name, Sir?"

"Is there anything I can help you gentlemen with?" Hugh attempted to keep his voice calm. "I can try and find another rabbit."

"Oh, no," the man said. "We were actually going to make you an offer. When was the last time you got to sleep on an actual bed? Have a decent home with running water and food in a refrigerator?"

This warm reception was much different from how Nate and Olivia had been treated a few days ago. Reggie had been right. They were going to take him right under their wing, and give him everything they thought he wanted.

"Lieutenant!"

The man turned his attention from Hugh at the sound of the voice. A third guard came through the trees. Hugh felt sick the moment he saw Olivia in his grasp. Her hands were behind her and locked in metal wrist cuffs. The third guard lifted his hand. Part of the uniform included a small projector in the palm of the gloves. When he lifted his hand, the image of Olivia, not injured, appeared to float in the air. Blue dots mapped out the bone structure of the projection, matching with the bruised Olivia struggling in the guard's grip.

The lead guard had a frown on his face, and displeasure washed over him. He looked from Olivia back to Hugh.

"Well, look who we found," he stared Olivia down. His eyes flickered to Hugh. "Sir, do you know this woman?"

Hugh's eyes bounced back and forth between Olivia and the guard. She looked at him with a glare, warning him not to say a word. "W-what? No! I've never seen her before in my life. She must have smelled my dinner and thought that maybe she'd get some."

"This woman," the guard held up a projected device with the profile photo of Olivia taken just days beforehand. The 3-D projection turned slowly in the air, "is a wanted fugitive. She's a dangerous criminal. You're lucky we found her before she got to your camp. Public disturbance, escaping guard custody, theft, and murder. What we're trying to say, mister?"

"Salinger. Dr. Hugh Salinger."

"Doctor?"

"Of psychiatry." Hugh nodded. His nervousness could not be hidden. Beads of perspiration trickled down his neck and his breathing became rapid. If he didn't get his body under control, it wouldn't just be Olivia they cuffed.

The guard watched him with concern. Through luck, or even just a wink from the heavens, the guard seemed to take his panic as a sign of fear of Olivia, not of the guards themselves.

"Psychiatry? Dr. Salinger, we could use a man of your talents. Have you ever heard of The Public?"

"Only rumors."

"Well, believe them. At least the good parts." The man smiled again. "Inside the city we have a home for you, food, a bath, clothing, and everything you ever had before the war.

There's a lot of good being done inside and we could truly use a man of your education and intellect. With new developments in medicine, plus the difficulty that we're having getting citizens accustomed to decent life, you would be greatly appreciated."

Hugh's eyes darted to Olivia. She struggled with the guard, trying to pull herself away until he shoved a power-gun between her ribcage. "It *has* been a long time since I've bathed."

The guard nodded. "It's settled. Come with me, and we'll get you in the transport. Did you know that just a mile east, and you'd start to see the tops of the city? Lucky for you, you were living right outside the city walls without even knowing it."

Hugh nodded. "Yes, lucky me."

....

The ride through the forest was dead silent. Neither the guards nor Hugh spoke to each other. Olivia had been tossed into a voltage containment in the back of the transport and the shock of touching the bars had finally kept her from fighting. Now she was silent.

This wasn't how it was supposed to happen. Olivia was supposed to be back with the others. Why hadn't she stayed behind? What was so important to her that she had to risk everything and try to break in on her own? Even her reasons didn't seem to be strong enough.

"I'm stronger than you think."

"Because I knew I needed to."

How could she have known?

When he saw the city looming before them, his chest started to ache with burning. He finally expanded his lungs and a flood of air relieved the ache. In a short time, he'd be like everyone else in there—complacent, calm, and caged. His body fluids drawn and children would be born with his DNA. The frosty bite of unease shook his body. The vapid, still, and sterilized smells of the guard transport wasn't helping the situation at all. It was worse than being in a hospital.

The transport glided through the gated archway and took them directly through the streets toward an odd building. Its symmetrical shape resembled a glowing gold and pale green rocket, about to shoot off into the sky. It looked barely convex on the north and south ends with each window reflecting the surface around it. At the base were three large arched entrances.

Hugh's memories of city life came nowhere in comparison to what he saw. Around on the streets, people sauntered as if it were any other day in a suburban neighborhood. However, there were no horns honking, no traffic jams. The commotion of business and the clamor of a real city were absent. Every person nodded politely to each other and continued walking. Some women carried shopping bags, other men communicated on projection viewers that popped up in front of their face. But it was the children that caught Hugh's attention. They seemed to have more fire in their eyes. Like the adults, however, something was missing. Each child had the look of secrets written on their faces. Secrets they didn't even know. They weren't like the others.

"Dr. Salinger. We've reached The Public hospital. I'll show you inside," the lead guard ushered Hugh out of the transport and the door silently slid shut behind him. When he turned back around, it was gone. Olivia was gone.

"Please, follow me, doctor."

Hugh felt empty already. He forced his eyes to look from face to face that passed him, hoping to see Ben, Sophia, or anyone from the community. Surely they hadn't all been killed. He gulped hard, and found it difficult. The thought of others being killed made him sick.

"Doctor Shilling, this is Doctor Salinger, PSYD," the guard motioned to Hugh. The doctor he was introducing him to was rail thin, with a look of irritation on his face. His eyes were a brilliant blue, and the structure of his face was perfectly proportioned—as he noticed many peoples' were. The eyes were straightly aligned, a nose that was neither too big, nor too little. No variation or imperfection. In fact, the entire city population was like Isaac had said—hand picked for their strong genetics.

"Dr. Salinger, welcome to Public One," the medical doctor's face relaxed and he extended his hand for Hugh's.

"Thank you, Dr. Shilling. You can call me Hugh for now."

"Very well, Hugh. Thomas here has told me that you are new to the city?"

Hugh looked at the guard. "Yes."

"Well, we're pleased to have you here. When you finish orientation, we'll be ready to help guide you through the rest of the process."

"Process?" Hugh narrowed his eyes.

"If you'll follow me, Dr. Salinger," the guard said at his side, "I'll be able to explain everything."

Dr. Shilling smiled politely at Hugh and turned to the nearest nurse. Hugh took a brief inventory of the hospital before he followed the guard. He was led down a hallway, brightly lit with natural light sources and into a single room. Inside it was set up like a small theater room. Semi-hard chairs in circular rows all pointing toward the center.

"Have a seat please, Doctor."

Hugh nervously found a seat and faced the center of the circle. Immediately, the lights went out and the hologram of a man stood in the center. Hugh had never seen him before in his life. The man was perhaps in his fifties with peppered hair, and dressed in a sharp blue suit.

"Welcome to Public One," the recorded man said. "In March of 2036, tensions between the world's nations reached a boiling point. On the 21st, insurgents dropped WMDs on Washington D.C., killing the President and many government staff members. This single act instigated one of the worse wars mankind had ever seen."

Hugh took his eyes off the hologram and glanced at the guard behind him. The man nodded to the recording, urging Hugh to keep watching. What for? He already knew all this.

"And so, using a stored fund from the CIA, in October of 2037, members of the government began preparations for a city. A city to protect its citizens and preserve the human race. This municipality was known as The Public. Though," the hologram smiled charismatically and motioned with his hands, "why tell you this? Odds are, many of you lived through and witnessed it. I'll tell you. I'll tell you everything."

The projection seemed to step forward, staring right at Hugh. "If, by the end of this presentation, you feel our offer is not comfortable to you, we will take that into consideration."

The presentation ended and Hugh struggled to close his mouth to swallow. So that's how they did it. Each and every single person in The Public, had at one point, known everything. Some having their freedom stripped if they didn't conform—others choosing to comply and aid in Public One's agenda. The guards. The doctors.

"Dr. Salinger?" the guard spoke up. "I'm afraid we need a decision from you."

Hugh closed his eyes before turning to look at the man. When he did, the guard placed a hand gently on the power-gun at his hip.

"You all truly believe this is the answer to what happened with the war?"

"I know I do. I lost everything in the war. Now I have it all back—plus more to spare."

Hugh nodded, his stomach flipping. "And if I choose to accept this, if I tell you I agree, I get the same benefits of the citizens?"

"Better than them, I think. You actually get to enjoy it."

"Then," Hugh carefully chose his words trying not to trip over his obvious disgust, "I think this is a brilliant organization. Yes. You can count on me."

The guard grinned and walked over to Hugh, holding his hand out.

"Welcome to Public One, Dr. Salinger. Please follow me to your initial exam."

—REGGIE—

istorted voices drifting in . . . and out . . . Olivia's hands burning with shocks of pain and electricity. She wanted to get out. "We want to welcome . . ." the voice died off as the tinkling of a bell somewhere in the distance took over. "Go to Hell," she growls. "Reggie," Nate says my name softly. Differently. Shivers tingle up my spine. The sound of a gun going off ripped through my ears once, twice . . . three, four. BANG!

A rippled breath shoots through my lungs as I push away, kicking free from my blanket. I can't get control of my heart. I'd heard the shots before. Normal handgun shots. I'd seen Olivia before, she was still there.

It was Nate. The way he touched me. It doesn't make sense. My reaction. What's happening?

I look over at Nate in the bunk across the cabin trailer from me. His arm is dangling off the side and his legs are too long for the short bunk. What's happening?

I can't look at him. Not right now. I push the blankets off and slip my feet into my boots that I set on the ground before I'd gotten in bed. The rich bitter odor of smoke lingers on my blankets, wafting when I move out from under them. The fire just feet away is still smoldering with pops and hisses. London is the only one still awake. He has a single stick poking around at the embers that glow and diminish.

"You're still awake?" I lower myself into a chair while he turns to look at me.

"Look who's talking."

"I already went to sleep."

London raises his eyebrow. "Your vision was that bad?"

I shake my head.

"Want to talk about it?" London's voice squeaks softly.

"No," I say a little too forcefully. "It's not that important anyway." The breeze blowing around the fire catches my hair intermittently, and puffs of smoke stream in my direction. London blows on the smoke, pretending that if he does, it'll make the smoke lean in a different direction. I can't help but smile.

"My hero," my voice now takes its turn to crack with the irritation of the smoke.

"Great," he smiles with his one crooked tooth. "I've never been someone's hero before. I should blow smoke more often."

I can't help but giggle. My laugh bounces off the aluminum-sided trailer homes like the crickets chirps off in the distance. I turn my head when an opposite trailer door closes. I'm surprised to see Audra walking out, holding a large sweater close around her shoulders with one hand. She looks at us and her eyes open a little more. She's startled to see us, but instead of walking back into the trailer to ignore us, like she's done the rest of the day, she seems to be having an argument with herself. She's hesitant, but her hand is planted firmly on the doorknob, with one foot propped on the step in preparation to pull herself right back inside. It takes her a few moments, but she quickly releases the doorknob and she looks over at me again.

"You're welcome to join us," I say softly. I move my chair closer to London so Audra can pull up a seat. Instead of walking, she shuffles her feet across the ground, sliding them over the dry dirt. She stops at the fire, looking at both of us like a doe—skittish, but curious and protective. Her eyes continue to bounce between me and London, then to the ground, and back to me.

"Would you like to sit with us?" London stands up and pulls out a chair for her.

"Who are you?" Her question is directed right at me. Now her eyes don't move. They're grinding into me. But she's not afraid. Just cautious.

"Me?" I ask. "My name is Reggie."

"No." She shakes her head. "Who *are* you? My son said something."

I nod. Her son looked at me this morning and asked why I glowed. Of all the questions, it was something I've never heard asked before; something I know I'll never forget.

"You're from The Public, aren't you?" she asks.

I nod. "Yes, I am."

"How can that be? You're too old. Not one adult has gifts. Only the children do. The only way he'd see that in you is if you were—" her eyes widen. "You're *it*. Aren't you?"

London looks questioningly at me and then back at Audra.

"I'm sorry," my head shakes, "I don't think I understand what you're saying."

"The precognitive. Isaac always told me stories about the precognitive the city had, but they were always just stories. Things he'd heard at work. My son, he—" Audra looked at the ground, still standing. Not moving. "He's like you. In a way. Both of my sons." She pauses again. I can't tell if she's hesitating to tell me more, or if she isn't sure of the truth. "Sam, my youngest, controls the emotions of other people.

The Public made us paint his room green to aid calmness in him, make him more sensitive to feeling emotions. Of course, with the population the way it is, he's never had to use it. Peter, who you saw, he can see things in others. Other children, at least. He was made to recognize the ability in others."

I frown at her use of "made." So crude. So distant. You make dinner. You make furniture. Not children.

"Peter recognizes those capabilities by a glow . . . he, he says that they glow. He's only ever said that about other children. Never adults."

I now know why she'd been so off-put by me. I'm not sure she fully understands, or cares for her children yet. How could she? Particularly with her understanding of feeling and emotions bombarding her from every angle.

"What color was Peter's room?" London jumps into the conversation. I look over at him, warning him that this isn't part of the conversation. At least not a part that's important.

"Red," she quickly answered. "Red to enhance the neurological pathways in his brain." But she doesn't seem fazed by the thought that The Public was telling her how to raise her children. Or in a sense, *their* children. "You're not what I expected," she says to me.

London makes a rattled jeering noise. "She's not really what *any* of us expected."

"How are your sons now?" I finally ask her.

Audra looks back at the trailer. "Better than I am. They don't have the emotions flooding back to them like me. Most of the time, I actually find the drug is still strong in my system. But, I was supposed to have my immunization," she catches herself and corrects her wording, "my shot, yesterday. Now, I can be perfectly content one moment and falling into sobbing fits the next. Isaac says it's the drugs wearing off, but it's hard.

I remember my mother going through something like this but it was when she was older, I think. I don't know, but it's not the same." She folds her hands together in front of her and looks down at the ground.

"Audra?" I speak softly. "Won't you sit down?"

"Yes!" She beams with such a wide smile, and I finally observe what she was talking about. I can't help but reel back into my chair.

"It's so amazing to meet you!" Her voice is so much louder than before, and I'm afraid that she might wake up the others in the community. "I never thought I'd actually learn that you were real, let alone meet you. Everything that has happened in The Public has advanced because of *you*! The technology, the chance to raise children without disease, it's all because they were able to study you! So many people who would have died outside."

She shakes her head, thinking over what she was saying. Her smile drops and she's now plastered with fury.

"People who would have been happy away from The Public. It was you wasn't it? You told them where my family *was*. My mother, my father, they're all gone! I was happy before you found me! You're a monster! You're not human, you're not human! *Who* does *that to people!?*"

My mouth drops, and I can't catch my breath. Audra has rounded on me and she's on her feet again. Somewhere in the back of my mind, I hear a door open and close, but I'm so focused on her fit. Audra bursts into tears and collapses on the ground. She rocks back and forth, holding her knees.

I push myself out of my seat and carefully walk over to her. My heart pounds, but I rest my hand on her back just to make sure she won't lash out at me before I draw her close and hold her. Audra's body shakes like a blade of grass in the wind. Soft footsteps come up behind us and I bring my head up to see who it is. A little boy, who looks to be no older than two is holding onto Isaac's hand. Instinctively, he puts his little pudgy fingers on his mother's shoulder and the shaking instantly stops.

"Mommy? You nee come a bed," his small voice says. He's extremely tired and I can tell that he's been woken up for this specific purpose. Dealing with his mother's mood swings must be keeping this toddler busy.

I pull my arms away from Audra. She stands up and then picks up her son. "Yes," she says calmly. Only the remnants of water on her face would ever betray her of crying. "It's late isn't it? I'm so sorry," she says to me.

With a free hand she brushes at her cheeks. "Like I said, I'm still adjusting. Come on," she looks down at her son. "Let's go." She kisses her son sweetly on the forehead and brushes his hair back.

Isaac stands by me as his companion and son leave the fire and go back into the trailer. "She's doing much worse than I did. I had very few mood swings when I came off my dosage. That's why The Public never noticed. But she's reacting worse."

"It will pass," I tell him.

He takes a deep breath and folds his arms. "I don't know what she'll be like when it does."

"You're worried she won't love you."

He finally looks at me, pulling his eyes away from the trailer.

"Not like you love her," I add.

Isaac nods and squints back at the trailer. "I'm sorry. I know Nate won't hear it from me, but tell him I'm sorry for leaving the way I did. I just wanted them safe, and I didn't care how I did it."

"We understand."

London shoots a glare my direction, but I pretend not to see it.

"You thought Liam and the others would make it out too. But you still had to protect your family."

Isaac shakes his head. "No. I didn't think that. I knew they'd get hurt and I'd still do it again if I had to. Everything."

I don't know what to say. I've never spoken with this man, and yet after experiencing what his wife went through, I can't help but feel sympathy, despite what he's done. He looks broken and tired.

"I'll tell him."

Isaac nods and his eyes sink to the ground. When he looks back up, he nods once. "Well, thank you. Sorry for Audra, again."

Isaac walks back to the trailer and quickly closes the door behind him. A lump is sitting uncomfortably in the back of my throat. I never knew the full extent to of what The Public was doing. I saw glimpses, but never the whole story. I have to lower myself onto the seat again and I drop my head between my legs, hoping that the spinning will stop. London's hand rubs along my back and he talks to me in soothing tones, but I tune him out.

Seeing what The Public has done to Audra and Isaac's family only heightens the severity of everything. Olivia and Hugh are in there.

What did I do? Why did I go there?

—NATE—

H ere. You might need this." Doran handed Nate a pack. "It's some first aid supplies. It's not much. I'm sorry we can't . . ."

"You have families to take care of. We understand." Nate nodded and lifted the pack up briefly. "Thanks for this. It'll probably come in handy." He tucked it into the bungee cord on the ATV. "Listen, uh . . . make sure you help—you know, Audra and the kids out. They aren't used to this. While you're at it, make sure you keep their husband and father alive. As much as I'd love to grind him into the ground, they need him."

Doran nodded and held out his hand. "Of course we will. Good luck, Nathan."

Nate looked at the ground and nodded, shaking his hand. "Thanks. You too, Doran." Nate turned to check on the others in his party and noticed London and Reggie standing with Audra and talking. "Hey! Reggie, London. We've got to go."

Reggie flinched, but didn't move. It was only London who turned and responded. "Coming!"

It was odd that Reggie hadn't said a word. It'd been like that all morning. He felt she'd deliberately been trying to avoid any contact with him, and yet, he wasn't sure why. Yes, he'd been a complete jerk to her before, but things were better, he thought. Now . . . he didn't know what to make of it. It was extremely irritating, and maybe it was all in his head. Even still, very few things about her made sense. At least now he felt he could trust her. Perhaps it was the fact that she was still having a hard time trusting *him*.

Audra hugged Reggie and the two women held each other for a moment. Reggie let her go and said something with a glance over to the two boys who were playing in the dirt. Audra smiled, wiping away a tear, and nodded. As the two ladies separated, Reggie walked over to Greyson's ATV before Nate called to her.

"Yo! Reggie. You're still with me."

Her face went flush. She turned to Greyson, "I'm sorry, I thought I'd be riding with you this time."

"It's all right, Nate. She can ride with me."

Nate lowered himself into the seat, confused, and feeling a little slighted. But, it was her choice. "All right. London, I guess you're with me."

When the four were ready to go, the engines revved and they took off, leaving the mobile community behind. If they succeeded in this, they'd be making life a little safer for everyone. Although he didn't want to admit it, he was a little disappointed that neither Doran nor anyone else had offered to help. But he understood. They thought their families were safe.

<hr />

Nate thought back on the events of the morning. While leaning on the rough burnt bark of a struggling tree, he looked up at the sky and tried to take it all in. Like déjà vu, he realized he'd done something similar to this a couple nights ago on the porch with Reggie. She'd been so entranced by the stars he realized he'd never actually taken the time to look at them before. The way she reacted to the world, took in its realness and beauty, surprised him. So many things about her were different.

Nate pushed himself back to his feet and kept walking through the trees. Around certain parts of the forest, much of the vegetation wasn't growing anymore. Skeletons of hemlocks, cedars, and firs were reaching out their boney arms and fingers to grab at something, anything to keep them alive. In an instant, the dead patches would end, and things looked like they might make it—desiring more than anything to live. He knew that feeling. He'd been living on that feeling for years. He was tired of it.

Nate leaned down and picked up a rock, hurdling it through the air. Before it struck the ground, a hollow clink rang where the rock hit. No object in nature made that noise and for a split second, he wondered if he'd hit a guard transport from the city that was out roaming the woods. Nate ducked behind a tree and listened.

There was nothing.

No noise. Nate looked around the tree and slowly moved forward. The trees parted and ahead of him a large boulder was placed in the center of the woods. But it wasn't a boulder. It didn't look like it was made by The Public either. This was older, but not by much. Perhaps only fifteen years. On one side of the rock was a set of wide double-set steel doors. Not made of titanium or the duralen metal that many of The Public's buildings and doors were made of. Bulky, heavy, dinged-up, forged steel. Nate ran his fingers along the seams of the doors, but there was no handle, no lock. It was a military bunker. There would be a key pad somewhere that would open it. How old it was, he wasn't sure. It could have even been built pre-twenty-thirty-five.

Nate continued to brush vines and crusted dirt off of the boulder, feeling along for a divot in the rock. When his hand sunk in an extra inch, he flicked away a large cobweb and the mud surrounding it.

These types of bunkers had been made before and during the war; mainly for high-clearance personnel with extra foodstuffs and weapons supplies—not for civilian use. This bunker had been completely forgotten about. Nate wasn't trying to let his hopes get up, but there was a good chance that the things inside had never been touched.

He pulled the face off of the keypad and looked at the wires that ran into the box—red, blue, green, and black wires with solder points. Nate reached into his belt and pulled out a large knife. He cut two wires, stripped them, and slid the knife back. His fingers twitched back and forth before rewiring the right colors and when he heard the hollow clang of steel, his breath caught in his chest. Nate peered around the corner at the doors. One had unlocked and swiveled open about two inches. Slowly, he moved around and slid his fingers between the doorframe and the door, pulling hard on it.

A gust of stale air met his nose—parch, dirt, dust. Inside, everything was dark and looked empty, but as his eyes adjusted to the light, he saw boxes upon boxes stacked along the walls, and a staircase —hundreds of feet deep. There was no way of knowing exactly how much was there until he got a good look.

With no LED on him, he wouldn't even be able to go deep enough to see what each box held. He'd have to come back with Greyson. Maybe there was a chance they'd be able to find supplies to help them through the city. Even a few of the right things would make all the difference.

He stepped back and put all his weight into the door, his feet skidding on the dead pine needles and dirt beneath his feet. With just enough space in the crack to pull it back open again when they returned, he started to back away. He watched the doors carefully before turning to jog back to the campsite.

The journey back to camp took him half an hour. Reggie and London were opening boxed ration meals and adding what little water they had to them. London bumped Reggie's shoulder and she returned it with a bump and a knock against his knee. It bothered Nate. He felt his chest tighten slightly, not wanting to focus on why.

He looked around for Greyson and when he saw him sliding out from underneath one of the ATVs, he hurried over. "Greyson, what's going on?"

"Hey, Nate. I noticed oil leaking underneath the four-wheeler and thought I'd check it out. Pretty quick fix. Where'd you slip off to?" he grunted, pulling himself up. A tendril of his curly blonde hair fell in his eyes and he wiped it back with a blackened oily hand.

"We've got a new development. One in our favor."

Greyson's eyes widened. "What is it?"

"You're not going to believe this. Before the war started, the government built a series of storage bunkers across the country. Most of them, however, were built after the war hit." He nodded with a tug at the corner of his mouth. "I found one. I mean, it looks like it was forgotten about because every single box and crate is still there. I mean, we're talkin' weapons, food, supplies, tech, things we've been without and definitely things that would make this plan a lot simpler. The problem is, with those two headed into the city tonight, we don't have time to go through it thoroughly to see if anything might help them."

"Holy sh—" Greyson ran his hand through the mess of his curly hair and looked over at London and Reggie. "That's amazing. Talk about good timing too."

"Yeah. I wonder if maybe we ought to push things out a day late. Get a good look at what's in there."

Greyson's eyes darted to Reggie and London. "Yeah." He nodded. "What will she say? Maybe she already knows what's in there."

"I don't know." Nate cleared his throat. "I haven't talked to her. Let's tell them, though. I almost wonder if we need to focus on getting them safely in *tonight*, and tomorrow, you and I can raid that thing. I don't want to call this lucky, but if I had to, I wouldn't be surprised if we found cloakers in there."

Greyson's eyes narrowed. "What do you mean?"

Nate smiled. "They were called L87s. The military developed them for the war. These were devices my grandparents only imagined in fiction. Only a few select missions in the states here were able to use them. That's why I'm hoping they might be in there. Soldiers would wear them anywhere on their person, and it masked heat signatures, movement, and scrambled any other tech not on the same frequency."

"Security cameras?"

Nate nodded. "Frozen. Not just a black out or cut to the power, but the frame would actually freeze."

"So anyone watching wouldn't notice anything wrong. Unless someone else was in the frame."

"Exactly."

Greyson rubbed both hands down his face and took a deep breath. "Nate, for the first time I'm thinking we might be able to pull this off."

Nate folded his arms and nodded again. "Yeah, me too."

"Hey, Nate. Greyson. We've got dinners ready," London called to them.

Greyson and Nate joined the other two for the meal and explained to them what had just been found. What it might mean for their part. London became increasingly excited. But Reggie sat listening in silence until Greyson asked for her thoughts.

"That would make sense." Reggie looked at Greyson as she spoke calmly. "I can guarantee those L87s are there. I had a vision I was telling London about. It wasn't anything in particular, but I did see Nate," she motioned to him briefly and then looked away, "walking through the gate as if it were his own front door. With no problems. No one stopping him. I just didn't know why."

"Are you kidding?" London smiled at her. "This is huge. This is monumental. I always wanted to be invisible."

"You do realize, kid," Nate cut in, "that it doesn't actually make you invisible? Just scrambles other devices."

"Potato Pot-ah-to. Right, Reggie?" London reached out and squeezed Reggie's knee and she smirked at him. Nate didn't like it. The two of them getting so close. His gaze remained fixed on Reggie's knee while he took another bite of food, chewing slow. It was just that London was only fifteen. That's what it was. Too young to be involved with a woman almost ten years older than him.

Nate cleared his throat. "That being said. I know what I'd rather do, but you two are the ones scheduled to enter the city tonight. It's up to you. Leave tonight as planned, or wait an extra day or two 'til we can find what we're looking for."

Reggie set her plastic ration tray in her lap and moved her tongue around in her mouth, still looking at the ground. "Putting it off a couple extra days . . . means Olivia's caught in there a couple extra days. I don't think we can afford that."

Reggie furrowed her eyebrows. "I don't want to keep her waiting."

"I agree," London said quietly. Even though his voice showed hesitation, his face portrayed none of it.

"You'll still have to go into the city tonight how we planned. No extra help. We don't have the time or the daylight to search through it tonight."

"Yeah." London finished off the last bite of his meal and then walked back to the truck.

Reggie calmly chewed the remaining spoonfuls of her own, keeping her eyes to the ground. She was easy to read as a whitewashed wall. When she finished eating, she stood up and moved back toward the nearest ATV.

He was sick of guessing. Sick of the evasiveness. Each time Reggie spoke of Olivia, darkness shadowed her eyes and it made him sick inside. She knew something was horribly wrong and yet she wouldn't say anything. Nate set his dinner on the ground and walked after her. He wanted to reach around and make her face him, but he couldn't. Instead, he looked down at her from the side while she pretended not to notice him.

"Reggie, what's happening to Olivia?"

Reggie moved her tongue around in her mouth, her jaw shifting, and she blinked a few times. Without looking up, she simply replied with a whisper, "She's not safe. I already told you. We just need to get her out."

She quickly dropped the last of her meal, two bites of tomato paste and re-hydrated meat cubes slopped to one side, on the back grate of the ATV before it clattered to the ground. Nate shook his head ever so slightly to himself, and watched her move back to London. He needed to know. And she wouldn't say. The vague answers were only pissing him off.

—REGGIE—

"All right, you guys know what to do?"

London and I both nod to Nate. I strap an LED light across my forehead so we can find our way through the night. Nate's gaze lingers on me for a moment, but he sighs and turns away. I know he's irritated. Maybe even angry. But I can't worry about that right now.

"Fine. Good luck you two. And remember that Isaac told us we can get into his home . . ."

". . . with the key pad. Four, four, three, eight, oh, nine," London finishes the sentence. "Believe me, I know. I had it memorized the last four times you told us."

I can tell that Nate is struggling to let London go. I grab London by the arm. "Come on. Let's get moving."

London starts to walk with me but stops to look back at Nate. "We'll let you know when we're in. We'll be fine, Nate."

Even I have to admit that London doesn't sound like the same kid I met a few days ago. Just a few days. That's all. His voice seems deeper, his confidence larger, and his patience for Nate's stubborn will is even steadier. So much change in such a short time, and yet I feel guilty because of it. Right now, I feel guilt about a lot of things.

"Good luck, kid." Nate licks his lips, and glances at me again. For once, I respond—offering a look that promises him nothing will happen to London; that I'll do everything that I can to keep him safe. I mean it. I owe him that.

London and I turn around and walk out of the woods. Our feet crunch on the dry rocky ground, the cloud covered moon barely peeking out at us.

The land seems to stretch on forever. The night air is stifling with heavy heat. It feels like the sun is still baking us in the middle of the night. Beads of moisture slither down my back, soaking into the light fabric of my shirt. I can still smell the remnants of destruction in the air, rising from the earth. Unnatural chemicals mixed with dirt and burned bullets and electricity.

"Any luck, Reggie?"

"Hmm?" I pull myself out of a stupor and look over to London.

"You haven't seen any visions, I guess?"

"Oh, no," I shake my head and kick at a pebble. "But I might be getting closer to figuring out how to get it to come. I think I might almost have it. It's just a little tricky."

I lied. I know he wants good news.

"Good. Because that area right over there is the pipe entrance."

I look around and realize that we've been walking by The Public for a while now. When we arrive, London lifts off the cover. Cool vapors rise from the hole, looking white and ghostly.

Before I can say anything, London offers me his hand to help me in. "No," I shake my head. "You first."

"You sure?" he asks.

"You've been here before," I smile. "I'll follow."

London quickly crawls into the misting pipe and I see him disappear into the darkness. "You got this, Reggie?" he calls to me.

I hesitate at the edge. "Yeah, I'm coming." I promised Nate that London would stay safe. I drop down into a crouch near the pipe's two-foot opening. The moist spray begins to soak my face as I step in feet first and drag the heavy lid shut over my head.

The moist air clogs my throat. Water droplets and dirt line the pipe walls. I force myself to move forward. The fit is incredibly tight. I don't know how London is fitting through this. He's larger than I am. My sharp hips keep catching on the walls and I have to pull forward with my elbows. The more I get stuck, the more my heart pounds. My head throbs and I reach out, clawing at the pipe wall as everything fades around me. Familiar tightening and pulling comes over me. My vision tunnels.

I can't breathe. There's so much pain. My leg. Water. So much water. I want to scream, but I can't.

The vision ends and I gasp for my breath. London calls to me from ahead. "Reggie? Are you coming?"

"London," my voice scratches. "The water!"

"What?" he breathes.

"MOVE!" I scream. "It's coming now!"

"What?!"

"Just go!"

London curses ahead of me. I scramble to squeeze through as quick as I can. Time wears on, the mist soaks my clothing, weighing me down. The light on my head flickers back and forth and I keep trying to look ahead to see London's feet. The haze is thick, and his feet are shuffling farther away. My fingers are numb from the cold, my knuckles stiff, but I have to keep pulling myself forward.

My breathing bounces off the walls of the pipe until I hear a roar. My throat closes off. The mist around me becomes heavier. It's coming. No.

"Go, London!"

I pull myself faster. The water dancing in the air suffocates me with the mildewing rank of the pipe and I can barely breathe. It's so humid. The roar becomes louder and louder. I can't look behind me, but I can hear it. It's coming at me like the roar of a helicopter. My elbows struggle to pull me through faster. The more I panic, the more my arms keep getting stuck. It's coming. The water. Thousands of gallons of water.

My arms keep pulling. My shoulders swivel from side to side. I have to beat it to the opening. The roaring beats through the pipe. Mist swirls around me so thick it's dripping off my hair and into my face.

London shouts at me, "I made it, R—"

The wall of water smashes into me from behind. It pounds into my back and slams my head forward. My face skids across the pipe floor and water fills my nose and mouth, burning my sinuses.

The thrust of water propels me forward far enough that I know I'm only feet away from the entrance to the pool, but I can't breathe. The water rushes against me harder, and my right foot is pushed so far forward over me that my knee is bent. My foot is trapped between the ceiling of the pipe and my rear. I can't move forward and the longer I stay the more I run out air.

My chest is burning, and all that surrounds me is chilling water and darkness. The force of the water presses my chest. I know I won't be conscious much longer. Spinning sensations roll in my head despite the fact that I'm moving nowhere. Ringing tinkles in my ears and white spots dance behind my closed eyes.

I can't feel the edge of the pipe.

Panic takes over me, but I keep trying to pull myself forward. My leg is still caught, pinched between the walls of the pipe and my body. The more I pull, the more I wedge my leg. Pain shoots through my knee. I try to twist my foot to the left, but it won't budge.

I keep reaching my arms out in front of me, trying to grasp onto something—a crack or divot of some kind to pull myself forward.

My lungs start to collapse on themselves—expanding and contracting rapidly. It's happening faster, and I'm getting light headed. The crush of water on my body is too much; I can't focus long enough to grab hold of anything. My hands are so tired. I'm so tired.

A hand wraps around my wrist and pulls me forward. Bolts of pain thread through my knee and up my leg. Screams escape my mouth, bubbling with the remaining air in my lungs. My wrist is pulled once more. Pain. So much pain. My leg shifts awkwardly to the left. My knee pops and mouth opens to scream again, but water fills to the back of my throat and it rushes down my throat, traveling into my lungs. Another yank pulls me forward and my head exits the water. A burst of water flows over my shoulders and I finally open my eyes. Rattling breaths and horrid coughs enter and exit my throat—I try to expel the water that overtook my lungs.

London yanks hard on my arms to get me through. My hips come through the end and he pulls once more. My body falls down on him and the water crashes around us. I break through the dark pool of ice water. It takes all the energy I have in me to kick with one good leg and pull myself to the surface. The water pours in around us, and the roaring rush of water fills the large concrete water reservoir.

"Reggie!" London yells my name.

"I'm," I choke on more water, grimacing at the pain in my leg, "I'm fine. The ladder!"

I head for the ladder and London rushes after me. I strain my muscles to pull my body up out of the roaring pool and I manage to stick my good leg onto the first rung and push up. I start to lift my other leg and my knee throbs with pain. The moment I apply pressure to it to push myself up further, it buckles underneath me and I slip on the ladder, falling back down into the water again.

"London!" My hoarse voice burns. "My knee! I can't get up."

"I'll go first and I'll pull you up."

London climbs up the ladder in a flash; his light blonde hair is plastered to his forehead and neck. He turns and lies on his stomach, holding his arms out. "Okay, go up as far as you can."

I grasp the ladder once more and pull myself up, stepping onto the first rung with my good leg. My hand shoots out for London's and he can barely reach me. He has to pull himself forward farther, putting his center of balance off to fully grab my hand. I hear him grunt to pull me up, but it's not enough. I bite my lip and put pressure on my bad leg to get me the rest of the way up, and then onto the next rung with my good leg.

"Just a couple more, Reggie," he pants.

When I hit the last rung, London reaches for the loops on my pants and pulls me over. I flop on the ground next to him, still coughing water to the floor. I inhale the concrete dust into my mouth, in and out. My breathing is rapid, but as it starts to slow down, I open my eyes. London is sitting next to me, his elbows propped on his knees, and his hands holding his head while he pants.

"You all right?" he asks, turning my direction.

"Yeah," I nod. My arms shake violently as I push myself up. I lean up against the wall. Water still rushes into the pool and the roar eclipses our heavy breaths. "We have to keep going. We can't s-stop."

"Reggie, your leg—"

"It'll be fine," I interrupt him, my voice shaking. "I don't think it's too bad, but I'll need some help."

London helps me to my feet, and I hobble around on my shaking leg. "Reggie, you can barely walk."

"I'll be fine, London. I'll make it work." I put my weight on the wall, leaning into it as I walk. My leg wants to crumple beneath me every time I step on it, but I reach the door and pull it open. London rushes over to hold it and I push my way through.

"You look ridiculous. Let me help you." London slips his arm around my back and I loop mine around his neck. With the extra pull on my side, I'm able to keep most my weight off my bad leg.

"Thanks, London. Let's go."

We hobble down the hallway and London guides us through. His teeth keep grinding together while he helps me walk. He's taking too much of my weight on himself, but it's helping us move faster.

When we make it out of the building and onto the street, London suggests we stop and rest. "No." I look at him sideways. "We have to get to the Tunnel. The sooner we get to Isaac and Audra's home, the sooner we can stop. But not 'til then."

London protests, but I pull us forward, nearly falling on my bad leg. He hoists me up and we almost make it up to a run-walk pace. I can see the signs on the streets leading us closer to the Tunnel. Shadows move around randomly. It's after curfew, so we continue to dive in and out of sight which slows us down. London peeks around the edge of a building and starts to motion for me before he shoves both of us down on the ground. A pair of guards are patrolling the streets.

"Lieutenant, do you smell that?"

My eyes flash open wide.

"Smell what?"

"I'm not sure. Moisture. Something else."

The guard points to the water treatment center. "It's Wednesday. Water."

"I dunno. It's different." The guard sets his hand on his power-gun. "I just wanna check it out."

"It's a smell. Let's keep moving. We'll be late for rotation."

Both guards continue on down the street and I wait 'til they're around the corner.

I grab at London's wrist. "Now."

London eyes me carefully. But he nods and reaches for my hands to carefully pull me up, wrapping an arm around my waist.

"We don't have time to cater to me. Just *go!*"

Without hesitation, he yanks me along and my knee strains. Behind my gritted teeth I hiss, "*Run faster.*"

Each step, each jostle, and every move we make toward the Tunnel feels as if my knee will rip free of the tendons and muscles. Every time London begins to soften for my sake, I bark a whisper in his ear to keep going. My knee won't matter if we both get shot.

"Reggie?"

"Keep going!"

We make our way to the Tunnel and get on board. The doors slide shut behind us and I collapse with a groan onto a seat. "Thank you," I whisper.

I hear him swallow in the silence of the train, and it begins to speed through the city. There's nothing said between us. London keeps looking out The Tunnel windows, and when we come to the right stop, he helps me up again. Every time my foot touches the ground, my knee gives out, but London keeps me propped up. It isn't long before we reach the house and London gets us in.

The door closes behind us. I hobble to the couch and fall onto it. London leans against the door. We both sit in absolute darkness. Time passes. Finally, London moves from the door and drops into one of the seats next to me.

"We made it," he whispers.

All I can do is sigh and try to ignore the pain in my leg.

"Reggie?"

"Yeah?" I whisper.

"This may not be the right time. But maybe it is."

"What is it, London?" I grimace, my knee shooting pain.

"Do you, with all the visions you have. Do you ever relive them? See them again, I guess. Like echoes?"

My head turns and I look at him. "What?"

"I guess I just thought that killing an enemy would be easy. Right? I mean, the guard. I just," he pauses and takes a deep breath, "I see it *all the time*. Do you ever have that?"

"I have a photographic memory." I pause. "So, yes. I see it all the time."

"Does it get easier?"

I take a deep breath and hold it within my chest, swirling around like my thoughts. I gently blow it out. "London, it's hard because you're a good person. One of the best. And when a good person takes someone's life, I think it's always hard."

"But will I stop reliving it? Do you ever stop seeing your echoes?"

"London," I can't lie to him. "If anything, they become more vivid for me. But I'm not like you. My mind works differently. If you want to ask someone about that. I think Nate would answer your questions better."

London's face falls. "That's what I'm afraid of." He sniffs dryly and runs and hand through his hair. "I can't end up like him."

A stabbing pierces my heart. The absolute silence of the home bores into my ears. I don't know how else to comfort him—what to do or say to ease his conscience. There's little to say when you're afraid of becoming your own worst version of someone.

—NATE—

The door on the boulder creaked loudly, reverberating through Nate's arms. Rust and dirt broke off and shot in different directions from the hinges. He and Greyson peered into the darkness and stepped inside. Boxes and crates rested upon boxes and crates. Some were small and simple, but others were extremely large with complicated locks and key pads. Nate pulled the hammer out of his belt loop and thrust the claw between two boards of one of the simpler wood crates. The nails squeaked as they came out of the tight wood, and when the lid popped off, Nate couldn't help but smile.

"We've got ammo in the crates." Nate fingered a key pad on a long horizontal case. "I think the longer locked cases here are the guns."

"What type of 'munition?" Greyson left the box he was trying to wrestle open and went to see what Nate had.

Nate reached in and pulled out a thin tube full of miniature metal spheres. The spheres were about a quarter inch in diameter.

"Military grade power shot? Thank you, God," Greyson said, leaning over the case. "Maybe he is looking out for us after all."

"I don't know about God, but it's definitely good. Let's see if we can get this longer case over here open. It's combo locked, but if we can rewire the panel, we might be able to get it to open."

It took them a few tries, some reprogramming, but the case snapped open. Both men grinned. "Power rifle. I may just have to kiss you, Nate." Greyson chuckled and looked to the back of the bunker. "I wonder how deep this goes."

"I'd guess about a mile. Wanna put on your LED and follow me down?"

"Yeah."

With their LEDs leading the way, Nate went down first. He curved along a few more stacks of crates and cases before he saw the beginning of a concrete stairway. Set into the stone wall was a titanium rod that led the entire way down. He was relieved to see that the stairwell only dropped down about ten feet and then moved forward again. If it was possible at all, things were getting darker. But the moment they took the last step, he could see a room just off to the left. No door. Nate walked through and found shelves of boxes. Each one stamped with a United States Ration seal. All food. At least two years worth for a small platoon. They found four other rooms—each containing the same amount of rations—kept cool and dry, and perfectly fine.

But it wasn't the food Nate was looking for. Soon, they'd be in Public One with London and Reggie anyway with plenty of food—most likely tasting better than rations. If he could just find the one item he needed, their entrance into the city would be too easy.

"What is it, Nate?"

"If they're in the bunker, they're not down here."

"What?"

Nate pulled a few ration boxes back into place and took his LED off, running a hand through his hair and placing the light back on. It seemed that everything in storage below where it was cooler was all food. "Remember the L87s I told you about? If any were stored in here, I think they might be back up top with the rest of the weapons—easily accessible if the military needed them. It'd make sense."

Greyson's eyes went wide.

"What? That look on your face, what is it?"

Greyson spun around. "Come on."

"What are you talking about?"

"Nate, remember that first case I was trying to open when we walked in? I couldn't get it open?"

"Yeah." The light from Nate's LED bounced around the walls and off the staircase. When they arrived at the case, Greyson's finger pointed at a stamp on the side.

"L87," Nate murmured. "Lot number 122875. United States of America." The case was only two feet in length, and about five inches deep. No wonder he'd initially looked over it. "It's fingerprint locked. That's why you couldn't get in before." Frustration coursed through his body, but he knew there had to be a way to break in. What would be the point of fingerprint locking a military weapon case? What one person could open it up? Unless it wasn't just one person that could open it up.

He reached to his pocket, pulling out his knife again. He had to see what kind of locking mechanism was on the case. He'd only seen two kinds. A secure storage lock, which held extremely sensitive information—usually only enough information for one fingerprint—and a network storage lock, which connected to a server. Its ability to connect to multiple information files was almost limitless.

"What are you thinking, Nate?"

"If I can find," he gently popped off the face of the mechanism, "what kind of lock this is I might be able to open it up."

"How?"

"Easy." Nate looked up at him with a triumphant smirk. "My own fingerprint. And the fact that this is a network lock, pretty much confirms that."

"What? How?"

"If . . . *if*, being the key word, this lock still has access to whichever satellite server it connects to, it'll match my fingerprint. I think this unlocks only for military personnel. At least, that's what I'm hoping." He carefully placed the face back on and ran his finger across the pad. The lock came to life and a short set of directions appeared on the screen. "Place Right Index Finger."

Nate pressed his finger on the pad. The words above his finger disappeared and the screen turned green. His own military identification came on the screen. An old photograph from his file—an unmarred sixteen-year-old. A set of bright blue eyes that had never seen war. A boy who still had family, with a bright future who had no idea of the darkness his life would become.

Innocent.

The next set of directions appeared on the small pad. "Identification Code." Nate plugged in his eight digit code—the familiar ripples of color radiating away from his touch on the pad. For a moment, he wondered if he'd forgotten it or punched it wrong, but a click was followed by a hiss of released pressure. Nate quickly pulled himself back. Inside the case, four sets of L87s sat. Waiting for them.

The journey to the city limits had been almost completely silent between the two men. Nate felt a nervousness he couldn't explain. It wasn't from The Public. It was even different from the nervousness of war.

Dirt grinded beneath their feet as they walked the few miles from the edge of the forested area to the walls of The Public. The weather had turned brisk on them again. Each puff of air escaping from Nate's nose or lips hung in the air. It was cold enough to be December. The bright lights of the large city ahead of them shone out like a mechanical sun rising over the horizon. But unlike the sun, they glowed only for themselves. Almost nothing outside city limits was touched by the lights. It was almost like the glow was being sucked back inside.

"Now would be a good time to activate your cloaker," Nate said, pressing his fingertip into his own device. It hooked in a loop around one ear, wrapped tightly around the back of his head, and then looped around his other ear. Greyson copied him as they approached the gate.

"You sure this'll work?"

"I guess we'll find out."

A few more steps. That's all they had before they'd be inside. Nate remembered what happened the last time he'd stepped through—a fist in the gut and a drug injection.

He walked through the gate, keeping to the outer edges, the shadows, just in case actual eyes were on them. Greyson followed him. There was no movement from the guard building. No one came out. But there were noises above the ambience of the night. From somewhere in the center of the city.

"How do we get to the house?"

"Follow me." Greyson moved ahead of Nate and they hurried toward the Tunnel. This late at night, past The Public curfew, it was odd that such noise was coming from the city. Nate hadn't expected to hear something going on.

Nate saw the entrance of the Tunnel in front of them. It reminded him of a simple rail-car station he'd seen in smaller cities years ago.

It stopped and double sliding doors smoothly opened. A dozen people began to evacuate the train and both men quickly ducked into the shadows. The group's feet almost seemed to glide across the ground with each step—so smooth and unpressed. Something wasn't right. It was after curfew. This many people shouldn't be out on the streets.

Nate and Greyson rushed to the Tunnel and the doors slid shut behind them. "Thank you for selecting Public One's transportation Tunnel. We appreciate your help in keeping our air free of pollutants and welcoming a more perfect tomorrow," a calm and mechanically content voice welcomed.

The city outside instantly disappeared. The car was moving fast enough that his eyes couldn't focus on just one image outside. A massive blur of black streaks and glows of green and white lights trekked by the windows. The stale smell of cleanliness and sterility surrounded him. The bright white of the interior was enough to make him squint.

Nate looked over at Greyson who had his head down, resting his elbows on his knees. The obvious anxiety of wanting to find Sophia was weighing on him. Just in the last couple days since they'd left the community, Greyson had aged. The circles around his eyes were darker, and pre-mature wrinkles gathered around his face, dirt caked inside crease of each one. His curly hair hung limp over his ears. Greyson was in a living hell.

As the Tunnel came to a stop, the contented voice returned and ushered them off. Without words, Greyson led Nate down the roads and they finally arrived at a home not unlike the others around it. Simple, but large. Geometric clean lines. A solitary light was on in the front window. Greyson pressed the pad on the front door, and they waited. Nothing could be heard from within, and Nate worried they'd come to the wrong home. But the door soon slid open smoothly and London's tired face greeted them. "Get in, get in. We're glad you guys made it. We were both worried. We've been sitting here wondering if anything had happened."

"With all the people out there?"

"You know about it?" London asked just as Reggie limped heavily into the room from the hallway.

London was dressed in Public attire. White from neck to toe. The short but straight collar of his neckline was only half an inch tall and stiff. The sleeves were long and the entire top looked heavy like a stiff jacket. It tucked into the belted pants he wore and they brushed right below the tops of his arches.

Reggie was dressed in a simple white bath robe. Her face. Her mousy hair were so different. It was still long, but braided into thick braids that wrapped in a twist behind her right ear, at the base of her neck. Her face was lightly painted with makeup. Some color on her cheeks, focus on her eyes. They were so bright. So silver blue they were almost clear.

She took another step with a limp and Nate dragged his gaze from her face to her leg. Her right knee was obviously wrapped with a brace beneath the robe she wore and looked over-padded.

"Know about what?" Greyson asked.

"There's what they're calling an Induction Ceremony tonight. The city officials will introduce all the new city 'members.' We heard about it on the television." London pointed to a large ninety inch digital display that was running silently across the white wall. Included with the weather forecast were news bulletins. Running over and over.

"I'm surprised no one saw you," London added.

"There was a lot of noise coming from the center of the city. Everyone is probably already there."

"London and I were going to go." Reggie shifted her weight. "Might be a good time to find out where they've placed Hugh and Sophia and the others." She took a couple steps forward, her eye brows diving under the strain.

"Then we're going too," Greyson took off his jacket.

"You'll need to get cleaned up," Reggie answered. "There are some more clothes of Isaac's in the second bedroom, but I don't think Nate will fit," she said as if he wasn't there. "London?"

"On it."

London left the house and disappeared outside.

"Where is he going?" Nate asked as Greyson moved down the hallway.

"To get clothes for you." She smiled and hobbled on a board-straight leg over to a seat.

Nate shook his head. "Where?"

"Let's say we'll be borrowing them."

He followed and sat down in a chair opposite. "Stealing, you mean."

Reggie half-smiled at him and nervously touched her hair.

"What happened, Reggie?"

"Hmm?"

Nate nodded toward her leg and she sucked in a deep breath.

Her hands reached for her knee and she tried to bend it against the brace. But the extra padding prevented her from doing much with it. "Nothing. Just something small. You should, uh, take the second shower in the master bedroom. London will have clothes for you when you're done."

Every ounce of him wanted to keep pressing her on the subject. But he thought better of it. She didn't want to talk about her leg, or anything else it seemed. Quietly, he stood, still watching her carefully, and knelt down in front of her.

"No, Nate. Please, I'll be all right."

He felt underneath the robe around the padded knee and looked up at her. "What did you wrap it with?"

"My shirt," she whispered and almost chuckled. "London helped. He felt bad it wasn't him that got hurt."

He narrowed his eyes on her. "What happened, Reggie?"

"I got caught behind London in the water pipe. With the water," she added, almost as if she'd forgotten about it. "He was fine. I made sure."

London, the one person Nate worried about most. She'd kept him safe.

Nate cleared his throat and reached down to lift her foot a few inches. The muscles in her legs tensed and he glanced up at her face. Pain had clamped her mouth shut and she looked up at the ceiling. This time, trying to be more careful, he ran his hand up her calf before gently lifting. The opening of the robe fell back over her leg.

Reggie jerked and hissed. Nate's eyes darted toward her thigh and back up at her face.

"Sorry," she whispered. "I wasn't expecting that."

"What?" He laid her foot down again.

Reggie blushed and shook her head. "Nothing."

It was too hot in Isaac's home. Nate pulled off the unbuttoned plaid shirt he wore and set it on the ground. His dirty t-shirt hung loosely on him.

"I want to get a good look at that. It could be a simple sprain, but if it's worse than that, we'll have to figure something out."

"I'll be all right," she repeated.

Against her protests, he gently felt around the knee. "I'm gonna re-wrap this for you." He looked up at her, hesitating. "You trust me?"

Reggie took a deep breath and met his eyes. "Yeah."

After examining the makeshift wrap, he found the end and untied it. The cloth was torn into wide lengths and wrapped tight. With each unwind, the cloth fell to the ground. When he finally saw her knee, he ran his fingers over the smooth but swollen purple skin. Goosebumps poked up on her lower thigh and down her calf. Slowly he moved her foot down and back up, watching the way the tendons and muscles moved, feeling for shifting. Nate saw Reggie grip the chair armrest and he released a sigh.

"Sprained. Not torn." He frowned. "But that doesn't make it feel any better. I'll wrap this better for you."

"Thank you," she whispered.

Nate looked up at her. In the kitchen Nate found two long white dish towels. He paused before returning to Reggie, not entirely sure why.

Though she wouldn't tell him the details, she'd watched over London just like she promised. If she'd been caught in the pipe, that meant she almost drowned herself in the process.

His pulse raced. He swallowed.

When he went back, Reggie was biting down on her nail, staring at the ground.

"These ought to work." He held up the towels.

Reggie gave him a tentative smile.

"Thank you," Nate said, wrapping up her swollen knee.

"What for?"

"For watching over London. I owe you."

"You pulled me out of here. I owed *you*."

"I was a dick. I owe you more."

At that, Reggie chuckled. "True."

Nate finished wrapping her sprain and ran a hand over the taught fabric. "This should work better."

Reggie's breath shook. "Thank you. You need to go get ready."

Pushing himself up, he left her and headed for the master bedroom. Minutes later, Nate stepped out of the raining shower and wrapped the light fabric "towel" around his waist. It was not the same fabric he'd been used to in a towel, but it worked better than anything else he'd ever felt. Water dripped from his long shaggy hair into his face and he mussed it with his fingertips. Electric titanium hair clippers and a razor had been laid out for him. He looked at himself in the mirror. He couldn't remember the last time he'd actually looked at his reflection. It was an odd feeling to not remember himself. Not that mirrors had never been available—he just hadn't needed one.

Nate picked up the clippers and turned them on. The light hum of the mechanism became louder as he placed it near his ear and buzzed his entire head. Tufts of dark hair fell to the floor around his feet. When he looked back at himself, his hair was only a quarter inch long. Not since the war had his hair been this short.

He stopped to stare at himself, the razor resting in his hand, thinking about Reggie. He couldn't stop thinking about her.

Shit.

What was he doing? Why her? Why now? Nate lowered the razor to the countertop and stepped back. He needed to shake it off. Olivia was waiting for him. She loved him. He was here to save her. Her, Sophia, Ben. All of them. There wasn't time to think about anything else. He'd have to compartmentalize whatever had just happened out there with Reggie; everything he was thinking about.

He picked up the razor again and completely removed any trace of hair on his face. A small jar of face cream sat out on the counter and he shook his head. London told him he had to use it. It would remove the look of weathering on his face. He needed to look pampered. He dipped his fingers in the jar and rubbed the cream around his face, dragging his hand down his cheeks, mad at himself.

The tingling happened immediately, waking up his skin, healing the hard and worn areas, and evening out the tan lines on his face. It continued to tingle and rejuvenate as he got dressed. He stepped out of the bathroom and met the other three. Greyson's curly hair was still long, but sleek with oils and pulled back into a ponytail.

"All right," he said, catching Reggie's eye and tucking it all away, "let's go."

REGGIE

Tranquil sounds emanate from the gathering. It's music I think. Strange. What I don't understand is that, music throughout history was composed to elicit emotion. And there isn't a single soul around us who can feel anything. So the music is void of any feeling except—uneasy satisfaction. The rhythmic ping, ping, ping . . . thrum, thrum . . . ping, ping, ping of a basic percussion is disturbing. The people we pass smile and nod at us, not feeling happiness, just unusual naiveté. A giant projection screen is coming from the side of the health building. The structure is pointed on the top and has curved sides. It almost reminds me of rockets that I've seen in visions. Sleek, streamlined, and smooth.

People chatter around us and I limp my way through, trying hard to hide it. They're all wearing the same style of clothing. No variation, no character in their appearance. Elaborate braids and twists in each woman's hairstyle. The men's are all slicked back. Little twinkles spring through the air like fireflies. I try to feel them, but I can't. The light travels over my hand and disappears. Each one the same. The twinkles dance with the melancholy beat of the sounds in the air—if you could call it music.

Greyson intently keeps his eyes on every face that passes him. He's looking for any familiarity. If only we could find Olivia, Hugh, or even Sophia, who looks so much like her sister, it would calm one of us down. But it makes me nervous being this close to those who could capture me. Close to Dryer.

All it would take is one person. One guard who's seen me before. I'd be back in my cell. And tomorrow morning my nightmares would return. Dryer would comb through my mind. Nate would no longer exist. Greyson would be gone, and I would never see London again.

"Where do we go? What's going to happen, Reggie?" Nate says into my ear. The warmth of his breath tickles the loose hairs near my neck.

I worry that my face is flushing and I drop it before two guards walk by me. "I don't know. Something about this feels familiar, like I've seen it." I whisper. Though, I do have an inkling. Perhaps that's why this feels so recognizable. I pray that it's not what I remember.

I turn to Nate, "We need to figure out how to get to Olivia."

I'm nervous not knowing what's going to happen tonight. If only I'd had a vision last night to guide me, perhaps I'd be calmer. My brain doesn't respond the way I wish it did. Instead, my mind follows things. Chasing after a thought pattern. Like a string left behind someone, wrapping and curling around anything it passes.

I know I can do it again. I just need to get to a place where I can be alone. Where no one will notice me.

I reach for London's hand and he grabs it. "Are you having a vision?" he whispers.

"Come with me."

London nods to get Greyson and Nate's attention and they all follow me around the side of a building. Walking is still difficult. The temporary knee brace isn't the most effective support. Any pressure still makes my leg want to collapse.

The sparkling lights in the air are not prevalent away from the crowds, but they linger around us. Blinking on and off. "London, I need you to balance me. I'm going to try to force a vision. But I can't be seen. If anyone sees what I'm doing—" Nate puts his hand on my shoulder, and I can't help but feel a leap of anxiety at his touch.

"We're keeping watch."

I take a deep breath and let it out. I close my eyes and lower my head, focusing on the pace of my breathing. Focus on my mind. Push out the pictures and noise around me.

The tinkering music swells and plummets through my ears. I let my mind wander to Hugh, imagining where he could be. I amble down a reflectionary path, from face to face. From possibility to possibility. Wind seems to be rushing around my ears, but I feel nothing on my skin. A tunnel of thoughts rushes by, and it's hard to focus on anything. The thoughts spin faster and faster. I don't know how to control it. I've never experienced this before and I don't know how to stop it. The rush becomes tighter and tighter. Pressure builds up behind my head, pressing me forward. I'm being compacted between two forces. A prism of colors explodes behind my eyes. My head feels shoved forward and slammed into a concrete wall. My jaw is locked shut and blood is rushing violently around in my skull. I feel like I can't breathe.

Something's happened. I buckle in pain, barely able to breathe. It's not right. *It's not supposed to happen like this!* What's happened to me? My head . . . my head. The back portion of my brain feels like it's exploded right out of my skull.

"Reggie!" London's voice is frantic. "What happened? Are you all right?" His thin hands grab the side of my face and his thumbs massage the joints of my jaw, easing it to release.

"I . . . don't know," I finally say. My voice is barely audible and shakes uncontrollably. I feel like the base of my neck has blasted in two. I raise my eyes and look at London. Greyson and Nate are behind him, their eyes wide. "My head. In the back." I reach around limply to cradle the top of my neck. It's fine, but inside, it's on fire. "It's the ch-chip. Something happened. That wasn't supposed to happen. Everything went wrong. I think it came from the chip in my head."

"I thought Hugh removed the transmitter." Nate narrowed his eyes.

"He did. This wasn't a transmission," I gasp, and close my mouth, trying to keep my jaw from shaking. "It didn't feel like that." My mind rushes at a thousand miles per minute, lacing around strands of thought patterns and events. Images set off colors of white and green. Sounds push them away and all of a sudden the sights around me become intensely colorful. With another loop, the colors behind my eyes spin and I can't handle it all. I can't slow the images down, and I squeeze my eyelids shut. The threading continues and I hold tight to London's hand.

"The chip feels like it's burning. I don't know how to explain it. But it's—" my hands still shake, "it's on fire. I felt as if it burst in . . . ."

I can't finish the statement. I can barely control anything. "It's just my head. It's never been—I don't know what I did. I did it wrong." I shake my head and try to take another deep breath.

"Can you walk?" London continues to hold me on my feet.

"I don't know. Something's wrong. What happened? What did it do to me?" I look down at the ground, my words continuing to spill out.

"That wasn't—" I start and stop. "I don't know. *Reggie, what did they do to you?*" I hiss under my breath. "What have you done?"

"Do you think you're going to be all right?"

I don't know how to answer. I don't know how I feel. Something's changed. There's a film of residue on my thoughts—like I'm trying to remember something, but the more I focus on it, the more it hides. Nothing feels like it should. I've never been normal; I've known that for years, but I never felt . . . I've never felt broken like this.

I'm not the same. Not the same as I've been and I can't figure out what's happening to me.

"Citizens of Public One," a familiar man's voice echoes behind me and I spin around, nearly falling over. Nate's hands steady me, and I instinctively jump from him. But my eyes are locked on the projection screen in the sky. Dryer's familiar voice. His face. A seething hatred bubbles in my stomach and I feel sick. "We welcome you this night. June twenty seventh, twenty fifty-five. You, who have all been generously rescued, found, and saved, are added to this day. We welcome our newest citizens of Public One."

As he talks, the faces of people I saw in my vision begin to show on the screen. A man, a teenage girl, the woman who looks like Olivia—I hear Greyson gasp—and a handful of others. Their expressions are gone, and they look through the screen with straight eyes.

"In two-thousand thirty-seven, war came to the boundaries of North America. The largest the globe had ever seen. The human race became an endangered species . . ."

Dryer's voice fades out and images of war and battle flash across the screen. My stomach rolls and the sights and sounds on the screen start to make my throat close off. Those are mine. My visions. They're showing my visions.

"Soldiers were dying in countless waves in overseas battles, and the country known as The United States of America would not survive. Only one year into World War Three, and boys started being drafted before the age of seventeen."

I look over at Nate and his face is stone. His eyes are locked on the screen, and the only time he moves is when he swallows. He was one of those boys.

"It was at that time, that a man who had devoted his life's work to peace and genetic research, saw a better path. In this area, this sacred ground, he began his work. Public One was the first of four governmental cities. In its first year, it consisted of only a few vacant buildings, one of them being the miracle tower. This great building, the Ponanki building, the tallest tower in the world was left still standing. This man, with the aid of brilliant architects, doctors, and the best remaining leaders in the United States began to join together to save mankind."

Pictures of Public One in its early stages fade in and out on the screen. It's just as I remembered it my first day. Small, and guarded by a tall chain fence. My face burns.

"Then the second miracle. Public One received new technology. Technology that allowed them greater protection. And during the remaining eight years of the war, that protection proved invaluable, bringing more than just warning, but the answer to human weakness."

London's wrist brushes against mine, but I don't dare look at him. We all know what the technology was. It was me. I came to them willingly.

"In an unprecedented time, only eighteen years, with the aid of willing scientists, physicists, geneticists, and other brilliant professionals, The Public has grown four-fold. Public One is the home of nearly three hundred thousand American refugees. With four Publics spanning the globe, the world's population is beginning to grow faster than we thought possible, in Europe, China, South America, and of course, North America."

More images play on the screen. People smile while shaking hands on the street, structures and buildings being built, and a young companion set holding a new baby in their arms.

"Today we welcome the new members of Public One. We owe it all to one man. I'm pleased to announce that our president, our governor and chief, the brilliant Martin Lobb is with us."

"Reggie," Nate hollers at me through a roar of applause, "who's Martin Lobb?"

I shake my head, mouthing, "I don't know."

⸺OLIVIA⸺

The soft wash of pale green lights. Cold metal around her wrists. A buzzing hum that swam inside her head.

Olivia's eyes could barely part, but when they did, the naked white room around her was the only thing to welcome her. She couldn't concentrate on anything. Her mouth was dry and parched, her lips cracked and peeling. With each movement of her head, the picture in front of her eyes rolled and rocked like the room was on a teeter-totter. The muscles in her neck couldn't hold her head up, and it slumped forward to her chest again.

Everything that'd happened to her, since she didn't know when, was a dark empty blank. The last thing she remembered was leaving the group, crouched into the back of the truck that Hugh drove. She didn't need to ask where she was. But how long had she been there?

For a few moments her eyes would open. Then they'd drop again, and the weight would pull her consciousness down with it. Even with the opening of a door in front of her, she was too exhausted and buzzed to know what was going on. Footsteps clapped against the floor and when they stopped in front of her, she took time to notice the shined black leather surface of the shoes. The cuffs of dark gray silk pants hit in just the right place.

"We worried about you there for a moment, young lady. Thought you might have had an allergic reaction to the drug. Glad to see that you're waking up." The voice rumbled like thunder. It was deep, empty, and if there was any emotion behind it, it was false.

"Where? Where am I?"

"Don't tell me you don't recognize anything. Oh, but then it wasn't you Charles questioned before, was it? That would have been your partner, Captain Naylor. He was quite the resistant, I've been told. It's too bad Dryer didn't kill him when he had the chance." The voice paused. "You'll be more cooperative, won't you?"

A crash of information came back to her as she remembered everything. Her eyes opened further and she looked up at the man across from her. His thinning peppered gray hair was slicked back, his face pulled up in a confident gaze.

"I'm in The Public," she answered.

He smiled at her. "Yes. Only this time we know *why* you came back. There is one thing I don't know though. Tell me, Ms. Woodstock. Why didn't Reggie stop you?"

Olivia looked from side to side, up her arms. They were raised above her head. She lay along an inclined metal slab, and her wrists were clamped to it. Down below, her ankles were also securely clasped to the bed. The sharp metal edges of the cuffs dug into her wrists. "Where's my father? Where's my sister?" She looked back at him, awake now.

The man shook a finger in front of her. "That's not the way this works, I'm afraid. You trespassed on private property and broke the law. You stole from me. I can't forgive that. There will be no bargaining. There will be no deal."

"Sorry. Who *are* you?"

"My name is Martin Lobb." The man's face fell and he folded his arms. "Which would mean nothing to you. You do understand the situation, don't you, Ms. Woodstock?"

Olivia sniffed. "How *do you* know who I am?"

Lobb walked a circle around her. "You mean, how do I know your name? Or how did we recognize you in the woods? I guess it doesn't really matter. Both answers are relatively simple. First of all, *Olivia*, the United States Government kept an . . . uncharacteristically close record of each citizen born between twenty fifteen and it's fall, in twenty forty-six. Your fingerprints, DNA print, and other identifying marks were on file just like anyone else's. Second," he came around her left side, "you didn't think you were that unrecognizable did you? Was the beating your idea or did you make some jokes at your negro friend's expense?"

"You're sick."

Lobb's lips drew up into a crooked smile. From a small rolling table near her, he lifted up a long spindle. "Have you ever seen one of these?"

Olivia looked at him, feeling sick.

"Your friend, Captain Naylor, has. Did a number on his face, I understand. Only a touch of the tip to skin can create the most horrific pain you've ever felt. My comrade, Dr. Dryer, prefers the non-invasive and, I should say, *humane* forms of affliction. Like this. But," he set the spindle back on the table and picked up a pair of old pruning cutters, "I'm not like him. I'm in it for the fun, Olivia. I want you to pay. You can't get something for nothing. You got Reggie, I get you. I just want to hear you beg for your life. If you don't you'll begin to lose each one of your fingers every day until I hear what I want.

When I run out of fingers, I'll move on to your toes. When we cut off the last one, I'll kill you. Then your father. While I'm at it, I might as well kill the rest of the occupants from your pathetic little nomadic tribe. They mean just about as much to me as the dirt between your toes. Except, it would be a real disappointment to lose Sophia. She's already partnered. Still, we already have everything we need from her." He tilted his head and smiled again. "So, you want to help me out?"

Olivia took her eyes off of him and set her head back, staring at the ceiling.

"I'll take that as a no." Lobb walked to her side, motioning to the camera. It floated through the air over towards them. He uncurled her pointer finger, placed the cutters around her digit and looked into her eyes. "Olivia, you have no idea how much I'm going to enjoy this."

She didn't move. Even her breathing was calm. If this was the way that she left the earth, she'd do it gladly. A promise of her life wouldn't keep him from killing her the moment she gave him what he wanted—she knew that well. Men like Lobb destroyed any trace of disturbance or rebellion. She'd known his kind. Her father had told her about the Hitlers, the Stalins, the Mussolinis. Every leader, every government had become corrupt and full of self-power. They never governed for the good of the people. Always for the good of the self. If Public One got Reggie back, they'd kill Nate, Greyson, London. All of them. Just to destroy any chances of their return.

"Nothing?"

Nothing.

In one swift movement, a piercing pain shot across her finger and down her arm. When the shock of losing her finger hit her brain, her mouth opened in a silent scream. It caught inside her lungs, in her throat, like a brick wall had blocked it off. After taking a second breath, the haggard sound of ripping vocal chords pierced her ears. The sound was ghostly.

"Olivia," Lobb's voice was hard and taunting, "come on. Beg."

──NATE──

"Welcome, everyone!" A man appeared on the screen. He looked to be in his forties, but something about his youth wasn't right. His salt and pepper hair was slicked back neatly, his dark gray suit was the perfect contrast to the deep crimson shirt and tie he wore. Crisp. Perfect.

"I'm not one to mince words, but suffice it to say, I'm very happy to be here to officially give a special reception to our new citizens. We want each of you to know that we are doing everything in our power to keep you safe. This is your home." Then, as if he knew Nate was watching, Lobb's face turned serious. "We'll do everything possible to ensure the safety of this Public. That includes ridding ourselves of true danger."

The camera zoomed out and off to Lobb's right, was Olivia, secured to a metal bed. Her index finger was gone. Blood seeped from the wound.

"No," he started forward, but Greyson grabbed his arm.

"This," Lobb continued, "is the beginning. This is how it starts. One virus. One person can destroy an entire civilization if not checked. It is my goal to make sure we can all rest easy knowing the threat is contained." Lobb lifted a pair of steel clippers and severed another finger.

"No!" Nate yelled.

"Nate!" He barely heard the simultaneous hisses of Reggie and Greyson. He cursed out loud, when the video went black and he rushed forward.

From out of nowhere, pain laced through his legs and they stiffened underneath him. A heavy blow landed against his chest and he fell to the ground. People around him parted, whispering. Not a soul seemed to realize that a tortured woman was just shown to them, let alone care that Nate's body had just been seized and thrust to the ground like an epileptic rag doll. But Nate's body continued to shake, each muscle experiencing the sensation of ripping away from the bones, separating from the tendons. Flashes of panic coursed through him, but even though he couldn't explain the agony he was in, he knew who was responsible. Two pairs of hands pulled him up and laced his arms over their shoulders. Nate barely managed to get out a gurgled form of Reggie's name, but it stopped just over his tongue.

"Reggie? What did you do!?" Greyson hissed at her.

"I didn't . . . I don't know!"

Hugh, dressed like a Public Citizen, hunched down and with Greyson, picked up Nate and got him to his feet. "I don't have time to explain," he hissed.

"Hugh?" Reggie gasped.

"Get him out of here. The guards can't see him," Hugh barked.

London and Greyson pulled Nate along, his legs dangling beneath him, trying to step when he could. When they were out of earshot, Greyson turned to Reggie again.

"I saw what happened! Don't tell me you didn't do it. You held out your hand and his body turned into a seizing board. Now, *what* was that?"

Reggie didn't say a word. Nothing. How could she stop him like that? How could Reggie do this to him? They couldn't take him away. He had to go to Olivia. He had to get her out.

"We have to hurry," Reggie's voice sounded thin to his ears. He could hear her lame leg dragging on the ground as she tried to keep up with them. "The Tunnel's here! Keep going, keep going!"

Nate was yanked onto the Tunnel and the door of the high-tech above-ground train shut behind them. The familiar greeting played over their heads, and he was placed into a chair. He tried to move his body, but it wouldn't budge. Not a single finger would twitch, not even his tongue would flick inside his mouth to speak. No matter how hard he tried, he had no control over his muscles. They failed him with each strained bit of energy he tried to use.

"Reggie, what in the world just happened? What are you not telling us!?" Greyson yelled at her.

"*I don't know*! I've never done that before, you have to believe me! There are a lot of things happening that I don't understand. My visions are changing, my abilities are growing, and the chip in my he—" her voice trailed off. She paused, holding her head in her hands. "That's what's happening. Whenever my chip was activated in the past, I would tense and crumple just like Nate. That lump," she pointed to him and he wanted to growl at her, "was what I became. What if . . . what if my chip has been taken over?"

"What do you mean, Reggie?" London asked her.

"There are two possibilities. Either Dryer planted a chip in Nate when they had him here—"

"Which, couldn't be possible seeing as if they've not used it before."

"Not necessarily," Reggie shook her head. "Dryer could time it whenever he wanted."

What's the other possibility? Nate wanted to ask.

"What else could it be?" Greyson sighed.

"It could have been me," she said, point-blank. "I just felt my head explode. I don't know what happened. There are a lot of things happening to me that I don't understand. There's a good chance it was me. What if my mind took over the chip? Or the other way around? Instead of causing me pain, it inflicts others?"

There was no sound from the other two.

"What are we supposed to do?" Greyson started. "Maybe Hugh, who apparently is *not* brain washed, could tell us, but unfortunately for us, he's still back there where we left him! We don't even know where we could find him in order to get him to answer the question—*if* he'd even be able to answer it. Who knows why he's not like the rest of them."

"Honestly, Greyson," Reggie interrupted, "If it was me that caused it, I don't know what's happening. You have to believe that."

"Of course we do," London spoke up. "Besides, if you hadn't stopped Nate like that, Hugh wouldn't have stopped him in time, he would have made even a bigger scene, and he'd be dead, not just paralyzed."

Nate wanted to yell. His jaw was clenched tight. His muscles frozen.

It was Greyson who spoke again. "How long do the effects last?"

He didn't want to hear it. Nate wanted to close his eyes, but they were splayed open, drying out and burning under the harsh lamp light above. Tears rolled down his face. His body tried to moisten the unblinking sockets.

"When they first triggered me," Reggie looked over at Nate with fear, "I was nearly comatose for twenty-four hours. Awake, but frozen in pain."

Comatose. Not able to do anything. He couldn't be like that. But he nearly was. With each movement of the Tunnel car, he was slipping off the chair, deeper and deeper.

"Each time it activated after that, the time lessened. After years of it, all I ever felt was the pain. He'll be fine. I don't think he was hit that hard."

"*That hard*? Are you kidding me? Look at him!" Greyson lifted Nate's body back onto the chair. "He's falling onto the floor and his jaw looks like it's wired shut, *Reggie!*"

The Tunnel came to a stop and Nate crumpled to the floor. He felt dead. In pain, fury, angry at Reggie and Hugh, but most of all, he just wanted Lobb for what he'd done to Olivia. He wanted the man's crushed windpipe in his hand.

Greyson and London picked Nate up by his arms, dragging him off. Traveling back to the home was a blur. London kept sagging under the weight of Nate's body, and street lights would bounce around in front of Nate each time he was nearly dropped. When they reached the house, Reggie quickly put her hand on the pad and the door slid open. His feet dragged across the floor before they set him down on the couch. Greyson picked his limp legs up and set them up for the night.

It was odd being conscious through all of it. He wondered if his eyes were even open anymore, or if he just thought they were open. Perhaps at that point, they'd dried up and fallen out.

All he could see over and over was Olivia's bloody hand, still glistening under the sick lights. She shouldn't have been there. He was supposed to protect her.

═GREYSON═

L ike every morning since they'd arrived, Greyson pulled
the light fabric away from the window with his pointer
finger. The brilliant sun outside pelted the scenery
around the house. It was like looking over the Emerald City.
The trees and plants were so green they almost sparkled in the
sunlight. Each person greeted each other with a smile—an
absent one, but a smile. If everything in this city wasn't so
horrible, he'd almost think that it was a beautiful place to live.
Absolutely perfect.

"You ready to go?" London walked up to his side,
fastening his uniform jacket closed.

"Yeah." Greyson's voice was husky. "Nate and Reggie
already left to check out the south end of the city. Thanks for
going out with me again. I know it seems pointless."

"No. No it doesn't. We all want to find Sophia. Hence,
why we're here."

Greyson gave London a weak smile and looked back
outside.

"I keep hoping I'll see Ben, too," London added. "You
know, if I had a grandpa, I think he'd be like him."

"What are you talking about? *If?*" Greyson said softly. "Ben *is* your grandpa." He winked at the kid and then quickly took his gaze back out the window. "Just because he's not your biological grandparent doesn't make him any less of a relative to you. I still consider him my father even though Soph and I have never been married." It was hard to say. He'd wasted so much time worrying about trying to find a minister or member of any clergy to marry them, and all this time they should have just considered themselves married. If they'd have done that, it'd be one last thing that he regretted never saying to Sophia. Not that he thought he'd never see her again, because he knew that he would, but—there was always an 'if.'

"You all right?"

Greyson bit the inside of his lip. He shook his head, but he couldn't take his eyes away from the window. "I don't know."

For the seventeenth time, London and Greyson left the controlled temperature home and walked outside. The bright sun reflected off the black streets, creating snake-like heat waves to radiate off the pavement. They had to be careful. They couldn't look like they were looking for someone, or even like they were strolling. Every movement was deliberate, like they had to be somewhere, had a job to do.

Greyson glanced from face to face. When he saw the long slender nose of one of the men from their community coming from the Public One Bank, he almost had to cover his mouth to keep from calling to him. Each time he saw someone from the community, his heart sank further, because it was never Sophia. All he wanted was her.

Maybe Reggie and Nate would have better luck on the other side of the city, he hoped. One of these days, he'd walk back into the home, and there she'd be, waiting for him.

Of course, wishing for that only made it harder. So, Greyson pushed it out of his mind. All he could do was continue on. Hours, he looked from face to face, walked through building upon building, and faked a calmness he didn't have. By lunch, London caught up with him and they both ducked into one of the cafés to eat. Neither said a word to the other. Greyson always ate too fast to get in any conversation. He just wanted to get back out.

People politely said "hello" and "good day" as they made their way back out onto the street again. It was a pattern. Look, eat, look, go home. More hours passed, and before they knew it, the streets' signs flashed that curfew would be active in thirty minutes. Another day. Gone. Still no Sophia.

They made it back after Nate and Reggie, who were talking quietly in the kitchen. Greyson ran a frustrated hand over his face and looked back out the front window.

As if he'd willed it to happen, the small groups of people outside parted to hurry to their homes, and a dark head of hair glided down the street. Greyson nearly fell over his own feet trying to get back out the door. The moment his eyes broke contact, he worried that maybe he wouldn't find her again. The door slid open and the glare of the setting sun blinded him. He raised his hand to shield his eyes, and scanned the groups again for her. He wondered if maybe he'd only thought he'd seen her . . . had maybe, wished so much for the chance to see her again that he'd imagined it.

But then he caught site of her again. She walked down the street away from him on the opposite side. Her arms swung comfortably at her sides. All clean and dressed in a white jumpsuit like Reggie wore—like all the women wore. Sophia's hair was pulled up into four different twists on the back of her head, wrapping like a well-organized striking puzzle.

Greyson had to hold himself back to keep from running. In all his people-watching, he'd noticed that Public citizens rarely ran in the middle of the day. With no panicked urgency to get anywhere or talk to anyone, there was no need. The moment he bolted toward her, he'd bring attention to himself. But the rhythm with which he moved his legs continued to beat harder against the ground beneath him. If only he could reach out and touch her, to have her see his face, then she'd remember everything and she'd want to leave.

But he also knew that even that was impossible. Reggie had warned him. When he did find her, she wouldn't be the same.

"Sophia." He barely had to say her name and she turned around. The sun bounced off her golden skin, lighting her up.

"Greyson?" Her smile didn't split her face like it usually did, but looked as if someone had told her a joke that she was giving a polite reaction to. "You live here now, too?"

His heart pounded and sunk all at the same time. "No . . . I mean, yes." He shook his head. "I need to talk to you."

"About what? Oh, Greyson. Ain't this city perfect? How wrong we were 'bout this. It's such a nice place. So much better here for us than the outside. In 'ere, they take care of us. We're not hungry, we're clean, and things are simple." As though someone had tapped her on the shoulder and reminded her, she raised her eyebrows. "Oh, I hope you don't mind, but I've been given a companion. His intelligence and mine, combined with our aptitudes and genetic traits, made us perfect partners. I'm sure they'll find someone for you, too."

The sink hole in his heart hardened and he wasn't even sure if his body was functioning anymore. "Sophia," he choked on the word, "I'm so glad for you. But would you mind coming inside to talk?"

She tilted her head in confusion. "Glad? Waddya you mean by that?"

Greyson's nostrils flared. "Please, Sophia. Just come talk with me. I just want to talk. To find out how you are."

"But it's curfew. How 'bout tomorra'?"

"It will only be a few minutes." He tried desperately not to sound like he was pleading with her.

Sophia looked around, but finally relaxed her face with an, "Of course."

He set his hand at the small of her back, leading her across the street and to the home where the group had taken up residency. The door slid open before they reached it and London beckoned them frantically with his hand. Sophia seemed not to notice. She quietly let Greyson show her the way in. The moment she was through the door, Nate grabbed her.

"No! Nate, don't!" Greyson shouted at him. "She won't fight."

"I'm sorry, Greyson." Nate clamped his hand over her nose and mouth. Each breath she took was a struggle, until her eyes closed and she passed out.

"What was that for!?" Greyson pulled Nate off Sophia's limp body which he'd just set onto the couch.

"She's all right, Greyson!" he hissed. "But she wouldn't have been cooperative for a blood transfusion if she were awake! A transfusion is probably the quickest way to get the drug out of her system, and until that's free of her body, even without emotions, she wouldn't stay. I had to get her to sleep somehow, dammit."

Greyson saw the small rise and fall of her chest, and shook his head, scowling. "You could have warned me."

"I didn't have time."

"Well, if we found Sophia out there, then Ben shouldn't be far, right?" London asked the group.

"Who's Ben?" Reggie asked.

"Sophia and Liv's dad." Greyson turned to her.

"So," she paused, "he'd be older?"

Greyson nodded. "Yeah. About sixty."

"No." Reggie shook her head. Greyson and the other two looked at her with confused faces. As if she knew where Ben was. "No," she repeated, her hand going to her mouth. "I don't think you'll find him."

"What are you talking about?" Nate prodded her.

"Haven't you noticed? Over the last couple weeks, I have. How old are the people here?"

Nate shook his head, not quite understanding.

"The oldest is maybe forty? Nate, Greyson. I think they're going to put him down. If they haven't already."

"What are you saying?" Greyson took a step toward her. "They'll kill him like a stray animal?"

"Does it surprise you? With everything you know about this society?" Reggie looked disgusted.

"Where would they hold him if they haven't?" Greyson stepped closer to her.

"The medical center. I think."

"London," Nate grabbed London's upper arm, "get ready. We need to go."

"Nate, they'll kill you. You won't be able to get him out," Reggie followed him into the kitchen and back out. "You can't do this."

"What if it was me, Reggie?" Nate stared at her, walking closer. "What would you do?"

Watching the two of them talk made Greyson freeze. The tension in the room rocketed.

Reggie jerked her eyes away from Nate and looked at Sophia on the couch. When she finally managed to look back at him, a natural rosy shade of pink flitted to her cheeks. "Nate, be *careful*."

He nodded, ran his hand along the small of her back, and met London at the doorway. Without another word, both men left the house. Greyson turned his attention back toward Sophia and dropped to his knees at her side. "What do we use for a transfusion? She won't be asleep for much longer."

Reggie cleared her throat. "Nate and I gathered these while you were out there." Reggie held out a small, long plastic tube, a bladder from an outdoor water pack, and a large medical needle. "The needle was in a medical kit, the tube we pulled from the piping on the chair." She pointed to a chair in the corner. The edges were cut up and the fabric hanging loosely. "What's her blood type?"

Greyson frowned at her and swallowed. "B-negative. I think. I'm A-positive, though."

"Don't worry. I'm O-negative. We'll need some of my blood first before we can drain a pint of hers." Reggie took the tube and fixed it to the opening of the water reservoir, then attached the needle to the end of the tube. She fixed the bag to the armrest of the chair, letting it hang before she sat down. Out of the pile, she pulled out a thick band of elastic and tied it around her bicep, tightening it with her teeth. "Hand me the needle," she said, holding out her hand.

"Would you like me to do it?"

"Have you ever inserted a needle into a vein before?"

"No. Have you?"

"No. But I trust myself more. Hand me the needle."

Greyson handed her the end of the tube. Reggie chewed on the end of her tongue and tapped the vein of her right inside elbow, and pumped her fist open and closed. Carefully, she slid the thick open needle into her vein and dark red liquid streamed through the tube like water through a straw. The bag slowly began to fill—faster when Reggie pumped her fist.

"How do you know all this?" Greyson whispered, brushing Sophia's hair out of her face.

"Do you want the scary version or the not-so scary version?" She almost chuckled.

"What's the scary version?"

"I don't know. Not that I don't know what the version is. It's that *I don't know how I know*. I just do. And not knowing about my past, or how I'm aware of things is a frightening experience."

The next five minutes were completely silent. Reggie filled the three liter bag only half full—still too much to take from her all at once. Greyson helped her remove the needle and she held a pad of gauze to the hole in her arm while she bent it. Her face had turned a very faint shade of gray, but she stood up and kneeled next to Sophia's body, ready to help further. Greyson had to hold Reggie up straight as her eyes closed. She tried to balance herself on her knees. With a second clean water reservoir, she attached the tube. A remaining dribble of her own blood came out of the tube, staining the white floor. When everything was set up once more, Reggie almost fell over.

Using her elbow, Reggie steadied herself on the edge of the couch. Then after putting the elastic band around Sophia's left arm, she tapped, and waited for the vein to protrude. When Greyson could see the vein, Reggie slid the needle into it. A slow moving stream of the contaminated blood drained from Sophia's system and began to fill the bag. It took much longer than Reggie's had.

"Reggie, you look awful. I can do the rest. You should go sleep."

"Are you sure, Greyson?"

"As long as you tell me what I need to do."

Reggie nodded. "Leave her needle in, and when the bag is half-full, switch bags." Reggie stood up and brought over the tall lamp from the corner and set it next to the couch. With a simple hook, she turned the lamp into an IV stand. The bag of her own blood was then hung on the hook. "Attach the tube to this bag and it'll drain right into her. Take the needle out and then tape her arm. She should sleep for quite a few hours at that point."

"Thank you, Reggie."

She nodded. "Of course."

Reggie staggered down the hall and out of site. At that, Greyson finally turned to look back at Sophia. As the blood left her body, her face looked even sicklier than Reggie's had. She'd only been drained of a quarter pint. He hated to see what she'd look like in five more minutes.

—NATE—

W here will we even find Ben?" London asked in a hushed tone as they entered the hospital. "He could be anywhere in here, and it's not as if we can simply ask them."

"Relax. We'll find him. But, we need to listen first."

"Why?"

Nate led him over to a long clear glass bench and sat down near the front desk. People calmly walked back and forth. London joined him, leaning forward over his knees. Nate brought his face lower to him.

"We can't imitate doctors if we don't know how they speak with each other, can we?"

London's eyes went large and he glanced back. "Nate, I'm *fifteen*. Who's going to believe me as a doctor?"

"All right, you'll be an orderly."

Nate sat down and London followed. Patients strolled in and out of the hospital, and he noticed that very few of them showed hurt in their faces. Pain, yes. The uncomfortable scowl that comes with minor throbs, aches, and tenderness. But no sadness, no misery, no anger. It was discomforting.

Never before had he imagined how large emotion's role was in every feeling of the body. Without sadness or resentment, the pain they felt was solely physical. Nothing more than that—just empty.

Nate observed the patients that would walk in, and speak with the attendant at the desk. Each one had a different story, but they were all so similar.

"We've had an accident. I slit my finger while cutting."

The attendant always replied—almost exactly each time, "That's inconvenient. Let me call the doctor for you."

At this point, a physician would come from the back hallway where a set of six elevator doors were, and walk up to the desk. "I understand we have a phalangeal wound. Please follow me and I'll heal that for you." So straightforward. No acknowledgment of sorrow or condolence to ease the patient's mind, because the patient felt no sorrow and needed no consolation.

"Nate?"

"Hmm?" Nate split his focus between the conversations around him, and London.

"What do you think of Reggie?"

The question yanked at Nate like a hook had pierced through his neck and wrenched him backwards. "Why would you ask that?"

London peered at Nate through slitted eyes. His gaze showed frustration and he quickly shook his head. "Never mind. Don't worry about it."

The spike in Nate's pulse started to abate, and his eyes jumped around London's face for a brief moment before he looked away.

Things with Reggie had become different.

If he was honest with himself, they'd been different for a while. Even before Olivia was taken. He knew Olivia's situation was part of the reason he continued to evade any thoughts of Reggie. It was a weight that pulled him downwards every day, filling him with guilt he continued to try and shove under the surface.

"No, actually, I *do* want to talk about it," London spoke up again.

Nate shifted his jaw forward. "About what?"

". . . the patient needs to be taken to level twenty-five for an x-ray. We will determine whether the bone is broken. I assume that it is . . ." a voice came and went through his ears.

"Reggie."

"You keep saying that," Nate whispered. "What about her?"

"I don't know, man. It's just, I really like her."

This wasn't news to Nate. It had been obvious from the start that London had a crush on Reggie. A bite of his own guilt rose in the back of his throat. He swallowed it down and turned to London.

"And?"

"Never mind." He expelled a huff and folded his arms, slumping in the bench.

"No, London." London's angst was annoying him. "You wanted to talk. So talk."

London shook his head. "I'm fine, man."

"You're not fine. You've got something to say to me? *Say it.*" Nate's tone was harder than he'd expected, but even though this was the wrong time to argue, and it wasn't what they needed to deal with at the moment, he forced it out.

London shook his head and turned from Nate. "If you don't know, Nate, then you're dumber than I thought."

"Listen, I may not be your father or brother, but I am in charge of you. Don't speak to me like that and just say what it is that you want to get off your chest."

"You think I'm *blind*, Nate? I see the way you've been with Reggie over the last couple weeks. I see the way you *look* at her. The way that you sometimes—" he shook his head, "You know I like her. I mean, *really like* her. You touch her like she's—" London harrumphed and shook his head.

"Listen, you may think you understand what you're seeing, London, but you couldn't be further from the truth. Reggie's just as much a friend to me as she is to you." Nate hissed.

"*Liar*," London answered through clenched teeth. "You're stupid if you think I can't see what you've been doing. What's worse is you're groping Reggie when Olivia thinks you actually love her."

Nate's eyebrows skewed above his eyes and he sat up straight, ready to lash out.

"No, Doctor. The patient is nearly fifty."

"Escort her to level seven."

Nate jerked around and watched an attendant move a woman from a seat toward the elevators. She was nearly fifty. What would be the point in healing someone they'd soon put to death? He didn't wait for a response from London. No matter how angry London was, this was more important.

"Shut up and follow me."

He stood up and starting moving down the hall. "Doctor," he gently called out.

A man in a white lab coat turned around. "Yes, sir?"

"May we speak to you in private?"

"What for?"

Nate realized there were very few reasons that someone with no emotions would have to speak in private. No embarrassment. No shame. His mind worked quickly. "It's so loud out here. I may have a hearing problem, and I need some quiet where I might speak with you."

"Certainly. Follow me." The doctor led them further down the hall and into an exam room. As soon as the glass panel door slid open and shut, Nate pulled the doctor off to the corner where he couldn't be seen, setting his hand over the man's mouth.

"London, the cabinet. Look for a drug called paralaxine."

London scoured the cabinet and eventually pulled out a small glass vial of liquid. "Got it."

"Get a syringe and fill it up only half-way."

London moved to the drawers, opening and closing each one. The doctor kept struggling inside Nate's arms, twisting back and forth.

Finally London found a small syringe and injected the needle into the top of the bottle. He fumbled getting the liquid into the syringe, but when he succeeded, he tossed it to Nate. Nate shoved the doctor face-first onto the hospital bed and pinned him down with his elbow. Pushing down as hard as he could into the doctor's back, he stuck the needle into the man's neck and pressed the liquid out. With a relieving sigh, Nate let the man fall to the floor and threw the needle into the biohazard drop. He stripped off his jacket and uniform top and set them on the counter.

"London, there's a set of white scrubs over there. Slip them on. Hopefully they fit."

Nate continued to undress, setting his white pants on the counter with the others. When he'd switched clothes with the doctor, he pulled a medical mask out of the dispenser and looked at London. The scrubs were nearly two sizes too small on the kid's lanky body, but it would pass. London frowned at him, but obeyed.

"Put on a mask."

Both men left the exam room and Nate led them to the set of glass elevators. There were no buttons, only a single pad.

"Excuse me, Doctor." A nurse stepped forward and entered a code on the keypad. "I need to get to level sixty." Nate and London followed her into the elevator. "Which floor?" She asked them.

"Seven," Nate tersely commanded.

"Yes, Sir."

The elevator smoothly moved up the shaft over the city. But it stopped at seven and the door opened. Without hesitation, Nate walked out, and London followed closely behind him. The door closed behind them, leaving the two nearly alone on the floor. An attendant worked at the desk ahead, moving files around in the projection in front of her. No other sounds came through the halls.

"Follow me." Nate walked up to the attendant. She had her bright red hair in a lavish flat bun at the very top of her head. Her blue eyes were bright and alive.

"Doctor, what can I do for you?"

"Check on the status of a group of citizens admitted three weeks ago. June twenty-seventh. We're here to make sure those over fifty were properly handled."

The attendant swooped her delicate fingers around the screen, looking for the information he'd asked for. He made careful measures to make sure he noticed the information she was looking at. What rooms were filled. Which names stood out to him.

"There were four groups that arrived that day. Many of retirement age. It looks as if eighty percent have already been retired—"

The tips of Nate's fingers went cold as he listened to her speak, but his eyes scoured the lists she had opened. And then, he saw him.

"—however, the last group is scheduled to be euthanized this afternoon. Is that correct according to your files, Doctor?"

"That's correct. Thank you."

She went back to the screen, her delicate hands flitting over the screen in the air. Nate paced around the desk and moved down the hallway without any resistance from the nurse. From door to door he looked for the matching number.

"Nate," London whispered at his back. "What are we looking for?"

"Ben's held in room seven eighty-three. He's still alive. The code is nine, nine, one, forty-two, seven. Can you remember that?"

"Nine, nine, one, forty-two, seven."

"Good."

Each hallway branched out, turning down different ways. And every turn was nearly devoid of people. The smell in the area was stale and putrid. So unlike the other areas of the hospital—it smelled like a normal hospital. One filled with disease and death. The layout was not unlike a labyrinth. So many rooms, so many options.

When they came to the right room, Nate watched the hall and London entered the code on the pad. The door slid open quietly. Lying like a corpse in a bed was Ben. Seven other hospital beds in the room were full. Each person asleep. Nate hurried to Ben's side and London started to unhook the tubes from his body.

"Paralaxine." Nate looked at the IV that ran directly into Ben's artery. "They're being pumped full of it," he groaned. "London. We're going to have to do this the old fashioned way. We need something to wake him up. In that cupboard over there should be, I hope, some adrinaphin. It'll need be to be shot into his spine to wake him up."

London crashed through the contents of the cabinets trying to find what he was looking for. "How do you know all this?"

"You don't survive a war without picking up some tricks." Nate leaned over Ben and whispered. "Come on, Ben. You gotta wake up if we're going to make it out of here alive. You need to be there for your girls."

"I got it!" London filled another syringe, this one, much larger.

"Throw it to me!"

London threw him the syringe and Nate rolled Ben onto his side. On the opposite side of the bed, London held Ben's body still while Nate placed the syringe in his right hand. "I'm sorry, Ben."

Nate pushed the needle slowly through Ben's back, directly into his spine. In order to keep the drug from overloading his mind, Nate had to be steady and slow in injecting. When it was empty, Ben's body began to twitch. London rested him back onto the bed while Ben's head jerked slightly from side to side, his fists clenching the bed beneath him.

"What's happening to him?"

"The adrinaphin is jump-starting his brain. It should only take two or three minutes."

An earsplitting alarm went off. The lights in the room became a bright blue and the atmosphere went cold. The lights pulsed in a rhythmic order. "Nate," London spoke up. "I don't think we have two or three minutes."

Ben's body was still jerking back and forth. Each vein and artery in his body was turning a deep shade of purple beneath his skin, the blood waking under the surface. The alarm screeched throughout the room. He and London were like the virus in a well-oiled machine.

Nate moved to the doorway.

"Nate!" London yelled. "We have to get Ben out of here or we'll never get out!"

"Not yet, London!" Nate looked down the hall to see a flood of guards exit the elevator. The attendant at the desk looked calmly down the hallway toward him. Their eyes met and she pointed methodically at him. He cursed and pressed the door pad. The door slid shut. Tremendous pain split through his elbow when he plowed it into the pad, sending sparks flying out of the wall.

Ben's eyes were fluttering, lost in a trance-like seizure. Not fully awake, but no longer stuck in limbo either. The throbbing of the blue lights flashing around them kept them calm.

Nate forced his mind to work faster to come up with a way to get them out of there alive.

"London, hand me a bottle of thermoxacin, paralaxine, and alcohol."

London reached into the cabinet, tossing each bottle to Nate. Nate's hand shot up, catching each one and setting it on the counter. He pulled out a Petri dish from a drawer and began filling it with the respective liquids. He wasn't moving fast enough. The pops and crackles coming from behind the door told him that the guards were only minutes from entering the room. The door budged the first half-inch, and London let out a yell.

"Nate?"

"Give me two seconds." Nate ripped off a section of the bed sheet and tied it around his mouth and nose. His hand shook, balancing the paralaxine bottle over the Petri dish. Only two drops. That's all he needed. Two drops.

"London," he said through the makeshift mask, "put that mattress over you and Ben on the floor, and cover your mouths. Now!"

London turned, shoved the bed over and Ben toppled to the floor. With the mattress covering the two, Nate looked back at the dish, and balanced the bottle once more. His fingers still shook.

One . . .

Two, three.

The last two drops came out too fast with his shaking fingers and the concoction exploded in a thick cloud of gas. The door was forced open and four guards rushed into the room. Nate raised the pit of his arm up to his face to keep from inhaling the gas, but his focus was already slipping. The guards grabbed Nate at the shoulders, but he fought, rolling his shoulders back limply. He had to keep his mouth and nose covered. He was almost smothering himself. Each guard staggered, and immediately fell to the floor. The walls around Nate danced and rippled.

"London," he whispered into his arm. "Stay."

Nate fell to his knees with his face buried in his shirt, a small crunch of his knees grinding into the floor caught his ears. The cloud of gas was beginning to dissipate, but it was still strong. They had to wait for the gas to filter through the whole floor, but not too long. Nate blinked, trying to focus his eyes, hoping with each hard press of his eyelids that the pictures in front of him would right themselves. He reached forward for a power-gun, dropped by a guard, and pressed himself off the floor, his knees aching. When he pulled the mattress back, he saw London laying flat on Ben's slowly moving body. A groan escaped Ben's lungs.

"Come on, London."

The boy shoved himself off Ben and pulled him up. Nate reached out to balance Ben on the right side while London held his left. Nate continued to lean on the wall, grip desks, whatever he could locate as they made their way down the hall. Ben's eyes were nearly open, and his feet were moving like gelatin below him. Nate was nearly falling over with him.

The attendant at the desk had already passed out and was draped over her chair. The paralaxine gas would keep each person on this floor cold for nearly two hours . . . and Nate barely trusted himself to make it down the stairs conscious.

"Nate, I can't do this on my own!" London grunted.

"I . . . I know."

London pressed on the stairway pad and a blast of crisp fresh air kissed their faces. Nate shook his head and tried to take a deep breath to clear his clouded head. The flashing blue lights and alarm reverberated down the stair shaft. Nate felt lost in a Tunnel of color and earsplitting sound. As if playing tennis with his inner ear, the unearthly screeching was knocking him off balance.

Once again, he took his bad elbow and smashed it into the pad behind him, breaking the ability for it to open. He reached out to the handrail and gripped it firmly, gripping tight to Ben's limp body.

"Nnn–" was all that slipped from between Ben's lips.

"Come on, Ben. We can make it," London coaxed. "Nate and I have you."

The men tottered down the stairwell. Nate slipped and nearly dragged both Ben and London after him.

"Nate!"

"I'm s—sorry. I've got it. I'm getting better," he lied. If anything, he was getting worse. He knew he needed to get Ben out of there before he allowed himself to collapse. Which, he knew, could be any minute.

Pounding footsteps came up the stairs below them and London shot Nate a panicked look.

"It's okay," Nate whispered. "I . . . I've got it." He raised the gun in his hand.

"But you can barely see where you're going. You've got to be kidding me."

"I," Nate blinked his eyes shut and held them closed for a period of time, "took out t-ten men in North Korea after being tear gassed. I can d —," he took a deep breath and opened his eyes, "do this. Stay down against the wall."

Nate funneled all his focus down the stairwell, watching for the first sign of movement. The moment a head was in view, even if it was blurred and twisted, he raised the gun and pulled the trigger. An electric pulsed shot glided through the air, cutting through the skull of the first guard, a second shot through the next, and two through the third. Cries belted out and the others held back. All these years later . . . Nate still hated what he did, but he was able to do it.

The swirling of the walls was getting greater. He was in a giant kaleidoscope. Twist the walls one way, and a new brilliant set of patterns and shades of blue surfaced in front. Nate felt along the walls of the staircase, continually holding the gun in front of him, watching below for any sign of human movement. He blindly beckoned to London behind him to follow, but didn't look back.

The first movement from the guards below triggered his finger and he took out two other men. He could only hear a few more voices. His right foot wobbled beneath him and he fell to a hunker before he forced himself back to his feet. He could feel the weight of bodies near his feet as he kicked them out of the way to allow for Ben and London to pass through behind him.

Five more lightning movements of his finger and the last three men fell to the floor. "All," he clamped his eyes shut again, and opened them wide, "all right, London. Let's get out of here." As they hurried out of the stairwell, Nate noticed clusters of people standing calmly against the walls. Sirens from the streets filtered in through the hospital as the glow of sunlight hit Nate's face. They were close. And he was able to make out three abandoned guard transports outside.

"Nate! Help me get Ben inside!" London pressed down on the guardian pad as the transport door slid up and open. Nate balanced Ben and hurried him into the transport, not caring how delicate he was with the man. "I'll drive!" London shouted. "You sit!"

The door slid closed after London and the transport whirred as he spun the wheel and bolted down the street. The line of seven other transports followed closely behind, sirens wailing—alerting every soul within fifteen miles that someone had stolen from them.

Nate's eyes were unfocused. A migraine cracked behind his eyes. Each passing color, turn of the wheel rattled his mind. He clamped his eyes shut, and they didn't reopen.

LONDON

Electricity crackled as it zipped past his head. London flinched as a blast nicked the side of the window, sounding like the chink of lightning against the side of the vehicle. They were well-outside the city walls now, but the other transports were still following close behind. Nate and Ben were unconscious. He had to deal with this on his own. If he didn't lose the transports, all three of them were dead.

London swerved around a large hole in the ground. The reverberating drone of the transport entered his ears, rattling his eardrums. Hundreds of ideas burst in and out of his mind, each one more impossible or stupid than the last. He didn't have the strategic brains that Nate did, nor the confidence. London's teeth bit deeper into his lip with each turn of the wheel. The nerves webbing throughout his body were shot. He didn't know how much longer he could hold off the transports. And he couldn't go back to the bunker and risk The Public finding out about it. The Public couldn't know how Nate, himself, and everyone else had even gotten into the city. That would mean death for all of them. Greyson. Reggie.

A power-gun rattled at his feet and he glanced down. His hand shot to the floor, picking up the gun that Nate had dropped as he fell into the transport minutes earlier. London struggled to hold the gun in his hand and steady. Keeping control of the transport meant he needed both hands. His fingers kept slipping around the grip of the controls, and he couldn't find the trigger of the gun. London glanced down and tried to make sense of what he was holding.

The transport lurched as it flew over a large bump in the hard ground. The gun flew out of his hand and he gripped the wheel again to keep the transport from careening out of control. Rattling echoed from between the controls and the window where the gun rested, humming against the glass. He reached forward and tried to keep his eyes in front, and on the gun at the same time. London gripped one side of the wheel with one hand, resting the butt of the power-gun against the other to control it.

He let go of the wheel with his right hand long enough to touch screen in front of him and the window to his left glided open. A burst of wind rocketed into the cab as they pitched to the right going a hundred and fifty miles per hour. In one jerky motion, he extended his left arm backwards out the window and shot out at the transports behind them.

No hit.

He pulled the trigger again, and bit down into his lip, drawing blood. The shot, again, missed hitting a single target. As London drew his breath, the transport dipped into a hole, jerking his arm to the side. His finger closed on the trigger and the gun clamored against the side of the vehicle. Like the blast of a bomb exploding, the shot hit the plasma tank of the first transport and it veered to the side, skidding across the rocky ground, grinding metal against stone, and flipping on its side. The guard driving close behind him, rammed into the underbelly.

London turned back around to watch where he was going. He brought the power-gun up near his face and looked at it. "Holy crap!"

With five guard transports left behind him, London jerked the wheel to a hard left. The transport swung around, and he bolted directly for the oncoming vehicles. The power-gun shook nervously in his hand, but he held it tight in his fist as he stuck his arm out the window once more and pulled the trigger. Two, three, shots crackled forward. The first punctured the front of the first transport, doing no damage other than making a simple seared hole into the metal. The second punctured the glass, hitting the lead guard. London saw the man's head fall limp to the side. Then the third shot hit the side of the transport. As if by a miracle, it passed through the plasma center. At its high speed, the transport lost control and its nose dove into the barren dry dirt beneath them, followed by the second as it rear-ended the first.

London whooped in excitement, nearly forgetting the other three. One of the transports fired multiple rounds at him, attempting to hit his plasma tank. Panicking, London dropped the gun and overturned the controls. The transport swerved out of control. He struggled to straighten the vehicle, but it kept sliding.

Off to his right he heard a crisp crackle as a power-gun fired, followed by a violent explosion.

"What the hell?" he whispered. It was then that he noticed Ben, panting and leaning against the door of the transport, the gun loose in his hand.

"Ben?"

"One more, kid." Ben handed him the gun and fell back again.

London looked out the window as the final transport sped toward them. He gripped the gun, firing round after round. He just hoped he'd hit the right spot. The final explosion wasn't as thrilling as the others, but one of his wandering bullets managed to hit the tank. The transport skipped and crashed over the rocky wasted terrain and ran right into their tail end. Their transport spun once and then stopped.

As if expecting a high-five from someone, he turned to the side. Ben looked better; conscious—but still struggled. It wasn't Ben he was worried about. Nate's skin had a slight pallor of green. His lips a light shade of blue. He had to get Nate to the bunker. He didn't know what would happen if he didn't.

London fumbled over the expanse of injections available at the bunker. Box after box were filled with drugs that could help, or make the situation worse. If only Nate were awake! He couldn't do this on his own!

London tossed another box to the floor and anxiously grabbed at his hair with both fists. "I can't do this," he screamed through his teeth. "I don't know which one!"

He grabbed at the countertop to calm himself and looked over the medical supplies once more. Which one would Nate pick? If they'd been dosed with a heavy amount of paralaxine, which they were, what did Nate use to inject Ben with originally? Ad—adrinaline? Adrinaphin!

London reached for a few more boxes, pulling them off the shelves and opened the first box marked *No. 938 Adrinaphin.* Syringes rolled out of the box and he grabbed one before running up the stairs.

Nate and Ben were still unconscious in the transport. Nate's muscles were tight and rigid. London pulled the cap off the first syringe and tried to roll Nate over onto his side.

London couldn't balance him on the chair with one hand. Nate's body rolled off the side and slammed into the floor of the transport.

"Sorry, Nate." London's voice shook as he lifted up Nate's shirt and guesstimated the spot where Nate had stuck Ben. Gently, he slid the needle into Nate's spinal column and pressed the drug into his system. When the contents of the syringe were all pressed out, he withdrew the needle and set it up on the seat. Nate's head jerked to the side. London jumped back, even though he expected the violent twitching.

Ben's voice almost groaned from behind him and London jumped up onto his feet. "Ben?"

"Hey there, kid."

London sighed and he struggled to breathe in again. "Ben! You finally awake?" London went to Ben's side and looked down at him. Ben's mouth was parched. Folds of dry skin were peeling from his lips. And his tongue, barely seen through his parted lips, was covered in a white film.

"I'll be right back."

London darted from the transport and back into the bunker. After finding a canteen of water, he ran back and held the edge of it to Ben's lips. "Ben, you need to drink something."

Ben's quaking hands reached up for the canteen. London held it steady and tilted it back toward his mouth. Water spilled over the sides of his mouth, over weeks of stubble, but as Ben started swallowing, London saw vibrancy coming back into him. The shaking slowed, and Ben was finally able to hold the canteen on his own.

"Keep drinking. I need to check on Nate."

Nate was still in a strange condition. With the mixture of drugs in his system, the adrinaphin may not have been enough, or even the right antidote to what Nate had breathed in.

"What's the matter with him?" Ben finally spoke.

London turned to see Ben pushing himself to a sitting position. His eyes were dilated, but focused. "He's inhaled some drugs. A gas he created in order to get us out of The Public. I gave him some adrinaphin for the paralaxine, but I don't know if that was enough."

"What did he mix?"

"Paralaxine, what they had you on, and, uh—" London swam through his mind, "thermoxacin, and alcohol."

Ben started to push himself up, but fell backwards into the chair. He whispered a curse and rubbed his head. "London. It's the Thermoxacin. He needs a shot of simple Methylphenidate."

London scrunched his eyebrows. "What?"

"Yes. It will slow down the reactions in his brain. The three drugs are battlin' each other right now. He'll never wake up. Run! Go, London!"

His heart hadn't stopped pounding since the alarm went off in the hospital. Now the sensation of a constant beating against his ribcage was harder and harder. His ribs were weakening and they just might have broken under the constant pumps. Flashes of what his life would be like if Nate didn't make it blurred through his mind. Nate took care of everything. He knew everything. Nate had to live.

The boxes of medical supplies spilled across the counter again as he knocked each one aside, looking for the right drugs. Finally, a box marked *No. 7310 Methylphenidate* appeared and he ripped into it. Small bottles clinked against each other and he reached over for an empty syringe. With both in his hands, he sprinted back outside and leaned into the transport.

"Ben!" he said, out of breath. His hands reached out and held the syringe and bottle to him.

"You'll have to do it, London. My hands . . ." Ben held up his hands. They were still under shock. How in the world had he hit that transport?

London gulped down a breath and ducked his head down in exhaustion.

"Yer gonna be fine."

There was so much confidence behind Ben's voice, London couldn't help but nod. He quickly removed the cover on the bottle and inserted the needle of the syringe into the top, drawing the drug inside. "I don't know how much."

"That should be good."

London pulled the needle out.

"Tap it."

"I know." London expelled the air from the syringe and kneeled next to Nate's side. Nate's skin had a sickly pastiness of yellow and his veins were a deep blue.

"Right into his artery, London. It needs to be circulated quickly to his brain."

With two fingers he felt along the stubble on Nate's neck for a pulse. It was so slow it was almost non-existent. He wouldn't last much longer. The needle slid in and he slowly pushed the plunger 'til it was empty.

The tendons in Nate's neck flexed and pulsed. Every muscle in his body became so tight that he started to convulse.

—NATE—

A beam of sunlight burst through the white clouds above casting glitter over the ocean as it crashed on the beach, licking it like a giant tongue. Seagulls squawked overhead as the smell of saltwater and fresh California air filled his chest. Tinkling of bikes, the low whirr of skateboard wheels, and laughter surrounded him on the pier. Nate turned his head as a hand gripped his shoulder. To his side, a gentleman appeared with a thick gray beard and thinning hair. He had somewhat of a belly poking out over the top of his belt.

"Hey, Dad."

"Son."

"Where's Mom? I thought we were meeting here."

"She couldn't make it. Got caught up back at the school doing detention duty."

Nate grinned and leaned over, resting his elbows on the railing of the pier. "That's Mom. How's she liking her class this year? They aren't driving her nuts like last year's class are they?"

"Oh, you know her. Even when it is a nightmare class she won't say a bad word about a single student. For some weird reason she says she loves it. Personally, after all these years, I don't know why she does. I could barely stand being around you kids growing up, let-alone spending six hours a day dealing with thirty strangers' children." He winked at his son.

"Thanks, Dad." Nate laughed. "Have I ever told you what a great role model you were?"

"Ah, there she is." His father chuckled as he looked behind Nate's back and motioned with a nod of his head.

Nate turned around and looked down. She wore a light blue sun dress, her silvery brown hair pulled up into a milkmaid braid on her head. She looped her arm gently around his waist and smiled.

"I wondered if I'd be able to find you."

"Hey, Reg. You ready for lunch?"

"Of course." Reggie went up on her toes as he leaned down for a kiss.

Around them, everything began to brighten. Light flashed off the metal spokes of bikes as they spun by, and the ocean was nearly impossible to look at. Nate covered his eyes, trying to shield them and pulled Reggie's waist closer to his body. The bright light spread across the horizon, engulfing the scenery around him. The sounds of the pier continued, unphased by the change. Nate squinted into the distance over the ocean. He couldn't make out what it was.

"Nate? What is it?"

"I don't know. It's . . ." He focused on the light. Something was moving within it. But that was impossible. ". . . it's probably nothing. Come on, let's go."

"Nate." His father gripped his arm, pulling him. "You have to go."

"I know, I just said that. Let's go to lunch. Then we can meet up with Mom when she gets off work."

"Nate."

The sense of calm in his father's face was unnerving. It wasn't normal. Something was off. As if he knew something Nate didn't. Anxiety shocked Nate's system and he narrowed his eyes as his *father. Before he could say a word, Reggie laced her fingers through his, pulling his attention to her.*

"You can't stay here. You have to wake up."

"What do you mean, wake up? You two are scaring me."

"Goodbye, Nate. I'll see you on the other side." Reggie pushed herself to her toes and kissed the corner of his mouth. She let go of his hand, and with his father, turned and left him alone on the pier. He hadn't even noticed the absence of noise around him.

The light grew until he could barely see two inches in front of his face. All he could say was, "No." The word clawed at his throat.

<hr>

Nate's eyes slowly opened up and he stared up at the ceiling. He couldn't move. Light flooded his vision. The fluorescence burned his retinas and he couldn't keep his eyelids open.

Through the haze, a blurred movement to his side caught his attention and he turned his head. His neck was stiff and it caught and popped with each movement of the vertebrae in his spine. Like a small bundle of twigs in a blender. London had his back to Nate. He was leaning over, speaking with Ben whose tears were running over his red cheeks.

Nate wasn't in Santa Monica. His parents were still dead. He dreamed of them constantly. But Reggie . . . she was the reason he couldn't move. She was the one reason he couldn't stay here. The dream, the wish to be with her. It was wrong here. What he wouldn't give to go back. In that world, it was okay to want her. It was better than it was here.

"Nate?" Ben's voice called from across the room. He'd taken his eyes from London.

No. He didn't want to go back to this life. Everything was so much worse. He closed his eyes, trying to draw himself back.

"Oh, thank the Lord. Nate, yer good. Wake up, son. You need to drink some water." He sniffed and wiped at the water on his face. "Yer severely dehydrated."

Ben shook Nate's shoulder, getting him to open his eyes again. "Sit up."

His arms shook as he reluctantly pushed himself to a sitting position. A glass of water was shoved into his hand and it sloshed over the sides, splattering his pants. The water continued to slosh inside the glass as he raised it to his mouth and drank deeply. He brought the glass down and took a breath. And he looked at Ben for the first time. Ben's eyes were swollen and scarlet. As much as he tried to smile at Nate, a dark pain reflected from his eyes.

London had told Ben about Olivia.

"Ben."

"Yer awake. You have no idea how worried we were."

Nate shook his head, ignoring his lightheaded state. The only words he wanted to say were, *I'm sorry*, but it wasn't enough. *I'm sorry* was a cop-out. What you said when you didn't know what else to say.

"Ben, I—"

Ben shook his head and cleared his throat. His head shook as if on a repeating track. His face burned a fiery red as it dropped into his hands, still shaking.

Nate set the glass on the ground next to him and leaned forward, his own body still trembling from all the chemicals, and took Ben into his arms. All the pain; it never got easier. "I'm so sorry, Ben. I should have stopped her, I should have kept her safe."

Ben's hand gripped at Nate's shirt, wringing it. "You couldn't. You couldn't have stopped her. Olivia has her own mind," he groaned, his voice dying off. "She's going to make it. She has to."

If he could have, Nate would tell him she would, but he couldn't tell him it'd be all right. He couldn't say they'd all be fine. He couldn't guarantee any of that. Nothing would help. Nothing that he could do. If he could only go back in time, so far back in time, he'd stop it all. He didn't know if he could do this any longer—live with the guilt of living, the shame of falling for her.

Ben's breathing calmed. He sat up, his head still hanging. "Nate, have they tortured her?"

What good would it do to tell him the truth? "No. Not badly."

Ben nodded, his face glowing red and splotchy. "God's watchin' out for her, ain't he?" He looked into Nate's face. Why? Why did he have to ask that question? And why did he have to ask Nate of all people?

"Of course," Nate whispered, the taste of a bitter lie leapt over his tongue. Was it a lie? He didn't know anymore. All he knew was Ben's daughter was in Public One, and in more danger than he was willing to tell. Whatever beliefs Ben had were the only thing keeping him together.

—REGGIE—

The clear warm water runs from the porcelain fountain tap coming out of the wall. My fingers swish back and forth through the wetness, playing it like a harp. When I pull my hand away, the water stops and the bathroom goes silent. I stick my fingers under the fountain again and the water runs out. I splash some water on my face then let my hair down. Looking at myself in the mirror, I can see how much more tired I look. Gray-purple hollows shadow my eyes, making them even darker. My cheeks have gained color, but they are sunken.

It's this place. Public One. It's draining me already. Everything has taken such a toll on me. And everyone else. Watching Olivia's face on the screen. It's been days, but I can't shake the pictures. The look on her face—the blood. It's even worse; the point that I had known before her. I should have stopped her. I could have stopped her, couldn't I?

I reach up and gingerly touch the back of my neck. Something is happening to me, and I don't know what it is. I don't trust it. No one should be allowed changes like these.

They're unpredictable and unreliable. Not to mention I feel as if I could die from them.

These last few weeks have changed me so much. For the first time in my life I'm actually starting to feel like I'm not human. Although I know it's not true, it feels like it is. I can see what Nate saw in me the first time he saw me. Something unnatural. Something machine-like.

I pull the lightweight linen robe off its hook and put it on before leaving the bathroom. The lights turn off on their own behind me and I walk into the front room. I'm grateful I'm able to walk on my leg without a brace now.

The full white couch envelopes me as I fall into it. I curl my legs up and hug them as I hear Greyson murmuring to Sophia in a room down the hallway. He's been trying so hard to get through to her. But it's more difficult on him that I think even I realize.

I lean my head to the side and shut my eyes. I try to push away the guilt I feel, and simply sleep.

The sun beats down on my face and I raise the palms of my hands. Blasts of power-guns shots ricocheting around my head. Faded voices and pounding heart beats. The images zoom in and out. "WHAT DO YOU WANT FROM ME?" Nate's voice cuts through the haze like a blade.

A rough graze against my arm, and his fingers are harsh and callused. The sun shines through again, and I can see its glow behind my eyelids. The picture shifts and my back is slammed against the wall. Nate's fingers lace through my hair, under my shirt and up my back as his mouth moves down my jaw. I dig my fingers into the flesh of his arm, pulling . . . pulling him closer.

Fire burns all around me and I feel as if I might go up in flame. I can't catch my breath, the air is so thick. No fire.

Dryer's face splits into a smile in front of me.

Screaming.

"Reg," Nate's voice Dopplerizes in and out. It's harsh as he breathes into my ear. My heart batters against my ribcage. His lips meet mine.

My eyes slowly open. My mouth is dry and I feel as if I can't move. Something raps from the back window and my eyes flutter over. The muscles in my body refuse to move as I see Nate standing at the back window, motioning at the front door. He's coming in.

A sudden urge to cry and scream all at the same time hits me like a million pounds. I hold it in and I hear the front door slide open then shut. Nate's feet move like hollow drums against the floor and come around the corner into the living space of the house. His buzzed hair has gathered dust, and his stubble is beginning to grow back in again.

"Hey," his voice rumbles softly.

"Hi. How are you?"

"A couple days of rest, and I'm brand new. How's, uh, how's Greyson doing with Soph?"

I find myself staring directly at him and I force myself to look away. "Not good. I'll go get him." I stand up, instinctively pulling my delicate robe closer to my body, and push past him without waiting for his response. I hear Greyson still speaking softly in the bedroom and I poke my head inside.

"Greyson. How is she?"

He pulls his head up. He's holding onto her hand, brushing it softly. "She hasn't woken up yet, but I think better." His face doesn't tell the same tale. Troubled shadows linger under his eyes, and his curly hair is looking more matted than usual. For the longest time, he just sits there, looking at her. But he finally stands up. "What is it?"

"Nate's here. Just got back."

Greyson looks back at Sophia, kisses her hand, and walks out of the room. I can't help but look at her. She looks so calm. So at peace, even though the weight on Greyson's shoulders suggests otherwise.

Instead of following Greyson back down the hall, I stay. The door slides shut behind me and I move over to the bed. The tube protruding from her arm continues to pump dark red blood into the bag hanging by the bed. This is only the second time in three days that she's had a transfusion. Each time I donate my blood, I'm exhausted, but I'm handling it all right. She's not handling it well, though. Her skin is so gray. If Greyson were doing this to her twice a day, I could understand the discoloration of her skin, and the struggle of her health. However, we've only done this twice in two weeks. My only assumption is the drug is making her body resist letting it go.

I reach out and take her hand, softly rubbing her smooth skin underneath my thumb. It pains me to know how much Greyson is hurting for her. And how much she's going through—this girl that I don't even know—the sister of one of the best friends I've ever had.

My mind flashes to Nate, and I shake my head. Over the past couple days he's been living in the forest with Ben and London, unable to enter the city with Ben. Why has he come tonight? The first time since they left. Admittedly, it's been nice not to think about him. Though I've missed him all at the same time.

The door slides open again, and both Greyson and Nate walk into the room. There's a new expression on Greyson's face. It's not as weighted as it was, but a sharp addition of stress has been added.

"Thank you for staying with her, Reggie," Greyson says to me while coming toward the bed. "Nate, you're sure this will work?"

"Greyson, I've been over this with you."

Greyson swallows and every muscle and tendon in his neck flex while he breathes out. "All right."

"What? What's going on?" I stand up from the seat and look at Greyson.

"Back in the bunker they found medical supplies," Greyson answered. "One of which is a military grade drug."

"It's not a drug," Nate cuts in.

"A *substance*," Greyson emphasizes with a touch of irritation, "that when injected into someone can kill off any foreign bodies."

"The military would use it on soldiers who contracted viruses and colds during war time. Keep the soldiers active. It was never released to the public. But I think that it might just be the thing to bring Sophia out of this." Nate shifted.

I look at Sophia the entire time he talks. As weak as she is I wonder if her body can handle one more invasive substance. "Will she be able to handle it?" I ask.

"I've told this all to Greyson. At the very worst, nothing will happen."

Behind Sophia's eyelids, her eyeballs are still. I've seen others sleep before. When they dream, their eyes always move, but hers are almost dead.

"Hand me the syringe, Nate." Greyson holds out his hand.

"Are you sure you don't want me to—"

"Give it to me," Greyson commands again.

Nate pulls a plastic syringe out of his pocket and takes a few steps before handing it to Greyson. He stands next to me, and puts his hands back in his pockets. I continue to keep my eyes on Greyson and Sophia. When the plastic cap is taken off, and the needle exposed, Greyson takes a deep breath.

"It needs to go in her—"

"I know, Nate. You already told me."

Greyson pulls on the loose neckline of her delicate slip. Just enough that her sternum is exposed. I look at his hand and it's shaking. In one movement, both Nate and I both reach out to grab Greyson's wrist.

"Let me do it," I glare at Nate.

Nate offers no argument and immediately pulls away. But Greyson yanks his hand out of my grasp. "I can do this! Why won't you two let me do this?"

I lash out and take hold of his hand again. "*This* is why. You're hand has no control, Greyson, and if you do this wrong, the injection itself might not do anything to her, but *you* could. I promise she'll be okay, but you need to let me take the needle. Please, Greyson. You shouldn't have to be the one to do this."

His head jerks over to look at Sophia and he finally nods. "All right."

"All right," I repeat. I still have to uncurl his fingers from the large syringe, but he finally lets go. Greyson moves around to the other side of the bed to hold Sophia's hand. The long thick needle in my hand is steady as I tug on her neckline again.

"Right in the center of her sternum," Nate coaches behind me.

I place one hand on her chest and raise the other in the air. In one swift move, the needle plummets into her bone and I press the plunger until it's empty. A torn gasp of air escapes Sophia's mouth and her eyes fly open, focusing on me. But it only lasts for a few moments before her eyes close again and she's asleep once more. I glance over at Greyson and notice him shaking. Both his trembling hands cup Sophia's.

I slowly pull the needle out and Nate already has a clean gauze ready for me. I put pressure on the needle's entryway and hold it there to stop the bleeding. After taping it down, all three of us watch her. I'm not sure what I'm expecting. Would it happen quickly? Would it take minutes? Hours?

A shuffle of feet move behind me and I turn just before Nate leaves the room. I look back at Greyson and Sophia. They need to be alone for a while. As I stand up and start to follow Nate, I hear Greyson's voice behind me.

"Reggie?"

"Yes?" I whisper.

Greyson is still fixated on Sophia. But he closes his eyes as he says, "Thank you."

"Of course." I hurry from the room and press my hand to the pad to close the door after I leave. I hear the front door open around the corner, but I don't see the point in catching Nate before he leaves. He knows I'm being evasive. How could he not? The hardest part is knowing why I'm doing this. I wish I hadn't had that vision. I wish I could forget it. The feel of his hands, the warmth of this mouth . . . I close my eyes and drop my head. I can't think about it. I simply can't. Not right now. Not with Olivia waiting for him, and not with what just happened with Sophia.

Before I can stop it, my bottom lip curls and pulls up. My face burns, and massive streams of water flow down my face. I hate feeling like this. If only I could get Olivia out. If only she could be here—things would go back to how they were.

—SOPHIA—

Somewhere in the back of her mind, chimes, like a grandfather clock, clanged in a dulcet droning. They were so faint, she couldn't make out if they were real or if they were a figment of her own unconscious mind. Colors moved and broke. Nothing was in focus. As if someone held a large sheet of waxed paper over her wide pulsing eyes. The artery in her neck, the veins in her arms and legs were pumping so strongly, she felt they might burst. Blood rushed to her head, attempting to lift the fog on her consciousness. A sharp image of man's face appeared and disappeared just as quickly. It was a face she knew well and would never forget. Greyson's whiteness had a touch of shadow mixed in as if someone had taken a thumb and smudged ash beneath his eyes.

Her head felt like it housed a twenty-pound weight as it rolled to the side. The tambour beating behind her ears melted with the clangs. A pressure encompassed her hand and her heart pounded harder, urging her to wake up. She had to pull herself out of this dissonance of color and sound—this merry-go-round.

Sophia could feel the tongue roll around her mouth as if it were dancing. She swallowed thick saliva and finally pressed her eyes open. This time, pictures were clear. She didn't recognize her surroundings, but none of that mattered. As her heart raced faster and faster in her chest, beating blood through her body, she squirmed her fingers, and immediately her hand was squeezed once more.

"Soph?" Greyson's voice crashed through the beating in her head and it immediately stopped.

She could barely catch her breath; her heart was beating so fast. If it didn't slow down soon, she'd hyperventilate. Her head was already so light that it might have been floating above her shoulders.

"Soph, do you remember—," Greyson's voice became indistinguishable as her mind sped backward. She remembered everything in an instant. The Public transports landing in the community. She'd just gotten out of bed when she heard the nearly silent whirr of their engines as they lowered. When she'd looked outside, she couldn't believe it. Dozens of men exited the two transports and within moments had crashed through each home, dragging women, men, and the few children out into the street. Two of the children had been killed.

Her heart pumped faster.

She could hear her own voice strangling and breaking to cry out as she fought back. But she wasn't strong enough to fight them off. At one point, her arms broke free and she bolted. Down the streets her feet carried her. She had to get away. She had to find her father. If they could escape, they'd be able to find the group that left.

A jolt hit her between the shoulder blades and she distinctly remembered how it felt as her face connected with the ground. The taste of the dry sweet dirt and blood as it caught in her lips and teeth. She couldn't keep her eyes open. The next thing she remembered was watching a man talk to them. It wasn't very long. What did he say?

Then, there was the hospital room.

Her eyes had flown open to find two nurses and a doctor standing around. Her head was secured to the bed, turned to the side. A case with two small glass vials sat on the counter. One of the nurses set another vial of blood into the case. That made three. The other six slots were empty. She couldn't make out the writing on the vials from where she laid. A piercing pinch in her stomach seized her attention away from the vials and she wanted to scream, but nothing came out. She couldn't move. Every limb was secured to the bed. The pinch grew more intense.

"How many eggs do we need, doctor?"

Sophia's jaw shook. Her eyes straining to look down at herself. They were taking her eggs?

"That's good. As long as we have two vials, they'll go a long way."

A large needle slid out from her belly and she was quickly sewn up. Blood. Eggs. She'd remembered what Isaac had told them. His first day in The Public they'd taken samples.

They did the same to her.

Her memory swam back again and she remembered walking into a brightly lit room. A man stood up from a chair, wearing a white top and pants. His copper hair was slicked back and his hazel eyes peered right through her with contentment. She'd been assigned to him. A companion. Yet, she hadn't panicked. She remembered the calmness, the serenity.

Sophia's mind raced faster and faster. Blurring through the last few days. The Public induction gathering, the powerful and brilliant Martin Lobb, and then she saw Olivia again. Her sister was alive. It'd been such a pleasant feeling to know Olivia was there.

A guttural screech clawed from her throat as she remembered one last thing. Olivia was there with him. The blood. So much blood.

"No!" she yelled, gripping at the sheets.

"Soph? Soph!? Babe, can you hear me?" Greyson's voice broke as he reached for her face and cupped it between his hands. His calloused fingertips whisked gently over her skin as giant tears fell from her tired eyes.

"Greyson?" her soft voice shook.

"Oh, thank you, God." Greyson bowed his head and pulled her trembling body against him. His arms held her so tight she thought they would never part. And that was what she wanted. The memories of everything rushing so quickly through her were too much. She couldn't think of them anymore. She couldn't think of Olivia—not now.

Her body was so tired she could barely lift her own arms to cradle the crooks of Greyson's elbows.

"Thank you, thank you," Greyson murmured over and over as he planted simple kisses around her forehead. "I'm so glad you're okay. Oh, God, thank you."

"Greyson?" A woman's voice called from behind Greyson and Sophia opened her eyes. The woman was slender, long, with light brown hair so mousy that it was nearly silver when it caught the light, matching her eyes. Her hands were neatly clasped in front of her, her fingers delicately laced together. Sophia had never seen her before in her life.

"Greyson, how is she?"

Greyson squeezed Sophia and kissed her temple before turning around to face the woman. A grin broke out on his face. "She's fine." He sighed and nodded, looking back and forth between her and Sophia.

The woman smiled and took a few small steps toward the bed.

"Who are you?" Sophia whispered.

"Soph," Greyson kissed her temple again, "this is Reggie. Remember the precog that we came to find?"

Sophia's eyes narrowed on the woman in surprise. Never in her dreams would she have imagined that the weapon Isaac had begged their community to go steal was an actual human being. Her father had told her of fantasy stories he'd read as a kid with people like that, but surely not in real life.

"Yes," she whispered. "That was you?"

The woman, Reggie, nodded. "Sophia," She seemed hesitant to speak. "Do you remember what happened to Olivia?"

Sophia dropped her head as her breathing quaked. "Yes."

Reggie came closer and knelt down next to the bed. Her eyes flooded with tears. "I am *so* sorry. I promise we'll get her back."

Sophia nodded and tried to hold her mouth from plummeting into a dark grimace. "Thank you," she said.

"Soph." A familiar voice traveled to her ears and she turned to see a figure had entered the room. Nate was dressed as he always was. Jeans, a t-shirt, and a thick flannel button-down shirt. His hair had been shaved close to his head, and it looked as if a month's worth of stubble was growing on his carved face.

"Nate." And she broke. Greyson held her close as Nate hurried close to put his arm around her. And there she was. Being cradled by two men she adored more than anything in the world. The man who would be her husband, and her closest brother.

"Olivia's being tortured," she finally whimpered. "They have her."

Nate hushed her softly. "I know."

Without noticing that Reggie had left the room during her conversations with Nate and Greyson, Sophia fell asleep. The drain of letting her memories flood back to her with the onslaught of emotions was too much. Sleep was a welcome respite. When she woke up, she found Reggie standing near the bedroom window, looking out into the midnight sky.

The moment she stirred, Reggie turned and gave a tiny smile. "You're awake."

"How long was I sleepin'?"

"Not long. Fifteen hours." She stepped away from the window. For the first time, Sophia noticed that Reggie was dressed in traditional Public clothing. But she didn't look like a citizen. And she definitely didn't have the emptiness that came with it.

"Where's Greyson?"

"Getting some sleep. He just left an hour ago. I made him leave. Do you want me to go get him?" She started for the door, but Sophia waved her hand as he sat up straighter.

"No. Knowin' Greyson, he prob'ly hasn't slept at all."

"He hasn't." Reggie shook her head. "Listen, um, I'm not sure what the men have said, but we're going to get Liv out. We just have to do it all at once."

"I know." She nodded. It wasn't fair, she wanted her sister back now.

The door slid open and Nate poked his head in. "Oh, you're awake. I didn't think you'd be up yet." His feet swished across the silky carpeted floor before he leaned over to kiss Sophia on the forehead.

Reggie cleared her throat and stepped back. Sophia's eyes quickly caught the nervous movement, and she glanced between the two. Nate's jaw stiffened, but gave no other notice.

"I'm going to slip out," Reggie whispered, giving Sophia one last smile before the sliding bedroom door closed behind her.

"I'm so glad you're all right, Soph."

"What was that?"

"What was what?" He narrowed his eyes.

"That. Between both of you. She got nervous, 'n you got irritated. What's goin' on? Is there somethin' I don't know 'bout?"

Nate shook his head. "It's nothing."

Sophia focused her eyes on him. "Are you raggin' me, Nate? I'm not five. I've known you fer a long time, and I know what I jest saw."

"I'm with Olivia, Soph. There's nothing between me and Reggie." The firmness in his tone was final. Though, it wasn't the tone that took her back.

"You're with Liv?"

Nate licked his lips, hesitating. "Yeah." He was done with the subject, and she knew that it would be impossible to get him to say anything else. Nate, she thought, what are you doing?

—NATE—

The breaking sound of water pulled Nate out of his stupor as it fell to London's shoulders, spattering to the dust on the ground while the kid trickled unfiltered water through his hair. Nate looked over to London as the boy ran another cup of water over his head, and shook the water off.

He looked back at the gun he'd started loading and slipped the sleek magazine back inside. Every time he thought back to what life was like for him a month ago, it made him shudder. Everything had changed, and yet nothing had changed.

His closest friend had died in front of him, and he still found himself living like a Nomad. A stranger was introduced to his life—Reggie. His thoughts rested on her more than he knew was healthy. He couldn't help it. This, he couldn't tuck away.

Weighed down, Nate leaned forward fingering the gun and thrashing himself on the inside. How could he be thinking about Reggie, when Olivia, the woman he was supposed to love was being held prisoner?

"Nate," Ben's silky voice broke the silence. "Somethin's bothrin' you. You wanna tell me what's up?"

Nate set the gun on the crate next to him, and sat down on the nearest case of weapons. He clasped his hands in front of him, covering the bottom half of his face as he leaned into his own guilt.

"Nathan."

"I'm fine, Ben. You know me. Nothing new."

Ben shook his head, his bottom lip gently pulling down. He looked to make sure London was out of earshot and spoke softer. "Nah. This ain't the same. And don't you lie to me."

"Really, Ben. I'm fine. There's just a lot on my mind. I know you don't believe me, but I'm handling it." Nate took a deep breath and cleared his throat.

"Nathan, I've known you fer years. If you think you can lie to me and brush me off that easy, you must be insane. Usually I know when to leave ya alone, but I have a feelin' this is differ'nt. Ya need to talk."

Nate picked at the dirt under his fingernails and dropped his head. He felt as if it'd been a good half hour before anything was said between them. "I," he finally spoke. "Must be the worst man . . . the worst *human being* in the world."

Ben's eyes narrowed and he sat down next to Nate. "What in the blazes are you talkin' 'bout, Nate? Is this about not wantin' to talk Reggie into usin' her abilities? We talked 'bout this. You said that the only way everythin' will work out is if she goes back into that buildin' and blows the guts outta every man in there."

Nate's eyes darted to Ben. He'd nearly forgotten what they'd been talking about. Reggie. The plan to get into Public One's headquarters. In detail, Nate had described to Ben all of Reggie's growing abilities, including what she'd done to save him the night he'd tried to rush The Public's main building when he saw what Lobb was doing to Olivia. He still remembered the ever-tightening twist of his muscles as his legs crumpled beneath him. The skewed rigidity of his jaw that kept him from speaking.

Then Ben had a thought. Reggie had intentionally stopped Nate, even though he was surrounded by thousands of people. One mind. One single brain that she had locked onto. If only she had the ability to lock onto multiple consciousnesses. It would be the only way they'd actually make it to the center of Public One. She'd need to collapse every man she could 'til they got to Dryer and Lobb.

"No, no. That's not it. I mean, I don't think she'll want to go in, but I know she'll do it."

He couldn't bring himself to say anything else. Not to Ben. Not Olivia's father. He was the last person he should be talking with about this. How could you tell the father of the woman you swore you loved . . . that you have feelings . . . No. No, it was sick.

Wasn't he just telling Olivia how he loved her? He'd meant it. He missed her that was true. He hurt for her, knowing what she was going through. What if he was just latching onto the nearest person? Why did it have to be Reggie?

"Do you think I'm a fool, son?"

Nate flinched.

"You *need* to talk, Nate."

He couldn't help but shake his head. It felt like acid was working its way through his lungs and burning through his ribs. "Ben, I'm fine. I promise."

"Dammit. Don't give me that."

Nate flinched. "Ben. *I can't.*"

"Nate." Ben's voice was gentle. Coaxing what Nate didn't want to let out.

In a flood of words, it came, and he couldn't stop it.

"Ben, I made a promise to Liv."

"What sort of promise?"

"She wanted to be with me, so I agreed."

Ben frowned. "Just because?"

"No!" Nate shook his head. "I love your daughter, I do."

Ben sat back against the wall, his face falling into a calm pool. Without even a touch of hesitation, he said the one thing Nate had been fighting back. "Yer in love with that Reggie precog, ain't cha?"

Nate's head flashed around and he stared at Ben. Ben leaned forward, his eyes darkening with pain. "Lemme tell ya somethin', Nate. I've been around. I've known fer years how my little girl loves you. Believe it or not," he looked back into Nate's eyes, piercing him to the core, "I saw the same feelin' in yer eyes. But you been guarded like a serial killer on death row. It hurt to watch my baby hopin' fer you. Yer walls would have destroyed any other woman. But I knew, I *know*, that you love her.

"Now, you made a commitment to Liv. A promise. Fer the first time in yer life, you opened up to her. It was all she ever wanted. I know you love her deeply in your own way. But, Nate I'm not blind. I see the changes that've happened to you. 'Specially since you stole, well, rescued that woman in there." Ben motioned in the direction of The Public. "She's caused somethin' to burn inside you that nothin' ever has, am I right? You come back every night from that city, glowin'. Maybe glowin's the wrong word. Whatever it is, it's still bein' forced down and hidden inside a black box, but I see it. That's somethin' I never thought I'd see again.

"Nate, I know you love Liv. You'd do anythin' fer her. But if you love this woman. Reggie. Even if they are just the seeds of feelin's. You gotta be honest to yerself. Honest to yerself, to

Liv, and honest to Reggie. If you caint' do that," he thrust his finger into Nate's chest, "*then* yer being disrespectful to my daughter. You figure out what you want, save my girl, and tell her the truth. Because this hidden thing you've got? It's not bad. You jest need to get it out."

Ben looked at him sternly. "Do you unnerstand me? Nate, yer just as much my son as if you were my own blood. Ya always have been. Though Liv may disagree with me, I'm not afraid to tell you—yer a fool if you throw this away."

Nate swallowed the bulge in his throat, trying to force it back down. He took a deep breath, and looked off in the distance toward The Public. How could he let Liv go through all this, just to end it? Just like that. One moment he was committed to Olivia, and then this.

He knew he cared for Reggie, but it was different. She was different.

"Ben, I don't know if I can do that. I still feel horrible, and horrible doesn't even begin to describe how I feel about leaving Olivia."

"Hold up, you will save her. Get me? You will. Liv will get over it. She's not the flower petal you think she is. Nate, you feel this way because yer decent. Yer the most loyal, but also the most stubborn and ridiculous man I've ever known. When you feel somethin's wrong, whether it is or not, you can't let it go. You won't let yerself, and there's yer fault."

"I can't let her go." Nate shook his head and ran his hands through his hair.

"Ya have to. You only get one of 'em."

"I don't want both of them, Ben."

"I know that. Lovin' Reggie don't mean you love my Olivia any less. You love them differently, and I un'erstand that. The fact that you love Liv is what will help you get to her, but don't dismiss what you *could* have."

Nate dug into the concrete floor with his boot heel and looked back outside. "What if Reggie doesn't feel the same?"

"How could she not?"

Nate raised an eyebrow at Ben. "You haven't seen her around me the past little while. She hasn't been the same, and I think maybe it's my fault. I don't know—"

"Lemme rephrase. How'll you ever know if you don't be honest? Like I told ya. Nate, yer gonna have to ask her to use her abilities when you enter the center of The Public. Gauge her feelings, then make a decision. Easy as that."

"I don't know." Nate shook his head.

Ben wiped at the sweat on his face and tried to smile. "Then you'll never do it." His bear-paw hand gripped Nate's shoulder briefly before he turned and walked out into the dusk with London, leaving Nate with his own thoughts again. He nearly had the entire strategy planned out. Why was it that the simplest of tasks, telling Reggie how he felt, was the most difficult to think about?

—REGGIE—

Yﾟou goin' to bed, Reggie?" Sophia looks at me. She's wrapped in her own dark blue robe and the light fabric hugs what curves she has. Her deep brown eyes look back at me like coal pits.

"Not yet. I, uh. I'm still trying to piece everything together before . . . Well, before everything happens."

Sophia nods and gives me a smile. "Don't think too hard on it, Reggie. Sometimes the right path is what you least want."

I narrow my eyes at her, not quite if she's actually referring to my visions. I see so much of Olivia in her. But at the same time they're completely different. Sophia is soft spoken. So unlike Olivia's brash yet authoritative character. Most of the time when she speaks, I barely notice she's been talking. Then there are other times when the simple words that she says cut me to the center. Like now.

"Thank you," I whisper. "Goodnight."

"G'night."

Sophia turns from the room and heads down the hall to where Greyson is already deep in sleep. The house is still. I look around, almost waiting for a noise or something to move.

My eyes drop to the floor and I pull my legs closer to me while I sit. Of course, I was only semi-truthful to Sophia. I have been piecing together everything I know will happen. Everything I've seen. I know those who will get hurt— severely injured. Clues and cues of what will happen have continued to replay for me. But I've finished. Truthfully, I finished a long time ago. Now, my mind runs over and over one vision. The only one that scared me and made me hurt all over.

Nate's hands. His mouth.

I close my eyes, trying to push it all out. It's insane. He's so in love with Olivia. I've been trying to reason with myself that perhaps what I saw was only a dream. The first dream I've ever had in my life. Pictures of subconscious stress that my mind has somehow visualized into a fantasy. It's something my mind's formulated together—something so wild it could only be a dream. Not that I've ever had a normal dream, but so many odd things have happened with me that I can't write anything off. Anything except what I've seen.

If I can just continue to ignore him, he'll go back to thinking I'm mad and I'll never have to worry about it again.

I think I'd rather have him hate me. I'd rather him hate me for what's happening to Olivia. I'd feel less guilty. Wouldn't I? After all, I am responsible. I should have stopped her. And they never should have come for me. It's because of me that they've lost so much. He knew that once. That hateful part of him I probably could have gotten used to. I know how to be around that part of him. But what I saw, what I've experienced already—I can't do it.

The soft swish of the door opening shoots icy shocks through my fingertips. I stand up from the seat as Nate walks in and the door closes behind him. His cheeks are flushed from the chilly evening, and it makes his eyes look even brighter, even in the dim lights.

"Nate. What are you doing here? We weren't expecting you 'til tomorrow morning."

"I needed to talk with you about tomorrow. Ben and I both think that the only way this plan will work . . ."

". . . is if I use my ability on the guards. I know." I feel my throat tighten. "I agree."

Nate nods. I feel my heart bursting with angst as he looks at me. "Is everything all right here?"

"We're fine." I assure him. I hope he'll simply turn around and wish me a good night, but I can see that there are other things on his mind. I don't know what they are, and I'd prefer to keep it that way. Although he continues to stare at me, I can sense the conflict in him.

I clear my throat and hug my body. "I was just going to bed. I'll see you in the morning."

"Reggie."

"Goodnight, Nate."

"*Reggie.*"

I stop, but I can't bring myself around to look at him. I know if I do, I won't be able to breathe. I can already feel it pressing down on my chest; nagging and pulling me.

My heart thumps louder and louder and I know he can hear it.

"Nate," I keep my voice even. "I'm *very* tired. I need to sleep, and I'm sure that traveling from outside has worn you out too. If you need, there's still a bed in the fourth bedroom available for you. I'll see you in the morning."

"Reggie, I just want to talk." His voice has a hardness hidden behind this pleading tone. So aggravated and almost cold. I hear him walking up behind me.

"At this time of the night?" I finally turn around and find him standing so close I have to back myself up and nearly hit the wall. "I . . . I really need to sleep."

He sighs and purses his lips. "Fine. Goodnight. I shouldn't even be talking about this right now."

I'm able to exhale in relief when he turns around. He curses under his breath and then stops. When he turns around, I take a step back. Please just leave, I want to beg him.

"No. I need to talk to you. Could you at least give me a moment?" he says, moving back toward me.

"Nate, I'm sorry. I'm sure it's important, but it can wait 'til morning can't it? I need the sleep. I think we *all* need the sleep."

He walks closer, standing directly in front of me. "I need to talk to you about something, and I don't want to put it off 'til tomorrow. Of course we need the sleep, but—"

"There's so much going on and so much—"

". . . I need you to listen, and I want you . . . ."

We both continue to talk over each other. Our voices rise until Nate breaks.

"You need to listen to me, Reggie!" Nate leans in to me, slamming the wall behind me with the palms of his hands. My heart has leapt up into my throat. His face is within an inch of mine as he presses me into the wall with the mere closeness of his body.

"Stop avoiding me! Dammit to hell! What do you want from me? *You have to talk to me!*"

"I can't!" I yell back at him. I feel my eyes burning and I fixate them on his face. Features that I've never noticed before paint the curvatures of his bone structure. An isolated dimple in his left cheek appears and fades each time he moves the muscles in his jaw. On his right temple a vein grows larger. A grunt rolls in his throat.

I know that if I blink, if I move, the tears will build—will spill over with the emotions I've been harboring for so many weeks. Anxiety. Fear. Guilt. Especially the strongest—desire.

Nate's eyes narrow and he tilts his head to look at me. He sees something in my face and I feel as if he's attempting to read me. I turn away from him to keep him from holding that look. I don't want to know what he saw. His fists leave the wall and fall to his sides.

"What's going on?" he asks cautiously.

I don't say a word. I can't.

"Reggie, what do you think of me?"

"What?" I spit back in a hushed whisper, looking up at him.

His face goes red with irritation and his eyes darken in the shadows of the hallway. "I asked you, what do you think of me? It's not a hard question, Reg."

Reg.

A collection of nerves and anger flutter within me. My heart is still beating, beating, beating, and it shows no signs of slowing.

"I *really* need to go to bed. Nate, if you stay, sleep wherever you like, but I think it'd be best if you were gone when I wake up."

I try to twist away from him, but Nate's hand lashes out for my wrist and holds me in place. His grip is gentle but unbreaking. Just the touch of his hand makes my lip quiver and I have to bite down on it.

"Let me *go*."

A strand of my hair flutters out of my braids and hangs directly in front of my eye. Like melting ice, the look in his eyes changes. The furiousness vanishes.

My ears scorch and my cheeks rise in temperature. I flinch as his hand comes up. I'm not even sure why. I know with one hundred percent certainty that he would never do anything to hurt me. It's something I've come to know about him.

But I *am* afraid. I'm afraid of what I'm feeling. I know that. I've known it for a while. I'm afraid of how stupid this is. I'm afraid that his feelings aren't for me. Not really.

He swallows and releases my wrist before he brushes my hair back. I can't move. I want to. It would be easy—and wise to turn now. To go to my room, shut the door and wait 'til morning. Until he was gone.

I'm stuck to the spot. Still feeling his shadow pass over me like a blanket.

"I'm sorry. I shouldn't have done that."

All I can do is shake my head. I close my eyes, clench my teeth, and try to understand why it is that I'm not moving.

"Reggie, I have to tell you something. I didn't come to talk about tomorrow. I did, but it's not the main reason. Something's changed. You and I both know it. You rarely talk to me anymore, and I don't know why that is. We enter the same room together and the tension's thick enough to silence a fog horn. We can't . . . *be* like that." He licks his chapped lips. "Not only does everything that we're doing depend on everyone being able to communicate, but, *personally*, I *wish* we weren't like this. I thought," he shakes his head, "well, I don't know what I thought, but I figured things were getting better. Better between *us*, I mean."

I hear the light pop of his tongue moving in his mouth and I swallow the dryness in my own mouth. It's true. For a while, I started to believe that the trust and acceptance in his face was merely a sign of friendship and mutual respect. Perhaps it started out that way. But he's not looking at me like that anymore. My knees shake each time I see it. I'm barely standing as it is.

"Reg, you're so different. Gosh, I don't even know how to put my finger on it. Because it's not your ability. I can't seem to put it out of my mind, it's like—" He groans in frustration. Another irritated puff of air shoots from his mouth and he pulls away.

Please finish. Please give up.

He paces slowly for just a moment before he turns to me once more. He looks as if he knows what to say again.

My eyes flash open when his left hand cups my face, followed by his right. He leans in and the heat of his breath graces my face. It melts my skin and my eyes close, taking it in. Being this close. Our lips meet and he gently opens my mouth with his.

"No!" I pull away, shoving him back. "What are you *doing*?" I hiss. "You love Olivia. I'm hurting too, but this is *wrong*. I *knew* it would be, and that's why I've been trying to keep you away." I run my hands over my face. I don't know—maybe in an attempt to erase what just happened. "I saw this coming. I knew it. I tried to keep my distance because I didn't know, and I still don't understand why you would do this! Why you would say this to me!"

His thick eyebrows drop and he frowns at me. "What? *This* is why you haven't spoken to me for *nearly a month*?"

"Yes," I barely manage to say. "Nate, I've had visions of this very moment over and over and I've really been trying to figure them out. Hoping that maybe things would change. I'd even be all right with things going back to the way they first were. I'd rather you hate me."

"*Hate* you?" He steps forward and I step back again. "I don't believe that shit, Reg. Why the hell would you want that? Do you hate *me*?"

"No," I firmly answer, shaking my head as it rolls back and forth along the wall. "It would be easier if I did. It's my fault she's being tortured." I keep shaking my head. Wet streams trickle down my face and I can't stop it. "*Olivia*, Nate."

"Are you saying you could *never* be with me because of Olivia? Or because you've warped your mind into believing it's somehow your fault that she chose, on her own, to go into the city with Hugh?"

"*No*. Yes. I don't know." I rub my eyes again, attempting to blot it out. "All I know is she's still alive; waiting for you."

"I know!" He swore. "You don't have to tell me over and over again. I saw it! And I'm hurting just as much as you are, and probably more. Because, yes. I love her. I haven't slept for days. Every good memory I have of the past ten years has always involved her. She was my friend, and I *love* her. Not," he stopped and sighed, "not like you think. I mean, yes like you think, but it's different. It's complicated."

I can't believe what I'm hearing. I can see in his face that he—no, I can't even tell what I see. His actions are suggesting he's two different people, with two conflicting belief systems. I can't even concentrate on my own thoughts, I'm so furious. No, I can't even say that I'm furious. Just having him this close to me is clouding every thought I have. I don't know what to say, or even how to begin to understand what *he's* trying to say.

My arms fold and I have to pull my gaze away.

"Liv and I are like siblings. And yes, in a way, even that's twisted because we've been together for a short period, and I blame *myself* for what's happened to her. I never should have given her a chance to come into this city. Reggie, I care for her. Deeply, believe me. But I never had the same feelings for her as I do—"

"What? For me? You don't know me."

"Yes, I do." He shakes his head. His voice is so tender that I feel I may melt with it. "Oh, I do. Reggie, you've had fifteen years to feel and see everything. It would be enough to destroy any normal person. But you have a greater passion for life than *I* ever have. You see the future, but you're so afraid of your own present. You have an immediate trust for people, which I think, or thought—was impossible, even the dumbest thing. As humans we're selfish, violent, and spiteful. At least that's how I *used* to feel. You treat London with the respect, as a man, that he's always wanted. More than I've ever given him. You kept him safe!"

Nate reaches out for my hand, turning it over in his palm. With his rough fingertip, he traces down the deep pink scar in the center. The scar from the knife in the kitchen. The light snags of his calluses sends chills up my arm. My face and chest burn.

"Reg, you're right. I love Olivia, and I hate myself for letting her get captured. But I *want* you. You've helped me realize," he licks his bottom lip, "how screwed up I let myself get. And what I've come to realize is that . . . wanting you doesn't mean I love Olivia any less. Pushing me away isn't what you want. I *saw it* in your eyes just now. When I asked you what you thought of me, I saw it. So believe me when I say it isn't just me that's in this anymore."

My eyes are frozen open, fixed on the ground. Is my pulse even beating anymore? I've spent fifteen years practically alone, in silence. With not a soul to talk to. No one but the sound of my own voice and the walls to keep me company. Silence was my lullaby. But this? This silence is deafening. It's driving me mad. He's waiting for me. I know I need to say something or do something, but I don't know what I should do. I know what I want to do, despite how hard I've been trying to stop it from happening. If only this was another time, under different circumstances. Perhaps then I'd be able to do something and not feel the burning guilt I know will eat at me if I let this happen.

The memories of my vision replay with each blink of my eyes.

I dig my fingers into the flesh of his arm, pulling . . . pulling him closer.

I can feel the touch of his skin before I even reach out. And it hurts. "Nate," I finally whisper. "I don't know how to be like this."

I don't look up, but I feel him. The warmth of him. He's moved close to me again, but this time I can't move back. "Well, lucky for us, I'm a little rusty too."

His callused hands run down my arms. He leans in and my eyes close. I feel his breath on the tip of my nose first before our mouths open together. He slips his arms underneath my robe, around the linen covering my waist, and draws me in tight. I breathe in deeply and I can hear it echo in the hollow of his kiss. I dig my fingernails into his arms, pulling his body closer. He was right. All I want is to hold him. To have him close. He saw it in me. He saw it before I even admitted it—he saw before I did.

Nate's hand moves under my shirt; running up my back then pulling down my spine. I raise myself to my toes as he kisses down my jaw line. My hands thread up his arms and around his neck, feeling each variation in his skin, each bump of every bone, muscle, tendon.

The fire I'd felt in my vision. It's so familiar. I feel as though I might not breathe again. My back slams up against the wall, and the reverberation carries down the hallway. Nate pushes me more. Our mouths meet again. His tongue licks the roof of my mouth and I feel a shiver run through me.

A sound comes from down the hall. It's ever so silent. Barely noticeable in the hallway but like a siren it screams at us. I recognize it as a bedroom door. My hands shoot out, pushing Nate off of me. Just fifty feet from where we are, Greyson stands with his arms folded, his face blank but the slits of his eyes are framed in dark circles. For a moment, all he does is stand there. I'm not sure I can look at Nate. My face and my entire body feel as if they're on fire.

Greyson takes a deep breath. "You both know it's two in the morning, right? Reggie, I think you need some sleep. I know *I* do. And, Nate?" He sighs and shakes his head. "Perhaps a cold shower?"

"Sorry, Greyson," Nate breathes.

"Just," he hesitates and looks into the bedroom, "keep it down." Greyson turns back around and the door slides shut behind him. I swallow hard and look over at Nate. He's staring right back at me. He frowns and shakes his head. "I should probably get going."

"W-we have the extra room, Nate."

"No, I really should go. London and Ben. They'll worry. Besides," he scratches his head, "dammit, I shouldn't have done this."

What? I want to yell at him.

Nate stops himself and turns back. With one step, he comes back and leans in to kiss me again. Our lips part slightly before he pulls back. His forehead rests on mine. But he doesn't pull back. He doesn't even try. I stand there, feeling the ache in my chest. My heart beats heavily against his chest, then he pulls away.

"Nate," I whisper.

I can't get a single thought to remain in my head, let alone another word to come out of my mouth. His footsteps tread softly away. The door of the house opens and slides shut. "Goodnight," I whisper after him.

"A re you sure this is his place?" Greyson whispers, taking a side-long glance at the home across the street as we walk by.

"I'm positive." I keep my eyes straightforward, avoiding any questionable actions on my part. It isn't often that a small group of people walk by a home three times in one day. I'd told Greyson and Nate it was dangerous, especially for Nate to spend so much time in the open. With each hum of a vehicle, he hides his face, anxious that it may be a guard transport. Despite the threat of being spotted by guards, they wanted to see Hugh's home for themselves.

"We're sure that he's not like everyone else? He's still . . . him?"

I barely nod. "Yeah, I think so."

"Let's go, then." Nate briskly steps away from me.

The three of us push away from the sidewalk, my own feet feeling heavy on the pavement before we reach the door. Nate places his hand on the door pad, and within I can hear the notification echo through the house. Hugh's movements can be heard inside before the door slides open.

When the door opens fully, his face registers a diminutive wisp of shock as he sees us, and in response, Nate throws the full weight of his body into Hugh knocking him back into the home and up against a wall. Greyson closes the door behind us.

"Nate." Hugh doesn't fight Nate's force but places his hands softly on Nate's wrists. "I know you're pissed at me for knocking you down the other night, but look at me!" Hugh struggles against him.

"Yeah, I can see," Nate grunts. "How the hell are you still the same?"

Hugh stops struggling. "If you'll let me go, I'll tell you."

With a final shove against the wall, Nate pushes himself away. "Talk."

"This isn't what we thought it was. Not exactly. I was under the impression that everyone here was forced into living this way. It's not true."

"What?" Greyson whispers.

"From the moment I was brought here, they took me into a room and showed a presentation. It told about the war, why Public One was created, and what the goal was. It told me practically everything. The processes, the people. I mean, it was definitely still sugar coated, but not enough to actually make it sound like a good idea. At the end, they gave me a choice. Lend my services as a fully-functioning citizen and help the system to grow in its goals, or . . . the alternative."

"You mean there are people here who know what they're doing?" Nate asked.

"The only ones who do are guards and staff. From the hospital administrators and doctors to the government. It allows them to make decisions without compromising the effectiveness of the choice."

"I'm sorry, but we have to move." I speak up, feeling sick to my stomach. "London and Sophia are on a schedule."

"Just like the plan?" Hugh responds.

"The plan," Greyson speaks up. "Has changed a little."

"What do you mean? What's changed?"

Greyson and Nate both look at me.

I chew on my lip. "I have."

It's like an impossible wall. The pressure. The anxiety. My pulse races so fast I feel my chest may burst. The building in front of my eyes burns my retinas. I can't look at it. I can't go back in, but I know I need to. If I don't, the building will always be there, always at my back, always promising to come back, to control me again.

"You can do this," I say to myself. "You're stronger than they are. They can't take you in again." My words feel hollow and empty, no matter how true they may be. A part of me just can't believe it. It wants to, but it can't.

"Reg?" Nate's hand gently rests on my back. "Are you sure you can do this?"

I whisper shakily once more. "You'll make it out. They won't win. Dryer is wrong. He was a liar, and you know that."

"Reg?" Nate's voice is genuinely worried.

I snap myself back to focus and my head slowly turns to look at him. His deep blue eyes bore into me. My strength lifts, but not much, and I nod to him. "I can do this."

"Are you sure? We can figure out another way."

"We won't have another chance, and you know that. I know Lobb is leaving The Public in only a couple hours. We'll never get to do this again. I can do it."

Nate presses the communication bud in his ear, turning it on, still gluing his eyes to me. "London. Are you there?" Nate nods as he listens to London's voice on the other end.

"London and Sophia are ready to head into the hospital. Reggie. Are you ready?"

Nate's hand envelopes mine and guilt washes over me. I pull my hand away. "Of course. I mean, I'm not sure if I can do . . . what you think I can do. It's not like I've had the opportunity to practice."

"You're not all going in without me, I hope."

I keep my eyes on the building ahead as all three men— Nate, Hugh, Greyson, turn to see the slender but tight frame of a man crouch beside us. The same face I'd seen in my visions the night before, and only once in person. It's Isaac.

I turn to study him. His eyes barely rise to greet us as he hangs his head and balances in a squat. He's not dressed like the rest of us. His filthy jeans are caked with mud, and soaked in water. His wet shirt has yellow sweat stains.

"I was worried you wouldn't fit through the water pipe," I say to him.

"Nomadic life's thinned me out a bit. Wait, how did you know?"

I squint at him and tilt my head. Although he knows exactly how I knew, I also understand how that still . . . doesn't quite make sense to someone else.

"You *knew* he was coming?" Nate buzzes in my ear.

"Of course I did."

"Why didn't you tell us?"

"Would you have let him?" I spin on him.

Nate takes a couple shallow breaths. "He has a family, Reg."

"Which is why I'm here." Isaac's voice is firm. "I ran when I shouldn't have last time, and even though I still think it was right by my family, I can't look myself in the mirror knowing that I could have done more."

"Audra made you, didn't she?" Nate smirks.

Isaac shifts his jaw and almost tugs up a smile. "It wasn't a decision made without her input if that's what you mean."

"How were you not seen?" Greyson looks Isaac up and down.

"Long story."

"Greyson," I cut off the conversation, "you don't leave the second floor 'til you see the sun balancing on the walls of the city. I know that sounds vague, but I need you to trust me. All right?"

"Got it."

"Once you get through to the security area, the code is 2637422. Three guards will be there. Be prepared. But you'll be able to communicate with London at that point and also open up all doors within the building.

"Hugh, there will be five men surrounding you at one point. I can't tell you *when,* exactly, because I don't know. But there will be one with a missing index finger—don't worry about him. His gun will misfire, but another man will raise his weapon to beat you across the skull. If you dart to the left, he'll miss you. After they're out, grab the gun that falls to the ground. You'll need it to keep guards off 'til the doors open. You'll need to escort everyone out of their cells.

"Everyone? Who will be in there?"

I squint at him. "Just don't scare them."

Confusion darkens his face, but he nods.

"Isaac?"

"Yes?"

"Go with Greyson." I glance down at his left arm.

"Your lives are more important than anything else. Protect yourselves at all costs. You'll have to."

A scream from Hugh. Three, four, five power shots. The sun hovers above the walls of the city and five guards crouch down. A gun cocks and I hear the low chuckle of a man. My blood dries in my veins. Another muted blast of the weapons and a fracturing yell bursts from Isaac. Blood pools at his feet.

I don't know where he's hit.

"Guys?" Greyson speaks up, pointing to the old watch on his wrist. "I hate to be the stick in the mud, but we've got to get moving. London and Sophia are watching the clock. If we don't move when we should, they'll be in trouble."

My hands run up the building as I pull myself to my feet. The others stay low to the ground and I feel a hand gently brush my thigh before grasping my wrist. Nate pulls me back down to his level and his eyes lock with mine. The others around us watch us.

"I'll meet you in there, all right?"

I nod, biting gently on my lip.

My throat tightens as Nate cradles the back of my head and pulls me in. Despite the conflict I feel, I don't want to let him go.

Greyson clears his throat. "Reggie."

I pull back and swallow. I can't take any more time. Without another word or acknowledgment of Nate, I stand and move quickly, still feeling as if he's right next to me. I pull around the corner, heading straight down the street toward the headquarter building.

The only home I'd known for fifteen years. Its cold exterior and polished glass walls cut through me. Guards are posted at the front doors. As I get closer, they place their hands on their weapons. At this moment, I look like any other citizen. The nearer I draw to them, the expressions on their faces change. Something in my demeanor challenges them. The power-guns in their hands charge, but they barely move. I don't know if they've recognized me yet. But they will.

I wait for the flicker of movement in the face of the guard to my right. I've seen it. He'll furrow his brows and immediately call for assistance.

His eyebrows crunch. His mouth parts. He knows.

"We need a squad at the north access. Alert Dryer, he's going to want to be here."

I raise my hands in defense, still slowly walking. My kneecaps are shaking uncontrollably, but I do everything I can to keep the fear from showing on my face. I'm straight. Resolute. I know that this will work. I've seen it.

The double doors behind him open and a group of seven men come out, each armed. The first guard rushes to me, and pulls my arms behind my back, securing my wrists with metal cuffs. "By statute 019, you, prisoner 0089, are being taken into custody of Public One. You have no rights. Anything you say or do is irrelevant and you will be held without a right to trial or questioning."

"I understand," I whisper as I look deep into his face.

Behind his ears, I can see a twitch. A shiver as he looks back at me with lively brown eyes.

Over the communicator I hear a faint, "Take her to the lab."

—OLIVIA—

Trickles of warmth ran down her arms. Red blood soaked her stained clothing and was now crusted onto the table. Today, Lobb made it through the last finger before she passed out. She was just beginning to wake again. The pain in her hand was nauseating. At any second, he could come back.

Olivia grimaced trying to pull her hand out of the wrist bar. Combined with the wetness of the blood and her sweat, the fingerless hand slipped through the bar relatively easy. The sharp edge of the bar cut along the joint of her thumb knuckle, tearing skin off. She hugged her hand near her frail body while throbs of pain contested up and down her arm. Her hand was on fire. Waves of cold rippled through her, followed by courses of heat. Hot fat tears streamed down her face, and it got harder to see with each blink of her eyes. But with her hand free, the only one without a bandage wrapped around a stump, she was now stuck.

"Think, Liv," she whispered to herself. "Think."

She attempted to squeeze the bandaged left hand through the cuff, trying to compress the bones so they could fit through the bars. The more she pulled, the more the sharp edges pulled at her skin and caught on the gauze, making it harder. Olivia screamed with gritted teeth, still hugging her stump hand to her chest.

When the doors slid open again, Lobb was the first to enter. A camera followed him in, hovering in the air, followed by two guards.

Lobb laughed a low mocking chuckle. "Where would you go?" He shook his head and walked closer to her, straightening his shirt cuffs—she noticed he'd changed his shirt; blood must have soaked the fabric that morning. He folded his arms. "I don't need you anymore anyway. Reggie's about to arrive."

"You're letting me go?" Her voice was hoarse.

"Of course. I just want to film a little segment with you beforehand. Is that all right?"

"Go to hell."

"I'm sorry about this, Olivia. I've really enjoyed these past couple weeks."

"Screw you." Olivia hocked saliva in the back of her throat and spit it directly at Lobb. The bubbled creamy dribble hit the center of his face and trickled down. The mocking sneer on his face disappeared, followed by a deep shade of scarlet. His arm lashed out, smacking her head back into the table. Olivia grunted, her chin dropping to her collar bone. She looked up to see him wipe his face with a silk handkerchief and then stick it back in his pocket.

"Turn on the camera."

She looked over at the guard, losing sight of the light above. A small blue light came on and Lobb looked directly at the camera. A joyful smile plastered his lips.

"Are we rolling?"

—REGGIE—

The guard hesitantly grabs at my wrist, and pushes me inside the building. The ride up the elevator is soundless. Until his voice crackles through.

"Welcome home, Reggie."

My head jerks up to look at a virtual screen, projecting Lobb's face in front of mine. "I hope the dangers of the country haven't destroyed you."

"You've destroyed me."

"Hopefully you've been able to see what a waste it's become," he continues, not acknowledging me, "the refuse, and uncivilized wildness. Everyone here has been saved from that. But you've tried to align yourself with those who've dared try to endanger us. Enemies. Charlatans. Breaking into our homes, threatening our prosperity, desperate to take what is not theirs."

I notice the distance the guards keep from me as the doors open and we step out of the shaft. My boots are almost silent against the smooth polished floor of my old hallway, making

Lobb's voice so much louder and grating as it follows me, the screen floating directly in front of my face.

"But try as they have, they will never succeed. Our city is powerful, our citizens are strong, and I have the power. I'm the protector. Not them."

The doors open as we reach the lab. My familiar chair is at an incline. Tubes, needles, and machines—as familiar to me as maybe a children's play room may be to others, but nowhere near as comforting. The whole scene makes my stomach flop over and I can't swallow. When the door behind me opens once more, I turn. Lobb's face is now gone, and I start counting down.

"One hundred, ninety-nine, ninety-eight, ninety-seven …" I count as quietly as I can under my breath.

"Quiet," the guard to my right growls.

". . . ninety-five, ninety-four . . ."

The butt of his power-gun cracks against my shoulder blades and I fall to my knees, breathing and grimacing against the pain.

There, standing in the doorway is Dryer. Dryer's hands are in his white lab coat pockets—slightly shaking. Not from nerves, but he's aged significantly in the weeks I've been gone. Stress, frustration, and constant tension have carved more lines into his face.

. . . *eighty-one, eighty, seventy-nine* . . .

"We knew it had to be you." He shuts the door behind him and then faces us again. "At first I couldn't believe it." His voice is like slime. Warm, with just a touch of damp coolness. It slips through my ears and slithers around my eardrums.

Numbers continue to countdown in my head. I block out everything he's saying to me. Greyson, Isaac, should be in the building by now, trapped. Hugh and Nate making their way through the other hallways.

. . . sixty-six, sixty-five, sixty-four, sixty-three . . .

"But I knew I'd see you again here. I always knew you'd come back, Dear. I told you that before. Remember?"

I think Isaac's been hit by now. It's getting closer.

"Yes, I remember," I grunt as I try to stand.

. . . fifty . . .

"I know you may think that by turning yourself in, you can spare the Nomads who took you."

. . . thirty-two, thirty-one . . .

"I'm not that naïve, Dryer."

He raises his bush eyebrows. "Then you must think you have a plan of sort. You actually think you can get out. Your fire never dies does it?"

. . . twenty-four, twenty-three, twenty-two . . .

"I have you to thank for that."

Dryer smiles. "I suppose that's true." He moves closer to me and I take a few steps back and to the side. Instead of coming for me, he walks to the chair he used to place me in every morning, grazing the surface of it with his finger.

. . . eleven, ten, nine . . .

"I can't wait to start working with you again, Reggie."

". . . four, three, two, one." I pull my focus off him, still remembering the face of each guard I'd passed. My thoughts spin faster and faster. I don't know if I'll be able to stop it. The rush becomes tighter. Pressure builds up. Two forces squish my mind. Colors explode behind my eyes. My head is shoved forward and slammed into a concrete mental wall. Energy radiates from my body as I see each face fly behind my closed eyes. The force explodes and finally the pressure alleviates.

I open my eyes to see all four guards who followed us in, clawing for relief on the floor, begging for relief from my mind. Their bodies are writhing. They can't control their own actions. Each muscle tight and unrelenting.

The look in Dryer's eyes tells me he never expected he'd be in this situation. Shock, fear, and even a dash of delight are spelled across his face.

"Well, Reggie. I should have learned years ago to never underestimate you."

"You always did spend more time in my head than I did," I hiss at him. "Give yourself some credit. You and I both know you never underestimated me."

Dryer smiles again, his bright white teeth matching the walls and floor. "An answer I'd expect from you, Dear. We've missed you. I don't know what you think you've accomplished. This," he waved his hand over the fallen guards, "is impressive, but it's a parlor trick, and it will get you nowhere. You can't stop this. All those people you *think* care about you are going to die because of you. There is no hope for whatever plan you have."

I narrow my eyes and shake my head. "I may have believed you once, but you forget what I can do. What I know."

"Reggie," he smiles, but it's a nervous smile, "I hate to be the one to tell you this, but you don't *know* anything. You never have. You *observe*. You see ripples. Events of things that *might* be. Life is littered with things that might be. Nothing is really set in stone, and it's always been that way."

"What are you talking about?"

Dryer takes a step toward us and I pull back. The doctor raises his hands in defense and stays still. "I'm not going to touch you. Reggie," he sighs. "You see the future, yes. An afterimage. But the ripple off a water droplet may see the rock in its path, but it can't see the twig falling from the tree above."

"Afterimage? What is that supposed to mean?"

"You already know. Don't you, Reggie?" He tilts his head and I see it in his face. The same skin-peeling look I'd seen every day for fifteen years.

"You mean the things I see are not certain. The future can change at the blink of an eye and I would never see it coming."

Dryer claps his hands—his soft, dark, disgusting hands. "There were so many reasons why I cared for you, Reggie. But your cleverness . . . it's what sets you apart. So you see why you won't win. Don't you?"

In a conditioned movement, a twitch starts at the back of my head and my chin lifts, because for just a moment . . . I almost agree with him. How could I not? Fifteen years of listening to him. The only person who's ever talked to me. Lied to me.

What Dryer says isn't right. It can't be. For years he's tested me, wired me, drugged me, and inflicted unimaginable pain on my body. He actually thinks I'm weak enough to believe him after all of the pain he's put me through. He always has. There's a bigoted pride he lives on and feeds off of, thinking his mind is somehow superior to mine because he managed to imprison me.

In all the time he's studied me, he still doesn't understand me.

"You're wrong. You don't know what the capabilities of my mind are anymore than I do."

"You still don't get it, Reggie."

"No! *You* don't get it! You never have. My whole life, I've been nothing but an insect to you. And you? You . . . have been *nothing* but a *disease*! You've fed off my mind like a parasite, starved me from the world, and sucked me dry! I grew up with no life! I've never lived, do you understand me!? I've never had a life until I left this place!"

"Reggie, Dear. You just don't understand . . ."

"*Stop*," I growl, "calling me that."

Dryer lowers his hands and frowns at me. "You're inexperienced. And you've been lied to by Nomads. If you —"

My chest tightens at the sound of his voice again. And I can't take it any longer. It's over. No more.

"*STOP!*"

It all happens too fast. My mind compresses, pushing in on itself as the prisms of bursting images and impossible colors slam against the back of my eyeballs. The power and pressure coming from my mind hurtles Dryer backwards in violent spasms, knocking him backwards. The life in his eyes disappears before he even makes contact with the wall. As he slides to the ground, a pool of blood trickles from his skull, down his neck, and puddles on the floor behind him.

—LONDON—

A bead of perspiration trickled down the side of his head. The vintage watch he wore on his thin wrist ticked slowly. With each hand movement, the pressure around his chest was building. He watched as people walked absently into the hospital and back out, oblivious to what would happen to their lives in just a few moments. And that was if the others even succeeded. If they didn't, he and Sophia were as good as dead. London had awoken that morning with every belief of possibly seeing the last morning of his life. Everything he did felt like the last time he'd do it. The last time he'd brush his teeth, the last time he got dressed. He didn't know if that was some sort of omen or just nerves.

The calm beauty of the day contrasted to the anxiety coursing through him.

"How much longer?" Sophia asked as she leaned forward on the bench.

"Three minutes."

London shook his wrist, wriggling the large watch downwards as the links clinked together. Tucked inside his uniform jacket was a small caliber power-gun. He could feel it pressing into his chest.

"Are ya nervous?" she asked.

"Do I look nervous?" London tilted his head over to look at her.

Sophia timidly smiled. "Very."

He let a rush of air from his lungs and Sophia spoke again. "I don't mean to say this the wrong way, but . . . how much do ya'll know 'bout Reggie?"

"What do you mean?"

"I mean, how well do ya know 'er?"

He knew exactly what she was getting at. From Sophia's point of view, they really hadn't spent much time with Reggie. Less than a month was surely not enough time to really get into someone's mind. But she hadn't talked with Reggie like he had. She hadn't really seen into Reggie's eyes like he had.

London dipped his head with the residual resentment that he felt toward Nate. He knew he shouldn't be as upset as he was, but the disappointment in the way everything turned out was there anyway. And it sucked.

"Sophia, if you're asking if we can trust her, the answer doesn't even need to be given."

Sophia's face flushed and she bit on her lip, nibbling on it back and forth. "I didn't mean to suggest she couldn't be trusted."

"Yes, you did." He lifted the watch up again to check the time. One minute. "But it's all right. You haven't gotten to know her, so I understand."

London licked his lips and looked out between the bushes again.

"London?"

"Yeah?" He turned back to look at her.

"Ya like her. Don' ya?"

"So?"

"Does Nate know?"

London sighed. "Yeah. We talked about it. I still think it's crap."

Avoiding Sophia's questioning gaze, London looked once more at the watch. Twenty-two seconds. Twenty-two seconds and the guards at the headquarter building would be too occupied to come to the hospital. Twenty-two seconds and he'd be rushing inside. All those years that he'd wanted to go with Nate, to be trusted, and now he was there. Just where he always wanted to be. It wasn't exactly how he'd expected it to be. Not that he'd imagined blazing glory, and not that he'd thought it'd be easy, it was just . . . heavier.

"Are ya mad 'im?"

"Whaddya mean? For Reggie?" London looked sideways. Sophia's eyes squinted and she looked away.

"It's not like I didn't see it coming. Besides, I don't think she liked me that way." London quickly glared at Sophia. Knowing Nate had moved in on Reggie still pissed London off. But he didn't have time to dwell on it. A group of guard transports left the side of the building, heading furiously for the headquarter building. Not only was it time, but the way was completely clear.

"Let's go," he whispered. Plants shuffled around with their movement. His hands shook furiously as he checked the placement of the gun beneath his jacket. A few people smiled at them with calm composures. Sunlight flashed a glittering reflection off the glass panels of the doorway. London's feet felt heavy, trying to keep him grounded, but he had the energy to keep moving. Not until it was over. He couldn't stop 'til it was over.

A sweet face pleasantly greeted them as they walked up to the main counter. "Hello. What can we help you with?"

"Who can I talk to about releasing the people from floor number seven?"

The woman's eyebrows scrunched, but she continued to smile. "I don't understand."

"What *doctor* do I have to talk to about releasing everyone on floor seven?"

"That's not—" she dropped her head, trying to look at something. "How do you know about the seventh floor?"

London ground his teeth together and reached for the gun tucked in the front of his Public issued jacket. He held it tightly at his side. "It doesn't really matter. You just need to know that we need to get everyone out of there."

The woman's smile disappeared. "I'm sorry, but we can't do that. Is there anything else that I can help you with? Are you injured?"

London lifted the gun and unlocked the safety at the same time. "Ma'am, I just need to get to the seventh floor. And don't touch the pad," he warned her as he saw her fingers flitter toward it. "In fact, Sophia, why don't you go around and make her a little more comfortable in the room back there."

Sophia cautiously walked around the counter and helped the woman back to an empty office room as the woman continued to nicely tell them that it was against the rules. "Great, London," Sophia said as she shut the door. "What do we do now?"

London immediately turned to the groups of people walking the lobby of the hospital. A few looked at them with tilted heads, attempting to process what was happening. Not a soul seemed to be truly bothered by the gun or their interaction with the woman. "We go to the elevator."

"Wait." Sophia glanced down at the projections the woman had at the counter in front of her. "London, I thought you said there were no security cameras in the city."

"There aren't. At least there weren't." He hurried around the counter, keeping an eye on the waiting families, and orderlies. Small shots of the hospital ran continuously through the projections. "I don't think it'll be a problem, though. All guards are at the headquarter building."

"Wait. Wait, what's that?" Sophia reached out and expanded the screen. It grew in size, expanding over the height of the countertop as the feed was zoomed in on. What they saw was a young woman lying asleep on an operating table. Her fingers were slightly disfigured from a birth defect and her short stature made her look more like an aged child.

A doctor took a long needle, and inserted it slowly through the woman's navel. The doctor compressed the long plunger and slowly pulled the needle out again, stopping blood with a gauze pad as it was removed. He handed the syringe to the nearby nurse and then his lips moved as he talked to the unconscious woman.

"What are they doing?" Sophia whispered.

London felt his face twist in disgust. They'd only talked about it once, but he knew exactly what was going on. "She's an incubator."

"A what?"

Even if he'd been older, and felt comfortable talking about such things, what he saw still made him sick. "The, uh, the incubators, that's what Reggie called them. The women who aren't good enough for The Public to use their DNA— whoever The Public thinks is a reject, they are the ones who have the babies. And babies are given to couples in the city."

"What?" Sophia's voice shook.

"The babies are genetically enhanced to be like Reggie. And the people they bring in," he looked at her, "like you, raise them."

A pale shade of green took over Sophia's face, draining of its normal rosy color. "Oh, no."

"Soph?"

A tear slid down her cheek and she brushed it away quickly. Her breath shook and she stood there silent. Her eyes darted back and forth, watching people walk around. It seemed as though she thought others were watching her.

"Soph?" London prodded again.

"London . . . I," her hand flew to her mouth. She took in another breath and reached her fingers up to brush the projected screen. When she touched it, her fingertips passed through the graphics. "I fergot. Russell, my companion, and I have a child coming. How did I ferget? London, how did I ferget?"

London stuttered. "I don't know, Soph. I'm sure it's the drug you had."

"What will happen to her?" she nodded toward the woman on the bed.

"I don't know." He shook his head. "I'm sure they take care of them somewhere in the hospital."

Before he could protest and get her back, she darted away from the front counter and headed for the glass elevator. London left the projection open and ran after her. Sophia slammed her hand onto the pad to open the elevator. Nothing happened. She pressed it again. No reaction. No numbers appeared, no elevator opened. London and Nate had obviously left their impression on the hospital. Years without a level of heightened security, and in one day that changed.

Sophia spun around, her eyes searching wildly. "What floor was that?"

"What floor was what?" he asked.

"The *woman*. What floor was she on?"

"Sophia, we can't go there right *now*. Our job is to go to seven first. Everyone on that floor will be euthanized. If we go after the incubators first, we may be too late to save anyone."

She shook. Even the deep rolling breaths she let out quavered. But she finally looked at him again, surrender in her gaze. "But all those women."

"They don't matter right now! All right!?" London yelled at her. He knew they only had a small amount of time. Reggie'd told him that. "They're still alive! I'm sorry. But we have to do this first."

She shivered, rubbing her arms. "All right."

London led her across to the doorway toward the staircase. For the first time, he felt like he was doing his assignment alone. No voice in his ear, no help at his side. He was leading Sophia. His job became that much more real to him.

He swallowed and fingered the gun in his hand. For once, it wasn't Nate. It was him. He was the one leading this and he had to get it right. He couldn't be indecisive.

The faces that passed by him all felt as if they were locked on him. Like they all knew what he was there to do, but not a soul did anything about it. He reached the door and swung it open. Inside, the same staircase they'd escaped through with Ben greeted them. His legs carried him as fast as they could, skipping and leaping over steps. Sophia's pitter patter feet followed behind, sometimes slipping when she'd anxiously misstep and clamor to hold onto the handrail. Each flight made his heart race faster.

Closer and closer to the seventh floor.

There weren't any signs of their struggle in the stairwell the day they rescued Ben. Nate's shots and the guard's shots that hit the walls were non-existent. As if they never happened.

He burst through the door and the woman behind the counter stood. It wasn't an ordinary nurse. The guard raised her weapon and London immediately got off a shot. The bullet missed her chest, and instead, hit her in the left arm, jerking her back. London continued to hold the gun up, steady. "You're going to let them all go for us. Then," he glanced at Sophia, "we want all the incubators out."

The guard smiled, grasping her arm. "You think so?" She grunted and her eyes flickered to Sophia. "You're a child. You don't know what you've gotten yourself into."

London rammed the gun to the guard's temple. "You're gonna let them go. Are you listening?"

A deep chuckle was followed by, "We believe in this cause more than you are invested in yours. You're nothing to The Public. Even if you manage to succeed this time, we'll rise even stronger."

"Let them out," London spat through gritted teeth.

"What if I don't?"

London stepped back and fired another shot into the woman's shoulder. She yelled in pain. "We'll do it without you."

GREYSON

Power gun blasts ricocheted off the walls around them. Depressed whirs of sound flew through the air.

Neither Greyson nor Isaac knew what they were waiting for. All they knew were Reggie's instructions. To wait. Wait for the right time—the perfect time. And who knew what would happen then?

Greyson leaned around the corner when it seemed like the firing had stopped. Around the bend in the hall a guard lifted his arms and aimed once more. Greyson's jerked back, his head missed by the shots. He could smell the singed hairs the electric charged shots grazed as they'd sped by his welcoming head. "Well," he sighed, "I didn't think we'd be stuck here this long."

Isaac gave a dry chuckle. "If we're going to share things we didn't think we'd ever do, I'd probably have to put this whole event at the top of my list. How about yourself?"

With a shake of his head, Greyson laughed as he double-checked the position of the sun through the window. "That's for sure." Greyson massaged his sore elbow as he leaned his head back.

Moments before, he and Isaac had slid into the hallway and he'd slammed his elbow into the access pad. It caused the door to seal shut behind them, but even so, guards still had firing privileges since the communication port between hallways was still open. There wasn't much cover except for the narrow recessed doorway they hid in. The guards could be seen behind the clear doorway, struggling to get the door open. Greyson's heart stopped each time the mechanics in the door whirred and then clanked.

Another shot blasted from down the hallway and pierced Isaac. With a gut-wrenching yell, he sunk lower into the corner, seizing his arm and holding it close to his body. Aromas of singed flesh and cloth filled Greyson's nose as he maneuvered closer to Isaac, careful to keep them both protected behind the wall.

"Let's see it."

Isaac hissed as he lifted his arm away from his body. The muscle tissue had disconnected from the tendons in his elbow, and although the shot had burned his flesh, blood still ran freely. Quickly, Greyson took off his uniform top, leaving his thin under-shirt on. He ripped a large section of the dense fabric off, using his teeth to start the tear. The blood wouldn't stop on its own. They had to tie it off before Isaac lost too much blood. Just above the elbow, Greyson yanked the knot tight, cutting off the circulation to the forearm. With the extra fabric from his shirt, he wrapped it around the injury to hold the muscle on. Isaac shook, gritting his teeth.

"You gonna be able to make it?" Greyson raised an eyebrow, panting heavily.

Isaac's eyes were red, squeezing together, and tears fell down his face. With each second he didn't speak, the darker shade of red his face glowed. When he finally breathed, he managed to get out, "I'll . . . uh, I'll be fine."

Greyson backed away again, and tucked himself against the wall. He swallowed as he looked around the corner once more, then ducked away from a flying chunk of the wall.

Outside, the sun was balancing in the sky. The window above them was situated just high enough that he could see the afternoon orb above the horizon, but yet it was at least a good ten minutes from teetering on the walls of the city like Reggie had told him. And knowing how Reggie operated, he didn't want to be the one to go against her warning.

"Hey, Greyson." Isaac peeked around the wall, automatically causing six more rounds to fire toward them.

"Yeah?"

"I never got to say anything to any of you, but," he held his arm tighter to him, "I'm really sorry about Liam. I mean, I won't lie, I really didn't like him . . . but, I'm sorry."

Greyson nodded. "You know, even though I'd known him for a number of years, I didn't know him very well. If you really want to apologize to anyone for not being there that night, Nate's the one to talk to."

Isaac crinkled his nose, which still hadn't quite healed from his last encounter with Nate. "Yeah, I think I might steer clear of him for a while. There are only so many times that your face can take a beating before permanent damage is done." His hands fidgeted with the tight fabric around his bleeding arm.

"I think he understands. At least, I think he can understand your reasoning behind it. You both . . ." Greyson paused as he listened to the whirring of the door.

Clank. They both jerked at the sound. The guards weren't through yet.

"You both have the same goal. You want to protect your family. It's just that you go about doing that in different ways."

"It was the only thing I could think of."

Greyson sucked his lips in for a moment. "I know." Up in the window, a few birds trailed across the sky, flying in a silhouette in front of the early evening sky as the sun balanced on the edge of the city wall. It was finally time.

"Let's go. Are you going to be all right?"

"I'll make myself be all right."

Greyson blew out through pinched lips before he rounded the corner. One guard lifted his weapon, but with the sun at the angle in the window, he raised his hand to shield his eyes. The guard fired and missed. Greyson's hand shot through the port and yanked on the weapon, wrenching the guard's body with it. The guard's head beat into the partition. Greyson turned his arm toward the other guards and fired off a set of repetitive rounds.

Over and over.

He hadn't even noticed the smooth movement of the door opening an inch. He didn't stop 'til the magazine was empty. Each guard was still, lying in the blood that seeped out onto the floor. Legs and arms sprawled and tucked underneath their bodies. The gun made a hollow clank as Greyson pulled the gun through the port toward himself. Tendons in his neck, and muscles in his face surged and flexed with adrenaline.

Reggie had done it. Even though she hadn't been sure it was even possible, she'd done it.

"We have to hurry." Greyson motioned for Isaac to follow him. He curled his fingers around the edge of the door and pulled on it. His arms strained, but he managed to open it just wide enough for them to slip through sideways. They stepped hesitantly around the handful of bodies on the floor.

Fluorescent lights above intermittently flashed above their heads as they ran. They passed hundreds of doors. Windows opened into giant rooms where labs stood vacant and silent. Sterilized countertops were clear. Digital projections still glowed in the air with numbers and DNA sequences that made no natural sense.

As doctors and technicians poked their head out of doors, Greyson raised the gun to them. "Stay inside!" The doors slammed shut behind them. Inside, they could be seen, raising their arms in defense.

Greyson and Isaac reached the end of the hallway, and carefully looked around the corner toward the security section of the building. When he looked back to make sure Isaac was ready to move with him, he stopped. Isaac had gotten held back, looking horridly through a wide window. After double checking the security hallway, he turned and moved to pull Isaac along with him.

But as he saw the thing that had frozen Isaac's feet to the floor, what he saw could only be called a nightmare in the truest sense. In a deep room below, nearly fifty children, all about five years of age, were connected through electrode relays. Projections flashed quickly in front of their small eyes with images, information, colors, and patterns. But what pierced Greyson through his heart was the jerking. What looked like electric pulses were rhythmically coursing through each child. Their heads tweaked with each pulse as their faces stared blankly at the projections in front of them.

"What is this?" he whispered.

"We were always just told they were trained. That they were given the best education possible. That's all we ever knew." Isaac shivered next to him. "My sons were almost admitted. Next year, Peter would have entered the program. They're just babies."

Reggie had told them about the "people" in cells. She'd warned Hugh not to scare them. Like anesthetized mice in cages, the children were experimented on.

The nauseous pull at his throat filled his senses. Greyson couldn't make himself to look at the children any longer. He didn't want to.

"Isaac, if we don't keep going we'll be killed before we have a chance to stop this. Come on." He pulled on Isaac's good arm, but Isaac didn't move. Greyson moved closer, his eyes briefly flitting toward the children. His stomach turned in knots again. "We'll get them out."

Isaac sighed and finally looked at Greyson, his face red. He simply nodded.

They pulled away from the window, leaving the children behind. Cautiously looking for guards along the way, they eventually found the security room. Greyson punched the code into the pad and the door slid open. Five guards were writhing in pain on the floor, still being affected by the blast from Reggie.

"Holy . . ." Isaac whispered under his breath. "Who is that?"

A man looked back at them from the security screen. Greyson froze. "It's Martin Lobb."

"Welcome to Public One. You must know you are illegally on restricted property. That's not acceptable. The Public protects what is ours."

"So do we, asshole," Greyson grunted.

"In order to show you, the extent we are willing to go, to save this city, I'd like to introduce you to a woman you already know."

The camera angle panned over. Greyson's eyes widened at the sight of Olivia strapped to a slat. Blood dyed the skin on her arm, crusty in places, still oozing in others. Her fingers were missing and saturated in red.

"Kill him!" Olivia yelled.

A guard reached over and smacked her.

Lobb looked back at them again. "We want our city to know, that they're safe. Safe from you. I will always put the safety of this city above any danger that threatens to destroy it."

Lobb moved closer to Olivia, and the camera was soon on both of them. But Olivia kept her eyes on the floor.

"Go to Hell," she whispered.

"This, is an enemy. Like you. She attempted to destroy everything I—we—hold dear." From within his jacket, he pulled a sleek silver power handgun out of his pocket and directly pointed it to her head.

Greyson leapt forward. "Don't!"

He barely heard the click of the trigger before the electric bullet seared through Olivia's skull.

—REGGIE—

The door slides open while Lobb continues to talk on the screen.

"We want our city to know, that they're safe. Safe from you. I will always put the safety of this city above any danger that threatens to destroy it."

Olivia groaned, "Go to Hell."

"This, is an enemy. Like you. She attempted to destroy everything I—we—hold dear."

I turn around to see Nate staring at the screen, breathing quickly. I don't even have time to turn around before I hear the piercing sound of Lobb's gun. I spin back to the screen to see Olivia's head hanging forward. Lobb steps toward the screen, handing off the gun as he does.

"You see, I'm not afraid to do what's necessary." He wipes his hand on a silk handkerchief. "This is mine. You can't have it." The screen goes blank.

The words echo over and over in my mind. "You can't have it."

I can't hear anything else over the ringing in my own ears. Olivia was just murdered.

I saw it.

We didn't stop it.

I can't move.

Why can't I move?

I can't stay here. I don't have time.

Forcing my feet to unglue, I twist around to Nate. His face is bright red, and he looks at the spot where Lobb's face was. He's shaking.

"Nate, we have to go find him."

He breaths shallow and rapid, looking right past me. His eyes flick to me and he doesn't even respond. Nate shakes his head and darts out of the room with me racing after.

Scarlet lights bombard us both as we run into the hallway. The guards from the hospital have arrived and they're waiting for us. Tucked around the hall corners, guards fired on us, their shots whizzing by. Some cut through my clothing. Another nicks my shoulder. Nate fires off twenty rounds, each going directly where he intends.

"Left!" I shout to him.

I try to center my mind on each guard and turn the corner. There are so many faces, I can barely focus. Three guards run from a hallway and I throw my fist out. My focus is too scrambled to use my ability. The next punch connects with a guard's throat. Another doubles over from Nate's shot. I shove another out of my way. He trips over a body. Nate shoots a third.

Another guard down. My head is rolling like waves exploding against land. So much commotion, but I have to keep taking them out.

There are so many of them.

"Down to the right!" I yell again, directing Nate. I know where he is. I know where he is.

My fists fly when my mind focuses on another. Nate's feet get kicked out from under him and his head cracks against the floor. With one swift kick, his boot lands on the kneecap of the guard. A gun flies out of his hands. Nate kicks him again, reaching out for the weapon sliding on the floor.

What was that? Seventy one, seventy two, seventy three men now? My head is pounding. There are so many, and I can't keep count. It's so hot in here.

Nate fires the weapon in his hands over and over, covering me from behind. "Go!"

I turn the corner, my mind finally resting and oxygen rushing to my brain. It's just down the hallway. The bright white hallway. Clean as ever with a few bodies strewn in clenched pain.

"I'm gonna kill him," I whisper harshly to myself, trying to keep from falling apart. I keep saying it over and over again; to remind myself to keep pushing.

I direct Nate up the shafts that take us to the upper level where I know where Lobb will be. The commotion and violence left behind us. It's suddenly so quiet. I can hear my heart.

There are only three doors on the upper floor. Three large rooms and I know exactly which one. I know each detail. The lavish décor and the disgustingly extravagant garbage.

The shaft ends and I rush toward the far right. I press my hand to the door and just as I'd seen before, it opens up smoothly. No request for a code.

Inside, I find an open office. Windows look out over the entire city. The polished marble floor squeaks against the soles of my white Public issue boots. In the center a pan of projected screens cuts the room in half. I don't recognize any of the information or images. At the other side of the screens, an upright rectangle-shaped chair back swivels leisurely around and a man smiles at both of us.

Martin Lobb has his hands in front of him, wiping them on a white handkerchief. Behind him is a screen of my reporting room. Dryer's body is still sagging on the floor. The image skips back and replays. I watch myself blast Dryer against the wall. The screen next to it shows Olivia. Again. Again. Lobb keeps repeating it.

"I saw what happened to Dryer, Reginald. Someone's changed a bit. Haven't we?"

Peripherally I see Nate raise his gun and shove its aim right toward the man in the chair still smiling. Smiling like he's won.

—NATE—

T he gun in his hand was steady. Aimed directly at the ridge between the man's eyes. If anyone on this earth deserved to die, he did. For everything he'd created and destroyed. For Liam. For what they put Reggie through for fifteen years.

For Olivia.

Nate could still hear Lobb's velvet voice floating over the projection screen. Out of the corner of his eye, Olivia's face and the shot of the gun. Her head jolting with the hit.

"I've heard of you," Lobb's voice was calm, no emotion in his face, but a clear and evident presence of coldness flooded his words. "Nathan Naylor. Yes." He nodded. "Dryer showed me Reginald, sorry, Reggie's files. The images we have of you on file are expansive. Quite detailed. Did you know that when Reggie became . . . passionate about a particular vision, the events were always more vivid? You know, you were famous in Reggie's visions before you stole her from us. For weeks leading up to her abduction you were all she ever saw. Why is that?"

He studied Nate's face, and Nate returned the gaze.

"If I wouldn't have known better," Lobb continued, "I would've said that she had a little interest in you before you met. Why? You can't possibly match her."

"Shut up," Nate barked.

"What am I saying? Of course you must know that now."

"You don't deserve to talk."

"Oh, I know you think that, but you'll want to hear what I have to say." His eyes flickered over to Reggie, scanned her from her toes up, and then back down again. Nate's finger tightened around the trigger and he took a step toward the desk.

Lobb smiled. He sighed and pushed himself up from the chair. His alabaster white hands looked like silk. "Don't worry, son. I don't look at Reggie like you do."

"Don't!" Nate took another step.

"You don't see it do you?"

"What are you talking about?"

"Nate," Reggie's voice bombarded him from the side. "He's stalling. Nothing he can say will benefit either of us."

The thick peppered eyebrows on Lobb's face rose. "Oh, but, Reggie. What I have to say *will* benefit you." His fingers traced the edge of his desk loosely and coolly while he walked around it, his other hand professionally resting in his trouser pocket where he'd just tucked the handkerchief.

Reggie didn't say a word. Nate threw his gaze at her for a moment. Long enough to see her frowning a look of curious antipathy on her face.

"You see?" Lobb grinned. "You want it. You want to hear everything. It's why you're still letting me talk. If you didn't care, like you so succinctly put it, I'd be dead already. You're curious and so lost within your own past that you can't even be sure you *want* to kill me!" Lobb smirked. "For instance, I'm sure you'd be very interested to know where you came from."

Even Nate's eyes shot open.

"You don't know anything," Reggie rumbled. "You know *nothing*."

Lobb chuckled. It was a sickly sweet noise that rumbled from his chest. "Oh, Reggie. If you only knew. It's important that you don't, however. You've changed so much over the years. Especially since I last talked with you."

"We've never talked before." Her voice shook.

"Of course we have." Lobb folded his arms. "You were almost ten, but you probably don't remember. I think the last thing you said to me was, 'Goodnight . . . friend'." The man grinned as if he were touched by the memory.

"I know you have questions about your life. Where you came from, your family, and even *what* you are. I know absolutely everything about you. I've known you since you were swimming in a tiny little Petri dish at the Los Alamos lab in New Mexico. You see, I made you. It wasn't exactly like a baking recipe, but I was the one who did what God couldn't. I suppose you could say I'm your dad."

"Don't make me sick."

"Reggie." Lobb held out his arms for an embrace. "Sweetheart."

Nate's finger tightened and a shot buzzed passed Lobb's ear, nicking it before hitting the wall behind him. If he'd wanted to hit him, he would have. It was a warning shot. Something told him to hold back.

The man ducked and grabbed at his ear. When he pulled his hand away, there was no blood. What the hell?

Lobb opened and shut his jaw trying to pop his ears. He whirled on Nate. The smile that was permanently plastered on his porcelain face was still there.

"Are you going to kill me for wanting world peace? Desiring a race of people superior to any before it? I've *seen* the horrors of this world. You have too, Nathan. I know you have. A mother? Jill. A father? Michael Naylor. Your siblings, Lou, Chris, and Dayna all killed in a blast. *Utah*, wasn't it?"

Nate's teeth ground against each other. As Lobb had said each of their names, the faces and memories came flooding back. Lobb had no right to say their names. Not them.

"My own wife," Lobb's voice softened, but a mix of scowling delight played on his lips, "my daughter. Killed at the hands of another. For what? Money. For the fifty dollars she had. Now she's dead. Gone. You know what that feels like. To lose your family. To have them *taken* away from you. There's nothing you can do. Even in the early years after the turn of the century, people were becoming unchangeable. No good could be done for us. So I came up with the only way to fix society. To cure the human race. There was only one way, and that was to start from *scratch*.

"We were ruined, Nate. Society was broken. I knew that the only way to fix it was to raise a superior generation. Stronger than any before. More gifted than we'd ever seen. To create a people that had the potential for perfection. Reggie," he looked at her, "see what she's become. Even a neglected intellect like hers, sharp as a knife. Physical strength and determination to exceed any normal woman. Abilities that make her far advanced to any person before her. Reggie, you were one of the first."

Nate half expected Reggie to lash out. But she stood quietly.

"Nathan." Lobb turned to him again, moving closer. "What I've created here. It's perfect. The children we've raised will grow, change the world, and the flaws of our natural state will have disappeared. What if disease no longer existed? What if there were those around us that could heal with just a wave," he ran his hand through the air, "of their hand? To eradicate negativity. Haven't you seen the greatness of Reggie's makeup? Gifted with an ability you and I could only dream of using. *She's* the future! Everything I ever wanted to create! Everything good about what I've created is in her. *Look at her*. You see the perfection of it, don't you?"

Nate nodded, molding the right words within his mouth. "You're right. To be honest, I know exactly what it feels like to lose my family. To feel like your whole damn world has been ripped out from under you. I lost my family. More than once."

He paused, licked his bottom lip, and calmly enunciated the next words. "This is for Olivia."

The gun shot and a single power bullet spliced directly through Lobb's forehead. His body shimmered in the air, a smile frozen on his face. His green eyes twinkled with what could only be described as repulsive delight, and then the hologram was gone.

expect Nate to lash out, shoot something, destroy something. The one man in the world he wanted dead, and he can't make it happen. Not today. We both stand still. The spot where Lobb stood just moments ago shows no sign of foot prints. He had us. In a way, he was right. We can't win. Not today. He's still out there. Others like me exist. Not simply the children Dryer and Lobb have bred. The first. I'm not alone.

Lobb is still alive.

"Come on, Reg. We still have work to do."

"Nate," I say as he turns for the door.

He stops and looks back at me. I can't read him. What I'm seeing isn't pain. Not frustration.

He takes a deep breath. "Yeah?"

"Are you not even angry?"

Nate glances at the spot where Lobb disappeared. Blank. Nothing. Then, he rounds on me. "Of course I am. I can't do anything about it right now, can I?"

I know he's right, but that doesn't alter the fact that I'm scared for him.

I feel everything moving very slowly. Each shot that Nate fires grows quieter and quieter as the buzz of charged bullets whirrs through the air.

It takes hours to disable the electrodes attached to each child. Their little bodies are so tired we have to carry each one out of the training rooms one and two at a time.

Lab technicians and doctors file out into the streets, Greyson leading them out. Like the guards, they've voluntarily worked on this for years.

I kiss the forehead of a little girl before I place her on the soft chair and turn to go back for another. I feel myself giving out. My head pounds like it's being hammered from the back. Though we've won this, Olivia's dead, Lobb's gone, and I can't say I'm at ease.

I walk out of the building and stand still in the street. The warm rays of the sun wash over my skin. Beams of light prickle the nerve endings in my cheeks and my forehead. I want to relish it, but I can't. I close my eyes when Nate stops at my side.

"What do we do, Nate?"

He doesn't say a word. Doesn't flinch.

"He killed Olivia. He's still out there. We took down two hundred guards today. Who knows how many exist still. There are three Publics still functioning."

"Reg, I'm really trying not to think about any of it right now. Not now."

I shake my head, but I don't argue. Pushing it aside doesn't make the issue disappear. No matter how many times Nate has used that tactic throughout his life.

I turn my back to the sun, let it melt into my hair, and face him. I want to take comfort in him.

No. I can't do this.

I turn away and try and take a deep breath.

"Reg?

"What?" I turn back.

"What's the matter?"

I shake my head. "What do you mean?"

"Something's bothering you."

I rub at my nose and look off into the distance. "You mean aside from Olivia, who neither of us want to talk about, and Lobb, who we didn't actually find," I say. My voice cracks and I shake my head.

"Reg, if you need to talk. I'll listen."

My eyes lock on the horizon. "He said I was one of the first. *One*. One of others."

"Reggie, you can't listen to him. There was nothing Lobb said that we can trust."

"I know, but why lie about that? What would be the point? What would he have to gain by lying to me about others like me? It's obvious I don't have a real family. But the others. Who are they? What if they're still out there?"

Nate sighs in frustration. "What if they are? If they cared, wouldn't they have looked for you?"

I turn on him, keeping my voice low. "What if they couldn't? What if they're just as much in the dark as I am?"

"If Lobb designed them, who's to say they're to be trusted either? If they even exist."

"Like you thought I couldn't be trusted?" I shouldn't have said that. I'm not fighting with him right now.

Nate grabs my shoulders. "Listen, Reggie, I know you want to dwell on this, but you can't. We can't afford to. Lobb is still out there. That's what we need to be focusing on. Not finding other people that may or may not exist. For all we know, he could have told you that to simply distract you."

"And killing Olivia? What was that? Why do that?"

He tries to keep looking at me, but he can't. I don't blame him. He releases me and looks to the ground.

"Nate, I don't feel right about this. You and me."

Nate hisses. "Shit, don't you think I haven't thought that too? So, if this isn't right, then what do you want me to do?"

"I don't know. All I know is that right now I need to find the others."

"Without me, then?" He steps back.

"Hey, if you thought that there was even a remote possibility that your family was still alive, wouldn't you do everything that you could to find them? What if it were Olivia out there?"

Nate drops his head and takes a deep breath. "Of course I would. What do you want me to do? Let you go off on your own?"

I don't answer. Just shake my head. "Nate."

"I'm not going to let you do it."

"No offense, but you can't stop me."

My eyes dance around his face—I try to study him. Chills travel up my arms and down through my body as he grabs my elbows pulls me to him.

"Reggie, I'm coming with you."

I shake my head and look at him with as much care as I can show right now. "Why? With all we've gone through, why do you want me to drag you into this?"

"I was dragged into this a long time ago. I'm finishing it with you. Whether you want me to or not."

ENCENDER

THE FIGHT IGNITES

A violent roar claws my throat. My fist tightens, and I thrust it down with fury. Sticky blood, smears of grime, and dried sweat coat my knuckles. Each movement of my fingers cracks open the scabbed crust. The tang of iron carries on the wind, thick in my nostrils. A drip of blood travels down my bottom lip. I lick it away and swallow. The leather strap that I keep wound around my hand tightens and strikes against the side of his head.

Once. Twice.

Acknowledgements

There are so many people who have been involved in this novel from the very beginning, and I owe them so much:

To my amazing Writer's "Support" Group. Wyatt, Liesel, and even Bri—without you three and your incredible talent, brilliant insight, and crazy minds, *Afterimage* would not be what it is.

To my wonderful friends at work, to my undergraduate professors, my honest-to-goodness amazing BFFs, and to all of you who freely offered help, encouragement, and enthusiasm along the way.

To Mrs. McNaughtan. In third grade you told me I should be a writer. I don't know how you saw it, but you did. Long before I did.

To all my beta readers. Thank you for all your feedback and support!

To two guys. Since I've never seen you again, you wouldn't know that it was your encouragement that persuaded me to publish this novel. Thank you. Now go flush your heads in a toilet.

Most importantly, to my family (both earthly and heavenly). Even more notably my dad, the reader; and my mom, the believer. You two gave me every opportunity in life. Not only to succeed, but to grow from my talents. I love you both so much.

Last but not least, thanks to all of you readers who have loved this book and the characters. I put a lot of my heart into this and I'm so grateful to be able to share that with you.

J. Kowallis grew up in northern Utah, graduated from Weber State University's creative writing program and lives in Utah with her Mini Schnauzer, Etta. She enjoys dreaming about, flying to, and writing about distant lands (real or unreal). *AFTERIMAGE* is her first novel. You can visit her at *jkowallisbooks.wordpress.com*.

CPSIA information can be obtained at www.ICGtesting.com
Printed in the USA
LVOW10s0448010116

468760LV00015B/258/P